THE WOMAN WHO LOVED JOHN WILKES BOOTH

THE WOMAN WHO LOVED JOHN WILKES BOOTH

by

PAMELA REDFORD RUSSELL

G.P. Putnam's Sons
New York

 Printed
simultaneously in Canada by Longman Canada Limited, Toronto.

SBN: 399-12132-3

Library of Congress Cataloging in Publication Data

Russell, Pamela Redford.
The woman who loved John Wilkes Booth.

1. Booth, John Wilkes, 1838-1865–Fiction.
I. Title.
PZ4.R9657Wo [PS3568.U768] 813′.5′4 77-18047

PRINTED IN THE UNITED STATES OF AMERICA

THE WOMAN WHO LOVED JOHN WILKES BOOTH

I

A SMALL TOWN IN SOUTHERN MARYLAND, SUMMER 1878 . . .

The old man eased himself down the front steps of the boardinghouse. After nearly fifty years with his stiff leg only stairs still gave him trouble. They set him off balance, forcing him to rely too heavily upon it. Otherwise, he moved with great rapidity and surety. It was only through others' eyes now that he would suddenly become aware of his infirmity. As at this moment, making his way down the stairs, the creaking of a rocking chair had ceased. Even with his back to the boarder on the stoop he could feel that she was watching him, nervous that he might fall, or perhaps hoping that he would. As he touched down on the dirt street, he heard the creaking of the rocker resume, and a sigh, either of relief or disappointment.

The leg was a memento of the uncontrolled rages of his youth. He had solved all of his problems, and created many of them, with his fists in those days. Then when he was seventeen he had gotten into a fight with a man. He couldn't remember why he had fought, not now fifty years later, not even five minutes after the fight had begun. He had just been a touchy cocksure fellow, ready with his fists. He could still remember losing his footing and being knocked into the street. He could still see the huge ale truck filling all the world before him, and the driver's face, frozen and unstoppable. He could still feel the bones of his leg being crushed beneath the wheels. It was a miracle that he lived, and some special gift, keeping his leg.

He had changed after that, not that he would ever be a man capable of deep introspection, but the limp metamorphized him from a burly young thug into something more vulnerable and conversely more sensitive to others. He did not often think of his accident, but death would never again be to him the strange and impossible thing that it is to those who have never felt its brush. He put it aside, and lived, and tried to forget its cold memory. The empty sleeves and the empty air where legs should have been on the soldiers he saw during the war were painful reminders. He would look at these men, and in their eyes was death, seen and momentarily escaped. Now, nearing seventy, death was ever present and inescapable. This was the reason for his presence in this little dusty town.

He limped quickly along the hot dry main street. In the beginning the townspeople had watched him closely. He was a stranger to them, and they were unaccustomed to people whose faces they had not seen all of their lives, whose voices they had not heard. As the weeks passed, and every day he walked through the center of their town, they grew used to him. They were a breed innately frightened of the unknown and deeply incurious.

This particular day, some five weeks after the old man's arrival, there was a carnival atmosphere in the town. Little boys in their Sunday best courted whippings by scuffing their shoes and soiling their clothes racing each other about the street. The little girls stood quietly in what little shade could be found, twisting their handkerchiefs, sometimes squealing at the grimy pinching hands of the passing boys, and watching. Ladies in white rested soft pale gloved hands, heavy with possession, on the arms of their men. Their parasols seemed like a reflection of the few small clouds floating overhead in the brilliant blue sky. Lemonade and cakes were hawked at intervals along the street.

A crowd had gathered around a large wagon covered in bright red canvas. It looked to be a traveling medicine man selling some magic elixir. The old man was walking past, thinking only of his destination, that small white frame house on the outskirts of town, where every day for over two weeks he had gone and been turned from the door, where once he had seen the shadowy form of a fair-haired woman in the window of an upstairs room. His thoughts were of these things, but the words of the peddler standing on the wagon made him stop.

The peddler had slick and shiny black hair, curling to auburn at his beard and neck. He stood, chest puffed out, shouting to the gathered people. A jet-colored dog lay in the dirt by the wagon. As the dog contorted, searching his belly for fleas, the sun shone on his gleaming coat. His master made similar motions looking for likely customers, but he shimmered only from his hair oil.

"The crime of the century! Inside this wagon you will see it happen before your very eyes! You will be there, and you will take part! And it only takes a penny. One penny! One penny to witness the crime of the century. That's all, I say! That's all. One penny!"

A young boy of eleven or twelve pushed excitedly through the crowd. He presented his penny and the man swept aside the wagon flap. The boy climbed inside. The man continued his harangue until interrupted by the boy who emerged red-faced and ran whooping among his townspeople and kin.

"I shot him! I shot him!"

The people began to laugh. The boy's excitement was contagious. The wagon man smiled grimly and greedily. It was going to be a very good day. The old man moved closer. This was no peddler of some cruel cure-all that raised hopes and then dashed them. This was not a hawker of some hair tonic which might well remove the buyer's scalp. He limped up to the wagon and held out a penny.

"I would like to be seeing this, sir."

It was the first time any of them had heard his voice. They averted their faces, suddenly uncomfortable. Even the oily vendor seemed ill at ease and reluctant, but he had never refused a penny in his life. He opened the wagon flap, slowly.

The old man went inside. It took a moment for his eyes to adjust to the darkness. Dimly at first, and then growing more clear and distinct, he saw a section of delicate white filigree railing, plunder from some burned-out manor house in Georgia most likely. In front of it sat a rocking chair, crudely built, with a red-tasseled velvet cushion at the back. In the chair sat a man, a waxen figure of great beauty and artistry. The old man stepped closer. The wax figure was a hauntingly accurate representation of reality. Only the glass eyes jarred the credibility. They were so cold and vacant, completely devoid of the humor and the melancholy, those two contradictions that were ever present in the living eyes. The figure was clothed in a rusty black suit with a shawl draped around its shoulders. In the darkness it seemed almost possible that the large hands resting on the arms of the rocker could move, that the sad compressed lips could open and speak. A few feet from the form in the rocker there was a pedestal with a revolver mounted upon it. It pointed, forever fixed, at the temple of the wax figure. There was a sign which read: PULL THIS TRIGGER AND KILL LINCOLN.

The old man, with trembling hand, squeezed the trigger, and through some macabre and intricate wiring, Abraham Lincoln slumped forward in his rocker and died, again, and again, and again. Anyone with a penny could kill him once more. He limped over to the figure, pulled the wires from it, and raised it upright. He reached out his hand and softly touched the face. Tears, the first he had felt since his leg was ground to powder beneath the wheels of that wagon, coursed from his eyes.

He stepped out into the shimmering sunlight. All around him there were upturned faces, squinting, sweating, horribly blank, and waiting. The peddler began to shout.

"It's the thrill of a lifetime. A little bit much for you, old-timer? Better go sit in the shade. Let the young folks have some fun."

"There will be no more fun today."

"Sure there will, folks. It is, I promise you, the thrill of a lifetime!"

He was easing the old man off the wagon, a hand under his elbow. The old man turned and drove his fist into the smiling sweating face. The man fell from his wagon to the ground. The crowd watched, not moving. He was wailing pitifully and loudly, writhing in the dirt, blood spurting from his nose and mouth. The old man grabbed him by the throat.

"Where did you get his face? Where?"

"Someone in Washington got hold of the death mask, made a pretty penny that fellow did. Lots of them figures was made and sold. I paid for it, all legal-like, paid over a hundred dollars for it, cash on the barrel head. I'm only trying to make a living, just trying to get by. Don't kill me, mister."

"You're afraid of an old cripple? I won't be killing you, that's sure."

"No, not now you won't, not with all these people. But maybe you might take it into your head to come back later and do it."

"You won't be here later. You are leaving now. Besides, if I had a mind to kill you I'd do it right here. Not one of them would lift a finger. You and I are nothing to them. It would only be another show, more thrilling as you like to say, because it would be real, and they'd have the added pleasure of watching me hang."

"There's already to be one hanging today. That's why I'm here. I go to all the hangings. It's good business."

"If one hanging is good, two is better."

"What kind of town is this? What kind of people are these?"

"You have to ask? They're the usual kind, no better, no worse, than any others. The kind to pay a penny for the thrill of playing at killing a good man."

He stood up. The crowd drew back and parted for him. He thought of all the coins they would have spent today, and then he saw all of them dead, and those coins, hot and wet from their palms, in their eyes, and he smiled. He limped on down the street, and was nearly at the end when he heard the trap of the gallows being tested with sandbags. He thought of the four nooses from a long-ago scaffold, and of a woman's black billowing skirts being bound at the ankle. A hanging was a reason for gaiety in this little dusty town, a time to drink lemonade and eat cake, and dress up in your best, and watch another human being die. Today had brought him to violence and to tears. It had been fifty long years since he had known these things.

He walked on toward the white house, praying that he would be admitted, that finally he could lay his heavy burden down, and leave this place forever.

She stood watching from the upstairs window as the old man turned from her door and walked off down the street. There was something familiar in his painful uneven gait that made her think she knew him. If she tried she could remember, but she did not like to look back. Memories for her were almost always sad. She leaned her face against the cool glass pane. How lovely the world looked from behind lace curtains.

"He come agin, Miss Annie. I sends him away like you tell me to."

She started at the sound of Mardella's voice. "Goodness, but you made me jump."

"Well, he come agin."

"Yes, I saw him from the window. Did he give his name this time?"

"No. He say jus' like all de other times dat he have to see you, dat he has somethin' fer you, but when I ask de name he won't say."

"I will not receive any gentleman into my home who will not give his name. He couldn't really be a gentleman and refuse."

"He gots his reasons, I 'spect."

She looked at Mardella and frowned. Mardella was nearly six feet tall. Her skin was light brown, but her eyes were black. She had a long neck which she arched when angry. It was arched at this moment. Annie saw and understood. They had been together for nearly thirteen years. They had little need of words to communicate.

"Mardella, why is he coming here? What does he want from me?"

"He says he gots somethin' fer you. He don't never say he wants nothin'."

"What on earth could he have for me?"

"It looks to me like he gonna keep on a-comin' till you finds out."

"He's a very old man, isn't he?"

"He ole, but he look more than he be. He had hard times. He done a lot of things he sorry fer."

"Della, how could you know such a thing?"

"His eyes tells me. Mos' folks tells more truth wid dey eyes than wid dey mouth."

"Like me, I suppose?"

"I say mos' folks. Not you 'specially, Miss Annie."

"You think I should see him?"

"I don't thinks you ought to go a-lettin' no strangers into de house, but . . . " She trailed off, looking steadily at the blonde woman seated in the chair by the window. She knew her better than any other living soul, and loved her better. It wasn't always easy to do either.

"You think I should see him?"

"I thinks it mighty mean to let an ole cripple man walk 'bout so much an' not never git to set hisself down."

"He's coming again tomorrow?"

"So he say. He come fer how many day now?"

"Every day, for weeks."

"I don't 'spect he up an' stop now. He come tomorrow. Sure, he come. I jus' made some lemonade, nice an' fresh. You like a glass, Miss Annie?"

"No, thank you, Della. I think I'll just lie down and rest for a while."

"I draw de curtains. You takes off yer shoes an' puts yer feets up on dat dere pillow. You look a litl' peaked."

Annie was left alone in the darkened room. The certainty of the old man's return both frightened and reassured her. It was hot and close but her hands were icy cold. She went to her tall black chiffonier, quickly ducking her head to avoid her image in the mirror. She opened the top drawer and brought out a small deep blue bottle. It was nearly empty. With shaking hands she tipped it to her mouth and swallowed what remained within. Then she carefully placed the empty bottle back in the drawer. She drew the spread off the bed and laid down on the cool white sheets. She stared at the gap of sunlight where the curtains did not quite meet. Then she closed her eyes, and as if that was not enough, she stretched her arm across her face. He would come again. He would come tomorrow. She chanted silently. He would come again. He would come tomorrow. That litany of dreadful certitude and her medicine lulled her to sleep.

At supper that evening she ate little. Her food grew cold before her. William noticed, but said nothing. He continued eating and chewing methodically and somewhat loudly. His wife was a delicate creature. He had known that when he married her some ten years ago. Indeed, it was her delicacy that made him want to join his life with hers. He considered her pale blonde frailty one of her great charms. He knew all about her sad and unfortunate past. He had even been a victim of it. Four days after his marriage to Annie, he was removed from his job as chemist in the Surgeon-General's Laboratory. The government had a very long arm and memory. William knew everything about Annie except what she really was, her feelings, her thoughts, her memories. And she was trying her best to eradicate those things within herself. She feared them, and could share them with no one. Only Mardella seemed to know her, and without a word spoken. It was the telling Annie found difficult. Living with William and his deferential pity had become hatefully easy.

She made William feel manly and strong, large and sure, a novel sensation for the serious-minded little scientist. He considered their union quite a successful one. She felt it not a union at all. The empty routine of her life, of which he was the biggest part, made her feel hollow inside and blessedly numb. Total detachment was her goal, and she had very nearly achieved it.

He watched her move her food around her plate. She was in one of her melancholy moods tonight. William knew all about those. He did not think about the origins of them. He was concerned only with their outward manifestations. That was enough. He indulged her in her moods, and in all things. Her deep silences, her delicacy, her refusal to go out into the world among people, her sweet wan expression, all were dear to him. William said nothing, asked no questions. He loved Annie exactly as she was at this moment. He ate his supper, and between bites gazed with longing across the table at his fine sad soft wife.

She was thinking of the old man. In her mind she kept seeing him walk from her door again and again. She knew that she had seen him before. She kept shying from the brink of remembrance and returning. And then it was before her. She had been idly watching William spoon rice pudding into his mouth. It was his favorite. A small drop of it clung to his close-shaven chin. Suddenly and shockingly, like turning a corner into the arms of a stranger, the memory, recalled, was there. It was compelling. She saw the old man, but he was younger. Not a young man really, more middle-aged. His back was straight, but still there was the same peculiar walk. He was no longer on her pleasant shady street, but instead walking unevenly down a long dark corridor with doors on either side and bars on those doors. She was seeing him not through lace curtains, but from behind bars, hard and cold. He wore a uniform, dark blue like a winter sky at night. His hair was gray only at the temples, and there was a pistol in a holster at his hip. He was not alone. A small woman in black walked beside him. Her hands were manacled and her face was covered by a heavy veil. Annie closed her eyes tightly to drive these images away.

"My dear, you are fatigued," William said.

She opened her eyes slowly. Now, gratefully, all that came into focus was his mild face with pudding on its chin.

"Wipe your face, William."

He embarrassedly put napkin to chin. "I'm afraid Mardella's rice pudding is too good. It makes me greedy and incautious. You don't look at all well, Annie."

"My head aches."

"You must go right upstairs. I will come up and rub your poor head until you go to sleep."

"Yes."

She rose obediently and left the table.

Mardella entered to clear away the dishes. Seeing the untouched food, she began to mutter. "Miss Annie, she done always eat like a bird, but dat man he make her stop all together."

"What's that you say, Mardella? What man?" he asked.

She looked at William. She felt that he should know what was happening to his wife and she knew that Annie could not tell him, or would not. Mardella thought that William was a coward. She did not blame him for this. It was simply what he was and there must be reasons for it. She didn't know what they were. She didn't need to. He looked at her and saw disapproval in her eyes where there was only sympathy and sorrow.

"Dat man who keep comin' round to see Miss Annie, dat man she say she don't wants to see, but I catches her awatchin' him from de window, dat man whose name she keep on askin' fer when all de time she know it. Dat man."

Mardella waited, hoping he would ask something further of her, but knowing that he wouldn't.

"That was a fine dinner, Mardella."

"I thanks you, sir."

She took his plate and walked from the room.

He carefully folded his napkin, and swept the few crumbs from the tablecloth into his hand. He placed them in a small pile upon the napkin. He always did this. It was more ritual than habit, the careful customs of a completely controlled man. He sensed Mardella's disappointment in him. He had wanted to ask her more questions, but he couldn't. He was afraid of the answers. Yet, the questions burned inside of him. He rose from the table and left the room. Slowly he climbed the stairs to his wife.

Annie was lying in bed. Upon entering the room, she had gone directly to the top drawer, but the bottle was empty. She remembered that she had finished it off in the afternoon. Tomorrow she must send Mardella into town for more. Even when she did not feel the need for it, it was important that she know that it was there. That empty bottle was like a broken promise. Why had she taken so much this afternoon? She wanted some tonight. She needed it to sleep. It was essential that she sleep. She couldn't bear to lie in the darkness and think and remember. Even though it was a warm night, she had closed the windows and put on her merino nightdress. It was softer than the cotton. It felt good against her skin. Besides, no matter what the weather she was always cold, especially at night. It was the darkness that chilled her. She could not stand to have the curtains opened at night. She felt exposed, sitting in a lighted room, and beyond the windows all was blackness where anyone could hide and watch her. She drew her long hair, freed for the night, across the pillow. It fanned out around her face. She heard his slow steps coming up the stairs toward her. She closed her eyes and feigned sleep.

Behind her closed eyes she saw the old man, once again younger and dressed in uniform, and the small woman in black was beside him, holding on to his arm with chained hands. The pair walked interminably down the endless dark corridor. She could feel her face pressed against the bars watching and watching them. It was not a dream for she was not asleep. It was real. It was remembered. Her eyelids quivered, she could feel them.

William was in the room now, turning out the gas jets, opening the curtains and the windows. She could not possibly open her eyes to face him and the blackness beyond the gaping windows. Now she had to stay with her memories. Why had she taken all of her medicine? Even a drop or two would have dimmed this man and these memories that threatened her.

He was undressing. He put each article of clothing away in its proper place. Standing naked before the chiffonier, he reached for his nightshirt and then turned and looked at his sleeping wife. He closed the drawer softly and walked to the bed. His small white body was covered with brown hair. He bent and kissed her slightly parted lips. She did not stir.

She felt his warm breath upon her face. The bed sagged as he sat down beside her. Behind her eyes she was seeing dark corridors. She preferred this prison, this recalled place of horror, to the one that she would see should she open her eyes. He was leaning upon the pillow and her hair. It felt as if it was being torn from the roots. Yet she could not move to free herself.

He unbuttoned her dressing gown and drew it open, tracing the blue veins lacing the pale swell of her white breasts. Through the open windows the moon shone brightly. Her skin looked silver. He began to rub and knead her breasts. He liked to think of her nipples as rosebuds, but had not the courage to tell her. He bowed his head and began to kiss and suck them. He sank his small teeth into them. They were so soft and good. He wanted to leave little red marks on them, his marks of love.

His pleasure and her pain, they had come to be the same. Her breasts would throb for hours after he finished with them. After he had gone to sleep, she would sometimes stroke them gently and guiltily. She would comfort them and herself.

He pulled back the coverlet, careful to fold it so that it would not wrinkle. Then he pushed her nightdress up around her waist. He parted her thighs and settled down upon her. She was still, her eyes closed, her skin cold and a little damp. He thrust deep into her.

She felt dry and breaking inside. She was like a corpse. Her thoughts were of death, a death to be met at the end of a long dark corridor on the arm of a man in blue. She wondered if all men like to spill their seed into corpses. It seemed so self-defeating. And William did not even do that. His fear was too great even for that. He rolled off of her, again catching her hair and tearing it. He moaned, and she knew, though she could not see, that his hands were covered in sticky substance, his substance. She heard him walk softly across the room and pour water from the pitcher, then open a drawer.

He returned to bed in his nightshirt. They lay beside one another, silent, not touching, isolated by their fears. The wide barrier of years lived together but unshared was between them. He forced his breathing into a smooth and regular pattern and prayed for swift sleep.

Tears squeezed out from the corners of her eyes. She opened them slowly. The moon had passed on. It was very dark. She got up and went to the windows. Outside she thought she saw a shadow move among the trees. She closed the windows and pulled the curtains. Tomorrow William would not question why he had gone to sleep with them open and awoke with them closed. He would not ask why. He would not ask when. He never did. He would merely awake and accept them closed as part of her day, as she accepted them open as part of his night.

Had something or someone moved in the darkness under her window? Did something or someone wait for her there?

Tomorrow she would see the old man.

II

He always came at two o'clock. At one-thirty she sat down in the parlor to wait for him. She had asked Mardella to show him in when he arrived. Mardella had not seemed surprised at this request. Annie had never seen her surprised by anything. It was as if she knew beforehand what was going to happen, what had to happen. Annie remembered the first time she ever saw her.

It was on a street corner. It was summer. Annie was standing, not watching, not thinking even, just standing. And then she had stepped out into the street in front of a fast-approaching carriage. Mardella had to have anticipated her action. She could never have pulled her back in time if she hadn't known what Annie was going to do. That had been thirteen years ago. They had been together ever since, and Mardella was still anticipating her. In the eyes of the world it was a mistress-servant relationship solely. It could be nothing else and yet it was everything else. They were two people who understood one another when no understanding should have been possible. They shared common ground where none should have been. She was white, Mardella black. There should have been an unbridgeable gap between them, but there was not. Mardella had only recently been free when she met Annie, but she would not speak of her origins. Only once had she come close to a personal revelation. Annie had told her all about herself that first day. It had spilled out of her.

After she had told everything, the black woman had said, "Mardella, dat weren't de name I borned wid. I takes de name Mardella. Mardella, a name from dat place where I from. When I takes de name I takes a little piece of home wid me. I think it a pritty name. I been given names by other folks in my life, but Mardella I gives to myself."

That was all she ever said, that first day or any other.

Annie heard the clock chiming two. She looked out onto the street. It was deserted. He wasn't coming. She had tried for weeks to wish him away, to drive him from her, and now he had gone. He wasn't coming today and she had to see him. She knew who he was. The man, his name, his walk, the part he had once played in her life and in her nightmares forever after, these things were unforgettable. She must see him, and seeing him, relive the painful times. It was essential to her, to the maintenance of her tenuous hold on sanity, to see him, to meet with him.

She watched the street and the clock alternately. The time went slowly past. He was fifteen minutes late, a half-hour, then an hour.

He had awakened late to a day stiflingly hot. From the window of his room in the boardinghouse he had looked out and seen the still and sweltering streets. The leaves on the trees had a thick coat of dust upon them, choking them. They looked weary and ready to drop at any moment. The old man felt just that way too. The town was sullen and silent after yesterday's excitement. There were very few people about. The air was heavy with heat. It was difficult to breathe. His sleep last night had been restless and fitful. He was tired, tired of this town, this house, this room. His weariness tightened. He was terrified by the intensity of the spasms in his chest. He sat down in the chair and closed his eyes.

It was past three o'clock when he awoke. He hurried into his clothes which felt as if they were lined with sand. The thought of the long walk in the heat made his heart contract in anticipation. He could not miss a day. He could not stop until he met with the fair-haired woman. He got up from the chair, slipped a little leather book into his pocket, and walked from the room. As he closed the door he thought that he had been denied all relief. Both death and cool breeze had remained elusive. It was necessary that he live within the furnace for another day.

It was nearly four o'clock, and she had all but given up when she saw him come around the corner. She concentrated on his shadow, elongated and black. She was not yet ready even after all the long weeks and hours of watching the man to really see him.

He looked up to the second-story window but there was no one. The curtain was so still it looked as if it had been painted upon the glass. Today had been the longest and the hottest yet. If this was to be their day of reckoning, it was the one when he felt least able to confront her and survive it.

Both were most reluctant to forsake the shadowy image that they held of one another in their minds.

He was at the door. She heard Mardella's footsteps and drew back from the window. The skin on the back of her neck was hot, her hands cold and damp. She stood, and her legs trembled beneath her. She thought that she would fall. Then she ran into the vestibule before Mardella could open the door.

"Don't. Don't let him in. I don't want to see him after all."

"De man's awaitin' out dere."

"I don't care. Let him wait. Let him wait until he rots. Let him wait forever."

"You an' me both knows dat he do jus' dat, he wait ferever."

"I can't. I can't today. Maybe tomorrow."

"Mebbee."

"I tell you I can't see him."

"I ain't sayin' nothin', Miss Annie."

"Yes, you are."

"I ain't. You hears me sayin' dat you gotta see dat ole man, dat you cain't go one more day an' not see him? Dat it be de cruelest, de mostest hardest piece of work I done ever see, if you don't? You see dem words a-comin' outa my mouth?"

Annie looked at her. She saw her hand poised over the doorknob, waiting. "Yes. Yes, I hear you."

"Den yer ears is a-playin' tricks, Miss Annie."

"Let him in."

He was about to turn away when she opened the door.

"You may come in, sir."

Annie had returned to her seat by the window. A shaft of late-afternoon sun pierced her left shoulder. She turned her head slightly and watched the dust mites swirl and drift in the light. She focused on one in particular, seeing its whole life and death in a moment.

He entered the room and saw her sitting grave and silent. There was a strange remote look on her face. She seemed older, thinner, and if possible, sadder than when he had last seen her. There was no gray in her golden hair. He realized with a shock that she was still a young woman. Sitting in the sunlight, ashen and desolate, she was barely thirty.

She heard him before she saw him, the heavy sound of the left foot, the slight dragging of the right. Watching him walk away from her down in the street while she sat above, separated by walls and locked doors, that was one thing, but to hear him, to feel him close beside her, in the very same room, that was entirely different and terrible.

"Good afternoon, Miss . . ."

"You needn't call me by any name. I wish that you would not."

"But you remember me, my name?"

"I do, sir."

"Yet, you always had your maid ask it of me."

"Yes, but only to see if you would give it, Colonel Wood."

"May I sit down?"

"If you must."

He pulled a straight-backed chair close to her. It was disturbing that an action so commonplace could be so sinister. She leaned back and away from him. He was very close. She raised her eyes to his face. He had grown incredibly old.

"I've been trying so long to see you."

"Yes, I know. It has been some weeks."

"It's been far longer than that. It has taken me years to come here."

"I would ask what has kept you away all of these years but what I really want to know is why you have come at all."

"I had to come. For years I couldn't. I was the impediment then. These last weeks you have been."

"Are you asking me for an apology? I find it perfectly reasonable that I would not want you in my home or anywhere near me. Do you not find that reasonable?"

"I do. After all of this time I very nearly did not come today."

"Why not today?"

"Because I knew that today you would see me."

"Do you read minds, Colonel?"

"Sometimes I wish that I did. It was just a feeling that I had, and it seems true, for here I am."

"Yes, here you are."

There was silence. The clock was ticking loudly. Outside, a child passing by was hitting the fence with a stick. It was a game. Every picket must be struck or the game was lost.

"You're wondering why I've come?" said the Colonel.

"Wondering? Wondering, that is a very light word. It does not begin to cover the questions that have arisen in my heart these past weeks. I had actually managed, not to forget you—no, never that—but at last to confine you to the dark part of my mind, the part I rarely use. I did not think of you when I ate my meals or brushed my hair or said good morning or good evening. Now I can do none of these things, nothing, in peace. You cannot help but know that your presence is unwelcome here, that you are abhorrent to me."

She put her hand to her mouth as if to physically scotch the flow of words, as if they were blood from a wound.

"I know that you hate me."

"You are wrong. I have neither the courage nor the anger any longer to hate all of those I used to hate. You disturb and upset me, but I haven't the strength for hatred. I'm much too tired."

"It was so long ago."

"It was yesterday. It is today. It never ends for me. It will live with me for as long as I live."

"I had to come here."

"And it seems that I, in my turn, had to see you. Perhaps you could tell me why you felt compelled to put us both in this unhappy position. Can you tell me why you have come? Can you tell me quickly, and then go?"

"Are you made of stone, Miss?"

"I only wish that I were. Am I to try and make this easy for you?"

"Yes. Can't you? I'm an old man."

"That means very little to me. I'm sorry that you are old. Sorry that you reached old age. I can still muster enough energy to eagerly hope for your death."

"You wish me dead?"

"Of course I do. There was a time when I wanted to kill you myself. I am not now capable of accomplishing that deed. That does not mean that I have ceased to dream of it."

"There are many who are gone now. Lane and Foster are both dead, by their own hand. Lafayette Baker, and the Secretary, and the President."

"Not enough, not nearly enough. Yes, I wished all of those dead, and many others. Unfortunately, most, including you, Colonel, still breathe."

"You can't mean what you are saying."

"I do. It is wise that you presented yourself to me and not to my brother. He is still strong and angry. He would probably kill you yet. And I would have the pleasure of crossing you off my long list."

"You must know that to your brother's grief is added the unbearable burden of guilt."

"You speak of guilt? You should die of it. You will not talk of my brother. I will not allow it."

"It was you who mentioned him. I had no intention of it. He is not the reason I came here, but I must say that his guilt must be very great. For it is he who killed your mother, as surely as if he had shot her with a gun."

"You! You come into my home and speak these words to me. You, the true murderer of my mother. You, her jailor and tormentor. You accuse my brother."

"I do."

"Leave here."

"I must stay. You know that what I say is true. I testified for your mother. Where was he then? In hiding. In flight. He was, and is, a sulking coward. He abandoned your mother, his mother, without a backward glance. He let her die for his crimes, his sins."

"Stop it. I won't hear these things spoken."

"You're right, Miss. You have lost all your strength and courage. I admired you when you were a girl. You met things head-on. You've become a very cowardly woman, hiding away in this house. You're a cripple much worse than me." He tapped his stiff outstretched leg. "I've learned to live with mine. Your disability is that you can't live at all, not in the present anyway. You can only live in the past with a lot of bitter dreams of retribution."

"You feel very good about yourself, don't you? You blame my brother so easily, so readily, to assuage your own guilt. You testified for my mother only to salve your conscience. It did a great lot of good, your testimony, didn't it? Didn't it, Colonel?"

"Nothing would have done any good. Nothing would have helped."

"You knew that. They all knew that, but I didn't. I didn't believe that the innocent died condemned. I kept thinking that there must be someone or something that could save her . . ." She sobbed suddenly, the tears building silently behind cold eyes. "Why have you come here, tearing open this old and horrible wound?"

"I had to come."

"Why? There can be no reason, except that you are still the same fiend you always were, the king of the Old Capitol Prison, the keeper of a thousand tormented souls. You reveled in your power over them then, and over me now. Your power to lock people away, to deprive their poor bodies of food and light and air, and to dispossess them of their very souls and hearts. We used to listen in our cells for your tread, the unmistakable sound of your walk. We would cringe and cower because you held total power over us. The feeling returned to me today when I heard you enter this room."

"You didn't know then and you don't know now what I was, what I am. I had no power in those days, only what was given me. I was another man's creature, his slave. I did his bidding then. He is dead now and I am free of him."

"Are you so very sure of that?"

"Yes. For what I do now you may curse or bless only me. This is my deed alone."

"You speak of the Secretary? It was he who was your master?"

"Yes. The last words he spoke to me, on his deathbed, were of your mother."

"How very touching."

"He said that she haunted him."

"No doubt she did. They say her spirit walks the rooms of the boardinghouse on H Street. I'm sure that it does. How could her spirit ever rest? I tried to give her peace. I worked for years to get her away from all of you, out of the hands of her tormentors and murderers, away from the prison where she died and where you buried her. Finally I was allowed to remove her body from that unmarked grave within sight of her gallows. Still she has no peace. It is fitting that none of you who killed her should have it either."

"Did you know that your mother kept a diary?"

Annie thought of all the times she had seen her mother bent closely over her little leather book. She had seen it in her hands as often as she had her rosary beads or her silver thimble. Her mother had rarely been without it, as she remembered.

"Yes, I knew that she kept a diary."

"Did you ever wonder what became of it?"

"No. There was no need to wonder. It was confiscated and destroyed along with all the rest of my mother's papers."

"It was confiscated, yes. And marked for destruction."

"And destroyed."

"No."

"Yes. It was destroyed."

"No."

"Yes, destroyed, as she was, by you and the others."

"I tried to save your mother. I failed. No one could have succeeded, except perhaps your brother. But I saved her diary, her words and her thoughts. I saved them for you. It was the last thing she asked of me. I've brought it here today."

"No. It was burned."

"I was ordered to burn it, after it was read by Baker and the Secretary. They gave it to me to burn, but I read it instead. Then I couldn't. I gave it back to your mother just before she was taken from the Old Capitol to the Arsenal. She had it with her almost the entire time she was in prison."

"I never saw it."

"I warned her to tell no one, not even you. It was a ghost book. It was ashes to everyone but your mother. It had to remain that way. The last day when I went to her she gave it to me to give to you."

"Why couldn't she just have given it to me herself? Surely, it couldn't have made any difference the day she died."

"But it did. You were watched always. You would never have gotten out of the building with that book. They wanted no record of her life, her innocence, even after she was dead. I was the only one who could have taken it from the prison, and I did."

"I don't believe any of this. It's some cruel joke. You only want to torment me further. Please go away."

He reached into his jacket and brought out the book. He held it awkwardly in both hands. She looked at the red leather cover of her mother's diary. It was cracking in many places. She closed her eyes.

"It's yours now. I promised her. It's yours."

"You are more monstrous even than before. My mother was finally dead for me, and decently buried like an ordinary woman in an ordinary graveyard. I no longer woke at night with the sight of her, hooded, swinging at the end of a noose, her skirts bound with rope, burning in my mind. She was dead. My memories of her were dead and buried. And then you came, you ghoul, you torturer. Well, I won't have it. I will not resurrect her. No one can make me do that."

"You contradict yourself. You accuse me of digging up corpses, and then you speak of resurrection. I am not a ghoul, but I do seek to bring her back from the dead for you with her book. All that is left of her is in it, and you refuse it."

"Yes. Yes, I do because I cannot bear it."

"You are a weakling and a coward. You were not always this way."

"No, I was different once. I was brave and stupid. I was young. I didn't know what fear really was. I had never felt it. I thought that life was beautiful and wonderful. I thought that people told the truth. I believed in honor and compassion and love. When my mother died, I realized that I lived in a world of hatred and injustice and fear. And I became afraid, and I began to hate. And I was unjust."

"Most of all to yourself. I remember the first time I ever saw you."

"I remember too. I was brought to your prison by soldiers."

"You weren't frightened then."

"I saw no reason. I had done nothing wrong. At that time I did not believe that the innocent were punished. I thought it was all some terrible mistake."

"You stood so straight and refused a chair. You looked me in the eye and answered my questions so quietly but so clearly, so firmly. You wore a long brown woolen cloak. You threw off the hood and pushed back a few strands of golden hair from your forehead. Your hand was so steady. You told me that you would answer no more of my questions because you were tired of them and of me. I don't think I ever admired anyone quite so much as I did you that night."

"I was seventeen years old. I was a fool. I might have been hanged for my spirit."

"You were released the next day."

"My mother wasn't. She was never released. You locked her away that night, forever. My mother, who was the gentlest of women, who never harmed any living thing. I don't think she ever really understood what was happening to her or why. She died not knowing. Is it any wonder that she has no peace, that she still haunts this earth. And I can't even remember her as she truly was. I've tried to think of her at the piano or braiding my hair when I was a little girl, but the other memories always intrude. I see her in that cell. I see her on the scaffold, even though I wasn't there. Well, those are not the memories I wish to cherish of my mother. I will not remember her as a murderess. That is not what she was. If I cannot remember her as my mother, as the good and kind woman she was, then I will not remember her at all."

"Her diary will give back that woman to you. She will once again be your mother, and not the woman who was hanged . . ."

"Stop! The two are indivisible."

"It's not true so."

"It is."

"No. There is something else, some other reason for your fear. Why does her diary make you so afraid?"

"This is how it must be."

"No. I don't think you're afraid of remembering your mother's death. I think you're afraid of discovering her life. If you read this book you would know your mother, what she thought and felt."

"No."

"Yes. Your mother has become a martyr to you now. She is no longer a real woman. Her death was so painful and so wrong that you decided not to live anymore, to completely withdraw from life. She is your reason for feeling nothing for anyone. But if you read her diary, you would lose your martyr and find your mother. You'd have to start living and feeling again. Well, go ahead, live your numbed life, but I'm keeping my promise to her, finally after all these years. I'm leaving her book with you. I could only come here because I thought that I was dying, but after seeing and hearing you, I suddenly feel alive. Compared to you, I'm young. You're the one who is dying. No, you're already dead."

He stood and placed the book on the table.

"Don't leave it here. Take it with you."

"No. You burn it. Then convince yourself that it was destroyed by others. That shouldn't be so difficult for you to do. One more lie, omission, evasion. Do as you will. It's yours now, as she wanted it to be."

"You said that you thought that you were dying, that's why you came here. Did you come looking for forgiveness?"

"I may have been looking for understanding, but I know now that you couldn't possibly give it to me."

"You're quite right. I couldn't. I cannot give what I have never received. Once I asked for understanding. My pleas were answered with laughter, Colonel."

She began to laugh. The sharp edge of hysteria gleamed through.

"Those men who laughed, Lane and King, they weep in Hell now."

She stopped laughing and looked up at him. "I only hope that you join them soon. You are condemned. You are afraid. That is why you are here, but you are doomed. I won't give you relief."

"You can't. Your mother did, years ago. I have her understanding and forgiveness. That's enough. You're right. I'm afraid to die, so afraid that I wanted your pardon too, but not any longer. I want only to be away from you, from this house, and this town, as quickly as possible."

He walked out of the room. She went to the window and watched him walk unevenly down the darkening street and around the corner. He was gone. She turned and saw the book lying on the table. She wanted to put the chair back in its proper place. She wanted to smooth out the rug. She wanted to forget that he had ever come. Most of all she wanted to throw the little red leather book into the fireplace and walk away and not return until there were only ashes in the grate. She was unable to do any of these things. Instead, she called for Mardella, who appeared immediately in the doorway.

"Mardella, I need some medicine. You'll have to go into town for me."

"Miss Annie, supper's on de stove."

"I don't care about that. I'm ill and I need my medicine."

"Yes, Miss Annie."

She turned and started out.

"Please hurry, Della."

"Yes, Miss Annie."

She went and sat down far across the room, shaking violently.

III

As soon as Mardella had come back from town, Annie went to her room with her medicine. She did not come down for supper. She remembered taking seven or eight drops, the most she had ever taken in one dose, and lying down on the bed in her clothes. She had fallen into a heavy sleep.

She awakened in the darkened room wearing a nightdress. Either William or Mardella had done this. She looked at him sleeping beside her and hoped it had been Mardella since the thought of him touching her was repugnant to her, especially when she was asleep. That she did not know what things he did, and that he might prefer to do them while she was unconscious frightened and repelled her.

She got out of bed quietly. The windows and curtains were open. She stood before them. There were no moving shadows this night. All was perfectly still. She noticed the top buttons of her gown were done wrong. It gaped open at her breasts. She turned and looked at William sleeping in their bed, but she could not see in the darkness that he was not asleep, that his eyes were upon her. She buttoned her gown. Without slippers or wrapper she went downstairs. William got up and went to the bureau. He took from her drawer a silk chemise. He returned to bed with it. He held it against him, then buried his face in it and wept. His sobs were harsh and racking. He began to rend and tear her chemise, but the tears did not cease.

Annie opened the parlor door and stepped inside. It was dark, but she could see that the chair in which the old man sat had been returned to its usual place. On the table stood a lamp upon a long lace scarf, and there was a small porcelain figurine from the H Street house. That was all. The book was gone. She fell to her knees and searched the floor. It was not there. She ran to the chair, throwing the cushions off, but it wasn't there either. From the darkness, across the room, she heard a voice. All the breath went from her body as if she had been struck. She had never in her life felt such fear.

"I has it, Miss Annie."

"Mardella."

She came out of the blackness. "I has it right here."

"Thank God, it's you."

She handed her the book. Annie took it. For the first time she held it in her hands. It was cool. Without thinking, she placed it against her hot cheek.

"I knows dat you don't want nobody lookin' at it."

"Thank you, Mardella. Come and sit down with me for a moment?"

"Yes, Miss Annie."

They sat down. She put the book on the table and then picked it up again.

"Della, do you know what this is?"

"I ain't been a-readin' it, Miss Annie. Ain't mine to read. 'Sides, I cain't read anyhow."

"I didn't ask if you had read it. I asked if . . ."

"I know what you is askin', Miss Annie. I ain't so sure dat I got de answer but mebbee I knows."

"What is it then?"

"I thinks dat it be yer ma's, dat's all I thinks."

"It is my mother's. It's her diary. Mardella, do you know what a diary is?"

"I thinks dat I do. It be when folks done puts dey life down in a book."

"Yes. That's just it."

"Dat ole man, he brung it to you today. Dat what he got fer you."

"Yes."

"How dat ole man he come by yer ma's book?"

"He says she gave it to him."

"You think he be lyin'?

"Yes, I think he took it from her."

"Why den he be givin' it back to you now?"

"Because he didn't want to die with it on his conscience. He was trying to make himself feel better."

"An' do he feel better, you think?"

"I hope not."

"You hates dat ole man."

"He was my mother's jailor, Mardella. He was one of the men who helped to kill her."

"Why he takes sech pains wid her book den? Why he keep it all dese years?"

"I don't know."

"What you gonna do wid it now? You be wantin' me to lock it away in de trunk in de attic?"

"No, Mardella."

"What you do wid it den?"

She looked down at the book and said nothing. Mardella stared at her until she looked up from her lap.

"I don't know just yet what I'm going to do."

"You knows, Miss Annie. You gots it in yer head to be rid of it. You gonna tear it up or burn it up or somethin' like dat. You ain't gots no right to be doin' dat, no right to do sech a thin', Miss Annie."

"I think that you have said just about enough, Mardella."

"Mebbee I has, an' mebbee I ain't. But I gots to say jus' one more thin'. You gots lots of yer ma's stuff. You gots dem pritty little knickyknacks an' her dresses an' sech, but ain't none of dem yer ma. Dey jus stuff. What you gots in yer hands, dat her words all writ down, dat her life in dat book, an' you ain't gots no right to do what you is thinkin'. Now I is goin' back to my bed."

"Della, I'm sorry. Please don't leave me alone."

She turned back and looked at the book. "You ain't, Miss Annie, dat be what I is tryin' to tell you."

She heard the door close. She sat in the darkness, and despite Mardella's words, she felt very alone. She stood and walked to the fireplace, carrying the book with her. She imagined it burning. The pages curling grotesquely like pleading fingers. She could smell the blackened paper, acrid. She could nearly taste the bitter ash. She closed her eyes, and when she opened them, she saw the small red leather volume before her, untouched and unburned, mocking her.

She reached for the matches by the andirons. She would burn it page by page. She struck a match, took the book and opened it. Even in the darkness with only the small circle of light from the burning match, her mother's small even hand leapt out at her. She knew that she could not burn her words. She shook the flame out.

If the old man had only come in winter, leaving uneven footprints in the snow. If there had been a blazing fire in the grate. Then she could have thrown it into the flames and it would have been consumed quickly and completely. She would never have opened it.

Again she struck a match, this time to light the lamp. She began to read her mother's words, knowing that now they would burn in her brain with a cold flame.

Saturday, October 1, 1864

Washington City

I have arrived. I have traveled thirteen miles of muddy road and I am in another world—through the splendor of the Maryland countryside in fall to this dirty, dirty city. The difference between

Surrattsville and Washington never ceases to amaze me, no matter how many times I may travel that muddy road.

These days, Surrattsville, most all of southern Maryland, seems like a land from one of the famous Eastern Shore legends. An evil spell has been cast. It is all stillness, and desolate, so desolate. The name of Maryland's curse is war. It goes on and on. Our crops wither in the fields. Soldiers are everywhere. Following them is the filth and flotsam which inevitably and historically has followed all soldiers since time began.

Our Negroes flee. They run to Washington and freedom, a poor, pitiful variety of liberty–terrible shanties in a place called Murderer's Row here in the city.

There are a great many Yankees here too. Surprisingly, this being the capital of the Union, there is nearly an equal number of secesh sympathizers. I try not to be provincial and petty, but it is exceedingly difficult to make these Washington folk out. If all goes well I may soon be sharing my roof and table with some. I wonder sometimes at my aptitude for keeping a boardinghouse, but I can think of nothing else to keep body and soul together.

I do not place the entire blame for the war on the North as many do, but I think that they were completely in error when they invaded the South. Invasion! It brings to mind thundering hordes of Visigoths clad in skins of animals–while instead we are treated to open-faced Illinois farmboys in ill-fitting blue, but cruel many of them, the sort to wrench the tails from field mice.

There has been rashness and haste on both sides. I am just a poor woman who does not understand such things, but it seems to me that this war is an enormous and terrible family squabble. The wounds go deep, deep. I hate to see division in a family, for I am a woman and a mother. It is my function in life to mend, to soothe, to weave and knit, to unite. It is perhaps necessary that this country be torn asunder, many have tried to convince me of this, but it goes against my nature. I mustn't express these feelings aloud. I must try not even to feel them. My one son is fighting for the Confederacy, and my other son, I fear, is intriguing for it. They may well give their lives for disunion, and I must support and succor them. It is they who are important to me. My feeble attempts at understanding politics are silly, and worse, disloyal. I am but a poor widow woman looking to support her family by taking into her home paying guests. I am aware of my rightful considerations, and I will keep to them.

Tuesday, October 4, 1864

I have begun my boardinghouse in earnest. I have already two boarders, a Miss Dean and Miss Fitzpatrick. Miss Dean is eleven years old and will be staying with us but a short time. Miss Fitzpatrick is nineteen. She will be a good companion for my Annie, even though she is three years older. Annie is old for her years. Both are essentially quiet and serious-minded, but with the eager happy-heartedness that is indigenous to youth. Miss Fitzpatrick is alone in the world except for her father, who seems to have little time and even less affection for the girl. She and Annie will be sharing the third-story bedroom. They will become great friends I think.

It is wonderful to have people to talk with again. Miss Anna Ward, my dear young friend from down in the country, is here teaching at a Catholic orphanage, and Father Wiget too is in close proximity at Gonzaga College. Both are within walking distance, that is, if Washington streets are ever walkable. From what I have seen to date they are usually rivers of mud, ankle-deep and filthy.

I am very glad to have Annie away from Surrattsville, however. It is time to be thinking of marriage for her. It will be difficult enough making a match out of a boardinghouse, but a country tavern would be quite impossible. All those sad-eyed men hunched over their toddies for hours at a stretch, hatching the Good Lord only knows what plans and schemes. My John will be joining us in December when Mr. Lloyd takes over the place. I wait for the time in great anticipation. John can only find trouble among those men and their intrigues. He is young and easily influenced. He sees it all as adventure, and I am unable to convince him otherwise. But there is danger here too—the draft. I could perhaps afford to buy him a substitute, but it would be very difficult. With Mr. Lloyd paying only five hundred a year rent, and the small amount I can take in here, we will barely get by.

Oh, if only Mr. Surratt had been wiser. He tried very hard, I know. It was not his fault that he never found his calling in life. God knows he was no farmer. He was a lost man, not really a dreamer–he had ceased dreaming, and not a petitioner nor an entreater–he asked for very little. He simply spent his time, wondering where the magic of his once charmed life had got to, when he had become a failure, and how he had suffered such complete defeat without even knowing of the battle. I miss him still, every day. He left me accustomed to shouldering responsibilities. At least I am not helpless. I was really a widow long before Mr. Surratt departed, alone in my decisions and dealings, and in my bed, while he played the genial host and gave away the profits of the place to curry favor in the county.

I fear for John and his desire to be liked, to be thought a good fellow. He greatly resembles his father in this, and in many ways. Isaac is like me, even in appearance. This is good luck, they say, for a boy to take after his mother. Isaac and his father never got on together. I regret it so. Isaac, our eldest, a youth who kept his own counsel always, close to neither of us, close to no one. He left home gratefully when the war began. It's been over three years since I have seen him. I don't even know where he is, even the occasional taciturn letters I used to receive from him have stopped. Strange that I do not miss him or fret over him as I do John, who is just a few short miles away from me and not in any immediate danger. Yes, John is like his father, not really admirable, but eminently lovable. I miss them both. And Isaac is like me, stolid and dull, and not the sort of person one would miss, or even think a great deal about. Mothers are not supposed to have preferences among their offspring, and yet they do, for they are only human.

Saturday, October 8, 1864

This tall narrow house is not my home. I have not had a home since father and little Anna left me alone so many years ago. Mother could not give me a home after she stopped loving me, and Mr. Surratt could not give me a one. My only true home could have been in God's house and I am to blame for not dwelling there.

I have another boarder. It seems that I am very good at running a boardinghouse. His name is Mr. Louis Weichman, an old schoolmate of John's from St. Charles College. He seems an amiable young man. He is somewhat timid. Yet, an unlikely but overripe conceit seems oddly present within him, a sense of great self-importance. He is now a clerk in the War Department, but he has tried many things, priest and teacher being two callings he pursued with some vigor, as much vigor as Mr. Weichman could muster. He is in search of himself. I fear that such a young man as he will not find his identity or destiny at the War Department. Perhaps it is the money that draws him. I hear that the pay is fair, and he seems not to mind in the least giving me thirty-five dollars a month for his room. It seems a great amount of money to me, but inflation has set in with a vengeance in Washington. Some rooms, I have heard tell, go for as much as one hundred and fifty dollars a month! When John comes, he and Mr. Weichman will share the room, so thirty-five dollars seems a fair price.

Monday, October 10, 1864

It is unseasonably hot in the city today. It is as if summer had decided to give us one last day to remember it by.

I was reminded of that day last June when I came from down in the country for a visit here with Father Wiget. It was to be a holiday, a respite from the tavern and my troubles, a long reviving conversation with the dear Reverend. It was Sunday. June the nineteenth it was, a hot day like today. Strangely dry, the dust blew in little whirlwinds through the streets.

We were early, so John decided to drive about Washington for a bit. After crossing through the barriers and over the Navy Yard Bridge, we swung to the left and drove toward the Arsenal. It suddenly grew very still and the dust settled in the streets. I remember thinking that Washington looked for all the world like a city under siege, with all the fortifications and rifle pits and the heavy anticipatory silence. We soon came upon a great crowd of people. John was forced to slow the horse to a walk and then a complete halt. He shouted to a tall man in the crowd, asking what it was all about. The man shouted back that it was the service for the poor young ladies. This shed no light on the event for me. John, who reads the "Star" regularly, had to explain to me about the sad occurrence. Eighteen young girls who worked at the Arsenal had been killed in an explosion a few days before. This was the service for them. It was sad, but solemnly beautiful too, all the mourners dressed in white. There was a large pavilion set up on the Arsenal grounds, draped in white. There were flags everywhere, hanging limp after the death of the breeze. The war has very nearly accustomed us to the loss of many of our precious young men. But these young girls, for them to die in a sudden and terrifying tangent of war, that was strange and horrible. Young girls were not supposed to die in wars. They were not to be exploded into pieces. That was the fate of young men in war.

Suddenly, all of it seemed so wrong to me, and I wanted more than anything to flee the scene, to escape this world gone mad, but the crowds and the heat closed in tightly, vise-like, and we were unable to move. I was forced to watch that tragic pageant and those shimmering tearful white players from my open carriage. I was late to Father Wiget's, and my holiday was ruined. Now, today too, is saddened by the memory of that day so many months ago. My mind has linked in memory this day and the one when those young girls were put into the ground. Both were hot and dry and still. I don't even know the names of the dead, but they haunt me. I assiduously avoid the Arsenal grounds to this day. There are ghosts there, souls prematurely torn from life. I cannot bear it.

Wednesday, October 12, 1864

Washington just does not deserve to be called a city, much less capital of a nation. It is a sprawling village, filthy and provincial. It is the hypocrisy of the city I despise. Alongside the ambassadors in their plumed equipages, pigs roam in the streets. Streets indeed! Mud holes they are, perfect sties, and no wonder the presence of pigs. Gambling dens and fancy houses abound. Young soldiers loiter everywhere. They are in blue and surprisingly in gray. The gray ones are prisoners who have been released after taking the oath of allegiance, or they are deserters. It is sad, sad, all this desperate drunken gaiety. But I suppose that all of these things are truly city-like. Perhaps the corruption, the dissoluteness, the unhappiness, they are the very things which qualify dirty little Washington as a city, metropolis of misery.

I tremble at the thought of John being thrust into the center of all of this when he comes in December. In the beginning I believed it would be such a good thing, but now I know Washington. If only he would settle down, perhaps with Miss Anna Ward. She is such a wonderful girl, steady and sound. She makes no secret of her affection for John. Presently she is absorbed in her teaching at the orphan asylum, a girl who can make her own way, but naturally and womanly enough she would prefer to be a helpmate and not stand alone. She is what John needs, stability, an anchor. That is what I always tried to be to Mr. Surratt, and yet he was not happy. His children and his wife, we were the net that entangled him, caught and held him. When we were courting I fell in love with his charm and his spirit. I did not suspect that those very qualities would turn to instability and irresponsibility.

Oh, perhaps, I did know. Perhaps those were the very things I did marry him for, his lightness, so markedly different from my somber heavy character, so fascinatingly different. Perhaps I am wishing my unhappiness on Miss Anna Ward, and the father's woe on the son. These two may not be a pair.

And what of my Annie? She is young. There is time yet, but youth by its very nature is short-lived and ephemeral. Whom will she marry? What nice young men are there for her? So many are dead. Of course, she need not marry. It would be comforting for me to have a loving companion for all the rest of my life, but that is really too selfish of me. Miss Fitzpatrick is nineteen, and she does not seem to have panicked at the prospect of spinsterhood, but my Annie, she is only sixteen, and golden blonde, and so fair. Surely she will have her chance at happiness. But is happiness to be found inevitably in marriage? I do not know. I fear that I have lived this long life and acquired no wisdom at all.

Saturday, October 15, 1864

Yesterday I would have been married twenty-nine years. That is a long time to be unhappy. Yet I have been unhappy for longer than that. I wish the war would end and I could return to the country, but even as I write I know that that would not bring me happiness.

No new boarders–the rooms stand empty–and I grow afraid. What is to become of us?

Monday, October 17, 1864

The carcass of that poor beast had been rotting in the street for days. Every morning I went to sweep the front porch, I would see it–and smell it. I love horses. We used to have a great many of them. Mr. Surratt for a time fancied himself to be a breeder of fine horses. The Army came and took them all away. Requisitioned was the word the young captain used. That was early on in the war. I remember once some Union mounts strayed from the encampment nearby and came to the farm. We fed them and put them in the empty stables. When the soldiers came to claim them, they offered me money but I could not accept. It would have been somehow too venal, accepting payment for what was pure pleasure. I wanted only one thing, to request of them that they be kind to the horses and to themselves and not go off to battle, to fight and die, but I said nothing. I only watched them ride away, powerless, knowing what their end would be.

Anyway, the city carrion cart came today to take the poor dead animal away. I am very glad of it. The man who drove the cart was an odd fellow. He seemed neither old nor young. He wore a Confederate gray forage cap perched on the back of his head. He called out good morning to me as I stood watching from the porch. From his accent I took him to be a Tennessee man. I asked if he was a prisoner. He said that he had been captured some months back, that he had taken the oath, and had then been given this job. It was this or male nurse, he said. I commented that it could not be a pleasant occupation.

He looked up from his work and he said to me: "I'm used to it, you might say. I used to bury the dead boys, that were my job in the Army. Dying, it smells the same, be it boys or critters. I'm used to it."

And then he returned to his grisly task and said nothing more to me.

Tuesday, October 25, 1864

We–Annie, Mr. Weichman, and I–went to the parade down Pennsylvania Avenue last night. It was a torchlight procession of surpassing beauty. There were shooting fires and Roman candles in a myriad of colors and hues. The reason for the festivities had something to do with the upcoming election. There was only the feeblest excuse needed, for the people are so war-weary and sad that they will grasp upon anything to help them forget their troubles for even the briefest of moments. There were many fistfights among the gentlemen. The combatants were those who held for Lincoln against those striking out for McClellan. But even the fisticuffs could not mar the spectacle for me. I went for the beauty of it, and closed my eyes to the rest. There is little enough loveliness in my life, and poor Annie's too. She was thrilled by it all. She stood on tiptoe, and her cheeks were flushed with excitement. Her eyes shone. She was easily as beautiful as the skyrockets. A shame that such a sight should be wasted on Mr. Weichman, a gentleman who shows not the slightest interest in young ladies. Annie does not care for him. She says that he reminds her of one of her father's hunting dogs. The first time she told me this, I knew immediately to which dog she referred, a large shiny animal, named Castor, who would mince along on his ridiculous big paws and slyly nip at all the other dogs, then run away. Annie is really very unusually perceptive for a girl her age and I will concede that she is right in a way about Mr. Weichman. He is a physical coward, but then that is not evil. It is moral turpitude that is abhorrent, and Mr. Weichman seems quite a moral and pious young man to me. However, those are not necessarily the most admirable qualities that a young man can possess when seen through the eyes of a young girl. Dash and valor—those are the gods of youth. I remember quite well.

The parade was lovely, but the crush of people lining the avenue was appalling. I lost my breath and felt faint several times. Mr. Weichman very solicitously took my arm on one very bad occasion. Yes, the old and feeble appreciate Mr. Weichman, and I fear that is what I have become, old and feeble. He accompanies me to church nearly every Sunday, and drives me about town. He lacks excitement, but he is secure and stable, qualities which I have come to admire, if only for their scarcity in this life. I suppose it takes living to truly appreciate them, and Annie has lived so little. I wish she would be more receptive to Mr. Weichman, but I saw her flashing eyes follow the soldiers on horses at the parade, and I know that it cannot be. I must not wish it to be.

Annie closed the book slowly. It had taken her so long just to read the first few pages. She felt as if she had been transported back over thirteen years. Reading her mother's words was like hearing her speak once more. It was as if she were sixteen again. She could feel the excitement she had felt upon their arrival in Washington, the love swelling inside her for something new and untried. She had not known, had not even guessed, her mother's fears and apprehensions. She had disguised them well, committing them to these pages and allowing no one to see. She had always thought that her mother had been as eager as she to leave Surrattsville.

Surrattsville. They had changed the name to Clinton after her mother's death. No one wanted any association with the name Surratt. It had come to mean something evil and foul. Her poor father. It had been the one great accomplishment of his life, being postmaster, having the town bear his name. Even that had been taken from him, but at least he never knew of it. He had been dead for a long time. She remembered the day he died. It was in August of 1862. Isaac was gone in the Army. John was still away at St. Charles. It had been just her mother, her father, and herself left at the tavern. That afternoon there had been a thunderstorm, very wild and fierce. It was so dark it had seemed like night. The air was hot and heavy. She had gone into the part of the house which served as the tavern, a long dim room with a bar along one wall and chairs all about. He was sitting at the bar, not upright but slumped forward, his head on his arms. The room was deserted. She went over to him and touched his shoulder softly, but he did not move. She called him. There was no response. She ran through the house looking for her mother and finally she ran out into the rain. She found her in the stables. Before she could speak, her mother did.

"Isn't it sad all these empty stalls. I hate it when things are not used. Everything is created for a purpose, and everyone."

"Mama, Papa is . . ."

"Is gone, I know."

"If you knew that, why didn't you go to him?"

"He didn't want me."

She remembered the conversation word for word as if it had taken place yesterday. She had not thought of it in years. They never spoke of him after that. It was strange now to read her mother's thoughts. Till this moment Annie had thought that her mother had deserted her father, if not in life, in death. She had let him die alone. She had never considered that her father might be guilty of desertion.

She walked from the parlor to the small room behind the kitchen, Mardella's room. She knocked on the door. It was opened quickly.

"You weren't asleep, Mardella?"

"No, Miss Annie."

"I want you to keep this in your room for me. Will you do that for me, Della?"

"I do dat wid pleasure."

She took the book and set it down on the dresser.

"You knew. I did want to burn it. I was afraid of it. I still am, perhaps even more now, but I cannot destroy it."

"I leaves it right here. You come an' reads on it as you cain." She felt proprietary toward the book, as the old man had.

"Mardella, how old are you?"

"Don't know fer sure. I 'spect I be 'bout forty."

"You're not so very much older than I. Why are you so much wiser?"

"I ain't. I jus mo' acceptin' den you is. I mo' forgivin' of folks. You cain't be so hard on dem an' on yerself, Miss Annie. You gotta bend or you break. Dat's how dis life is."

"Yes, I suppose so, Mardella. I'll be coming in for the book every once in a while."

"You come as you cain, Miss Annie. De door be open to you. It be day pritty soon. You gotta try an' gits some sleep."

"Yes, I will."

"An' Miss Annie?"

"Yes."

"I don't wants to see you a-roamin' round des house at night widout yer slippers. You gits yer death of cole."

She stepped quietly into the room. William had not moved. He lay on his back, his mouth open, snoring slightly. She got into bed beside him. He had left her very little room. Her leg brushed against his but he did not stir. She looked at his slack unconscious face. He knew nothing of her night. He knew nothing of her. She thought of her mother, and of all the people who live in the same house, eat the same food, breathe the same air, but never share a thought. She closed her eyes and tried to go to sleep. It was impossible.

She got up and went to the chiffonier. She took only two drops of medicine. It was not enough to make her sleep, but it would ease the cold cramped feeling she had in her stomach. She looked at her face in the mirror, but all she could see was a silhouette. She tried to remember how she had looked when she was sixteen. It didn't seem that she had changed so much. Yet she must have. At sixteen she would not have understood her mother's words of unhappiness, but now she could. That must show in a face.

She wrapped a shawl around her shoulders and sat down in the chair. She couldn't go back to that bed and lie awake listening to him breathe until dawn.

Her mother had thought that she was beautiful. She was always telling her so, but she must truly have believed it. She had written it in her diary. She could feel her mother's hand on her hair. She leaned back in the chair and smiled. Even now her mother would think that she was beautiful. Her mother loved her. Those we love must have a special kind of beauty. The kind that does not alter or die. The kind that never changes, no matter how many years may pass. At that moment, she wanted more than anything to read further of her mother's book.

IV

The next day, she missed his coming. She had not dreamed that this would be so. She was watching for him at the window when Mardella came into the parlor.

"Miss Annie, I's goin' into town to do some marketin'. You needs anythin'?"

"I'll go, Mardella."

"What's dat you say?"

"I'll go into town."

"But you never . . ."

"I know, but I want to go."

"Jus' as you say, Miss Annie. I tells you what we be needin' fer supper."

She felt very strange out on the street. She was frightened and yet exhilarated. She had not walked any distance in years. Her breath was coming fast. She knew that her face must be flushed. It felt very hot, yet the heavy sadness she had carried with her for so long was being lifted from her.

The stares of the townspeople made her feel vulnerable, naked. She walked into the store and it seemed to her that all conversation ceased. She could not approach the clerk and ask for the things she wanted. She could not speak. Panic rose up within her. She could no longer see faces, only pairs of staring questioning eyes. She ran from the place, upsetting a shelf of materials, calicos and laces. A ream of red ribbon rolled after her, as if it were chasing her from the place.

She ran all the way home. Her hair had come loose from its pins and was streaming around her face. When Mardella opened the door, Annie flung herself into the house. Tears had begun to run down her cheeks. Mardella said nothing. She simply led her into the kitchen and sat her down at the table. When Annie had taken several drinks of water and started to twist her hair back in a knot at her neck, Mardella spoke.

"Miss Annie, what happened?"

"Nothing."

"I sees you come a-runnin' up de street like demons was after you. I couldn't git to de door quick enough. Somethin' happened."

"Nothing, really. I was fine. I was enjoying the walk, but when I got to the store I felt that everyone was looking at me."

"Dey probably was."

"What do you mean? Why should they look at me? I'm no different from the rest of them."

"You is different, Miss Annie. You done live in des place fer a lot of years an' dey ain't never seed you come into town. Deys bound to look. You gotta 'spect dat. Didn't you know dat dey gonna be a-lookin' long an' hard at you when you ups an' comes a-walkin' in after all dese years?"

"I guess I didn't really think about it. I just wanted to get out of the house. I just wanted to go to the store like an ordinary woman, and shop, and come home again. I didn't imagine it would be so difficult. I'm sorry, Mardella, I didn't get the things you needed."

"I go an' fetch 'em, Miss Annie."

"I think I may have done some damage in the store. I ran into something. The clerk called after me. I'll give you some money to pay for anything I may have broken."

"Yes, Miss Annie."

"And the basket, your shopping basket. I must have dropped it somewhere. I feel such a fool."

"Don't be worryin' 'bout none of dat. I finds de basket. I goes right now."

"Do take some extra money to the store, for the damage."

"I will, Miss Annie."

Mardella left her at the kitchen table, her head in her hands. The basket was in the road not far from the house. Mardella picked it up and dusted if off. There was a pale blue hair ribbon beside it. She put that in her pocket. Then with the basket over her arm, she raised her head high and approached the town. She entered the store and scanned the room, looking the customers in the eye. The shopkeeper was on his hands and knees tracking down the stray spools of thread and ribbon rolls which Annie had upset. Mardella stood over him, tall and menacing.

"My mistress says she wants to pay fer anythin' she done broke."

The man looked up at her. "There was do damage done. Was the lady taken ill suddenly?"

"Yes, she ain't well. She ain't strong."

"I understand. It's for your mistress that you always buy the laudanum. Will you need any today?"

"No."

He stood. Mardella still towered over him. "Well, now what can I get for you today?"

When she returned to the house the kitchen was deserted. She put the basket on the table and went to her room. The book was not on the dresser. She walked to the front of the house. Seeing the parlor door was closed, she smiled and went back to the kitchen.

Annie sat in the chair by the window, the book in her hands. Her mother's tight script noted the date, October 30, 1864, almost fourteen years ago. Annie began to read what had happened to her mother's life on that day so long ago.

Sunday, October 30, 1864

A wonderful old man came to the door yesterday. He stayed the night. He left his mule standing outside. It was a mangy-looking beast, but then so was its owner, Jess Moran. He had been sent to me by an old friend from the Maryland Shore. Jess Moran smelled of the sea. His clothes were crusted white with salt, and his eyes were the bluest I have ever seen. He just sparkled. And by merely looking at him, one could see that he loved every single moment of life, calm weather or foul. This morning at breakfast he told us the reason for his visit to Washington.

"I've come to surrender again."

"Surrender?" I asked.

"Again?" asked Annie.

"Yes, I surrender once a month."

"Captain," I said, "I don't mean to pry, but what do you mean, you surrender every month?"

"Just that. Every month I come into town and I pick myself a likely-looking young officer, young ones is the best. I tell him that I'm a Confederate, an old Reb, who's tired of fighting. I tell him that me and my mule have come to surrender. Well, the young officer takes us to an office and I sign the oath of loyalty. I ain't false swearing neither, Miz Surratt, I believe in the Union. I always have. Then usually we get around to the mule. The young officer he asks me if I would like to turn in my mule to the Commissary Department. They would pay me. About that time I say to him that me and my old mule been through the whole war together and that it would be mighty hard for me to sell him. The young officer he thinks for a minute, and then he says to me, what if, to save my feelings, I gave him the mule and he took it to the Commissary Department and sold it and then he gave the money to me. Then it wouldn't be so much like I was handing over my mule for money. He would be doing it. Well, then I think on this for a minute, and finally I say, it's a deal. We shake hands. I go over then and say goodbye to the old mule. By the time I'm finished there ain't a dry eye among the three of us, not mine, nor the young officer's nor the mule's neither. He takes him then by the old frayed rope and goes off to the Commissary Department. Later, the young officer gives me the money."

"Surely there must be an easier way to sell mules than going through all of that, Captain."

"Well, you see, Miz Surratt, it's always the same mule. I've only got one."

"But how is that possible?"

"That mule is mighty attached to me. He can't stand no other man riding him or messing with him. He only likes me. Well, when I say goodbye to him before the officer takes him, I whisper in his ear where I'm going to be later on, and he runs off from the Commissary Department and joins up with me. We go back home with a little money from the United States government. I figure they can afford it. And we sure can use it, my old mule and me. We've been doing it for many a month now."

Annie was concealing a smile behind her coffee cup. She asked the Captain, "You say that you whisper in the old mule's ear and he understands what you say, Captain?"

"Sure he does."

"He must be a very intelligent mule."

"Jebediah, he's smart, but not near as smart as some critters I know of. This is a mighty fine house, Miz Surratt. I'd be much obliged if the next time Jeb and me is in town you'd permit us to stop again."

"It would be a pleasure, Captain."

The Captain is the sort of man that when you think of him you find yourself smiling. I've been thinking of him and smiling all day long.

Wednesday, November 2, 1864

Washington is without doubt the paradingest town. Last night the reason for celebration was the emancipation of Maryland, a rather dubious reason I think. Maryland has had heaped on her head one hardship after another, mainly because her people tried to remain neutral. Our Negroes began to flee from Maryland long ago. Many planters and their families are starving because there is no one to work the fields. Those who do remain, mostly women and children, fill their days with prayer and supplication. The emancipation of Maryland! If only it were true, and Maryland, that once happy land, was truly free to pursue her peaceful and productive life.

Last night watching the torchlight procession, the red flame flickering on the black faces in the darkness, my mind traveled back some thirty years to that little farm, Condon's Mill. Mr. Surratt inherited it from his Uncle Neale. It was our first home. I came there as a fresh bride of fifteen. Our hopes and dreams were so new and bright then. We were rarely apart for a moment, Mr. Surratt and I, in those days. There was so much to learn, to discover. I can still feel his strong arm about my waist. He could span my waist with his two hands, that's how small it was. I had to stand on tiptoe to put my arms around his neck. Our first night together, dark and still, my white gown with Mother's embroidery upon it against my bare skin, lying in that big bed, alone and trembling, waiting for him, this man I really scarcely knew. And when he entered the room, the wind gusted up outside and the leaves rushed about on the ground. He stood for a moment on the threshold. Then he called me to him. I slipped out of bed, my bare feet cold upon the floor, and went shyly up to him. He touched my face softly and then began running his hands all up and down me. My shivers came up through the silk. I quivered and felt things that I had never known, had never heard of, things which Mother and the nuns had never spoken of, things which the girls at school had never whispered of. I thought that perhaps I alone in all the world could feel them. The tiny buttons I had sewn so carefully, which ran the length down the front of my gown, were undone one by one, until he bent and kissed my naked breasts, and told me that soon I would have a son to suckle, his son. Then he picked me up in his arms and carried me to bed.

Once, one hot autumn noon, I took his supper to him out in the fields where he was working. He had taken his shirt off. He gently pushed me backward onto the warm soft soil, lifted my skirts, and took me while I looked up into the vast blue sky and felt the blazing midday sun on my face. I kept one of my soil-stained stockings from that day in a drawer for months afterward. I could not bear to wash it. I wanted it to remain penetrated with sweet Maryland earth and memories.

I was very soon with child. We were so happy then, happy as we would never, never be again.

One night when I was late into my third month and sleeping very lightly under my new unaccustomed weight, I was awakened by a loud crackling sound. Our room was smoky but bright as day. I woke him from his heavy slumber. He was up in a moment and pulling on his boots. I went to the window and saw our barn and fields covered in flame. Then a large figure ran across the yard and stopped for a moment. It was Elijah, the boy Mr. Surratt had bought three weeks before to help him out on the place. He wore no shirt. His chest was wet and shining black. His skin had a red cast to it. He stood, his head raised and fists clenched, spellbound by the fire. Suddenly he looked toward the house, staring at the window where I stood. It was impossible that he could see me, perhaps only my white gown, but I felt that his black eyes were staring straight into mine, burning, consuming me. He turned and began to run, long powerful strides. At first I thought that he was going for help. Then I knew in my mind what I had known in my heart from the moment I looked into his eyes in the firelight. He had set the fire, with one prayer, hoping we and all our kind would perish in it.

Our farm was totally destroyed by the conflagration. We never again saw Elijah, but he was in truth a prophet. That night foretold what our life would become. The dream was shattered. I knew then that God had seen fit to punish me for the promise I had made to Him and broken, the convenant I had betrayed. I lost my baby that night, and I lost my husband. He was never the same man again, the man I had loved and worshipped so much that for him I had dared to forget my vow, but God did not forget. In the long years ahead of us, he was only that man again for flashes, for tantalizing moments. I waited only for those, and the rest of the time, I tried to understand and indulge the man he had become. He realized that night that life could deal him blows that he was helpless to fend off. He began to fail and fail. He never fought again. It would have been the same if during the fire one of the beams of our house had fallen upon his legs and made a cripple of him. He would forever need support. He found it partially in me, and partially in a more steady and silent source, the warm amber liquid sealed in a bottle.

Last night, seeing those faces, so proud, in the firelight, I thought of Elijah and his revenge and his prophecy. I wonder, did he know that by ceasing to be a slave and chattel, and becoming a man again, that all of those things were taken from another man. It takes an overly introspective woman to interpret the event, I suppose. That fire burns still within me. I did not lose myself as Mr. Surratt did or discover myself as Elijah did. I was just the woman who caused it to happen, who watched it all turn to ash, and I must bear the burden of understanding.

A woman is not taught to prize herself, but to guard, to esteem, and protect the attentions and affection which others give to her. A woman defines herself and makes her happiness through others. She does not look to herself to see herself, but looks instead to others, and relies, indeed lives, upon what they see. That is not to deny the existence of an inner life in women, for I believe that we are spiritual creatures. Our souls are beautiful, made so through the sufferings which all of us endure, but all of that is secondary to the matter of primary importance in a woman's life–the effect which she can produce in others, that is the reality of her life, the purpose of her existence. A woman needs response. A man must stand alone or at least believe that he can. A man can choose, while a woman must demur. He is stalwartly what he is. She is what others believe her to be. And yet, did not Elijah when he took my husband's faith leave me bereft and alone that fiery night so long ago? Am I not to this day alone? I have only known one woman in my life who can stand alone. My mother. She has the strength of a man, but I do not. I want to play upon the stage again. I want response, precious response. I want my image reflected in the dark, liquid, loving eyes of a man, just once more. I am nothing now. I am so alone. The days go by so swiftly, and soon I'll be too old–perhaps I am already.

Monday, November 7, 1864

Washington is being abandoned. The reason for the present egress is the election. Everyone is going home to vote, for there is no voting in the District of Columbia. Being a woman I know little of voting, but I do know that Washington is nearly deserted. Trains leaving the city are filled to capacity.

Sometimes I wish that I could get upon a train, without ticket or destination. Just ride and ride until I saw a likely spot, and stop there for a while, and then resume my journey once more. I wish that I could do this and leave no one behind me wondering where I have gone, and have no one expecting me when I arrive wherever I do finally arrive. I think sometimes that would be quite wonderful. It is, of course, impossible. I would be lonely and frightened if I did not know where I was going or to whom, but there is the chance that I might not be, that I might just love my journey without design, objective, or goal.

It's not that I feel fettered by obligations. I just can't imagine where they all came from. It seems not so very long ago that I was young and free. How did it happen that the responsibilities multiplied so quickly? Husband, children, servants, the farm, the tavern, now the boardinghouse, the boarders, friends, relations, near and distant, merchants, people I owe, and those who owe me. And where am I in all of this? Who am I? I'm buried under all their needs and desires, their hopes and fears, their triumphs and defeats.

I would miss my obligations and responsibilities, I know that. And yet, it is tempting to think of that train, that journey without end that I shall never make.

Tuesday, November 15, 1864

Mr. Lincoln is again the President. Parades and processions abound. I grow weary of them. They are unseemly really while so many continue to suffer hardship and torment. Yesterday an old countrywoman came to the door. She spoke little. Her dress was roughly made, but she wore it with dignity. She seemed to me to be in great need of a sympathetic ear, but was loath to admit it. She finally told her story, a tragedy really, but spoken through without tears, stoically. We went into the parlor. I took up my sewing, and she sat with her great gnarled hands very still in her lap. After a silent time she sadly began.

Mrs. Eva Tull had ten sons. She said, with a mother's pride, that they were good boys, a little thoughtless and wild, but good boys all. When the war broke out they were eager to become soldiers, eager for their childhood games to become real. At least Mrs. Tull was spared the sorrow of a family divided. All her boys believed in and were anxious to fight for the Union. Soon, too soon, all but one of her sons were wearing Union blue. They left her behind on the little farm in northern Maryland, and if their eagerness pained Mrs. Tull, she did not say.

Her "old man" had died five years before, so she was alone with only little fourteen-year-old Caleb, her youngest. That was in 1861, the year it all began. The first year of the war took five of her sons, with only Zach surviving his wounds long enough to return home to die. The others had fallen and were buried somewhere in Virginia. She put up five crosses, made with her own hands, in the family burying ground. Her "old man" was no longer alone. Within another year's time, there were four more crosses standing above empty graves. Mrs. Tull had but one son left above the ground, the youngest, Caleb. Caleb was fifteen by now and wild to be off and avenge his brothers. She was understandably reluctant to let him go. He was her only son left on this earth, and her favorite at that, her last little baby, born when she was forty. She had nursed him until he was four years old. One autumn night in 1863 he ran off. She never even got a kiss goodbye. As his breakfast cooled on the table the next morning, she went to look for him and found him gone. Now she was truly alone. He wrote sporadic letters which she read with great difficulty, and treasured. Then they stopped. After almost a year of silence, she received word. Caleb had been wounded and was in a hospital in Washington. She was given no idea of the seriousness of the wound. She did not even know which hospital, assuming in her poor country mind that there would be but one. She came in the rain, through the rejoicing crowds. She made her way from hospital to hospital—searching. Finally she found him. He was dying, his young life ebbing swiftly. She was with him when he died, but he never knew her, never knew anything. He just slipped away in silence, much like the night he ran away from the farm.

This time she pressed her lips to his cheek and though he could not respond, at least it was better than watching his breakfast grow cold and knowing he was gone without a touch.

She told me the story from beginning to end without a tear. There is a certain capacity for sorrow. Once the limit is reached, there is mercifully only numbness. This poor old woman had reached the limit. She sat before me, silent and still and stunned. I could say nothing to her. There was nothing that she wanted to hear anymore, perhaps nothing that she was capable of hearing. All was drowned out by the voices and the laughter of her ten dead boys. I took her upstairs to a room. That was, after all, what she had come for and not my poor paltry words of sympathy, so terribly insufficient and shallow-sounding. She laid down upon the bed, careful not to put her big solid boots upon the spread.

After an hour or so I brought her a cup of tea. She had not stirred. She was in the exact same position as when I left her. Her eyes were staring up at the ceiling. The room was growing dark. I started to light a candle. She spoke, asking me not to. In the same even tone in which she had refused a lighted candle, in the darkness so that I could not see her face, she told me that she would be unable to bring Caleb's body home. She had used all the money she had in the world in getting here. Except for a few pennies, there was nothing left. She said that the thought of another cross above another empty grave made her want to crawl into the earth and fill one. I offered her supper because in the face of such sorrow I knew nothing else to offer. She refused. This morning before she left, she tried to give me money for the room. I did not take it, would not, could not. It was very early, and I tried to persuade her to stay to breakfast. Again she said no. She went upstairs and gathered her small bundle of belongings. I wanted very much to embrace her, but something held me back, fear of breaking down and causing her to. I believe if once she began to weep she would die of it. I watched from the window as she slowly walked off, a bitter gray cold morning, but I'm sure she never felt it. Later when I went up to the room she had occupied, I found the cup of tea, cold and untouched, the spread carefully smoothed, and her few pennies on the bureau. Then I wept. Oh God, end this war soon, and then I will join in the parade and rejoice. But even if the war should end tomorrow, it would be too late for Mrs. Eva Tull and her ten sons, and how many others?

Sunday, November 20, 1864

I have given Mr. Weichman some money and he has arranged through the War Department to have Caleb Tull's body sent home to his mother. I know that I am sending her death, but I hope that she may now live, at least survive without that last unbearable sorrow. It could be the bitter November cold that deadens my spirit and turns me against this city, but I think not. I have seen Washington at its so-called best, in spring, with everything green and cool, but still there is filth and decay and coarse rough people. In fact the juxtaposition of spring and such foulness makes an even more glaring example of Washington's gross ugliness. At least dirty gray weather seems to fit with the rest here. Spring in Washington is like putting a pink ball dress on a week-old corpse.

Most all the soldiers I see in Washington are either drunk or dead. Funeral processions and barrooms abound. Strange that both taverns and coffins are made from the darkest blackest wood. I think that most of the people spend most of their time drinking, or mourning, or shuttling between those two occupations. There are signs posted everywhere declaring that no man in uniform is to be sold or served liquor. It seems, to say the very least, to be a very highly disregarded law. Facing the specter of death, horrible death and agony daily, makes the soldiers seek many kinds of transitory relief. Fancy houses flourish here in Washington. Poor frightened boys, many of them not much more than children, who thought that a jaunty plumed hat or a newly grown mustache would make them fearless men, flock to these houses, seeking another kind of proof of their manhood and their courage. There are always those who are willing to make a profit from misery. There are many of them in this city. I have seen soldiers with Bibles, but they are few, very few. Bibles do not bring the immediate satisfaction of bottles and women. Immediacy is of the utmost importance to these men who can put no faith in tomorrow–moment to moment they live–the only surety in life is death.

Thursday, November 24, 1864

Still there are no new boarders–none of a permanent nature at any rate. There are only poor pitiful transients, lost and alone in the city, the kind I hate to take money from. They are mostly women, looking for the men that they love, men they haven't seen in years, long years, men who are usually dead.

Today an old Negro woman came to the door looking for work. She was obviously country-bred, led here by glowing tales of freedom. She appeared to be sorely disappointed and disheartened. I advised her to return to her folks. She said that they were no more, that the old place had been burned, and that all those who had lived there, black and white, had scattered the good Lord knew where. She was a tall woman, but stooped from years of labor. She was thin, so thin that her bones stood out from her skin, and her eyes were glassy with fever. She told me that she had a little girl to feed. She looked to be near sixty years. She seemed to read my thoughts. She explained that the little girl was her grandchild, that they were now living near the big white house where Mr. Lincoln lived. I knew of the place, a settlement of filthy hovels which had sprung up, poisonous and evil, like a toadstool–freedom land. Human life meant absolutely nothing there. All was misery, disease, and desperation. She said that they shared a room with thirteen other people. She cared little about her own hunger which I could almost see but she would work for food, food to sustain her child's life. She cared only for the child. She would not take anything from me unless she worked for it. I realized that she was adamant about this, so I set her to sweeping the mud from the front porch. She could barely hold the broom. I saw her lurch once and then grip the banister in white-knuckled fury at her lack of control. She had an innate and indomitable dignity. As I watched her from the window, I wondered how anyone could ever have owned this woman.

I gave her some cornbread and ham for the work she had done. She told me that they would eat today and tomorrow on it, but I knew only the child would eat. I wanted to tell her to provide for herself, to protect herself, for without her the child would surely die, but I could not find the proper words. As she was walking away, trudging barefoot through the sucking gray mud, carefully holding the precious package of food to her thin chest, unaccountably I was reminded of Mrs. Eva Tull. We are all alike in sorrow, all the same in pain. I thought of all the things I had wanted to say to Mrs. Tull and had not, the missed opportunity. This loosened my recalcitrant tongue, and I called out to her. Come again tomorrow, I said. To sweep, I added. She turned and nodded her head. How many more strays can my meager budget accommodate, I wonder? Do I love being kind? Or do I love being loved because I am kind?

Friday, November 25, 1864

Thanksgiving Day. I went to Mass this morning accompanied by Mr. Weichman. I had hoped that Miss Anna Ward could join us for Thanksgiving dinner, but she felt that she should remain with the children. John came in from the country. I wanted him to feel that everything was going well with us, that we were happy and prosperous. Dinner was an extravagance. Prices here in the city are an outrage—21¢ a pound for coffee—but at least these things are obtainable. There are many who are quite literally starving in Maryland, all throughout the South, and even right here in Washington.

After dinner I played the piano. I do not know why I continue to try to play. I am no longer any good at all. It's something I thought I would never lose. I feel like the faded beauty who is inexplicably drawn to her glass every morning to scrutinize her face and her loss. Every morning she approaches with renewed hope—perhaps today my beauty will have returned to me—but it never does.

No one seemed to notice my poor showing at the piano. We sang and made merry. Later I tried to speak privately with John, but he managed to evade me. He seemed happy and carefree enough, but as the evening wore on I sensed that he had other things on his mind, things other than turkey dinners and singing ballads. His holiday mask dropped for a moment, revealing a preoccupied and worried man. Yes, that was it, he had become a man. There were lines beneath his eyes and etched in his brow. His face was no longer smooth and boyish. He had lost weight, which he could ill-afford. All of this in little more than a month. Of course, he has always been thin, even when he was a child. I worried so about him. He ate and ate and never gained a pound. I will be glad when he comes here to stay and I can keep my eye on him. This sudden maturity paired with that surface and obviously counterfeit jaunty air frightens me. He is hiding something. I know it. Perhaps it is best that we did not speak this evening. He might have told me what I did not want to hear.

Sunday, November 27, 1864

The days immediately following Thanksgiving were grim. Holidays are special, days of heightened emotion and feeling. They are difficult days to come away from–like descending from a lofty summit–it is far easier to breathe back on the plain, but the view is not nearly so wonderful and grand. Annie feels this, I know. Yesterday and today she spent languishing in her room. This life is boring to her. And why not? She is young and craves excitement. I well remember how I used to love to dance. Oh, that wonderful special feeling, to glide across polished parquet floors in the arms of a handsome young man, a young man with whom one could so easily fall in love. There is no other feeling quite like it. Of course, by the time I was Annie's age my dancing days were over. When I was not yet seventeen I had already lost one child and was growing large with another, Isaac. Please God, I can keep Annie from that. Children are, after all, the second chance, the new life to live again, are they not? No, I suppose they are not. I wish sometimes that I was anything but a human mother. I wish that I could have given birth to my young and then left them, forgotten them, never known them, just have given them the precious gift of life and gone my way, leaving them to live as they would, or as they could. I cannot bear to see Annie stumble, but then I cannot run after her as I do that little calico kitten, trying to prevent the hurts which teach and are inevitable. The kitten is far too quick for me. He is hopelessly entangled in my yarn or caught in the lace curtains before I am even aware of what is happening. I can only believe that Annie will be too quick for me too.

She has just come into my room and asked to go to one of those "hops" at Willard's Hotel. I was right, but I did not expect it quite so soon. I have no idea where or when she even heard of such things. I told her that I would think about it. I suppose we must go. I cannot refuse her. She has so little pleasure. Why do I dread it so? Perhaps because I will be relegated to the chaperone's couch with such finality. I may as well hang a sign about my neck declaring that I am decrepit and finished, that pretty blonde girl dancing with the tall officer is my daughter. There is nothing like having one's nose rubbed in old age. I will wear my black bombazine. It is appropriate for funerals, and this is really the death of my youth.

This is terrible of me–I am wishing that I could have remained forever a slender dark-haired girl in a white dancing frock. I really should be more careful in my wishes, for they could be granted to me by some cruel and whimsical power. I would hate to remain forever one thing, even such a pleasant thing as young. I would be caught, I'm sure, at that one dreadful moment upon entering the ballroom, apprehensive, palms damp beneath little white gloves and heart beating wildly behind ruffled tulle, ever uncertain, faint, afraid. So then I do not wish for eternal youth, for it is only so wonderful because it is not eternal.

I suppose that it is on to the "hop" with Annie, in a different incarnation, no more fresh flowers in my hair. All my flowers are old and dried, and pressed between the pages of dusty books, but they hold some lovely memories which all the fresh ones have yet to attain. And so it should be. I only wish that I could remember but a tiny bit better.

Tuesday, November 29, 1864

The Captain and his mule Jebediah came to surrender again. I know that he is a larcenous man, that I really should not allow him in the house, but I could no more turn him away than I could one of my own children. He is so charmingly candid about his fraud and thievery that somehow it seems all right for him to do the things that he does. He told us a lovely story this evening as we sat in the parlor. Annie began it by asking if his mule would be comfortable out in the cold all night long. It is a bitter November evening. The Captain twinkled his eyes at her.

"You're a real animal lover, ain't you, young lady?"

"I suppose I am."

"There ain't many who'd give a thought to an old mule. I'll put your mind to rest. Old Jeb, he's used to the cold, likes it even. Sometimes at home when there's a real fiercesome gale, and it's so dreadful cold that no man will stir from his house, I'll look out the window and I'll see Jebediah. He'll have come out from the barn. I never close him in or tie him up. It don't do no good. He stays where he likes and goes where he wants. Anyway, he'll have come out of the barn and he'll be standing right in the midst of it, breathing in that cold air, snorting and prancing. He likes the foul weather, old Jeb does. We're much alike that way. Many times I'll go out into the night and join him, stand right beside him and do my snorting and prancing. Now, young lady, since you're such an animal lover, I've got a tale I think you'd like.

"Well, it begins with two raccoons. Now coons is feisty beasts. They're small, but quarrelsome. Well, these two coons, they were different. They were friends, not mates nor nothing like that. They were just friends, pure and simple. They liked each other. The rest of the animals, and the other coons too, they couldn't understand these two, how come they was so peaceable and fond of each other. The rest of the critters took to talking about and criticizing these two coons, and the coons heard them one day. They began to wondering if maybe there wasn't something wrong with them. The bigger of the two said to the smaller.

"'Perhaps we should try to fight like the others.'

"'You mean argue?'

"'Well, I don't know. What should we argue about?'

"'I don't know.'

"'Maybe we should just commence rolling around and biting one another as I've see the other animals do.'

"'But I'm so much bigger and I'll hurt you. I think we should just argue.'

"'You begin.'

"'I want you to get out of my forest. There's not room here for both of us. I want you to leave right now.' And the little raccoon turned to go. 'Where are you going?'

"'Why, I'm leaving. I love this forest and I hate to leave it, but I love you more, my friend, and if you want me to go then I will.'

"'Wait. I don't want you to go. I was just trying to start an argument.'

"'Oh.'

"'I don't think that we're very good at this.'

"'Nor do I.'

"'Shall we just stay friends as we are and let the others talk as they will?'

"'Yes, let's please do.'

"And the two coons did just that, young lady."

Annie smiled and said, "I like that story, Captain."

The Captain is one man I could never turn from my door.

She looked up from the book and noticed for the first time that the light was fading. William would be home soon. She had been reading for hours. She had begun with the Captain and ended with him. She remembered him very well, his tales, his wonderful approach to life. He had made her mother laugh, something she had rarely ever seen her do. He had made them all laugh. She reached up to her hair for a ribbon to mark the page, but there was none. She remembered that she must have lost it running from town. She took the thin black one that she wore at her throat and put it between the pages. She was dreading the next passages, the reliving of a time that had been so happy. She did not want to be reminded of her first love, her only love. Seth.

She thought of her mother, her quiet kindness, her inability to express her feelings, her great sympathy and love for others. But her mother had never seemed to be a person or a woman. She had been merely her mother, with no further existence beyond that. That she felt pain, so deeply, that she could speak to no one of it, that she felt forced to confine her emotions to the pages of this book, made Annie sad. She hated herself for not reaching out to her mother. She hated herself for being sixteen and totally absorbed in herself. She hated herself for not seeing that her mother was in need.

Hardest of all to realize was that her mother had known love and passion. To visualize her mother and father embracing, to think of them touching, lying in a bed their bodies pressed close, or out in the fields on a hot day her father plunging deep inside her mother, to think of her mother walking slowly back to the house her thighs damp and sticky from him, it was unthinkable.

She envied her mother, and she knew her not at all.

V

Mardella was stirring a large kettle on the stove. Annie entered and sat down at the table. She held the book in her hands still, reluctant to let it go.

"Mardella, what was your mother like? Are you like her?"

"I don't know. She die when I a tiny baby."

"Your father then?"

"I only knows but one thin' 'bout him."

"What's that?"

"He white."

She looked up from the boiling pot. Her eyes, through the steam, were veiled.

"I wish I had known my mother better. As I read, I find that I really didn't at all. She felt things, thought things, that I never guessed. Is it always that way between mothers and daughters, do you suppose?"

"I s'pose. I knows one thin' sure, it be a rare gal don't grow into bein' her ma someday."

"I'm not at all like my mother."

"Mebbee you is different from mos' folks."

"I'm not anything like her, Mardella."

"I never did meet de lady, so I cain't be sayin' one way or de other. All I knows is dat mos' gals, black or white, dey mebbee don't start like dey ma, but dey comes round to bein' dat way, even if it jus be a way of sayin' a thin' or smilin' or a part in de hair or a movin' of de hands a certain way."

Annie touched the gold hoop earrings that she wore. Her mother had always worn that kind. She had never thought of it till now. She wondered how many other things there were that she had never noticed or remarked. She went to Mardella's room and put the book away. She came back into the kitchen.

"Did I break anything at the store?"

"No, Miss Annie."

She heard William calling her name. He was home and looking for her.

"Thank you, Della."

She left the kitchen. Upon seeing him she tried to smile, but faltered. She accepted his usual kiss on the cheek then rubbed the moisture he left away. He looked very young to her. He had such a bland smooth face, very little expression. She wondered if he felt things just as her mother had without her knowing it. Did he hide his feelings or were they merely non-existent.

Yet he had been what she wanted and needed. She felt that he asked nothing of her, and she gave nothing. He offered her only safe emptiness, with no true understanding. She accepted that and gave the same in return. She wondered if he was as satisfied as he seemed with this existence of theirs.

"Did you have a good day, Annie?"

"Yes."

"What did you do?"

"I read most of the day."

"What did you read?"

"Just a book." It occurred to her that perhaps she was being unfair, unkind, to him. But then what did it matter that she never really responded to him, that she skimmed along the surface, that she never expressed her thoughts to him. Annie couldn't believe that he wanted those things of her any more than she had ever wanted them of him. William wanted a wife, a kind of marionette, who danced only to the properly pulled strings and never dared to take a step on her own, but what if she was wrong? What if William did want more than that? She thought of her mother, how blind she had been to her wants and needs. She wondered what would happen if once, just once, she told him what was really in her mind and her heart. Perhaps then he would reveal his, but did she want to know? "Really I had rather an upsetting day."

"Did you? I'm sorry."

"Yes, I went into town."

"It was a fair day for it."

"Yes, the weather was wonderfully fair. It wasn't the weather that disturbed me. It was just that I very nearly went mad in Kirby's dry goods store. It seemed to me that everyone was watching me and that their eyes felt like fire burning into my flesh, and I wanted to scratch their faces till blood ran, and I wanted to throw things and break them. I ran from the place. If I had stayed I would have done all those things. I would have lost my mind. I'm not completely sure that I haven't. So you see, William, I did not have a good day."

He looked at her for a moment, trying to read the seriousness of her words. It was so unlike her to say these things. He was disturbed and frightened by her words. He did not know how to answer. He wanted to say something calm, soothing, to make the look in her eyes go away. He wanted to forget what she had said. He feared what she would say next, what she might ask of him. He felt as if a vial of explosive was sitting across the table from him. He shifted uneasily in his chair. Her gaze was steady, but she seemed not to be seeing him. Her glassy eyes were fixed on his face. He wanted this to stop. He wanted their life to be as it had always been. He did not like this change in her. He wanted her as she was before.

"Perhaps we should look into your diet, my dear. You may well be eating something that doesn't agree. That happens. I'm sure that it's nothing serious. A matter of diet, no doubt."

"No doubt."

"Speaking of diet, what wonder has Mardella concocted tonight? We will be dining soon?"

"I would imagine. We always dine at the very same hour. It hasn't varied in years."

"Yes, that's true. I have always believed that regularity brought peace of mind. Knowing what to expect of life, that is true happiness."

"Aren't we living proof of it?"

"I beg your pardon, my dear. What is it you said?"

"Nothing, nothing of importance."

"I am very glad to hear that you are enjoying the weather and going out a bit. You stay too close to the house, Annie. Loving your home as you do is a truly feminine trait, and it does you credit, but there is such a thing as being too confined."

"Is there?"

"Yes, there is."

"And how does one know, William, when one is too confined?"

"I'm not sure that I understand . . . ?"

"Does one feel as if one is being choked, that the air is being strangled off at one's throat? Does one want to scream at the walls and the chairs and at you, William, scream and scream until finally no further sound will come forth? Do these things indicate to you being too confined?"

"I am unsure what they indicate."

"Perhaps improper diet."

He pulled his watch from his pocket. In desperation he looked to routine to solve this situation. "I believe that it is supper time. Shall we go in?"

"Yes, of course."

They ate their meal in silence. He glanced up at her furtively from his plate. She thought that he might be afraid that she would begin screaming at any moment. Perhaps he feared that she might sail a dish of boiled potatoes at his head, or begin drooling and gnashing her teeth. She had terrified him when all she had been trying to do was explain herself. Perhaps she really was going mad, but it seemed that he was the crazy one, with his obsession for the expected, his love of order above all else. Yet those were the very things that had drawn her to him years ago. She could not despise William because she had changed and he had remained the same. But she could not help but feel that he was only trying to give her what she wanted, what she had come to expect from him. Somewhere there was another William, a man she did not know. There was something in rare moments that flickered in his eyes. She had never wanted to look any deeper, into William, or herself, or anyone else.

The old man and her mother's diary had turned her careful world upside down. She had descended into a kind of walking sleep after her mother's death. She was afraid, terribly afraid, of everyone and everything. She looked at William. Perhaps those were the only things they had ever shared, fear and a great reticence for life. Now, suddenly, she wanted more.

"You are not eating your supper, Annie."

"I was thinking."

"I see."

"William, do you care to know what I was thinking about?"

"Of course."

"I was thinking of my mother."

"You know how that upsets you. I thought you had put that entire episode aside forever."

"My mother was not an episode. She was my mother, and I can't put her aside forever."

"I thought that you had. I suggest that you do. It only disturbs you, pointlessly. There is nothing to be done. It's over."

"It can never be over for me. It's always with me."

"Annie, I don't know you tonight."

"Tonight! William, you've never known me. Do you think because you crawl on top of me in bed that you know me?"

"You are fatigued, and overwrought."

"I am not!"

"Lower your voice. I think that you should go upstairs."

"Please listen to me."

"I will not listen to that. We have a good life, quiet and serene, a house where no voice is raised, no blows are struck."

"We have no life at all."

"You may not realize what a fine and rare thing we have."

"We have nothing, I tell you, nothing."

"There are houses which are hells on earth, where there is only misery, cries, shrieks, moans in the night. I know of these things. You do not. Go upstairs now, and take your medicine."

"How do you know these things? Did you live in a house like that once?"

"Go upstairs."

"Did you live in a house like that as a child? Did your father strike your mother? Please, you must tell me. I want to understand." She got up and went to his chair. She bent on her knees before him. "Do you think you are being kind, to me or to yourself?"

He stroked her hair. "Yes."

She jerked her head free. "You are not."

She stood, and left the room. She entered the bedroom and started toward the chiffonier and the blue bottle inside, but stopped. He had told her to take her medicine. Did he prefer her in a stupor? Certainly she had wanted it for a very long time, but not now. It wasn't that she was any less afraid. She was terribly frightened, but the important thing to know was why she was afraid, what and whom she feared. Her medicine gave her relief. It deadened her. Suddenly she wanted to be alive, to answer her questions. She wanted to feel, even fear.

She thought of the first time they had ever given her the medicine, to calm, to sedate her. It was during the trial. She was called to testify. She knew what she wanted to say. She wanted to convince those stern men in the blue uniforms that her words were true. She wanted to save her mother. She wanted so many things, but it had all gone wrong. Seeing her mother, veiled and chained, it had all gone wrong. And the questions they asked of her. She was carried fainting from the courtroom. It was then that the Army doctor gave her morphine. He had eased the wounded and the dying boys with it for four long years of war. He could ease her pain too. There was nothing the medicine couldn't relieve, no torment it could not allay. That was the beginning of it. She was called later in the trial to testify again. That time she fortified herself with the medicine. She had done much better, but still her words did not save her mother. Nothing saved her mother. Only the medicine delivered her, but it condemned her too.

Late in the night she went down to Mardella's room. She was sleeping. Annie quietly took the book and walked to the parlor. She stirred the fire and added some logs. It blazed up nicely. She was glad that it had been a rather cool evening and Mardella had lighted a fire. She took a cushion and placed it on the floor and sat down. She stared into the flames, seeing her brother John. It was easy for her to conjure his image. He looked so much like her, the same fine blonde hair, the same sharp features, the same gray eyes, but more wintry and remote even than hers, she thought.

She remembered him far better than Isaac. Isaac was so much older than she. He had gone off to war when she was only twelve. He had been no part of the boardinghouse days in Washington. And for better or worse those were the most vividly recalled days of her life. She couldn't see Isaac at all, not even the boy Isaac from their childhood. He had been big and silent and dark. He had frightened her, though he had never played any of the cruel pranks upon her that John had. She had sometimes wondered why Isaac had not been named for their father. He was the oldest son. After reading in the diary of the lost baby she realized that it had probably been intended to be John Surratt, Jr. Isaac had come too soon upon that loss. They could not give him the name meant for the dead baby they still mourned. Years later, when they were given another golden infant boy, when the pain had subsided somewhat, that child was named John Surratt, Jr. She wondered if Isaac had ever wondered. If he felt cheated, hurt, unloved. That was the reason, perhaps, for his darkness and his silence. He had been wonderful during John's trial, strong and dependable, a rock. How she wished he had been at their mother's trial, but they had rushed it so, so terribly eager for vengeance. Isaac was still making his way home through the devastation, across razed acres, up from the ruined South, as they tried her. When he finally arrived she was dead.

Isaac was out West somewhere now. She hoped good things for him, a family who loved him, something he had never possessed. She opened the book to the ribbon-marked page.

Wednesday, November 30, 1864

This evening Annie, Miss Fitzpatrick, and I went to the "hop" at the Willard. Such preparation, primping, and palpitations, it was truly amazing. We arrived at ten o'clock, the girls in white and I in my black bombazine. I looked for all the world like a big ominous onyx between two little sparkling diamonds.

The large bare dining hall had had the tables removed and there was an orchestra set up at the far end. The room was really quite an ugly affair, but it was transformed by the laughter and the music into a thing of beauty. Annie's pretty cheeks glowed–she danced nearly every dance. There was one young officer in particular who seemed quite smitten with her. Miss Fitzpatrick did not dance nearly so much. She sat beside me, her smile pinned on her face like the nosegay at her waist. I noticed that she was unconsciously tearing her fan into little pieces. When she realized what she had done, she started, as if some other hands than her own had been at this mischief. She quickly hid the pieces from sight.

I suppose that there are people born who do not have one moment of happiness vouchsafed for them in life. Miss Fitzpatrick is such a person. Her father is employed by the government, and travels a great deal. She never knew her mother. She is very much alone, boarding in a house of strangers. She is not really so very plain, but there is an anxious and unattractive look to her face when in repose. She tries to overcome this by a kind of studied gaiety, very contradictory to her true nature, and grating, like a piano slightly out of tune. Her forced smiles and giggles show such conscious effort that they bring only pity and puzzled frowns.

Now Annie is not without her serious side. She may even have inherited a streak of melancholy from me, but she is as capable of change as the Washington weather. Her happiness is bright and genuine. Her smile's like the sun. Perhaps it is because I view her from a mother's fond and prejudiced vantage point. That may indeed be what is lacking in Miss Fitzpatrick, the total loving fondness of a mother, the sort of unquestioning and uncritical love which inspires one to be better than one is, to try and never disappoint . . . Mother approved of me when I dressed in white and went to balls. It was the thought of me in black that she hated, the coif I loved that she despised.

There was a young man who caught my eye at the "hop." He was escorting two young ladies whom I found out later are a senator's daughters. He was striking, all dressed in black. His hair and mustache were dark too. Yet, there was nothing somber about him. His eyes had a depth and intensity which was burning. He compelled attention. If I felt like the dull and forbidding onyx, then he was surely a black opal, on fire. His luminous eyes made the color black not one of mourning and sorrow, but of joy and bright promise, and excitement. He and the young ladies made an elegant trio. I did not believe that I was still capable of lapsing into such schoolgirl ecstasy, but all it took was a pair of enchanting black eyes. He could be my son, and I his mother, I am sure. Miss Fitzpatrick pouted because I kept forgetting to call her Honora. I must try to remember.

Thursday, December 1, 1864

The first day of the last month of the year. I have embarked on a new enterprise, and I hope that the day is auspicious. I have begun serving meals in addition to letting rooms. Of course, I will have to add some help in the kitchen. Cookie and Dan will no longer be enough. The old woman, Dulcey, who has come faithfully every morning to sweep the porch, I think would be ideal. I grow nervous.

Perhaps I have been precipitous. There is more to this undertaking than I had imagined. It seems that to make money one must spend.

John will be here soon, as Mr. Lloyd will be taking over the tavern this month. I thought for a time that with John living in Washington he would be safe and that I could stop worrying about him, but I can see now that his presence here will be a mixed blessing. Washington is a hotbed of Southern sympathizers, and I know that John will be drawn to them as a divining rod to water. Now Mr. Weichman, though quite vocal in his championship of the South, has at least taken a job which affords him some protection. It seems the height of hypocrisy, however, to be in the employ of a government that one detests and despises and wishes to bring down. John is not guilty of such self-serving dishonesty, but he could be drafted, or worse, thrown into the Old Capitol Prison for his beliefs. The Secretary of War, Mr. Stanton, they say has jailed thousands, men and women, guilty or innocent, with reason and without. The man has the blind and cruel zeal found only in a patriot. Perhaps it is not for nothing that his name, Stanton, rhymes with Danton, another famous patriot. Stanton–Danton–the Temple Tower–the Conciergerie–the Old Capitol–the Arsenal. Secretary Stanton has not yet instituted the guillotine, but he is a patriot so we must wait and see. Danton too was a lawyer, as is Stanton, strange the coincidence. Why is it the men of the law who feel so free to ignore it. I tremble for John.

Saturday, December 3, 1864

John has arrived from down in the country. He and Mr. Weichman will share a room. They are good friends and seem to enjoy one another's company greatly. Theirs is a friendship not just of memories, but one that continues on through to the present and the future, renewing itself and not relying solely on past intimacies. I hope that John will be influenced by Mr. Weichman into a calmer and more cautious way of life. I cannot imagine Mr. Weichman ever doing a daring or dangerous thing. Of course, I wouldn't want John to lose his spirit or his courage, but a slight diminishing of those two qualities which he has in such abundance would do him no harm. As a child I am sure that Isaac must have been equally reckless. He was a daring boy, but a stoic. He never made a show of it. He probably hid his wounds from me, while John considered them to be badges of his courage, emblems of pride. It occurs to me that John was rather thoughtless even then, caring little about the worry and consternation he caused, enjoying and reveling in it, in fact. And Isaac, taciturn and uncomplaining, I wonder what hurts he concealed from me. It's strange that my sons seem to have found their way into the wrong occupations. If John is involved in some sort of intrigue, Isaac would be much more suited to those clandestine operations. And Isaac is in the Army, where John should be, indulging in soldierly heroics.

I have always felt that life held something either very good or very bad for John. I pray for the former, but fear the latter.

Annie is considerably perked up by John's presence. They look remarkably alike, more so now than as children. Yet their temperaments are very dissimilar. John teases her unmercifully at times and takes a rather masterful air in his treatment of her—very brother-like and manly. She seems to enjoy it. Annie will make a wonderful wife. That seems impossible and far away—Annie married and with a family other than this one—yet it will be very soon. I wish sometimes that I could see the future. Not mine, I have very little future left, I will be forty-five years old this coming June. If only I could see the future of my children, my mind would be eased. I don't know why I worry so, and about things which will probably never happen, things which will only have an existence in my frightened imaginings early in the morning before the sun has risen and I have not slept.

When I do sleep I have strange dreams which wake me with a jolt, in terror, and I am unable to go back to sleep again. There is one recurring one which makes me grow cold just thinking of it. It is the only dream I have ever had of myself. I wonder if dreams really do portend the future, acting as signs and omens. Oh, perhaps I would rather not know what lies ahead. Maybe I would be more content with a long chain of dreamless nights and heavy slumber.

Annie closed the book. It seemed that she could read less and less of it at each sitting, because more and more it summoned forth memories for her.

The "hop." She and Honora had discussed it at night for weeks before she had broached the subject with her mother. She had not thought that her mother would understand. Yet her descriptions of the feelings just before a ball were so true and right. It amazed her that her mother had actually known what she was feeling. She remembered how she had felt that her fate hinged on that evening. It had been a wonderful and a terrifying feeling. She and Honora had talked of it. Why didn't she and her mother speak? She could have told her so much, eased and soothed her, and she wanted to, Annie knew that, but she hadn't. And she, poor woman, had been so afraid that she was old and finished. Yet, Annie remembered thinking how white her mother's skin had looked, how black her hair, and the grace with which she walked. Why? Why hadn't she taken her hand, or kissed her cheek, told her that she looked beautiful in her black bombazine? They had had so much to give one another, and somehow every opportunity had been lost, such a waste, such a pitiful waste. All the words never spoken, but thought. All the love never shown, but felt.

That night at the Willard she had met Lt. Seth Kierney. After that the breach had widened between her and her mother. Soon it became impassable. The joy that her mother had seen in her in early December, she had attributed it to John's coming, but it had been Seth. Seth had made her so happy. Why had her mother disliked him so? He was good and kind. So was her mother. Good and kind people should like one another. Yet they did not. They saw only the bad things in one another, Seth and her mother.

Seth. Why did he have to die? And if he had to die, why couldn't he have died before she ever knew him. His life would have been cut short by only a few months. They only had such a little time together. She would rather have had none at all. There could never be anyone like Seth for her again. Annie looked into the flames and tried to find his face there, but she could not. She thought of the picture he had given her. She could see it. He was standing stiff and unsmiling, in uniform, with a rifle beside him, and behind him was a screen with flowers and trees painted upon it. She hadn't looked at that picture in years. It was strange that she could remember it and not the man. But she did remember Seth, the tone of his voice, the way he wore his hat tilted back on his head, his hands always warm, his mouth, how it felt to kiss it, but she couldn't see his face. She could feel him, remember his touch and smell, but she couldn't see him anymore.

She recalled the day in late December when they had met at the Smithsonian Institution. She had sensed her mother's disapproval of him from the first time he visited the house so they arranged to meet elsewhere. She and Honora had said that they were going to Mass. They left the house together, walked for a while, and parted. She had felt sad seeing Honora go off alone, knowing that she was meeting no one, that she would spend the next hours by herself, and then return to the corner, and meet her, and go home again. She wanted to call after her. She wanted to really go to Mass with Honora and forget Seth, but she could not. She went on to the Smithsonian.

They had walked and walked together. She told him that the Smithsonian was like a castle to her, the turrets and the high stone walls. He told her that in the spring all the grounds surrounding it were covered in flowers, little white ones, growing wild everywhere. It was as if they were living hundreds of years ago, during medieval times, she had said. They decided then that she was to be his lady, and he her knight. She gave him her handkerchief to carry into battle. It had been the most beautiful day of her life.

The fire had gone out. It was almost dawn. She quickly returned the book to Mardella's room and went upstairs, but she did not go into the bedroom. She went instead down the hall to the door that led to the attic. It was dark there, but she knew what she was looking for. She remembered where she had put it thirteen years ago.

In the small pocket of the lining of the big striped trunk, she found it. She could not clearly see it, but she knew that it was the picture of Seth. She left the attic and went into the room. William was sleeping. She walked to the chiffonier and put the picture in the drawer, and then she took out the bottle. She swallowed enough to make her sleep. She got into bed beside him. The man next to her was not her knight nor she his lady, because he was not Seth, a boy who had been dead for thirteen years. Annie felt an overwhelming sadness and grief.

VI

That morning she received a letter from her brother John. It was disturbing, and yet it presented her with an opportunity. She folded the pages after carefully reading them and put them in the pocket of her skirt.

She walked into the kitchen. Mardella was washing dishes.

"Della, have you ever been to Baltimore?"

"Yes, Miss Annie, I has."

"You know the city?"

"I lives in de city fer some years."

"I never knew that. You have a secretive soul, Mardella. You know everything about me and I know nothing about you."

"Ain't nobody livin' knows everythin' 'bout somebody else. Dere is things dat cain't be tole, cain't even be guessed at. Dey's de things dat in a body's head."

"It's true, so true. I wish sometimes that it wasn't so. Reading my mother's book, it's almost as if I could see inside her mind."

"You think dat's a good thin'?"

"What do you mean?"

"You might jus' run up 'gainst somethin' you don't wants to be seein'."

"I was afraid of that in the beginning, uncovering so many things I had forgotten, feeling the old pain again."

"Dat ain't my meanin', Miss Annie. I ain't talkin' 'bout rememberin' things, feelin' 'em all over agin. I's talking' 'bout new things, things you might never knowed nothin' 'bout before."

"There has been that sort of thing already in the diary. My mother lost her first baby. I never knew that. She never spoke of it, but I'm glad to know it now. It helps me to understand her in a way I never did when she was alive. I'm glad for these things."

"I jus' hopes dat you is gonna be glad 'bout all of 'em, Miss Annie." A pot slipped from her soapy hands and fell to the floor. She bent and picked it up. "I's sure glad it you, ole black pot, an' not one of dem pritty little china dishes, dem's mighty breakin' things." She put the pot back in the water.

"Would you like to go to Baltimore, Mardella?"

"You is thinkin' of goin' to Baltimore, Miss Annie?"

"Yes, but if you'd rather stay here I can very well go alone."

"I 'spect I likes to go wid you."

"I thought I'd pay my brother John a visit."

"It be a long time since you seed him."

"Yes, a very long time."

"He be happy to see you."

"I hope so. There's something I have to discuss with him. He may not like what I have to say."

"Cain't always be sayin' nice things to folks, much as we might likes to."

"Della, did you drop that pot on purpose?"

"I don't know what you means by dat, Miss Annie."

"I think you do. I won't break so easily as a china plate, Della, I promise. I'm stronger than you might imagine."

"I be lookin' forward to Baltimore, Miss Annie. I likes dat town."

Annie smiled. It was good to know that someone knew you well.

Mardella knew her very well and, in her way, loved her too. She went into the little room off the kitchen. For the first time she actually looked at Mardella's room. It was stark and bare, devoid of any personal possessions. She wondered if Mardella locked those kind of things away or if she had any at all. It troubled her, this room, so empty, revealing so little about its occupant. She took the diary from the dresser and went outside to the back stoop.

She brushed off the rocker. The seat was covered with thick dust. She sat down. It would be another hot day. Already, at only ten in the morning, it was warm and still, no sign of a breeze. She rocked herself gently and looked over at the empty chair beside her.

When they had first married it had been summer. They had spent long evenings on this porch, not speaking, but sitting in silence growing used to the other's presence. She had not thought of happiness then, only of peace. She remembered her mother's words in the diary about her wedding night and she recalled her own, how similar and yet how different they were. She had felt the things her mother felt, but she had hidden them. She and William had walked from this porch in the darkness and climbed the stairs. He had come to her, embraced her, but he did not remove her gown. They lay on the bed and she missed feeling his skin touch hers. He had lifted her gown only enough so that he could enter her. He had done it tenderly and there was no pain, but then he had suddenly pulled away from her. She felt as if she had been torn. Then there had been pain. She felt a sticky wetness on her stomach. William had gone and gotten a towel and wiped it away. He spoke finally, slowly and with reluctance.

"Do you understand, Annie?"

"Yes."

"I'm afraid . . . I . . ."

"Please, don't. I understand, William. Just don't, please."

She had turned from him then. Early in the morning before he awoke, she got up from their bed and in the pale light she took off her gown and stood naked, looking at a spot he had missed with the towel. It was dried and caked on her skin. She put a finger to her mouth and wetted it. She rubbed the spot and touched her tongue. The taste was salty, like tears.

Annie stretched her feet out into the patch of sunlight and began to read.

Sunday, December 4, 1864

Tonight has been a revelation. I have felt so worried and alone lately. There is no one really who could understand. Anna Ward is kindness itself, but she is just a girl and cannot fully comprehend my doubts and fears. She has no children, no husband, and is only twenty-two years old. Still, she is a true friend and she has helped me set my feet upon a path this evening which will lead to clarity and stability. My religion, upon which I have relied for solace and refuge for so long, has failed me. The beauty of it has paled for me. The thrill of the pageantry and ritual is fading. This evening Anna Ward introduced me to Maria Carbini, and a devout faith, an abiding belief, was born, perhaps reborn, within me. She is a revelation. She looked into my eyes and I knew that she saw into my very soul. She told me things about myself that could not have possibly been known by another living being–but she knew.

She is a small woman, and at first glance ordinary enough looking, perhaps fifty years of age. She was dressed in black with a shawl around her of some strange, lovely, and soft material which I could not identify. Shw wore her gray hair in a chignon. Her skin is dark and smooth, extraordinarily smooth for a woman of her age. That is just the first of many discoveries. Upon closer inspection one begins to realize that she is totally and completely extraordinary. Her eyes are a clear blue, her gaze penetrating. She rarely looks from the face of the person speaking to her, but fixes the speaker with an unflinching blue stare, making the one who speaks acutely aware of his words. And when she talks, which she does not often do, or at least never frivolously or lightly, she uses no gestures. Her words and her compelling soft voice convey her thoughts and observations succinctly. She has no need of gestures.

Maria Carbini knows things. She knows the past, and the present, and the future. More importantly to me, she knows my past, my present, and my future. She told me that soon I would fill the house with boarders, but that my financial difficulties would continue, peaking in April of this year coming. Then at about that time money would no longer concern me. She told me that I should have married my first beau, Henry Warfield. I started when she said the name. I had not heard it spoken in years and years. I had no wish to trick her, but more to test her seemingly incredible abilities, when I asked her if I had married Henry Warfield would I have been spared the fate of being a widow. I knew full well the answer. She smiled, which I had not seen her do before, and said that I would have been Mr. Warfield's bride and widow within the same year, and I knew that she spoke the truth. Shortly after I refused Henry Warfield he was tragically killed in a hunting accident.

I then asked her why she said that I should have married him, surely being a widow at fifteen could not be a desirable destiny, a life spent alone. She smiled again, and then her face grew somber and she spoke. I can recall her words exactly. "You would have been spared having children. One of your children is inextricably bound up in your sad fate." Her words made me tremble, but she would say nothing further on that topic.

I asked about Isaac. She told me that he was safe, that she saw him standing beside a river, that he wore a tattered uniform of some dark color. She told me that he had grown a beard. She predicted that he would return unharmed from the war, but that she saw some obstacle or barrier preventing our reunion. John, she said, was headed for a very cold place, very cold. I saw goose bumps raise up on her flesh as she said this. I realized that she felt the things that she saw, actually lived her prophecies. She told me that I was right to fear for John, but again stopping short at the crucial point, refused to say more. I asked her if Annie would marry. She answered affirmatively. I asked if her husband would be a soldier. She said no, that the war would be long over before Annie married, and that her husband would be a scholarly man, a scientist perhaps, quiet and serious.

I asked her if there was any way that she could tell me if Mr. Surratt was happy in the afterlife, happier at least than he had been here on earth. She said that yes, there was a way. Then she grew very pale. It is not tonight, she said. It is not meant for this night, but there is someone, not your husband, but someone who wishes to speak with you, someone in the beyond who wants to warn you, she told me. Then she said, it is a child or a baby. I felt a chill as she said this. She asked if I knew who this might be. I said no, quickly, too quickly. I felt trapped, caught in her blue gaze. Then she said it was time for me to leave, but that we would try to contact those who sought me, if I wished it, four days hence.

So I must wait in a kind of dread, a kind of anticipation which feels like hunger until—what? I cannot sleep. Her words keep running through my mind. My thoughts return again and again to my "sad fate" and to the child who has a warning for me. Is it little Anna? Sleep is impossible.

Thursday, December 8, 1864

These four days have been interminable, days of cooking and mending and making conversation when my mind was a million miles away. Finally this day arrived, and perversely I was almost sorry.

These things are seen in disbelief, understood with difficulty, but to speak of them, to attempt to describe, that is near impossibility. I went to Maria Carbini tonight with four days of carefully culled skepticism, but it was shattered. I believe in her powers, though I now know her to be a cruel and hard woman.

Tonight, through Maria Carbini, I spoke with the dead, indeed communicated with one who had never lived at all except for three short months within my womb.

We sat in a darkened room, the gas jets turned low at a plain table with a light cloth upon it. We held hands across the table, linked only by our little fingers. A momentary revulsion swept through me upon touching those long thin hands in the darkness. They were cool, not much substance, not like flesh at all, like thin strips of ivory covered in parchment.

After a moment I felt a kind of vibration which seemed to be coming from her body and feeding into mine through our hands. Then the table began to shake, violently. When she spoke, saying that she felt the presence of spirits, two of the lights sputtered and went out. It was quite dark. And then I saw it. Rising beside me, disembodied, was a tiny white hand. It seemed to glow, but appeared at the same time very solid and real. It reached out to me, but failed to touch. Then it disappeared. I heard a faint wail which might have been the wind, but sounded like a baby's cry.

Maria Carbini said in her low voice that there was great difficulty here, great trouble, that the spirit had a message for me of great significance, but that it would be delivered only with effort and struggle. I saw the face. It was not hers, not little Anna's, as I had expected but a little baby's face. It seemed to be floating in the darkness across the room from me. In a wavering voice, it told me that it was the child lost so long ago, the night of the fire. It moaned and cried for the life it had never lived. I felt the emptiness and the agony of that night returning. I was jolted from my painful revery by a piercing cry, and then the words, the warning, came. It told me that I should be wary, that troubled times were coming to me, brought by a man who would at first cause only happiness and laughter, but later death and despair. The voice continued, "This man will die surrounded by smoke and flame, but the fire will not consume him. He will not burn, but he will die, die as I did, engulfed in a brilliant hot blaze." And then as if a curtain had fallen before it, the face of my poor dead baby disappeared. I was left in the darkness with only the cold spare hands of Maria Carbini for comfort, and small comfort they were.

It is over, she said and lit the lamps again. I asked her what it meant. She would say only that I held the answer within me, that it was not for her to interpret the spirits. I felt suddenly that she did not really care either about my present fears or my ultimate fate. She seemed merely pleased at yet another demonstration of her power. I had expected more of Maria Carbini, but hers is a cruel genius, not tempered by compassion or pity. I wonder if she is immortal or inhuman, or perhaps both.

I wanted to leave that house and never return. It was sin and blasphemy for me to have come to her. I offered her money. I thought that she would refuse it, be insulted by it, but she calmly accepted it as if it were only her due.

As I left I saw in the darkened hallway her deaf son, standing and watching me. She had spoken of him to me. When he brought in tea that first night, she explained that he had never in his life uttered a word, but that he was endowed with greater powers. He had frightened me then, a huge sad dull-faced boy, but coming upon him suddenly in the darkness I was terrified of him. He moved slowly and haltingly away from me down the hallway making no sound—a stealthy tread and no voice with which to speak—his enormous ape-like arms swinging at his sides ending in tiny white hands. I left that house forever.

Friday, December 9, 1864

Annie's young officer from the "hop" paid a call today. Annie was aglow. His name is Seth Kierney. I wish that I could like him, but I cannot help but feel that he has come to try and take Annie from me. I've always known that she would marry and leave one day, that is the natural order of things. I didn't know that it would be so painful. Her eyes follow him everywhere. He is a boy of some grace, it's true, but I wonder if he is quite right for Annie. Ridiculous, I suppose. No human being is ever absolutely right for another, but I want Annie to be the happiest that she can be, and I doubt this boy. The question is, is there a boy to be found anywhere I would not doubt?

She danced with so many officers. There were so many likely youths. Why this one? Why has he come here? Why do Annie's eyes follow only him? He doesn't seem in the least extraordinary to me. Our conversation over tea was most awkward. He has very little to say, to me, anyway. Annie came down and his words came swiftly and smoothly. He never once glanced back to me, but then why should he?

I left them in the parlor as I knew they wanted to be left. I felt miserable and alone. I wonder, is it the threatened loss of my daughter which makes me feel this way? Or is it that I once had what she is having now, I know the sweetness of it, and I can never have it again? Am I as wretchedly selfish as all that? I wish that there was someone who could reassure me, who could tell me that every woman, every mother, feels as I feel now, but there is no one I could confess this feeling to. I wonder if my mother experienced this with me. She is not dead. My mother lives. I could ask her, but she would not see or answer me. She wants to be dead to me, but why? Why? She is so far from me, that old woman who lives down in the country, not in miles but in heart. It all began so long ago, this estrangement, this distance between us. She shared my grief when little Anna and Father left us, but she never truly understood how alone and abandoned I felt. She never understood the solace I found in the Church. Sometimes I think that she hated me and the Sisters. Sometimes I think she even hated God. Her hatred and my faith were of the same cloth. They kept our pain at bay. I wonder if my mother's hatred has faltered as my faith has, but I am afraid to ask.

Annie barely touched her food at supper this evening. I told her to eat, but she only smiled at me, and said something about it being impossible to eat, that eating was ordinary and mundane. I suppose that it is, but I wonder does she know how difficult it is for me to provide mundane things like food for her. I wonder, does she appreciate my efforts. Does anyone? Of course, they don't. Why should they? All of my accomplishments are dull and lackluster.

I'm feeling very sorry for myself tonight. No one else will pity me, so I must pity myself. I wish that I could tell Annie what I'm feeling, but I cannot. It has always been quite impossible for me to express my emotions. The words won't come. I want the people I love to just know somehow the way I feel. They should know because I love them and they love me. I want Annie to understand me without explanation. I am not fair and I ask far too much.

Annie is so young and she is happy. She thinks that she is in love, and who am I to say that she is not. Do I wish that I was young and happy and in love? I do wish that. And perhaps I am being given that through Annie. I must try to believe that it is so.

Saturday, December 10, 1864

I have put in another advertisement for roomers. I must take in a little more money. I do not know where money goes. I try to be frugal, a good and wise manager, but still financial stability remains illusive. Of course, prices are a scandal here in Washington. And now John is here and he brings people occasionally. It is necessary to be hospitable and cordial, though I must say I have served tea to the strangest collection of John's acquaintances. They all seem to be forever looking over their shoulders. John avoids Miss Anna Ward these days. She feels it, I know, and it hurts her. One-sided love is a cruel thing, one of the cruelest of things. It is usually women who suffer of it, in silence and forbearance and for lengthy periods of time. Our province is pain. It must be borne, like children and disappointment.

I think that I will prepare an oyster loaf for supper tomorrow. John loves it so.

Tuesday, December 13, 1864

It is very late. The house is asleep. I have turned out all the lights, the fires have burned low, and the doors are locked. We are safe and secure, but outside it is bitter cold. The wind howls through the streets at night and prowls on the corners by day.

I cannot sleep. First it was my dreams preventing it, and now it is the memory of Maria Carbini bringing forth the old pain and a new fear. Yet I was tempted to go to her again. Perhaps this time she would tell me pleasant things and I would not have to take hold of those hands to hear them. It gives me strange comfort to know that someone knows the outcome of my life. It makes me believe that there is some pattern to it, some reason for it. If I am destined to remain in Washington, I know that I will be unhappy. I love the country, most especially my Maryland. Here, in the city, nothing is what it should be, and very little is what it seems. I pray for the end of the war, the end of winter, and the end of Washington. War, winter, and Washington, a very ugly and malevolent triumvirate.

There is a rage in the city these days, relic-hunting. People go to the White House and take sofa cushions, cut pieces of brocade cloth from chairs, take pictures from walls, and vases from tables. I wonder why people feel compelled to take souvenirs. Do they have so little faith in their memories, their capacity to call forth recollections? Must they have some small physical piece, some property to remind them? How must Mr. and Mrs. Lincoln feel? Do they ever know the safety and security, the warmth and dreaming, that so many take for granted behind their locked doors and before their banked fires at night in this city? Must the President and his wife sometimes wonder that perhaps the relic-hunters would like to cut small pieces of them too, to remember them by? I have never put much value upon my privacy. It has always just been there for me. If someone recognized me on the street, it was a friend, of course. But Lincoln, so many recognize him whom he does not know, has never seen. He cannot know that because someone knows his face and his name that that person is his friend. But he belongs to them all. He is their President, and he knows them not. It must be terrifying . . .

December. Twelfth month. Last month. Another ending. My life has filled to the brim with endings and with deaths. My life, more than others I think, has been made of these things. And it does not grow easier, saying goodbye. Why do those I love always leave me? Why do they? Why?

Late night thoughts, they give me shivers. I must go to bed. I must sleep. In the morning it always looks better, except lately it hasn't. It doesn't change lately. I have late night thoughts mornings and afternoons these days. These days I shiver all the time. Daylight, dawn, no longer frightens away my fears. My fears are unafraid now. I cannot drive them from me.

I hate it here in Washington. I wish that I were back in

Maryland, but I fear that there I would hate it too. Geography is not at issue. I am. And I am terribly afraid that my hatred is not for the places where I rest, but for myself. Late night thoughts, leave me tomorrow, please.

Her mother had never mentioned the name Maria Carbini to her. There had been a woman who had told the future, but Annie had known nothing of this woman. The book had trembled in her hands as she read the words that were said about her husband, not a soldier, but a scholarly man, quiet and serious. Her mother had not told her. She had believed the woman's prophecy, but still she had not told her of it. She could not understand this. Had her mother been too involved with herself, to bother about telling her that small scrap of information. That couldn't be true. Her mother wasn't capable of such selfishness. She dropped the book at her feet. The sun had gone from the porch. It had to be nearly noon. The heat was intense.

Perhaps Mardella had been right. Perhaps there were things better left unknown about another. It hurt her to think of the names and the people in her mother's life about whom she knew nothing. Maria Carbini, the prophet. Henry Warfield, a dead beau. And who shared her name? Who was little Anna? Did she really want to know? These mysterious interlopers were taking her gentle, soft-spoken mother, who always wore black and a sad half-smile, away from her. Who was this woman who had been her mother? She found herself thinking that if she could discover who that woman had truly been, that then she would find herself. Maria Carbini had been right. They were inextricably bound up together. She was afraid. Most of all, she feared the entrance of the black-eyed man whom Maria Carbini had seen dying in flames and smoke. She knew who he was, who he must be. She knew that within the next few pages of the book at her feet he would be there. And she was afraid.

January 1, 1865, New Year's Day, her birthday, her seventeenth birthday, that was the entry in her mother's diary that she dreaded. That was the day he had come into their lives, and from that moment on, all had been lost. She got to her feet unsteadily. She left the book where it lay and went inside the house. She walked past Mardella without a word and climbed the stairs to the room.

The curtains were open. The white light from the windows blinded her. The pain behind her eyes was unbearable, excruciating. She hurried to the chiffonier, took the cork from the bottle, and tipped it heavily to her mouth. She left it standing open. The cork fell to the floor. She walked over and drew the coverlet from the bed, but the expanse of white sheet made her close her eyes upon it. Her forehead and upper lip were beaded with sweat, as she lost consciousness.

Mardella came into the room expecting what she saw. She carried a damp rag in one hand. She closed the curtains, crossed to the bed, and looked down at her mistress. Her breathing was steady, if heavy. Mardella loosened her bodice, and wiped her face with the cool cloth.

"Poor baby lamb, what make you do dis?"

She walked over, and with a hand to her lower back which ached constantly, she bent, picked up the cork, put it in the bright blue bottle, and opened the drawer. She held the bottle in her hand for a moment, looking at it closely.

"She need you. She need you bad. I know dat, she'd of jumped outa de window long 'fore dis widout you. You ain't no good, but you keeps her livin'. You an' me, us keeps her livin'."

She put it in the drawer, shut it away, and walked from the dark room.

VII

She opened her eyes and saw the curtains closed. She could not remember pulling them. It must have been Mardella. She sat up slowly. The pain was gone now. She felt only a stale dryness all through her. She stood up and looked in the mirror. Her eyes were black-circled, her hair hanging loose at her shoulders. She looked like a mad woman. All she needed was spittle seeping from the corners of her mouth.

It must be nearly four o'clock. William would be home soon. She must clear her mind, fix her hair. There was little she could do about her eyes. She wanted to tell him tonight about Baltimore. She had to see John.

She was standing in the doorway of the dining room when Mardella came in from the kitchen.

"The table looks lovely, Della."

"I thanks you, Miss Annie. I cooks somethin' special fer you tonight. You thinks dat you cain eat?"

"I'll try. What's the surprise?"

"Now, if I tole you it wouldn't be one no more."

"No, it wouldn't. Della, I left the diary on the porch this morning . . ."

"I puts it away fer you."

They heard the front door open and close. William entered the room.

"Good evening, my dear." He kissed her cheek. "Good evening, Mardella."

"Good evenin', sir."

Mardella returned to the kitchen.

"You look tired, Annie."

"I didn't sleep well last night."

"I'm sorry to hear that. Tonight is another night."

"Yes, there always seems to be another night."

"Perhaps it is the heat. You do suffer so in the heat."

She saw an opportunity in this. "Yes, I do. I was thinking that I might visit my brother in Baltimore."

"Is it cooler in Baltimore?"

"Ever so much cooler."

She smiled, feeling her face would crack.

He looked at her and ran a finger under his stiff collar. "It might be good for you at that."

"I really think that it would. I really do."

"You seem very anxious, Annie. We will discuss it later. Right now, I'm ready for supper."

"I don't know how you can eat in this weather."

"It is best not to dwell upon things when nothing can be done. I don't feel the heat as you do."

"Mardella has made something special this evening."

"I will go and wash up."

"Do you really think that I might be able to make the trip to Baltimore?"

"Perhaps."

"It's just that I think it would be a pleasant change of scene, and the weather is so much cooler there."

"So you have said. I believe I said that we would discuss it at another time. I am not so sure that I could do without you."

"Oh, but . . ."

"We shall speak of it later."

He left the room. She thought of him running the soft white wet soap in his soft white wet hands, and she cringed. She had to get away from him, if only he would let her go. Those hands of his could squeeze and grab her, hold her fast. They had before. She could feel them on her hair and her face, her neck and her breasts, her waist and her thighs. She could feel them everywhere.

She sat down at the table. He re-entered after a short time. He smelled of soap. Mardella came in with the soup. They ate without words. He bent closely over his bowl and consumed the hot liquid quickly and loudly. She watched him, lifting an empty spoon to her mouth over and over again.

"You put me in mind, Annie, of the lady who claims to be reading but never turns a page. The soup is very good. You should try some and stop pretending to eat."

"I didn't think that you would notice."

"It is very irritating. I do not know why you bother to come to the table at all."

"Because you have always insisted upon it."

"I ask very little of you, Annie. Perhaps, I ask too little. You should learn what it really is to be a wife. I have indulged you far too much."

"You've always seemed perfectly satisfied with me."

"Perfectly satisfied, until lately. The dissatisfaction began with you, Annie. You have changed."

"I'll tell you why if you want to hear. I would love to tell you why."

"I do not wish to hear. The only thing that I want is a return to normality. I want you to be what you have always been."

"And what is that?"

"My wife."

"You just said that I didn't know what it was to be a wife, that you had indulged me too much."

"And I have. What makes you think that I would let you go running off to Baltimore on a little holiday without me?"

"How can you object to my visiting my brother?"

"That is not all that this trip is."

"What, pray tell, is it then, William?"

"It is not the weather. And it is not your brother. You are meeting someone."

"Meeting someone?"

"Yes, you have taken it into your head to become a runaway wife."

"I don't know what you're talking about."

"You do know. You have met with him here in this very house, my house."

Mardella came in to take the soup dishes and serve the main course. She put each bowl and plate carefully upon the table, and then went back into the kitchen. He took her plate, heaped food upon it and handed it back to her.

"I don't want it. I can't possibly eat all of that."

"Take it. You will eat every bite of it."

She sat with her hands folded in her lap and stared at him.

"I don't want it."

"Eat that food, I tell you! You will do as I tell you."

His voice was shaking.

She took a mouthful but could not swallow it. She choked into her napkin and started to get up from her chair. He was around to her side of the table in a second. He pushed her back down.

"I want to go upstairs."

"You are not going anywhere unless I tell you that you may. Eat your supper."

"I can't."

"You will. You will if I have to feed it to you."

"I don't understand any of this. You're mad to think that there is another man. There is none. I want to go to Baltimore to see my brother. I'll tell you why . . ."

"I know why. I know why you want to go to Baltimore, and it is not to see your brother."

"It is. There's no other reason."

"Eat that food." He was standing over her still. She looked up into his face. "Eat."

"No."

He pulled her from the chair and shook her by the shoulders. He pushed her back down in front of the plate.

"You are my wife. You are mine. You will do as I say. Eat your supper."

"William, why are you doing this?"

He did not answer. She was afraid of him for the first time. She realized that she had lived for years with a man about whom she knew nothing. She had no idea what he was capable of doing. She had no idea who he was. She began to choke down the food on her plate. She couldn't taste any of it. She chewed and chewed but there was no moisture in her mouth or throat. She felt as if she was trying to eat huge handsful of straw. He ate steadily. She didn't see the effort he was making. Finally her plate was empty.

"I would like to go now."

"No, not yet. I would like to see you eat some more potatoes."

He took a large spoonful and dolloped it onto her plate.

"I'm going to be ill."

She felt the food rising up in her throat, bitter and foul.

"You are not going to be ill. You are going to eat your potatoes, or you will be very sorry."

She pushed back the vomit with mashed potato, swallowing both together. Mardella came in to clear the table. Annie rose from her chair.

"Where are you going, my dear?"

"Up . . . upstairs."

"No. Stay and have dessert with me. We will go up together."

"I think I'll go up now."

"Stay."

She sat back down. Mardella took her plate, looking closely at her.

"Miss Annie don't look at all well."

"She is fine, Mardella. Bring in dessert, please."

"Yes, sir."

Dessert was a lemon meringue pie. That was Mardella's surprise. It was Annie's favorite. Her mother used to make it sometimes, on Sundays. She looked at the pie and tears welled up in her eyes. She brushed them away, but more came. She ate her piece of pie. He ate his. He folded his napkin, as always, and walked around the table, slowly this time. He put out his hand and helped her from her chair. He kept his hand firmly under her elbow all the way up the stairs and into their room. He guided her to the bed. She sat down.

"Will you let me tell you what is happening to me? Will you let me try to explain? I have changed. It's true. There is a reason for it. I want to tell you about it."

"I know the reason."

"No, you don't. There was a man who came here . . ."

"And he is your lover."

"No. He's a very old man."

"Mardella said that too, but you both lied. He is a young man. He is your lover. You planned to meet him. Was it just to be a few days in Baltimore or were you going to run away with him?"

"No. No. No. You have to listen to me. There is no man."

"I saw his picture."

"What picture?"

"It is in your drawer. He's in uniform. Did you know him during the war? Did you know him before you knew me? When did you take him as your lover? Has he always been?"

"The boy in that picture is dead, and has been for thirteen years. I loved him, but he was never my lover. I wish that he had been. Perhaps then I would have known something other than the revulsion and disgust I feel whenever I'm near you." He turned and walked to the door. He bolted it and began to unbuckle his belt. She ran for the door. He grabbed her as she passed him and spun her around. He ripped open her bodice, and started to tear at her skirts.

"Disgust and revulsion, that is all I have ever given you? Now you will know what those things really are."

He dragged her to the bed and threw her down upon it. He was breaking her stays in his hands. He tore her pantalets open. She was not fighting him, but only resisting, trying to get away. He held her down with one arm, taking off his belt with the other. She was almost completely naked now. Her chemise hung in tatters around her. Her hair was loose. He turned her over on her stomach. She tried to crawl away until he raised his belt and struck the first blow. She stopped. She did not cry out, but lay there very still. She wanted him to beat her. She wanted to be punished. Then he threw his belt aside and he was on top of her, pushing inside of her. For the first time, he did not pull away from her at the last moment, but stayed, filling her. Then he rolled away from her.

After some time she heard him get up and walk to the door, unbolt it, and go downstairs. She did not move. Then he was back. She saw that he had a plate of butter in his hands. He came over to her and began to smooth it on her back. His hands felt good upon her. She wanted to take them, all soft and slick from the butter, and rub them on her breasts and her stomach and her thighs. She wanted to feel him inside her again. She turned to him, but he looked away. Then he stood and went to the bureau. He took out a cotton nightdress and returned to the bed.

"Sit up. Put this on." She did so, silently. "Have you nothing to say to me? Don't you wish to call me a beast?"

"No."

"I am a beast. All men are beasts and all women make them that. I thought you were different, but you are the same. You are a wanton, like all the rest."

"I don't know what to say to you, William."

"There is nothing to be said. You transformed me into my father tonight. You did that. I hate this night. And I hate you. And I hate myself."

"I'm sorry."

"Go to Baltimore. Go soon. Go tomorrow. Go to your lover."

"I have no lover. You are the only man I have ever had."

"You are a liar. I cannot stand the sight of you. I can only return your revulsion and your disgust. That is all I feel for you now."

"What did you ever feel for me?"

"I loved you."

He stood, crossed to the other side of the room, and began to undress. He folded all of his things neatly and put them away. He came to the bed and lay down with his back to her. She wanted, for the very first time, to reach out to him, but she did not.

VIII

She boarded the train that morning feeling anxious. It was much like her ill-fated walk into town, but she knew that this time there was no turning back. She was placed in the "Ladies' Car," which was by far the nicest of any of the cars, reserved strictly for women. She thought that it was interesting that women were treated so well by men while all the time men viewed them as their property. Women were allowed almost anything except the luxury of being human beings. William had felt free to beat her, to force-feed her, because she was his. His anger was so great because his property was, in his mind, threatened. That was all she was to him. And yet, she thought that once late last night she had heard him sob and that sound had made her want to weep. It disturbed her that his brutality had sparked a response in her, that in his anger she had for the first time felt William's love. It had been so strong in the darkness, but in the bright light this morning she had felt unsure and William had been gone.

The train began to move out of the station, picking up speed rapidly. She remembered right after the war, the trains had moved at a snail's pace. It took hours to go the shortest distances. She reached into her pocket and touched the diary as if it were a sort of talisman. She watched the countryside pass by out the window. She thought of all the people who lived out there, people she would never know. Her world had become so small, small and stifling. She had chosen it because it had seemed safe, but she realized now that she had been slowly dying in it. She was frozen, but she felt the thaw had begun. She only hoped that some of the person she had once been had survived the long winter.

She brought out the book and opened it. She felt strong enough now. She had taken a first step toward the future. This was the right moment to confront the beginnings of her troubled past. She began to read.

Thursday, December 15, 1864

Today a new Supreme Court Chief Justice, Salmon P. Chase, was sworn in. The old one, Chief Justice Roger Taney, died a short time ago. He was a Marylander and a Catholic. He hated slavery and yet he and his court upheld its legality, its existence. He exorcized it from his home and plantation, but gave it permission to flourish in the rest of the country. Then he was a man of contradictions. The man who replaces him is probably the same. We are all confederates in contradiction, being human. I distrust their justice. Perhaps I have seen too much injustice from them.

Today in the kitchen Dulcey was scrubbing pots. I walked in and noticed that close beside her stood her little granddaughter. Dulcey told me that her name was Genevieve. She is a beautiful child, light-colored, huge hazel eyes, and softly curling black hair. She is maybe eight years old. Dulcey asked me if it would be all right if she brought her along with her from now on. It was an odd conversation. It keeps playing in my mind.

"Genevieve, she good chile. She be real quiet. She help me too."

I asked her then if the child wouldn't be far happier at home.

"Home. Dat place ain't home fer us. It be where us sleeps an' eats.

Ain't no home to nobody. Dere be thirteen of us dere. It a place full of folks an' misery. Genevieve jus ain't happy away from me, an' I ain't from her."

I said that there couldn't be much for her to do shut up in a kitchen all day long. Children like to run and play, I said.

"She be better off. Dey after her all de time at de other place."

I didn't understand what she meant by after her.

"After her. De men, dey after my baby already."

I looked at the lovely child Genevieve. She sat at her grandmother's feet, toying with the hem of her skirt. She didn't lift her eyes to me. She didn't even understand what we were speaking of. She was busily twining the strings of Dulcey's apron around her slender wrist.

"I always keeps her 'side me nights. I wants to in de days too. She sech a little thin' an' she gits hungry. She don't know nothin' 'bout men. Dey gives her sweets to touch her, she done tole me 'bout it. I don't wants her growin' up into her ma. I be much obliged if I could brings her wid me days."

I told Dulcey that she certainly could. I cannot stop thinking about it. This is not a just world, Salmon P. Chase. Do you know that, I wonder? Do you know that this is a world where innocence is corrupted, where goodness is denied, and justice is merely a word used by selfrighteous and blind old judges? Yes, I know that justice too is blind, but at least she is a woman. She can understand humiliation and pain. And you, Salmon P. Chase, what of you?

Saturday, December 17, 1864

Lt. Seth Kierney has begun to make a nuisance of himself. I believe that I am a hospitable woman, that is my nature and my training, but he wears thin his welcome. Is there not a war going on? Shouldn't he be off somewhere fighting it? I don't understand how he manages to lounge around Washington all the time. Did I say Washington? I should be more specific. I should say H Street. He is here constantly. After he had gone this evening, I spoke to Annie about it.

She had walked him to the door, and stayed far too long for decorum's sake or my taste. She came back into the parlor, flushed and breathless. I plunged in, not in my usual manner, I must admit, but it had been building within me for days and it just spewed forth. The conversation went like this.

"Anna, what have you been doing out on the porch all this time with Lt. Kierney?"

"I've been kissing Seth."

"Anna!"

"You're angry?"

"Yes, I am. And I'm disappointed in you."

"You would never call me Anna unless you were very upset."

"I am very upset."

"But why? Because I've been kissing Seth?"

"I am very surprised at you. You are behaving in a manner most bold and brazen. You are disrespectful."

"I'm sorry, Mother. I don't mean to be. I'm in love. I could lie to you and say that it was the cold that took my breath away and made my cheeks red, but it is not the cold. It's Seth. Yes, I've kissed him, and I will again. I love him. I won't lie about it."

"You're too young to know what love is."

"No, you're too old."

"You have a very sharp tongue, child."

"Mother, I'm sorry, truly, I am. I don't want to hurt you. I love you."

"And you love Seth?"

"Yes. I can love you both, Mother. It's very easy."

"Does he love you?"

"Yes."

"Yes, and he wants you all to himself. I can see that in him. He'll want, he'll demand, all your love."

"Mother, you can't demand love. It must be given. I give my love to Seth, as I give it to you. He would never ask me to stop loving you. You don't know him. He's so wonderful."

"I don't know him and I don't want to. I don't want him in this house ever again."

"Mother, please. Don't do this."

"I don't want him here."

"I don't understand you."

"I have no need to explain myself to you. I'm your mother. You will do as I say. Lt. Kierney is no longer welcome in this house. You will not see him again."

Annie just turned and left then, without another word. I don't know why I said those things. It was so unlike me. I know that she must have been surprised and hurt. It wasn't that I wouldn't explain. It was simply that I couldn't. I don't like the boy. He's not right for her. He is shallow and facile. I write these words and they are perfectly true but I know that they are not the real reason. I don't want him here. That is all. He brings it back too vividly, all that I once had and lost, all that I once felt and can never feel again. But how can I ever tell this to Annie? I cannot.

Saturday, December 24, 1864

Christmas Eve. Honora and I went to late Mass. It was quite moving and beautiful, but I cannot help but miss the voice which once spoke to me, giving me blessed guidance, and has now gone still. I am sad, and yes, resentful. I feel forsaken. Yet I realize that it is I who turned from God and not He from me, not until I broke my promise to Him did He turn away. Once the Church used to calm me and give me serenity. Nothing else could do this until Mr. Surratt. I took him and his strong arms to hold me. I chose him. Our days together were so short-lived but so sweet. They are gone now. He is gone. I am alone. I no longer have the Church and the heavy solid peace it gave to me. I have nothing. I am utterly alone.

Annie is ill. It is Lt. Kierney, I am sure. Honora told me that he has gone back to the lines. Annie has been in bed for two days. This morning she asked me for a hand mirror. When I asked her why, she told me that she felt as if she had grown old overnight, that she was positive she had sprouted a fine collection of gray hairs and wrinkles. She said that being sick, regardless of age, made one old. I know that what she really meant was to be in love and have the object of that love far from you, that is despair. I wish that she could have told me that, but I know that I have made it impossible for her to speak to me. I regret it, but I do not know what to say or do. It has gone too far. Perhaps I could make some blancmange to soothe and cheer her.

John brought home a little tree for the parlor. It is very pretty and smells wonderful. He can be so thoughtful one moment and so utterly careless the next.

Still no response to my advertisement and my every thought is of money and money and money. I hate it so. This, the holiest of seasons, and mine are the least sacred of thoughts, how to obtain another load of coal, a cord of wood, a peck of beans.

I look at the little tree upon which we have put red ribbons and white candles. It is a lovely thing, but it is dying, cut off from its roots, its sustenance. It is green and freshly scented now, but soon it will turn brown and hard, and when one touches it the needles will fall in clusters. Annie came down in her wrapper. I looked up and saw her standing in the doorway watching me, and I knew that we were thinking the very same thing, the same sad thought about our pretty little tree. I wanted to say something, but I did not.

Everything and everyone I love dies. Why is it so?

Sunday, December 25, 1864

Christmas Day. It is night now. The day has been a long one. The streets were icy and treacherous. Paying calls and even church was impossible. Now, in the dim stillness of the house, I think of Mother. How she would hate and conquer the quiet of this house. Yet she herself was so still and silent last week when I went to see her. Brother Zadoc came and told me that she was ill, maybe dying. I went out to the farm, and as I sat by her bed, looking at her face, I realized the last time I had seen her had been at Mr. Surratt's funeral, three years ago. Zadoc says she is much improved this week. I hope that she is well enough to enjoy today. She loves Christmas and all holidays. Her image, from my childhood, rushes up in my mind so clearly—her words, her stories—but always her joy of living shining in her face. Last week, as she lay in a stupor, it was there. It will always be.

Some of her stories made me quake in fear as a child, but her tales always ended with human courage and that strong indomitable will to live which she herself shares with all of her characters. Her stories of her frontier childhood in Georgia frightened me most. Those were harsh days. She learned to love and value life, but she learned unremitting hatred too.

There was an old tradition among people in those parts, a macabre practice which my mother witnessed once, and told me of, in vivid detail, many years later. It was shortly after Father and little Anna had gone. Mother had marked me as a survivor. I would have stopped her midway in that terrible tale, but there was never any stopping Mother. I shall write it as it plays itself in my mind, in my mother's words, just as she spoke them to me over thirty years ago.

"My mother was a widow, as I am, and as you may very well be, Mary. We are destined to outlive the men we love. That is the fate of strong women who have a penchant for weak men. I was about twelve years old when Katherine began to come around and visit. She was odd-looking to me. She had a large wide mouth with full lips. They always looked slightly bruised or as if she had just gorged herself on currants, red, but with a bluish cast to them. Her hair was blonde, fine silver baby hairs caught the sun at her temples. Her eyes were big and very nearly black. She was very pale but her hands were brown from laboring on her husband's acres. She wore shirts carefully buttoned to the throat but across her breasts the fabric strained and swelled. Her wide hips swayed beneath heavy skirts. She would ride up to our place at dusk and sometimes later on an old bony horse, and sit on the step of the front porch. She rarely came inside. She would keep hold of the reins as if she could only stay for a moment.

"I never took part in these conversations. They did not interest me. I had heard older women talk before, always about disease and having babies. It bored me. So I steered clear of Mother and Katherine, until one day when I discovered that Katherine had been weeping. She had arrived with her straw bonnet pulled low over her face, but my sharp young eyes did not miss her swollen red-rimmed ones. Women, in those days and that particular place, did not shed tears easily. I had only seen Katherine's husband once. Mother and I had stopped by the place when they first came. He emerged, huge and bare chested, from the barn and eyed us angrily. He was old but powerful-looking. I had thought at first that Katherine was his daughter, but when she came out of the house he had put a heavy arm around her shoulders in a most unfatherly way, not tenderly but more as if to restrain her. He glared and spoke no more than three words to us, but Katherine was voluble and friendly even with that proprietary band of iron about her. We never went again, but Katherine came to visit us after that. I felt sure that her tears this day had something to do with her husband and for once I wanted to listen to what was said on the porch in the growing darkness. I sat down under a tree in the yard not far from them and strained to hear.

"I could only make out a few words but they were enough to confirm my suspicions. The husband was one of that special breed of men who are enormously and hideously cruel. He had a collection of thick black bullwhips which he used with devastating effect on the animals about the place and on Katherine. She was used to the beatings and the backbreaking work. She had been given to her husband when she was little more than a child by her father, a man of similar temperament. She spoke of endless nights, with the windows open, when it was cool and dark outside. She was forced to lie in their hot bed, long after he had heaved off her. The sound of his heavy snores drowned out the blessed sounds of crickets and frogs and the other gentle living things she loved, until she longed to put a pillow to his face and stop his breath or her own. As I listened in the yard to these words they made little sense to me, Mary, as I am sure they will make little to you now, but try to remember them. It is important for a woman to know of this."

I have remembered, Mother. I have remembered well. I am sitting on a dark and dreadful Christmas night and all the house is asleep. I wish that I too could sink into total dreamless oblivion for a few precious hours, but your words force themselves into my mind and onto the page. I am helpless to stem them.

"I heard Katherine tell my mother that her husband's younger brother had come to live with them. She said something about how the sun played upon the muscles of his back when he worked in the fields, how his eyes were clear and blue, how they always seemed to be watching her, how his face was young like hers, not lined and gnarled and old. And his hands, big, with thick flat fingers, and sometimes how when she handed him something, their hands would touch.

"Suddenly she slapped the reins hard onto her hand, and stood, saying that she must leave. My mother stood watching her ride off until she disappeared. She had never done that before. I walked over beside her and asked her about Katherine's trouble, but she would just look at me and say that it was a great trouble and that she was afraid for Katherine. I had never heard my mother say that she feared anything. It impressed me deeply, but I did not understand it. We didn't see Katherine for nearly a week, and when she did turn up again it was in the dead of night. My window faced out on the yeard. I was awakened by the sound of hurried hushed voices. I got up and looked out my window, but all that I could see was Katherine's old thin horse standing in the yard.

"I stayed at the window, and finally there was silence. I saw Katherine come from out of the shadows and slowly mount her horse. The moon was full that night, and as she turned, I saw her face clearly. If I had not seen her horse and heard her voice, I would not have known that it was her. Her face was a white grotesque mask, swollen and puffed. She raised a hand toward the porch, in farewell to my mother, the moonlight showed it to be covered in long red gashes.

"Three days later a crowd of neighbors, loud and feverish, arrived at our place. Mother and I had lived those days in silent and forbidding tension. We did not speak, but merely waited for what was coming. The neighbors announced that there had been a murder. We knew that it had been at Katherine's. I remembered her bruised white face. I was not surprised. Mother did not seem so either. She merely took her place, straight-backed and hard-faced, in one of the wagons. She told me to stay put. I stood watching the wagons go down the road, but all that I could really see was a horribly hurt moonlit face. After they were out of sight, I saddled a horse and followed.

"The farm was still, unnaturally hushed. I stopped my horse so that I was hidden by a clump of trees. In the middle of the yard there was a body covered by a blanket. It looked large, too large. I felt somewhat relieved. I was getting ready to dismount and take a look at the corpse when the door of the house opened. The neighbors came out leading Katherine. My mother followed behind, still ramrod straight, but her steps were very slow. Katherine's face in the sunlight was mottled blue and purple. The red gashes I had seen on her hands continued up her arms and covered her long slender neck. Her shirt was torn and her large white breasts could be seen, though she fumbled at them and at the torn cloth, trying to cover herself.

"The crowd was moving her toward the covered form in the yard. When they reached it, they stopped. Someone stooped and uncovered it, and I saw Katherine's husband, a huge gaping wound in his skull. It looked to have been done with an ax. My mother came up and stood beside Katherine. It looked for a moment like the beginning of a funeral service of some kind, but it proved to be an entirely different ritual. It was a trial. The neighbors were Katherine's judge and jury. She was to be tested. One of the women stepped forward and began to strip the clothes from Katherine. Her head was bowed. She was slowly divested of her torn shirt and chemise, her skirt, her petticoat, and her pantalets. She wore no shoes or stockings. She stood naked. Her back was to me, a white beautiful back, dappled by the sun, but with long scars running down to her soft rounded buttocks. A man roughly reached for her and pushed her down to her knees beside the body. Then he reached for her hands. This would be the proof of her guilt or innocence. He took them both and plunged them deeply into the wound. Katherine struggled and the veins roped in her neck, but the man held her fast.

"Everyone, except my mother who had closed her eyes, leaned

forward in anticipation. The man pulled Katherine's hands out and thrust them into the eager faces. Her hands were clean and free of blood. The neighbors drew back in disappointment. One by one they took to their wagons until Katherine, crouched still as stone over the dead man, and my mother were the only ones left in the yard. Mother drew her away and began to hand her her clothes. I came out from the trees. Mother said nothing, just looked at me. We buried Katherine's husband, and then she came home with us.

"She stayed with us for a time, and then she went off one day, with a young widower who had three sons and was on his way West. Before she left she told my mother what had happened. I'm sure that she was the only living soul Katherine ever told. I eavesdropped.

"Her husband had found them together in the barn, naked, his brother deep inside his wife. It was not their first time together. Something just drew them, pulled them, every time they were near each other. The brother leapt through the window and ran off. Katherine had not been quick enough. He beat her until she lay senseless and bleeding on the floor. He bound her with rope and went off to track down his brother. She freed herself and made her way to our place. I never knew if Mother had tried to make her stay or not. As Katherine told her story, she paused for a moment at that part and went on without a word.

"From our farm she went to their secret meeting place, where they had met for weeks after her husband had gone to sleep, the place they had been in too much of a hurry to go to that night. She knew that was where he would be. He wanted her to run off with him, but she said that he would hunt them down, that they would never be free of him. And so the brother went back to the farm with an ax. When Katherine found what he had done, she sent him off. She knew that she and her words had prompted it, but she also knew that her lover was too much like her husband, too much his brother, for all his handsome face, his wide blue eyes, and his soft touch. And she knew how short a time it would be before he turned against her.

"She told my mother this just before she left for the West with the widower. He sat in the wagon outside waiting for her. She put her old life behind her and began again. That was the right thing. Katherine was after all only sixteen years old. And that is Katherine's story, a woman's story."

I suppose that it always takes a man to free a woman from another man, so she is never truly free, but even without freedom, there can be strength and a kind of reverence for living, for enduring, for continuing. Is that what you looked for in me and found that I lacked, Mother? Is that why you will no longer look upon me? If you cannot respect me I will understand, but love me, Mother, please. I need your love.

Annie closed the book and thought of Katherine's story. Why had her mother been able to only copy it down in her diary and not tell her? Her mother had heard it from her own mother at a far younger age. In reading it, Annie could not help but think that it was a story of horror but of hope too. She had to believe this. In light of what had just happened to her, she had to believe it. It terrified her that William could inflict such pain upon her, that he could, as he had described himself, become a beast. Yet there was something good in it. He had spoken of his father. The man must have been a monster of temper, totally at the mercy of his moods. William must have hated him, to say with such disgust that he had become his father. William had been driven so deeply within himself that she had come to judge him strictly from his surface. They were two of a kind. His father had been his tormentor. Her mother had made her what she was.

Could she love William? She did not know. She knew that she hadn't loved him. He had been a refuge for her. When she thought she might be able to discard that refuge, he had sensed it. He had given her desire to leave him the wrong reasons, but still he had tried to prevent her going. In that effort she had seen something, perhaps a small hope for them. She abhorred the violence and the jealousy, but there was caring beneath that. She felt that his apathy over the years had been far crueler than what he had done the night before. She felt that possibly she could love him, but she had left him.

She had this to do first. She had to find her mother. She had to know the woman whose death had caused her retreat from life. She had to find the woman who caused her to lose thirteen years of her life. She had to understand this woman. Then she could find herself.

If, after this journey had ended, she could return to him, perhaps then they could build something. The foundation of numbness, the careful edifice of polite detachment, must be torn down. They had made a beginning. She had seen a break, a crack, in him. By leaving as she had, she might be allowing him time and reason to seal it over, but she had no choice. Leaving him did not mean that she would never return. She hoped he knew that. She was not rejecting him, but the life they had had together, which had been no life at all. She would wish that they could truly share a life together, but first she must find herself, learn what she could be to herself before she knew what she could be to him.

She knew that through the horror and the pain that living often is, you must keep believing in life. That was Katherine's story. Why, years ago, hadn't her mother told her of Katherine? Perhaps then she wouldn't have shared her mother's grave all these years. Perhaps she wouldn't have wasted her life, making her own body a tomb.

IX

The train was leaving the Washington City station. She could see the Capitol building, its dome shining under the noon sun. It would not be long and she would be in Baltimore. She opened the book and began reading again, the rhythmic sound of the train in her ears.

Tuesday, December 27, 1864

Christmas has come and gone once more. I realize that I spent the greater part of it in melancholy revery, but how I did need to escape the present, my financial worries, my troubled thoughts of my children. John has taken off on some sort of secret excursion. He left early Monday morning, with no explanation. I came down in my wrapper and found him preparing to depart without even a goodbye. As his mother I feel that I have some rights, and I told him so. He looked at me steadily, so large and masculine, and impatient. He kissed my forehead, saying that I would catch cold, ordered me back to bed, thereby neatly evading all my inquiries. My son has learned to be a man very quickly. I watched him stride confidently away from me, mount his horse, and ride off down the street. He did not wear his hat and the sole bit of December sunlight settled on his proud golden head.

Annie grows pale. She alternates between languor and a kind of frenzied activity. She is, by turns, snappish and sweet. She actually slapped poor Mr. Weichman the other day. Afterward they both stood in astonishment, looking at one another. Mr. Weichman fled the scene. Honora began to laugh in that stilted odd way of hers, but for once I was grateful. I too laughed and told Annie that she really must give up beating upon the boarders as we couldn't afford to lose any. She started to laugh then, but quite hysterically, and ran up to her room. She would not come down to supper. Mr. Weichman treads very softly around her now. It is rather comical. What will become of this brave lad I cannot say, but I would hate to ever be in need of Mr. Weichman's courage. I fear that it is a commodity in short supply. I apologized to him for Annie, but he waved me off as if eager to forget the entire incident. Well, so be it. And Annie and I–we are merely polite to one another these days. She tells Honora what is in her heart, not me. I have only myself to blame for it.

I have placed yet another advertisement for roomers. Money is running dangerously low after the holiday expenditures. I have found that people love to collect on bills at the beginning of the new year.

Saturday, December 31, 1864

This is the last time I shall write 1864 in this volume. I am not sorry to see this particular year pass, but just the thought of this–any–another year passing is frightening to me. We, the women, tick off the years on our fingers, the war years . . . 1861, 1862, 1863, 1864, and now 1865 is waiting to be counted. Still it goes on, and we tremble for the time when one hand will no longer accommodate our calculations, the terrible tolls . . . father, brother, sweetheart, husband, son.

I went to early Mass this morning, accompanied by Mr.

Weichman. The rest of the day was spent planning meals, and trying to stretch the life out of a poor penny. I will retire soon. I can hear the revelers in the street below. It is, after all, New Year's Eve. My thoughts are of John. I pray that he does not return hollow-eyed from lack of sleep, the mud thick upon his boots, for then I will have to know that he has crossed the river into Virginia, and I do not want to know. It looks to be another long night.

Sunday, January 1, 1865

The house is quiet. Everyone has gone to church. My head was aching so that I decided to stay home. We are rushing headlong toward the end. Down in the street they're still drunk from last night's Holland gin and joy.

But soon comes the reckoning. Time is running from under me like a horse gone wild. I live on, but my youth is dead and gone. Annie is seventeen today. Seventeen years ago today she was born. It was a difficult delivery. I have three children. I lost one. More has been asked of other mothers. John is in my thoughts always, but what of Isaac, my good and steady son? Please God, I would not be asked to sacrifice my Isaac as Abraham was asked by You to sacrifice his. I confess I do not think of him often, but I do love him. I do not want to lose him . . .

The first day of this new year is nearly gone. It is late, but I want to write of this. His name is John Wilkes Booth. He is the one from the Willard's "hop," the escort of the senator's daughters. John brought him here tonight. Imagine my amazement. I cannot think where they would have met. He was extremely gracious, a famous actor evidently. He has toured the country starring in plays. Not being a theater-goer, I do not know of him or his illustrious family. He spoke of them with the most charming modesty. When I mentioned the Willard's "hop," he even pretended to remember us. I am sure that he is unaccustomed to being entertained in a boardinghouse, but he did not betray by look or word that he was in the least condescending. Still, suddenly I feel bitter. Mrs. Mary

Lincoln can spend two thousand dollars for a ball dress. She can parade in white and fresh flowers like a girl, while I must grow old, counting pennies, wearing black bombazine, and running a boardinghouse. I can taste the bile rising. It fairly chokes me. When he smiled at me he seemed to read my thoughts, to understand. His black eyes took in everything.

He made my shabby parlor glow, shedding a kind of light upon it for a moment, and then it became even shabbier beside his brilliance. I am sure that he will not come again. He was only being polite. He was merely kind. He would not care to visit us again, I am sure. Yet he did stay longer than courtesy demanded. Yes, he did.

Annie closed the book and put it back into her pocket. The train would be arriving in Baltimore soon. They had just gone through the tunnel. She had left so hurriedly there had been no time to send word to John. She would be an uninvited and unexpected guest, not a particularly auspicious combination. Mardella had stayed behind to pack her bags. She would be coming on the train tomorrow. At least with no bags she would not look as she stood on their doorstep as if she intended an extended stay. She had never been sure if John's wife cared for her or not. Victorine was a chatty sort, but with all of her chatter, she was always watching John, trying to anticipate his every want or need. Annie didn't imagine that John was an easy man to live with. She had adored him as a child, but he had been cruel to her, hurting her feelings, pinching her, making her cry. Obviously from her diary their mother had felt much the same way she had about him. He had been her favorite child, that was clear.

They pulled into the Baltimore station. It was early afternoon, and she began to walk to John's house, remembering the city from her visits to her cousins years ago. Everyone was a stranger. None of the faces were even vaguely familiar to her. Then she saw a man standing a few feet in front of her, a small-boned man with chiseled features, black hair and mustache. She looked more closely, her heart beating fast, he was shorter and swarthier, but for a moment, she had been reminded of Booth. Really the man looked nothing at all like him, but John Wilkes Booth had been in her thoughts just waiting for the slightest excuse to surface.

She thought of the first time she had ever seen him. It was her birthday. They had had a small celebration, a cake, a few presents. Louis Weichman had given her a bottle of violet water. Honora had given her a lace handkerchief. She couldn't remember what her mother's gift had been. John had not even remembered that it was her birthday. He had been gone for several days and returned that evening with Booth.

The actor wore evening clothes, and he was remarkably handsome, as her mother had written. After that their recollections diverged. She had felt that Booth was patronizing them, that his every word was calculated for effect, that he was one of those people who want everyone to admire him, whether he respected them or not. She thought him an insecure and strutting peacock.

Later that night she and Honora discussed him. Though she did not know her mother's feelings at the time, they corresponded with Honora's. Honora had been much impressed by his looks and his manners. When Annie had given her opinion of Booth, Honora had teased her, saying that she only had eyes for Seth. Remembering her first love, wishing things had happened any way but the way they had, Annie continued walking through the Baltimore streets to her brother's house.

X

She turned on the street she remembered as John's. It had been nearly five years since she had seen him. She thought of John's children. They would have changed tremendously too. She walked up to the yellow house with white shutters and lacy curtains showing in the windows, and rang the bell. John's wife answered.

"Annie. Annie, honey. Is it really you?"

"Yes, Victorine, it's me. Hello."

"Come in, honey. What brings you to Baltimore? There's nothing wrong, I hope."

"No, there's nothing wrong. I know my coming is rather sudden. I would have written, but I guess I just felt like being impulsive. It's so dreadfully hot down south, I just escaped you might say."

"Johnnie's in his study. He's going to be so surprised."

"I'm sure he will be. I don't want to disturb him. Maybe I could wash off some of the travel dust first and then go in to him."

"Of course. How stupid of me. You come right up the stairs with me. I have a room that will be just perfect for you, but where are your bags?"

"Mardella is coming up with them tomorrow."

"You still have Mardella? I must tell you, honey, that big Negress just scares me to death. She is, how would you say it, so formidable."

"I don't know what I'd do without her."

"I suppose. You sure you're just escaping the weather, Annie, honey?"

"Yes, of course."

The room was small and crowded with ruffled chintz. It was on the curtains, on the bedspread, on the pillows, and the rocker and the little footstool that stood before it. Victorine, after several more veiled looks and probing questions, left her alone. She washed her face and hands, and smoothed back her hair. She wanted to see John as soon as possible. She came out of her room and Victorine appeared at her side almost immediately.

"C'mon, honey. I just can't wait to see Johnnie's face."

They went down. She knocked softly on the study door and opened it. He spoke before looking up from the papers on his desk.

"Victorine, what is it that you want?"

His wife bit her lip at the obvious impatience in his voice. "Johnnie, there's someone here to see you."

He looked up. "Annie."

"Hello, John."

He rose from behind his desk and walked over to her. He took her hand rather stiffly.

"Isn't this just the biggest surprise, Johnnie? Aren't you so excited to see Annie after all these years?"

"Yes, Victorine."

"I think we should have a nice long chat." She sat down in the nearest chair. Annie and John remained standing. He looked at his wife. She stood up quickly. "I just remembered I have some things to do in the kitchen. I can't stay. You all enjoy yourselves. Get reacquainted, you know. I'm going to fix something real special for supper."

"Thank you, Victorine, for being so kind."

"You're entirely welcome, Annie, honey, and I mean that."

She left the room without exchanging another word with her husband.

"Sit down, Annie. It's been a very long time."

"Yes." She sat down on a small settee. "I came because of your letter."

"Surely there was nothing in my letter that would have provoked such a precipitous trip as this."

"But there was something."

"What?"

"In your letter you mentioned a lecture tour."

"Yes, I believe I did."

"Are you still planning on it?"

"I certainly am. I was just going over my notes."

"You mustn't do it."

"I don't think I understand you. You're telling me that I mustn't make this lecture tour?"

"Yes."

"And why not?"

"It's indecent. I shouldn't have to tell you that."

"You don't know anything about it."

"I know all I need to know. You plan to give speeches publicly about our mother and the circumstances of her death. You want to exploit and carnivalize it. You hope to make money from it."

"I want only to clear our mother's name and mine."

"You do not. You wouldn't choose this way if you did. You only want to feed and satisfy your own grandiose conceit."

"I want to come forward and tell the world what I know, the truth."

"Then why didn't you come forward at her trial?"

"You, my own sister, say that to me?"

"It's time I said it. I've felt it for years."

"Have you? Have you really?"

"Yes. You let her die for you, die in your place. And now you propose to make money talking about it to a lot of people who once howled in the streets for our mother's death. No, you never heard them. You were safe in Canada, but I heard them. I heard them, you cowardly bloodsucking leech."

"I heard them, Annie. I hear them still, every day of my life."

"How very sad for you."

"What's wrong with you? Why are you coming here now and saying these things to me? Are you running away from your husband? Why are you traveling alone?"

"What has that to do with any of this?"

"I'm trying to understand what is prompting this irrational behavior on your part."

"You think I'm mad, is that it?"

"I have no idea. All I know is that this person who has come into my home shouting epithets at me that my own worst enemies wouldn't use, this person, is not my sister. I want to know what has happened to you. Why have you suddenly taken to jumping on trains, arriving unannounced, and spewing forth invective?"

"I've come alive. I've been resurrected after years of being dead."

"I'm very worried about you. You are making no sense whatsoever."

"Oh, but I am. I'm making too much sense and that is making you very uncomfortable. Six months ago I would have received your letter announcing your lecture tour and I would have been shocked and angry, but I would have done nothing. But not now, not anymore."

"And what has brought about this miraculous change in you? Becoming a runaway wife?"

"You say that the way they used to say runaway slave."

"That is exactly how I meant it."

"John, do you think of Victorine as your property?"

"Yes, I do. She belongs to me. However, that is not the subject under discussion here."

"Isn't it? I think it is. You think I have escaped from my husband, that I have taken some kind of illegal liberty for myself. And because I have done this, I feel free to say these things to you.

You may be correct in a way. I suppose I am a runaway wife, but that is only an effect. It's not the cause. Our mother is the cause."

"Annie, I think that you are a very confused little woman. I want to help you in any way that I can. You need help."

"You're afraid to discuss Mother with me, aren't you? You'll give lectures to strangers, because they will accept what you say and not question you, but you won't speak of her to me. You're afraid."

"I am not."

"I was afraid, John. I immured myself in a house for thirteen years. I closed my mind to her and to everything. I couldn't face the pain of remembering, so I forgot and I died. Then just a short time ago a man came to see me."

"What man?"

"Colonel Wood."

"You didn't receive him? You didn't see him?"

"I turned him away from the house for weeks. I didn't want to see him, and then I felt I had to."

"And he said something to you? He told you something that turned you against me?"

"He said many things to me, but very little about you. I wouldn't allow him to speak of you."

"Thank God you still have some loyalty."

"It had nothing to do with loyalty. I wouldn't allow it because I was afraid he would say things about you that I had thought for years. He made me see what a terrible coward I had become and how I was wasting my life. I couldn't accept what he made me see. I was very cruel to him. I'm sorry for that."

"You're sorry? That man killed our mother."

"No, John. He didn't. Many people are responsible, but he isn't one of them. Those who loved her and those who hated her must share the blame for her death. In particular, one mad and evil man, but he is dead and gone. You are responsible and I. And Mother, herself."

"I cannot believe what you are saying."

"All of us are to blame, John. We committed numerous crimes.

We were selfish, blind to anything but our own desires and despairs. We didn't listen. We didn't speak out. We none of us knew what went on inside anyone else. And we didn't care. John, Colonel Wood returned Mother's diary to me."

"She didn't keep a diary."

"Yes, she did."

"It was a trick, Annie."

"No, John. It's a little red leather book. You must have seen it."

"I don't remember it at all."

"It is Mother's. I had always believed that it had been destroyed, but Colonel Wood saved it."

"He told you that, and you believed him?"

"Not at first, but I do now. There is no reason for him to lie."

"I tell you it must be a forgery."

"Only Mother could have written it. I recognized her hand immediately. And the book itself, I had seen it a hundred times. It's no trick."

"Let me see it. Do you have it with you?"

"Why? Do you want to include portions of it in your lectures?"

"Let me see it."

"I don't have it."

"You do."

"Maybe I do, but I must know your reasons before I hand it over to you."

"Who are you to decide, to tell me that I can or cannot see it, to question my reasons?"

"I can only tell you how I felt when first confronted with it. I wanted to burn it."

"I wish to God you had."

"That is what I am afraid of, John, that you will want to destroy it. And it must not be."

"What does she say about me? Did she blame me? Did she hate me?"

"She loved you, John, loved you best. Whether she blamed you or not, I can't say. I haven't been able to read the last of it. It took all my strength just to begin it. I've come to Booth in the last few pages I've read. John, why did you bring him to the house? Why?"

"I've asked myself that a thousand times."

"And what is the answer?"

"There is none."

"An explanation then?"

"You didn't know Booth. I remember the first night I met him. It was winter and the war was going badly. I had been carrying messages, papers, for the Confederacy across the Union lines for some time. Did you know that I was a courier, Annie?"

"I suppose we all guessed it, but we never spoke of it aloud. I know that Mother worried about you, and I did, but we never said why we worried. It was like so many things in that house, always there, heavy and unspoken."

"It was exciting when I began as a courier, but that paled. I was approached in the first place because I knew the area so well. They knew I had taken over for Pa as postmaster after he died. It was strange, after a while I began to feel just like I was delivering mail again. I was tired of the mud and the same boring routine. I wanted to do something important, something earth-shattering, something that would win the war for the Confederacy and make me a hero. It was then that I met Booth. Louis Weichman and I were walking down Pennsylvania Avenue. It was cold that night and the wind cut like a saber. Just ahead of us I saw a man standing beside a lamppost. He was wearing a long black cloak. He turned as we approached and the light fell upon his face. And I knew that he was waiting for us, for me. Louis greeted him as if he were surprised to see him, but I remember thinking that it was intended."

"It wasn't destiny. It was Weichman."

"It was Boooth. He was at the center of it all. He dominated. Yes, Louis knew him. They had gone to school together before Louis had come to the seminary. It was no accident that night. Nothing Booth ever did was by accident. It was planned that I should meet him that night. He knew that I was ready."

"Ready for what?"

"For almost anything that would help me escape my life. I had visions of the war ending and going back to the tavern and being a postmaster. I couldn't stand it. I wanted more than that. Being a courier had not given me what I craved, and so I was ready for Booth."

"How could he have known that? How could Booth have known what went on in your mind?"

"Perhaps Louis told him of my disenchantment. I would like to think that, but I don't believe it."

"If not Weichman, then how?"

"Booth. He just knew. He knew me."

"That first night, did it begin then?"

"Yes. We walked to a barroom near Ford's Theater. They knew him there. Men kept coming up to the table, smiling, shaking his hand. It was warm and dark and the whiskey was strong. We talked of the war. He stretched out his high black boots. They had silver spurs on them. He spoke loudly of the Confederacy and the Cause and dared anyone to challenge him. Of course, no one did."

"But it was dangerous."

"Yes, he was dangerous to be around. You felt that always when he was near, danger, hazard, even fear. You never knew what he might do."

"Was it then he spoke of the plot?"

"Yes, Louis excused himself, as if by prearrangement, and Booth and I were alone. He leaned toward me and said that he had gathered around him a few loyal men, that the future held great things for these men, but that they must meet the test. They must be true and unafraid. It was then I told him that I was a Confederate courier. I wanted to impress him. I wanted to be one of his few loyal men."

"Why?"

"Because he was offering me the chance to be a hero and that is what I had always wanted to be. He was the adventure, the excitement, I had craved, but which had always eluded me. I mentioned that my mother ran a boardinghouse in the city and that it would be a perfect place for us to meet. I wanted to belong."

"To Booth?"

He looked at her for a moment. "To his conspiracy. I would have done anything."

"Even involved your mother?"

"Yes, but I never thought it would go the way it did. I never wanted to kill anyone. That wasn't the plan. We were going to abduct Lincoln, take him to the South, and force an exchange of prisoners. We were going to win the war."

"But that changed?"

"Yes, we started too late. The war was all but lost. It all began to go wrong. That's when he began to talk about assassination. That's when I quit him, Annie."

"Yes, you quit him. You went to Canada."

"I went on a mission. I was carrying messages for the Confederacy."

"Still trying to be a hero?"

"No. I just couldn't stand to look at myself any longer. I suppose I was trying to redeem myself, I wanted to think that I was an honorable man."

"Honorable! That was a very honorable thing that you did, John, going to Canada to deliver papers for a government that was lost and leaving all of us at home hopelessly entangled with Booth and his mad plots."

"I had to get away from him. I wanted no part of murder."

"But what about your family?"

"I didn't believe that you would be harmed. I had no idea that Booth would really do what he said he would."

"You believed him enough to flee to safety in Canada."

"You hurt me, Annie. I never thought that you, my own sister . . ."

"That's just it, John. You never thought. You never thought about anything, or anyone, but yourself, your schemes, your heroics, your adventures. Selfish, incredibly selfish. You grew very tall, John, but you never grew up."

"I did grow up, Annie. Shall I tell you the moment I grew up? I had been in Canada, in hiding, for several months. Everyone was looking for me, hunting me. I was staying with people. They were my only source of information. I couldn't be seen in the streets. These people told me that Mother had been arrested. When they told me this, I wanted to go home immediately, but they said that that was exactly what the government wanted me to do. They told me that she was being used as bait to catch me. They said that just as soon as the government realized that Mother wasn't going to draw me into their net that they would release her. I believed them. Then there was no word for a long time. It was decided that I should leave Canada. One afternoon, in the rain, I was taken to a train station. At the station I saw a newsboy calling out an extra. Something important had happened. I couldn't hear him. They were rushing me along toward the train which was beginning to leave. I caught hold and jumped aboard. I raised one hand to say goodbye to the people who had hidden me for so many months. The newsboy had come forward into the rain and was holding up the paper as if only for me. I couldn't hear his shouts, but I saw his lips moving, and the big black print of the headline beginning to bleed in the rain. MARY SURRATT HANGED!!! That is the day, the moment, I ceased to be a child. I began then to know the consequences of my actions, the horrifying outcome."

"John, how can you think of giving speeches about this?"

"I have to explain myself. I have to make people understand. I can't go on living otherwise. Don't you see that?"

"Yes, I see."

"You blame me still."

"As I said before, John, we are all to blame. That is the truth of it. I came here looking for someone to hate, I confess that to you. There hasn't been a time in the last thirteen years when I haven't hated someone. I had lived so long with hate I didn't think I could live without it, but I think now that I can. I don't hate you, John."

"Please don't, Annie. I hate myself. That is enough."

"Do you wish that I hadn't come?"

"Yes."

"Oh, John, don't you see? I never would have had this

understanding of you. I would have accepted your lecture without a word, attributing all the wrong reasons to your doing it. I would have gone on thinking that you let Mother sacrifice herself for you. I would have hated you silently for the rest of our lives. Now you can truly be my brother again."

"You don't mind the idea of the lecture tour then?"

"No, not now. I believe that it is necessary. It is important that people know your truth."

"My truth, you say that as if there were other truths."

"Do you think there is only one?"

"Yes. I swear what I say is the God's truth. I never thought that she would die. I didn't think that they could kill her. I swear it."

"I know, John."

"You believe me?"

"Yes. John, I do have Mother's diary. Would you like to read it?"

"No, I don't think so. You read it for me, Annie. You tell me what she said."

"I will, John."

"How long are you planning to stay?"

"I don't know really. I've said what I came to say to you. I would like to visit with the children and Victorine and you for a while. I'd like to feel a part of a family for a few days anyway."

"You should have one of your own."

"But I don't."

"Will you stay long enough to hear the first lecture?"

"No, John. That is your crucible. I have my own. Reading Mother's diary, I realize how unhappy she was. If only we could have talked, it might have been different."

"Perhaps not, Annie."

"No, I blame myself for not being to her what that little book was, always ready to listen, always open to her. I have to know what makes all of us so reluctant to share our feelings. I think Mother is the key. That's my trial, my test, to find my mother, and myself."

"And after you do, will you go home, Annie?"

"I'll try to go home. I'm not sure that I will still be welcomed there, but I will try. John, owning a woman, possessing her, won't make her stay, but loving her will, if, that is, she loves you in return. Go back to your work. I'm going upstairs to rest for a while."

"Annie, don't stay from home too long."

He stood and so did she. They embraced.

"I care very much for you, Annie. And I cared for Mother, as much as I am able to care for anyone."

"Thank you, John."

She left the room. Victorine happened to be dusting near the door.

"My, my, didn't you two have a nice long visit."

"Yes, we did."

"Families are wonderful things. 'Course I never had a brother, but I have six sisters. Why, when we get together, the talking's liable to go on for days, I tell you."

"Victorine, I think I'll go up and take a little nap. It was a long train ride."

"Of course, Annie, honey." She started up the stairs with her. "What did you and Johnnie talk about? Old times, I suppose."

"Yes, old times."

"Do you think Johnnie's looking well?"

"He hasn't changed."

"Maybe he looks a little tired to you?"

"No, I don't think so."

"We have a real good life, Annie."

"I'm sure that you do."

"Johnnie's a devoted father and a wonderful husband. Do you think Johnnie's happy, Annie? Did he say he was?"

"Victorine, we really didn't talk much about the present. More about old times, like you said."

"Of course, honey. He's happy. It's just that he locks himself away in that little room so much of the time, and you know, I never do know what's going on in that man's mind, and he never says. He just stares out from behind those big gray eyes of his. You know, honey, you have eyes just like his. I'll bet you two got them from your daddy."

"No, our mother had gray eyes."

"Oh, well. Now you take me. Whatever pops into my head comes right out my mouth, and even if it didn't you could see what I was thinking right on my face. I have one of those faces you can read real easy. But Johnnie doesn't, and you don't. Like right now, I sure wish I knew what you were thinking, but I sure can't tell."

"I'm thinking that I want to have a nice long talk with you, Victorine, but right now I'm just dead on my feet."

"Of course, honey. You take a nice nap, and we'll talk later."

"Tonight. We'll sit up till all hours. I'll be your seventh sister, even if it is just by law and not blood."

"Annie, I have a confession to make. I never liked you much before this. You always seemed mighty cold and standoffish to me. Now I don't think that I have changed. I think you have, honey."

"I have, Victorine. I have."

XI

She entered the ruffled room and sat down on the bed. She wondered if William missed her at all. Probably he wouldn't today, but maybe tonight. It occurred to her that tonight she might miss him too. She reached into her pocket and took out the diary. She lay back on the bed, propped herself up on one elbow, and began to read.

Monday, January 2, 1865

No more the holiday spirit in the streets. The new year is beginning now in deadly earnest. The faces round the breakfast table were early morning puffy and sour. Mr. Weichman had slept in such a way as to leave a long red scar from his eyebrow to his chin. It made him look rather fiercesome, not at all like himself. Of course, anyone who knows Mr. Weichman even a little would realize that the only way in which he could obtain a wound would be at the hands of a wrinkled bedsheet.

Turning away from the troubled expressions, I stared into my coffee and saw dark and beautiful eyes, the same liquid color, staring up into mine, his eyes. My hand trembled, and his eyes spilled out onto the white tablecloth. I know that I am a fool. But still I wonder if he will come again. What, indeed, in this tall and dour, grim, and narrow house would draw him? His life is so full of happiness and brilliance, and gaiety, and success. Why would he even recall for a moment this sad place or the poor old woman who resides in it? Perhaps a shrug of pity, a shiver for the ugliness of it, but he will never come again. If I could wish away all my wrinkles and gray hairs, and half my years, even then he would be too beautiful, way beyond me. He is for the likes of young milk-skinned senator's daughters, not middle-aged boardinghouse keepers, or even little dark-haired provincial belles from upcountry Maryland which is the best I ever was. It is a sad day when one realizes that one's own small greatness lies in the past and not the future. It astounds me that I even think of him at all, but I cannot stop. I listen for the sound of horses stopping outside the house. I strain, I pray, but they all go past. I tell myself that if I could but see him once more that then I could forget him and this ridiculous fancy, but he does not come.

I am an old and settled woman. I had my hopes, it's true, but I am resigned now. Can a pair of mesmeric black eyes change all that in one evening's time? I thought that I had faced all the cruel tricks that life had to play upon me, but life, it seems, saved the cruelest for the last, when I am weakest. Now he comes. Now, when there is no chance of having him. And I am unable to explain to him what I once was. I cannot whisper that my neck was once slender and creamy white, that my hair was glossy black like his. Beauty is as impossible to evoke as pain. This is bitter, bitter beyond all belief. How can I persuade him that I was once young and beautiful without him turning from me, my present self, my age and ugliness, in horror and disgust? For am I not living proof that he, that I, that everyone, will some day, inevitably, grow old and ugly? I must not dredge forth my memories of my white shoulders, my soft full lips. All my past glories must remain only in my mind. For, by being past, they are not only pathetic and pitiful, but deadly prophetic.

It is best that he does not come again, that I never see him again. I must be pleasant and placid and regain my resignation to life. I must be old and settled once again. And if he should come, I will hide my pounding heart beneath black bombazine, and never let him or anyone see my folly, my shame, this insane infatuation which I hold for him.

Friday, January 6, 1865

I feel that my children live lives of which I know nothing. John and his mysterious trips and friends. He tells me so little, only what he wants me to hear. Isaac, I know nothing of him, not even if he lives. And Annie. Her defection is nearly total. She is much closer to Honora these days. They are always together. They go to church and shopping and paying calls, and when they are in the house, they are upstairs in their room with the door closed, against me, I feel. None of my children confide in me. I must take the blame for it. Do I seem to them so incapable of loving and understanding them? I do love and understand. I do not judge. I am approachable. At least, that's what I want to be. Perhaps they know, can feel, even before I, that I would fail them. I have failed them so often before.

Of course, at the moment Annie cannot forgive me for forbidding her to see her lieutenant, but I hope she will thank me one day. She is so young and it is so easy to be hasty. I just don't want her to live a life of regret. She is wrong to think that I know nothing of love. I realize that I must seem to her old and dried up, incapable of passions, but she is wrong. Yet I cannot tell her that John Wilkes Booth is constantly in my thoughts. She would be shocked. She would think me a terrible fool and would be right in thinking it. I simply cannot tell her that I have known love and know it still. I could not frame the words for such a revelation.

My children do not see me as a human being. I am merely their mother, just a word really. Perhaps I could be more to them if there was not that easy identification. I try not to define them as merely sons or daughter. They are not just words to me, not just my dear children, but I am to them just one word. I am Mother. That is all. I am more than that. I want more than that. Why can't I tell them?

Sunday, January 8, 1865

He has come again. I had given up hoping when this evening he walked through the door with John. He took my hand. He smiled. He spoke to me as if I were the only one present. I was shocked that the picture I had carried of him in my mind was so diminished by the reality of him. His eyes gave off a light, a glow. It simply cannot be remembered. It must be seen.

I wish that he would never come again, and I wish that he would stay forever. I am in turmoil. My life had settled into a vague unhappy rhythm, empty church services without real faith, empty household duties for strangers without real love. I had accepted it. It is a most unpleasant discovery to be made, that in the sedate middle years one is still at the mercy of fate. There is a theory that in middle age one is safe, that life is mostly over. If, sadly, most of the pleasure is gone, then, happily, so too is the pain.

It is the time of remembrance, for long smooth uneventful days. All that is shattered for me now. All the physical ravages of age do not nullify the need to love and to be loved, this need is ageless. I thought that the days of dreaming of a kiss, wishing for an embrace, wanting to feel the touch of a man had gone. It is not seemly even for a young woman to desire these things, but I desired them, I confess, when I was young. I desire them still.

Even when I was young I could not express what I felt. I could not confront my need. I thought somehow that my husband would know, would understand. And he seemed to, he lured me from my true path in life, he tortured me with a brief glimpse, and when I rose up to meet him, responded fervently, he drew away from me forever. God punished me for my passion and my betrayal. He left me alone with a small memory which grew in my lonely brain into something unreal and impossible. But it is real. It is possible. A woman can love to be touched, embraced, kissed, she can even crave these things. She can give them to the man she loves. That is real. That is possible. At least it is when young and supple white bodies invite touch, but not when one is old. I am dreaming again. God keep me from it. Yet I know that it is You who gives me these dreams to punish me.

Wednesday, January 11, 1865

John has introduced yet another strange character into our midst, two, in fact. The one is a low and rough man. He speaks but little, and when he does there is a heavy accent. I guess it to be German. This is not a poetic or learned Teuton, but a dirty and small man with the ugly darting eyes of a trapped muskrat. He has no brow at all. His hairline reaches right down to his bushy brown eyebrows. He has not one redeeming quality, no stature, no presence. He is not even sinister. He is comical. When asked his origins, he muttered something about "Port Tobacco." The girls immediately dubbed him "Port Tobacco," though his name is Atzerodt or some such German mouthful. "Port Tobacco" is quite an appropriate appellation, not only because that is his home, but because of the constant presence of a thick wad of tobacco wedged in the left side of his mouth.

I cannot imagine what John or Mr. Booth could see in this horrible little gnome of a man. However, the gentlemen sequester themselves nightly for several hours at a time upstairs in John's room. I had almost forgotten the other member of the group, Davy Herold. He is not memorable. Usually late, he will come in breathlessly and talk with me for a moment before going upstairs. He mentioned once that he had been raised by his mother and six older sisters. He is used to the feminine response and atmosphere. I dropped my ball of yarn once and he reached for it with his left hand, then he stopped, as if still feeling the blows delivered long ago, and slowly brought forth his right hand. He had been trained against Nature by some superstitious person, probably his mother, who believed that to be left-handed was to be a creature of the

Devil. I too am superstitious, but I have a deep and abiding belief in the ultimate rightness and wisdom of Nature. I would imagine that when he is alone in his beloved Maryland swamp, he shoots his gun and kills, destroys, with his left hand, because he was never allowed to pick up a cup, or write his name, or throw a ball with it.

I cannot help but wonder what these clandestine meetings are all about. I fear that they may be playing cards. Mr. Booth's presence calms my fears somewhat. He could not possibly be involved in anything wrong or bad. I look into his eyes and there is such beauty and clarity there, though it is difficult to look beyond the surface of them. I sometimes think of them as mirrors and I wonder if Mr. Booth doesn't perhaps merely reflect what one wants to see in him. I wonder where is the real Mr. Booth, but I cannot gaze for too long because my breath begins to come fast.

Saturday, January 14, 1865

I sit here in the midnight quiet of the house and all is still and I try to convince myself that this day was real and not just another of my impossible dreams. If I put it all upon paper, every detail, every small moment, then perhaps it will become real to me.

I was alone in the house today, sitting by the parlor window, letting the warm afternoon sun heal and revitalize my poor swollen hands. They give me such pain sometimes that I cannot sew, or write, or play the piano, all the things which occupy and please me. They were throbbing with such force this morning that I winced at every movement. I wondered if it was not some sort of punishment for my thoughts and dreams of him. I stretched them out on the arms of the old rocker. The sun was pouring warmth into them. I was feeling better, almost at peace with myself when an open carriage drew up and stopped before the house.

It was he, dressed all in black, like a lithe shadow, unreal in the bright sunlight of the unseasonable hot and fair January day. The sight of him brought such joy to me, and such dread, for my peace had departed as it always does upon his arrival. I am always afraid that I will show too much, reveal myself to him. Yet I yearn to tell of my love. If he laughed, then perhaps my pride would come to my rescue and all would be over.

These thoughts were going round in my mind as he walked into the parlor. He was admitted to the house by Cookie, who is always too busy in the kitchen to answer the door unless it is Mr. Booth. His appeal is universal, it seems.

I spoke first.

"Good afternoon, Mr. Booth. I'm afraid that you find only me at home today. John has gone off somewhere without telling his poor mother. The young ladies are out enjoying the weather. You must try to content yourself with me."

"That is splendid, for it is you I came to see."

"Me?"

"Yes, Mrs. Surratt. I learned this morning that I must take care of some rather urgent business in Maryland. I have heard you speak with such fondness and yearning for your home, I thought perhaps you would like to accompany me today. Is this an entirely decorous request on my part? Surely it would be proper for you to allow me the pleasure of your company this afternoon. Our acquaintance is not of long duration, but there is a depth which belies its brevity. Do you not feel that too?"

"Why yes, Mr. Booth, I suppose that I have felt that. I had assumed the admiration you inspire in all quarters would accustom you to such occurrences. It must be quite commonplace for you, though not for me. I am just a poor widow who goes very little into the world."

"That is the world's great loss. It is true that people who have seen me on the stage, or have heard my name, think that they know me. Sadly, Mrs. Surratt, that is almost never the case. Very few people really know or understand me. It is rare when I encounter a sympathetic soul such as yourself. I don't think that you believe, as many do, that my life is all gaiety, applause, and admiration. I know that you see more deeply than that. Perhaps you even see my great loneliness. Do you, Mrs. Surratt?"

He had come quite close to me as he said this, standing above me in the shadow, the shaft of sunlight from the window missed him by inches. The darkness was quite appropriate to his revelation. I wondered for a moment if he was enough of an actor to realize this and to place himself there purposely, but he is not a poseur. He was telling me that he is lonely.

"I suppose that I might have suspected that you are not entirely what you seem, but then, Mr. Booth, none of us are."

"Exactly. I feel, for example, that you are not what you would have the world believe you to be. Will you ride with me to Maryland this afternoon, Mrs. Surratt?"

"Yes."

Driving through the countryside of Maryland we spoke but little. It was so strangely warm and spring-like for January. A brilliant and unnatural sun blazed in the crystalline blue sky which looked almost hard, and brittle enough to crack. The land was desolate. We drove past many abandoned farms. It was all very eerie, and barren, and sad to look upon. But being beside him I felt such elation, such happiness, that I felt able to ignore the plight of Maryland just this once. After all, I had been mourning it for years. He himself was very moved by the sad spectacle.

"Someone must be made to pay for this."

His voice shook with anger as he said it. I was watching his hands holding the reins. Mesmerized by his eyes, I had never before noticed his hands. They were the most beautiful I had ever seen, long thin tapering fingers, a gold ring initialed JWB. His hands were like a woman's, but on a much larger scale. My thoughts were only of him, but to be polite I made some stupid statement about Maryland and then quickly returned my full attention to the contemplation of his beauty.

It surprised me greatly when we stopped at my farm and tavern, leased by Mr. Lloyd. Mr. Booth's business was with that very Mr. Lloyd. It concerned buying some property. Mrs. Offut, Mr. Lloyd's sister-in-law, and I had tea while the gentlemen talked business in the other room. From Mrs. Offut's conversation I fear that my tenant, Mr. Lloyd, is a drunkard. She was full of harrowing tales and regret at her unfortunate sister's marriage to such a man. He is already behind in his rent. Mrs. Offut inspired in me the fear that it would always be so. Mr. Booth and Mr. Lloyd did not converse for very long. I noticed that Mr. Lloyd's hands were shaking and his face was most pale except for two very red patches at the cheeks. This seemed to confirm the sister-in-law's stories. Mr. Booth and I were in the carriage when Mr. Lloyd leaned close to Mr. Booth and whispered something. I heard only two words. They disturbed me greatly. After a time on the road I asked Mr. Booth about it. He stopped the carriage. His face was turned from mine. Then he turned toward me. He asked if I would like to walk about for a bit. I said yes. He helped me from the carriage. His hand rested on my arm for a moment longer than was needed. I could feel him looking down at me, but I could not lift my eyes. He took my hand and raised it to his lips.

"Dear Mrs. Surratt, your hand is trembling. Are you so troubled by what you heard?"

"It just seemed so very strange, what Mr. Lloyd said."

"What was that?"

"I heard just the two words, widow and camouflage, but he looked at me when he said them. I am a widow, Mr. Booth, and I cannot help but wonder what you are trying to conceal, to hide."

"I dare not tell you."

We stood beneath a leafless tree and a futile wind rose up to blow the foliage to the ground, but the tree was already bare. So the wind aimlessly tossed my skirts and ruffled his black hair.

"I don't understand, Mr. Booth."

"Will you call me Wilkes? It will make it so much easier. My mother calls me Wilkes."

I swallowed the bitterness which rose at the thought that I reminded him of his mother, and said, "I will call you Wilkes as your mother would. It would be most improper otherwise."

"Not as my mother, I beg of you. I am not good at dissimulation." He took my hand again.

"Again, I do not understand. What is it that you are hiding, and how am I being used to hide it?"

"I hate the suspicion in your eyes. It is from you that I am hiding. I am concealing my impossible love for a woman."

"What woman?"

"A woman, beautiful and sad, a widow."

I could hardly bear to listen. "What has that to do with me? Why should you want to keep this from me?"

"Because you are the woman of whom I speak."

I felt faint. "It cannot be."

"I cannot remain silent any longer. There will be no further camouflage. Thank God and Lloyd, for once his loose drunkard's tongue be praised. It has forced me into the open."

"This is impossible."

"Don't." He raised a beautiful hand to my lips. "Please don't say that. I love you."

"This is a dream, a mad dream. It cannot be that you have wanted me as I have wanted you. Why me, old and ugly, while you are so young and beautiful? There is no reason for you to desire me."

"There can be only one, I love you."

I do not know how I had the presence of mind to say what I said next. "It is not in the least remarkable that I should be enamored of you, as I have just most incautiously revealed, I fear. That is not notable. You are easy to love. You have been loved and admired all of your life. But I, I am different. I . . ."

He stopped my words. He took my face into his hands. I wonder, does he know that he also held and holds my heart? "You are beautiful to me. You look at me and your eyes understand. I know that they do. There is wisdom and love and acceptance of me in your eyes. I could tell you anything. You would not think me a coward if I told you of the time when I served in the Virginia militia. We were sent to the hanging of John Brown. I was only a boy. The sight of the life being wrenched from that old man's body, the horrible jerking, the death throes of him, the stiffened black tongue, how it sickened and appalled me. How, though he was guilty of the most heinous, vile and evil of crimes, I wished at the moment of his death that he could live, behind bars, of course, but live, and not have his life so hideously torn away from him. I could tell no one else this. I never have, not family, not friends who have known me for years, but I can tell you and be assured of your understanding and acceptance."

"Yes, it's true. I do understand."

"I could tell you of my mad father who had funerals for every living beast that died on our plantation, how I inherited his almost insane regard for life, but how too, in youthful rebellion of him, when I was eight years old I killed an entire litter of kittens, and presented them to him, in a basket, their little bodies matted with blood, how I watched his tears and did not cry until later when I was alone and the tears began and would not cease. I can tell you that and your dear sweet eyes widen, but you do not condemn me. You do not abandon me. Your gaze never falters. You continue to look straight into my heart and soul. Now do you understand why I love you?"

"No."

"Come here." He drew me close and looked at me so long and so hard that I had to lean against him or fall to the ground. "I love you because you want me to, because you have willed it. I love you because you are not what you seem. We are liars, both of us. I have need of you, and that is irresistible to you."

"I must go. It is getting late. Look, it's growing dark."

"Don't ever think that you can escape the darkness or me."

He turned from me then and I followed him back to the carriage. We were soon in Washington. He looked at his watch.

"I don't want to let you go yet, Mary. It's early still. Have tea with me at the National."

"Is that where you live?"

"Yes. Will you have tea with me there?"

"Yes."

And so we had tea at his hotel. He held my hand across the table and said little. I can still see the tea in the china cups and the little cakes sprinkled with sugar on the silver tray. And his eyes.

We did not stay long. He looked again at his watch and said to me, "I must return you, but I do not want to. Do you believe me, Mary?"

"Yes."

And I did believe him as I looked at him, but it is now as I sit in this quiet darkened house alone that I have difficulty believing. I do not know what will happen beyond this day. He is right about me. I am not what I seem. Trying to be what I seem to be, I walked away from him and the darkness today, but the fantasies in my mind tonight are what I really am and what I really wanted this afternoon in the country. I wanted to lie with him. I wanted to feel his hands upon me. I wanted his mouth on mine. I wanted him within me. I wanted to feel the wind on my naked skin. I wanted to crush the red and brown fallen leaves as I writhed beneath him. I wanted to smell of their sweet decay. I wanted to take his black hair in my hands and pull him closer and deeper. He let it stop today. He let it ebb because it was not the right moment, but it is true, I will never escape him. Today was only a brief abeyance. I want him and the darkness more than life.

She heard Victorine knock at the door.

"Annie, it's nearly supper time. Are you awake?"

"Yes, Victorine. I'll be down directly."

Her mother had been in love with Booth, and he had professed to love her too. She wondered if perhaps her mother had not just written a dream or fantasy. It was so very strange. Was it possible that the whole time she had been in love with Seth, feeling things that she thought only she could feel, that her mother had been dreaming of the very same things? It explained so much. The sudden arguments that had sprung up between them about Seth, the bitter words. It must have been, as her mother warned her about Seth she was really warning herself about Booth. She remembered once coming into the parlor and finding Booth and her mother standing by the fireplace. She had had the odd feeling that Booth had moved quickly away from her mother just before she entered. She had thought very little about it at the time, but now, she wondered, had they been embracing, had their mouths been touching, had he bent her back across his arm and kissed her throat, and hearing her footsteps had they parted, and stood side by side staring into the flames?

They had, she felt that they had, as surely as if she had seen it. Booth could move like a cat. He had the instincts of a cat, the ability to sidestep danger at the very last moment. Her mother and Booth. She put the book in her pocket and went down to supper.

XII

The children had changed. She remembered them as babies. She watched their faces as they ate their supper. All sorts of things filled their minds now where once there had been only emptiness. She smiled at them frequently, and they smiled back, polite children. They must surely think her a strange old bird, their Auntie Ann.

"Hasn't Willie grown, Annie?"

"He certainly has, Victorine. He's almost a man."

"I'm nearly ten, Auntie Ann."

"Ten, that's a great many years."

"It sure is. Miranda is only eight."

"Eight is very nice too." She smiled at Miranda. She was a quiet and grave little girl with fair hair like her father's. She wore it tightly braided. She was thinking as she looked at the child that she might have had a little girl like Miranda, just her age. She couldn't think of anything else to say so she just smiled.

"Mama, may I be excused?"

"But Miranda, you haven't had any pudding."

"I don't want any, thank you."

"I'll eat hers."

"Yes, Willie. You may have it if Miranda is sure that she doesn't want any. Miranda, honey, are you sick?"

"No, Mama, I feel fine. I just don't want any pudding."

"I don't think I care for any either. Perhaps Miranda and I both could be excused, and we could take a little walk."

"I would like that, Auntie Ann."

"Would it be all right, Victorine? John?"

The parents exchanged a glance. Victorine answered, "Of course, Annie, honey, you two have a good time, but don't be gone too long."

"We won't, I promise."

"Miranda, take something to put around your shoulders."

"It's warm, Mama."

"Do as your mama says. It might get cold real sudden."

"Yes, Mama."

The street was quiet. Most everyone was at supper. A few rocked slowly on their porches, silently watching the day hang suspended for a moment in twilight. The little girl took her hand, but she did not look down, nor did the child look up.

"Miranda, do you remember me? You were very small the last time I was here."

"I don't remember your face. When Mama told me that you were here I couldn't think what you looked like, but I remembered a kind of feeling."

"A feeling?"

"Yes, when I thought of you I felt something soft and cool and smooth. I don't know why."

"I do. I brought you a quilt, blue satin on one side and yellow on the other. You were about three years old. That's what you remember."

"I still have it, I think."

"I'm glad."

"Mama put it up in a closet. Why would she have done that, do you suppose?"

"Perhaps she was saving it for you."

"Auntie Ann, do you think that I look like you?"

"Yes, very much."

"Shouldn't I look like my mother?"

"What do you mean?"

"Don't most little girls look like their mothers?"

"Sometimes they do. Sometimes they take after their fathers, as you do."

"Do you think that Mama talks an awful lot?"

"She likes to talk."

"I guess so, but sometimes I get very tired of listening."

"Well, she's your mama and you love her. Just try to remember that when you get tired sometimes."

"Papa doesn't talk very much at all, but I like what he says. I like his voice. I like to listen to him. You don't talk very much either, Auntie Ann."

"No, I don't."

"When I grow up I want to be like you and Papa. I don't look like Mama and I don't want to act like her either."

"Maybe you'll change your mind about your mama. That happens."

"Maybe, but I don't think so. I don't think I'll ever like Mama's talking. It hurts my ears. Besides she likes Willie better than me anyway."

"No, Miranda. She loves you very much."

"She loves Willie better."

"Why would you say a thing like that?"

"Because it's true. I heard her say it once to Papa. I had a bad dream and I got out of bed and came downstairs and I heard her say that no baby would ever mean to her what Willie meant because he was first. It's not my fault that I came second."

"I don't think you understood your mother. I'm sure she didn't mean it that way."

"Oh, yes, she did. Auntie Ann, do you have any babies?"

"No."

"Maybe you'd like to take me home with you. Since we look alike we could tell people that I was your little girl."

"Miranda, I think that's about the nicest thing anybody's ever said to me, but your mother would be very hurt. She'd miss you very much, and you would miss her."

"No, I wouldn't. I'd miss Papa, and maybe even Willie, but not her. She doesn't love me."

"Should we turn back? It's getting dark."

"Yes, Auntie Ann. Will you think about taking me home with you?"

"Miranda, you could come for a visit. We would have a wonderful time, but you can't ever be my little girl. You're your mother's daughter. Remember this, Willie was her first little boy baby, but you were her first little girl."

"I suppose so, but I still want to be like you, not her. Mama is fat and she talks too much."

"Miranda, please listen to me, and try to understand what I say. You mustn't judge those you love so harshly. All of us have reasons for the things we do. Sometimes we don't know what other people's reasons are, but we must always try to remember that the reasons are there making them do the things that they do. Maybe your mother talks so much because she is afraid."

"Afraid of what?"

"Of people not liking her."

"If she'd stop, people'd like her a lot more."

"Miranda, are you afraid of anything?"

"Yes."

"What?"

"I'm afraid of the dark."

"And do you have a lamp by your bed?"

"Yes, how did you know?"

"I guessed. Most people who are afraid of the dark have a lamp by their bed. Did your mother give you that lamp?"

"Yes."

"Has she ever teased you about being afraid, about needing your lamp?"

"No, never."

"She loves you, Miranda, that's why. She doesn't want you to be afraid. She knows that someday you're not going to need that lamp anymore, but that right now you do. She doesn't want you to be afraid of the dark, but because you are, that doesn't mean she loves you any less."

"Do you suppose that Mama will ever stop talking so much?"

"Maybe, someday."

"I hope so. Do you really think she loves me?"

"I know she does."

"She isn't really fat, you know. She's nice to hug, soft. Sometimes she says very funny things, and we all laugh, even Papa."

"We're home."

It was dark and the lamps were shining yellow in the windows.

"Isn't it pretty, all lit up, Auntie Ann?"

"Beautiful."

They walked inside. Miranda ran upstairs. She came down a few moments later and into the parlor where they were sitting. She was carrying the quilt.

"I found it, Auntie Ann. May we put it on my bed, Mama?"

"You'll stifle, Miranda. It's summer, honey. Don't you know that? You'll just burn up with that on you."

"Please, Mama."

"You are the most stubborn child. If you just have to have it, I suppose so. I just know you'll throw it off in the night. I just know it. My goodness, how many years has it been since you brought that to Miranda, Annie? Why, it must be five. She was just a baby really. I remember when you came to see us. We weren't living here then. We were just up the street, in that funny little house on the corner with the crooked floors. Do you remember, Johnnie?"

"Yes, I remember. I think I'll go into the study for a while. I have some work to finish up."

"Mama, can we put the quilt on now?"

"Hush, Miranda." She was watching her husband. "Johnnie, I declare, those four walls in that little bitty room see more of you than your own family does. Aren't you going to say goodnight to the children?"

"Goodnight, Willie. Goodnight, Miranda." He walked from the room.

"C'mon, babies. Say goodnight to your Auntie Ann. It's time to go to bed."

"Goodnight, Auntie Ann."

"Goodnight, Willie."

Miranda approached her. She put her thin arms around her neck.

"Goodnight, Auntie Ann."

"Goodnight, Miranda. Can we go for another walk tomorrow? Maybe a longer one?"

"Oh yes, I would love it."

She walked from the room, trailing the quilt. Victorine's voice could be heard all the way up the stairs.

"Miranda, honey, pick that up from under your feet. You're going to trip on it and fall down the stairs. I knew a lady once who fell down some stairs. Now, don't laugh. It was a very serious thing. Why, the doctors said she would never walk again, but she did. Now, pick that up, Miranda. You're going to fall. Willie, don't skip steps like that. Stairs are not to play on. Willie, stop that. Miranda, are you certain sure that you want to put that on your bed? It's too hot, don't you think, honey? It's dangerous to get too hot when you sleep. Do you know what? You can get sick as a dog from it. I know, I've seen it happen. My baby sister Betty, your Aunt Elizabeth, she always wanted to sleep in her wool nightdress, didn't make a bit of difference to her, winter or summer. She was the sickliest child I ever did see. Willie, if you don't stop skipping steps you're going to drive me to distraction."

Her voice faded away. Annie put her head back and closed her eyes. In a few moments she heard Victorine coming back down the stairs.

"Miranda certainly has taken a shine to you, Annie."

"Yes. She's a very sweet child."

"I suppose she is. She's mighty like her papa, kind of hard to get close to. Now that Willie, he's bright as a new penny, always laughing and talking. He's easy to love you might say. You know, some folks are just that way."

"Yes, some people are born with the sun and they just carry it with them wherever they go."

"That's just it, honey. Annie, is everything fine with you?"

"Everything is getting a great deal better."

"Was there something wrong?"

"Yes."

"Is that why you came here? You and Johnnie talked for such a very long time. I can't imagine that it was all just about when you two were children."

"Mostly we talked about our mother."

"Oh, you didn't. You couldn't have, honey. Why, Johnnie won't hear her name mentioned. He just won't hear it. I've tried time and again to talk to him about your mama."

"Victorine, hasn't he told you? Don't you know what he is working so hard on?"

"No, he never tells me. He won't even let me into that room to dust. I guess he thinks I would try to spy or something. I guess he's probably right. If a thing is just lying about I can't help but read it. It's just my nature, you might say."

"He's writing about our mother and his experiences with John Wilkes Booth and the assassination."

"Why would he do a thing like that?"

"He's planning to give a series of lectures."

"But he can't. He mustn't. We've lived so quietly. Folks have finally forgotten all about it. Doesn't he care what this could do to me and the children? You know, my mama was dead set against my marrying Johnnie. She took to her bed for a week over it. But I was determined. I wanted to marry Johnnie more than I've ever wanted anything before or since. He had only been out of prison for a month. You remember. Well, finally Johnnie charmed Mama. He could always charm the birds right out of the trees when he wanted to, and we were married. You remember."

"Yes, I remember."

"Oh, Annie. He just can't do this to us. You must talk to him, convince him not to do this thing."

"Victorine, that is exactly the reason I came here. He wrote me of his plans, and I couldn't believe it. I was angry and shocked. I came here to tell him that he just couldn't do it, but Victorine, he explained to me that he had to. And he does. He must."

"Why? Why must he ruin our lives?"

"He wants everyone to know once and for all that he did not willingly let his mother sacrifice her life for his. He can't live with the knowledge that people consider him a coward and a self-serving murderer."

"Everyone who knows and loves him knows that those things aren't true."

"Do they?"

"Of course, they do."

"I don't think John believes that."

"I remember once right after we were married, Johnnie decided to take out an insurance policy. One of the questions they asked was if his mother was living and if not; how she had died. Do you know what he answered them? He wrote down that his mother was deceased, that she had been murdered by the United States government. He never did get the policy. Now what makes him do things like that?"

"Victorine, do you understand John at all, really?"

"I ask myself sometimes that very question. When we were first married Johnnie was a stranger to me, but I expected that as the years went by and we lived together I would come to know him, but it seems I came to know him less and less as time passed. We've been married over ten years. We have two precious babies, and I don't know that man at all. He just becomes more and more a stranger to me. And now this . . . this lecture business. What does he mean by it?"

"Victorine, I think it might be better after the lectures. The idea that everyone hates him for what he did, that they can't stand him for living and allowing his mother to die, that has been festering inside of him."

"What does he care what a bunch of folks who don't even know him think of him? Annie, he knows his family loves and understands."

"He doesn't know that, Victorine."

"Of course, he does."

"No, Victorine. Our brother Isaac left and went West right after John's trial. Neither John nor I have heard a word from him since, but do you know the last thing he ever said to John?"

"Why, no. I never even met the man."

"Isaac said to John that he stood by him during the trial, that he had seen him through it, because they were brothers. But, he said, blood didn't make it any easier to look him in the face. Blood didn't make him hate or blame him any less. And then he left."

"Poor Johnnie."

"Victorine, I told him the same thing this morning, just in different words, that's all. It was the first time I had the courage to do it, but I had always felt as Isaac did. For the first time John told me what he went through in Canada, how he learned of our mother's death. Has he ever told you the story?"

"No, but . . ."

"Victorine, he has to tell you and the world. If he doesn't he will stay forever in that room, isolated, afraid that even his own wife and children hate him."

"But the children must never know. Oh, he mustn't do this. People will start talking again. It'll be in the papers. Willie and Miranda's schoolmates will hear about it. And Annie, they mustn't know."

"They must."

"No, I want it kept a secret."

"Secrets, Victorine, have a way of turning into lies. Do you want to lie to your children? That's what you'll have to do to prevent them from knowing."

"How can I tell my babies that their grandma was hanged?" Annie flinched as if she had been struck. "Oh, honey, I'm so sorry. I wasn't thinking. I only meant . . ."

"I know what you meant."

"It's just that they're so little. They can be hurt so easily."

"It's their legacy, Victorine, not a pretty one, I admit. Perhaps you should have listened to your mother and not married John. You had to know that this would happen one day."

"I didn't even think of it. He was so handsome and I loved him so much. I couldn't think past the next time I would see him, much less ahead ten years. I was a silly girl, Annie. I didn't think of consequences. I only thought of what I wanted at the moment. I guess now all that I am is a silly woman, rattlebrained and empty headed. Oh, Annie, I can't tell my babies this."

"Victorine, it may not be as bad as you think. John may, probably will, speak in empty halls about his personal obsession, but speak he must. Perhaps the newspapers have printed all the words that they ever will about my family and its unhappy twisted fate. It may be that no one, anywhere, wants to read or hear another word about the death of Mary Surratt. I don't. I want to know about her life. Not her death, I watched that. If you would like, Victorine, I will tell Miranda about her grandmother."

"No."

"I want to very much."

"No."

"They have to know. It is best they hear it from family and not strangers. John will tell Willie, I'm sure of it."

"No, I don't want it."

"Let John tell Willie and I will tell Miranda."

"I feel sort of like my mama must have felt the time she took so sick. We all thought that she was dying, so did she. She spent one whole day deciding where each one of us seven girls was to go, where we would be happiest, if she died. I feel that way now, as if I were giving my babies to the ones who are able to do the things I can't do for them. I know that you will tell Miranda better than I ever could, but I can't help feeling that I'm dying a little bit. And Willie, my poor little Willie."

"John will do fine with Willie, a man telling a boy, a father his son. He's bound to make it heroic. He'll tell him first of his adventures as a Confederate spy, then his escape from Canada across the ocean to the Old World, his time in Italy as a papal zouave, his capture in Egypt. It will be an epic, I'm sure. Willie will never know the reality of a terrified woman being led to the scaffold by her priest. His father could not possibly tell him the story of a woman, alone, desperate at the thought of growing old, afraid of her feelings and desires, enduring, yielding, always and fatally. Only a woman could tell that story. Only a woman could understand it."

"That's not what you're going to tell Miranda?"

"I don't know exactly what I'll tell her. I've always been so afraid of words, the damage they can do. Once I said a thing I felt committed to it, forever. I am beginning to feel that I really know my mother, that I could tell Miranda what a wonderful woman she was, and I could speak of her flaws too. A few months ago all that I had of my mother was the memory of her death, the injustice of it. That is all I would have been able to give Miranda of her grandmother, but now I believe I can give her so much more than that."

"Annie, honey, Miranda is only eight years old."

"You don't think she'll understand what I'm saying?"

"I don't, honey."

"Don't you know that when I described my mother's life just now, I was describing yours too."

"I have a good life, a perfect life."

"Victorine, how long will John stay down in his study tonight?"

"I don't know."

"How long does he usually stay?"

"Sometimes he gets very tired and he falls asleep in his chair."

"Sometimes?"

"Yes, sometimes."

"How often, Victorine?"

"I don't know what it has to do with any of this. Johnnie and I have a good life."

"How often does John sleep in his chair in the study?"

"It's not your concern, Annie."

"Victorine, you asked if there was anything wrong in my life and I told you that things were getting better. Now I'll ask you, is there anything wrong in your perfect life? Can things get any more perfect for you?"

"Why is he so cold? Why are you so cold? Why does he despise me so much that every night he would rather sleep sitting up in his chair than share my bed? Why does he hate me? I get so frightened that the words just start to come and I can't stop them. All that I'm trying to say with all those words is love me, love me, Johnnie. And as the years go by, I get more and more frightened and I feel he loves me less and less and there are more and more words. I hate you all, you heartless silent tribe."

She ran from the room. Annie sat for a moment. Then she too rose. Walking past John's closed door, she thought of knocking and going inside, but she stopped and reconsidered. She went up the stairs to her own room. She had only a small satchel with some night things and her medicine in it. She took out the bottle and tipped it to her lips. When she needed her medicine, she needed it badly. She did not recognize it as a craving or a thirst. It never occurred to her that she wanted her medicine. It only seemed that without it she became irritable, unable to concentrate. Then she took her medicine and these things disappeared. She made no connection between the two. She took out the book and began to read.

* * *

Wednesday, January 18, 1865

My hand trembles as I try to write this evening. Events are confused. My mind is in turmoil. This quiet house became bedlam tonight, and I am afraid, desperately afraid. Something terrible has happened or is about to happen.

John left immediately after dinner. He had been preoccupied throughout the meal, much the same as he had been during the holidays. I wanted to ask him what was wrong, what was troubling him, but the barrier was up, impossible to penetrate.

After he had gone, Mr. Weichman went up to his room. Annie, Honora, and I went into the parlor. Annie read aloud while Honora and I sewed. Annie has such a sweet clear voice. It is usually such pleasure for me to hear her, but tonight it grated upon me, everything did. I was on edge. John had infected me with apprehensions as tangible as a fever.

Annie grew weary. She is very pale and silent these days. Sometimes she hardly seems real to me. I know her so little. She is like a lovely vague shadow in the house. She kissed me goodnight with her cool soft lips and went upstairs. Honora soon followed her. I knew that she would brush Annie's long fair hair. They would lie side by side and talk into the night. I remembered Cecile, a girl from the convent. She was all those things to me that Annie is to Honora. It is hard to imagine Cecile as anything but what she was the last time I saw her over thirty years ago, fresh and fair like Annie. How I loved to kiss her. Her lips were so soft and sweet. In the night she would come to my bed and we would hold and warm one another under the thin blanket. Just before dawn she would slip back to her cold bed. I could feel her shivers from across the room.

I was alone in the parlor, wishing that he would come, seeing his face, feeling his touch.

It was warm beside the fire, the air hot and soft, divinely suffocating, like sinking into thick feather quilts and pillows. My fears for John were fading. The warmth suffused me. I suppose I slept then. I dreamt of Mr. Booth and Cecile. They were standing in a forest. They began to dance, whirling and whirling, faster and faster. She wore a white dress, made of transparent material. She broke free of him and twirled alone into a beam of sun slanting through the trees, and her long white legs, her thighs, her small high breasts could be seen in silhouette, as if through a diaphanous white fog. She sank slowly to the ground. He reappeared. She laid back and lifted her dress away from her body but covering her face. She was naked. She put one hand to her breasts and the other to the soft golden down between her thighs. He stood watching her. Both were very still. Suddenly he was transformed into a great gray slavering wolf . . .

I awakened with a start. I did not know how much time had elapsed, but I felt a cold draft of air and I saw John enter. His face was wildly white and frightened. He did not say a word to me, but ran up the stairs, taking them two at a time as if demons were after him. He even left the front door open in haste. I started to close the door when Mr. Booth appeared. He looked like some supernatural nocturnal being who only came alive in the darkness. He was wearing a long black cape which slipped from his shoulders and fell to the floor. He too looked wild, almost savage, but there was no fear in his eyes as there had been in John's. There was an intensity, an excitement about him that I wished I had inspired.

I asked him what had happened. He looked at me for a moment and he recalled the wolf of my dreams. Then he ran up the stairs without speaking. I picked up his cloak, and held it close to me and waited.

They soon came down. John carried a bag. I asked him where he was going, but he seemed not to hear me. He looked only at Mr. Booth, spoke only to him.

"It's all at an end, you know."

"What? What is at an end?" I asked.

He brushed me aside like a moth. "They will be after us now."

"Who? Who?" I was growing desperate. I seemed not to exist for either one of them. They could neither see nor hear me. Finally Mr. Booth spoke and his voice shook with emotion. I was jealous of that quavering. It was absent when he spoke to me.

"I need you, John."

"You need no one." John turned away. Mr. Booth went swiftly out the door which I had forgotten to close. I called after him. I did not know that I had called him Wilkes. I did not realize that tears were streaming down my face until John turned and looked at me and saw them.

"He'll . . . he'll be back. He forgot his cloak. He must come back."

"Mother, for God's sake."

There was something like hatred in his voice. He knew what I was feeling, but how he knew I will never know. He saw my love and my desolation as if he too felt them. I realized that the hatred in his voice was not for me. It was turned within.

"John, tell me what all of this means."

"I cannot. It is all unbearable, unspeakable, but I'm out of it now. Please God, I'm out of it. I must go, Mother."

"Where? Where must you go? You are my son. You will not leave my house in the dead of night and not tell me where you go."

"I'm going South. I don't know any more than that myself."

"When will you return?"

"I don't know." He looked at me strangely, his eyes rested finally on Mr. Booth's cape which I still held to me. "He won't be back. You would do well to burn that."

"What are you saying? Of course, he will be back."

"No, he won't, and you should thank God that he won't. John Wilkes Booth is the Devil incarnate. He is evil personified. I curse the day I ever brought him here, and pray I do not live to regret it even more than I do this night. Burn that cloak. If anyone asks, deny that you ever knew him. Goodbye, Mother."

He left me then. He closed the door on my farewell. I don't understand any of this night. I only know that it was terrifying.

Annie woke to find the book open beside her. It was dark still. She had read only the one entry from January 18 and fallen asleep.

She had taken more medicine than she had intended. She got up and began to undress for bed.

She slipped in beneath the covers, stretched and sighed and flung her arms out. She felt at that moment that it was wonderful to be in bed alone, but unconsciously she was listening for his breathing. She turned. She was alone and there was only silence. She took one of the pillows and held it in her arms, pressed her face down into it and went to sleep. It was nearly dawn.

XIII

She slept until ten in the morning. She looked around the strange, sunny, ruffled room, and for a moment could not think where she was. She felt tired, as if she had not slept at all. She dressed in the same clothes she had worn the day before, glad that Mardella was coming today with the trunk. It would be good to see Mardella's face, to have her near.

She went downstairs. The parlor was deserted. The door to John's study was still closed. She walked through the dining room into the kitchen. It was bright and spotless. Victorine was sitting facing a window. There was a bowl of batter in her lap. She had stopped stirring. The spoon had slipped down into the batter.

"Good morning, Victorine."

"Annie. You gave me a start. I was watching the children. Oh, goodness, the spoon's all covered with batter. Mercy, what a mess." She cleaned it with her fingers and put them in her mouth. "I'm making a chocolate cake. I love chocolate cake. Do you? Did you sleep well, Annie?"

"Fine, thank you."

Victorine concentrated on her batter for a moment. Annie looked out the window. The room became heavy with silence.

"There's some coffee on the stove. I didn't know you were such a late sleeper. My sister Emiline was that way. We used to come in and tear the covers off her bed, and two of us would sit on her, and the rest would tickle her feet. Emiline married an old preacher, can you imagine. He must be twenty years older than her and sour as curdled milk. Well anyway, I don't suppose she needs to worry about her feet getting tickled in the morning anymore."

"I don't suppose so."

She got up and was pouring the batter into a pan. "Oh, goodness, I forgot to butter it. The cake'll stick for sure. I don't know what's the matter with me."

"Victorine, about last night . . ."

She didn't look up. "You know, Annie, honey, I can't imagine what got into me last night. I thought we'd have a nice pleasant little chat and I got all gloomy. I'm not generally like that. I just don't understand it, but I do apologize. I hope you'll forget everything I said, honey. I was just being a silly goose."

"I didn't think so."

She looked up from the pan. "Well, I was, and that's that. You have to promise me that you're not going to think anything of it. You promise me now."

"I promise, Victorine. I think I'll go out and talk with Miranda."

"I don't think you'll need to, honey. I sort of explained in my own little way to the babies this morning."

"What did you say?"

"I just told them that a long time ago their grandma got herself into a little trouble, but that it was all forgotten, and if anybody should say anything about it to them, they just weren't to listen."

"Do you think they'll accept that?"

"They seemed to, honey. Children don't dwell on things like we old folks do. That's part of being young, I suppose."

"Victorine, I told you last night . . ."

"You promised me that we were going to forget all about last night."

"But I feel that I've hurt you somehow."

She was putting the cake in the oven slowly and carefully. "I don't understand you, honey. You haven't hurt me. Now if I were to come back an hour from now and reach in that oven with my bare hands and take out that cake, that'd hurt me. I would have blisters on my hands for weeks, but, honey, words can't hurt like that. You didn't raise any blisters on me last night."

"There are many kinds of hurts, Victorine."

"Well, honey, I guess I just don't feel them. You're just too sensitive, Annie, and you imagine things. My sister Sally was that way. She had a little friend that nobody could see but Sally. Mama thought sure she'd grow out of it, but Sally never did. She was mighty good at imagining things, Sally was. Those children are awfully quiet out there. What do you suppose they're up to?"

She walked to the window and shouted out, "Where are you, Willie? Miranda? Don't you be running off now. You stay close in the yard. Some gypsies might come and carry you off. It happens all the time. I knew some children once who were carried off by gypsies. They never saw their mama or papa again. Don't you go running off now. You hear me, Willie? Miranda?"

There was no answer but she seemed satisfied and turned away from the window.

"You never did tell me, Annie, honey, do you like chocolate cake. I hope so because I make an especially nice one."

"I'm sure that you do, Victorine."

"You going out, honey. It's early yet to meet the train. It won't be in for hours."

"I promised Miranda a walk today."

"Oh well, you two have yourselves a fine old time, but don't you be gone too long. I'll start to worry."

"Afraid the gypsies will get us?" Annie smiled.

"You two'd be a fine prize. I hear tell they're partial to blondes, honey." She smiled also.

"We'll be careful."

"Mind that you are, Annie. Mind what you say and do." She stopped smiling.

"Victorine, are you trying to be subtle?"

"I don't know the meaning of the word. I'm just warning you about the streets of Baltimore these days. Why you're just a little country girl and not used to the city anymore. I know when Johnnie and I first moved here, I was scared senseless by it all. Just be careful, Annie, honey, that's all I'm saying."

"We won't be gone long."

"Have a good time."

She walked out onto the porch and called to Miranda, who appeared from around the corner of the house.

"Are you ready for our walk?"

"Yes, Auntie Ann."

"Good, let's go."

They were out of sight of the house before the little girl spoke.

"Did you see Mama, hiding behind the curtains watching us leave?"

"No, I didn't."

"Well, that's what she was doing, though it's awfully hard for Mama to hide. A little white kitchen curtain just won't cover her. Auntie Ann, I slept without my lamp last night."

"That's wonderful, Miranda."

"I was a little afraid at first, but I was more scared thinking about what it would be like than after I'd done it."

"That's usually the way things are. We imagine that they're going to be far worse than they could ever really be."

"Auntie Ann, Mama said something real funny this morning."

"What was that?"

"Well, she started talking about my grandma. She said that she wasn't her mother but yours and Papa's, and that she had died before I was born. She said that my grandma did something wrong or got into trouble or something like that. What did she mean?"

"Miranda, I don't think your mother wants us to talk about it. You are her little girl, and she believes she knows what is best for you. I can't argue with her or go against her wishes. It wouldn't be right."

"But what did my grandma do?"

"I'll tell you this much, she did nothing wrong."

"Mama lied about her then?"

"No, I didn't mean that, Miranda. It's a story I don't think you would understand right now. Someday you will. And I hope that when that time comes I can be the one to tell you."

"But I want to know now."

"Miranda, if someone had taken your lamp from you last week, do you think you could have stayed in the dark and not been afraid?"

"No, I don't think so. I was still afraid then. It was only last night that I wanted to try it, that was the very first time."

"There is a time for everything. You were ready to sleep without your lamp last night, and I am so proud of you, Miranda. Telling you now about what happened to my mother, your grandmother, would be like taking your lamp away from you last week. I don't think that you're quite ready yet. What I would like to tell you about now are the good and wonderful things about your grandmother. I don't think your mama would mind it. Really, that's all I ever wanted to tell you about, because that's the important part, that's the part you should know. Her troubled days can wait to be told, maybe forever."

"Was she beautiful, my grandmother?"

"Yes, very. She had eyes like ours, but her hair was black. She had the whitest skin and small soft hands. She played the piano wonderfully well."

"I'm learning to play the piano."

"That's good. That would have made her very happy."

"Tell me more about her."

"She had a low and sweet voice. She wore golden earrings, like mine. When she walked into the room she carried the scent of violet with her. In fact, it drifted ahead of her, announcing her. I remember that there was a little white kitten who used to chase her wide black skirts because the swaying of them drove him mad and she was rarely still. She didn't laugh or smile often, but when she did, it was like the sun breaking through clouds."

"Did she ever cry?"

"I know that she must have, but I only saw her cry once."

"When?"

"One time when I was very cruel to her."

"Oh. Was she afraid of anything, like the dark?"

"She kept all of her fears secret, locked deep inside of her. She never told me of them. She never told anyone."

"But shouldn't you tell someone when you are afraid?"

"Yes, Miranda, always. Fears love to be kept secret because that is when they are strongest. Most of the time if you speak of your fears they disappear, like magic."

"Would she have liked me, do you suppose?"

"Oh Miranda, she would have loved you."

"Was she very old when she died? My Grandmother Lily was ever so old. I remember, I saw her lying in bed and her hair was long and white, and when she closed her eyes and stopped breathing, everyone cried. Mama told me she had gone to heaven. Mama lifted me up and I kissed her face and Mama has a lock of her hair in a locket she wears around her neck. Was my other grandmother old and sick like that?"

"No." Then quietly almost to herself, "She should have been. She should have died in bed with all those who loved her around. She should have grown old. She should have closed her eyes and gently let go of life. She should have."

"Auntie Ann, are you crying?"

"Only a little, Miranda. I envy your mama. I wish that I had a locket like hers."

"Mama says it will be mine someday. What if, when it is, I give it to you? Would that make you feel better?"

She knelt down beside the child and took her in her arms. "I love you, Miranda."

"I love you, Auntie Ann."

She stood up. "We've gone a very long way and I promised your mama we wouldn't be gone long. We had better turn back."

"Auntie Ann, if my grandmother wasn't old and sick, then why did she die?"

"I think that you must wait to hear about your grandmother's death, Miranda."

"Will someone tell me when I'm ready to hear or will I just know?"

"I think you'll know. In the meantime, Miranda, will you do something for me?"

"Yes, anything."

"Love your mama. She needs and loves you very much. You see, Miranda, all the things that I've told you today about your grandmother, my mother, I took for granted at the time. I never knew that I loved my mother so much until she was gone, and then it was too late to show her or tell her. Miranda, give her your love while you can. Years from now when you find a glove that smells of violet or a book filled with her words and the hand is familiar, but the words are the words of a stranger, I pray to God that you do not feel that love welling up inside of you and know that you cannot give it to her, and you did not give it when you could."

"I'm not sure I understand, Auntie Ann."

"I'm sorry, Miranda. I was talking to myself more than to you. You did understand about your mother, about trying to appreciate her while you have her."

"Yes, I think so."

"Good. And you will try?"

"I'll try, Auntie Ann."

They walked the rest of the way in silence. They came up the back porch and into the kitchen. Victorine was at the sink. She turned at the sound of the door.

"I thought the gypsies had gotten you two sure."

"Mama, something smells wonderful."

"It's my chocolate cake, Miranda."

She came up behind her mother and put her arms around her waist. "Oh, Mama, I just love your chocolate cakes." She walked swiftly from the room.

"I've never known that child to ever do anything like that in her life. I declare, you could knock me over with a feather. She's getting right sweet, Annie, honey."

XIV

She was late getting to the train. Mardella stood beside her trunk.

"I was gittin' ready to take out on my own, Miss Annie."

"I'm sorry I'm late."

"I has a letter fer you, Miss Annie."

"From whom?"

"Who be sendin' you a letter?"

She handed her the envelope. It had her name upon it and was sealed with red wax. She recognized William's hand.

"Did he say anything to you, Mardella?"

"He didn't say nothing 'cause I didn't never seed him. He done took off, don't know where. Dat was laying on de table las' night. He didn't come fer supper. I left dat house standin' empty dis mornin'."

"I don't understand. I suppose he'll explain in the letter."

"I 'spect he do dat."

"Mardella, we won't be staying here long."

"Jus' as you say, Miss Annie."

"We'll leave for Washington tomorrow or the next day."

"Washington?"

"Yes, Mardella."

"What be dere? I thought we was done wid dat town."

"It isn't necessary that you go if you don't want to."

"I goes wid you, Miss Annie. How is yer brother an' de family?"

"They're fine."

"Dis place sure done growed."

"Yes, it's changed a great deal. I remember coming here when I was just a girl. I thought it was the most beautiful, the most exciting place I'd ever seen. Now it just seems rather large and very dirty. I guess I've gotten old. I just don't like cities much anymore."

"But you is goin' to Washington?"

"Yes, I think it's time to go back."

"Where we be stayin'?"

"The Willard seems as good a choice as any. There will be ghosts and memories everywhere. There'll be no avoiding them."

"Not lessin' you steers clear of Washington, dere ain't."

"Well, I'm not going there to visit ghosts. I'm going to see someone who is very much alive."

"Who dat?"

"You'll find out soon enough. You probably already have a guess anyway, I'm sure. I have some very lovely recollections of Washington. I was sixteen and in love there. That's a very special thing."

"Well, I didn't know you in dem days."

"I wish you had. I was much nicer then in many ways."

"You is nice enough dese days."

She smiled. "Only you could say that, Della. You know me well enough to know my intentions. Well, Della, this is the house, the white and yellow one."

"I's mighty glad of dat. My arms is 'bout to break right off."

"Oh Della, I should have carried one. It's such a long way. I intended to."

"I knows it, Miss Annie."

They smiled at one another and walked inside. There was no one about. They climbed the stairs and entered her room.

"What is dis place?"

"It's my room."

"If dis ain't de frilliest place I done ever see in all my born days. I 'spect dere be ruffles on everythin' dat's rufflable."

"You're certainly right about that."

"You wants me to unpack de trunk?"

"Not everything. We won't be staying that long. I would like to change out of these clothes. They were gritty enough from the train yesterday, but stepping back into them again today was awful."

"Why don't you takes yerself a little nap. I'll unpack an' lay out some fresh things fer you. I 'spect dey's got a place fer me downstairs somewheres."

"Yes, Victorine told me that there's a nice room off the kitchen that you can have."

"I just hope it ain't ruffly frilly like dis one."

"Poor Mardella."

"It just' dat ruffles don't serve no purpose. Dey jus' catch de dust, dat's all."

"I think I will rest for a bit, perhaps read a little."

"In de book?"

"Maybe. Maybe the letter."

"Is you takin' good care of de book, Miss Annie?"

"Excellent care, Mardella."

"Good. Now, I gonna tote dis trunk down to my room. Dere ain't no place fer it here wid all de ruffles. I brings up some things fer you later."

"Thank you, Mardella."

She left the room. Annie began to unbutton her basque and untie her skirts. She stood in her pantalets and chemise before the glass and looked at herself. She ran her hands across her breasts and down her hips and thighs, then turned and slipped down her pantalets. Over her shoulder she could see the red marks he had left upon her with his belt. They were still bright and angry-looking. She remembered that night as a dream, wondering why it was that at the moment he was hurting her, punishing her like a naughty child, why it was at that moment she had come closest to loving him. Probably his letter was an apology or plea of some sort. She would read it later. She took the book to bed with her instead.

Friday, January 20, 1865

These past days have been a maze of disbelief and misunderstanding. John has gone off, run away. I do not know why. All that I know is that his departure reeked of escape. From what? From whom? What has he done?

And Wilkes. Since I called his name out into the night, it seems foolish to keep referring to him as Mr. Booth. He is Wilkes to me. Why has he gone from me? Am I to be left with only his cloak? Is that to be my souvenir of him? Am I to be reduced to the likes of the relic-hunters?

Annie and Honora came in late this afternoon. They have been going out a good deal lately. I told them that I did not approve of their being out so late. As if prearranged, Honora went upstairs and Annie told me that she wished to speak with me. We sat down on the sofa in the parlor and Annie took my hand.

"Mother, I have no wish to lie to you or deceive you."

"But you have been?"

"Yes, I did not want to, but you have been so unreasonable about Seth. I had to do it."

"Is this conversation to be about Lt. Kierney?"

"Yes."

I removed my hand from hers. She looked so happy. I wanted to be happy for her, but Wilkes had gone without a word and Seth Kierney stayed on and on. I told her that I had no wish to discuss him.

"Seth and I are going to be married."

"Has he written you about this?"

"I've seen him, Mother."

"But he went back to the lines."

"Yes, and come back again, and gone and come back again. I've been seeing him right along."

"Where? When?"

"Wherever, whenever we could."

"After I asked you not to."

"You told me not to, Mother. You did not ask."

"You are seventeen years old. I am your mother. I have every right to tell you what you will and will not do."

"But you never told me why."

"That is not necessary."

"It is. I want to know why you dislike Seth, why you don't want us to be together."

"He'll hurt you."

"He loves me."

"That is no safeguard. Love always brings more pain than pleasure."

"We're going to be together and happy forever."

"He'll leave you one day."

"No."

"And if he stays, then he'll change toward you and toward everything you thought you had together." I didn't want to say any of these things but I could not help myself. I was thinking of Wilkes and Mr. Surratt. Why should Seth Kierney be any different? They either stay and grow to despise or they flee. I hated to see Annie's face as I spoke to her.

"I won't hear these things, Mother. They're not true, not for Seth and not for me."

"You don't care what I say. You don't believe that I know of what I speak."

"I don't want to believe. Mother, has your life been so terrible to bring you to this?"

She was asking about me. She was doing what I had pleaded that someone do. And I could not speak. I could not tell her. Why can't I reach out and take what I need and give what is needed?

"You are determined to marry him then?"

"Yes."

"When?"

"After the war is over."

"That could be a very long time."

"Seth doesn't think so."

"I'm sure that the lieutenant knows better than I. And do you intend to continue with these clandestine meetings?"

"No. Seth is going back to the lines soon. He thinks he will be there until the end. I had hoped that he could come to the house to say goodbye."

"By all means let him come, if it's to say goodbye. I only wish that it would be permanent."

"You want him to be killed. That's what you're hoping for . . ."

"No, I meant . . ."

But she wouldn't let me finish. I only meant that I hoped they would reconsider their marriage plans after they had spent some time apart. I only meant that perhaps she would meet someone else. I only meant that things change, but she wouldn't let me finish. I will never forget what she said to me. There is no going back after this night. I will always remember her words.

"What are you, Mother? Is it just that you are old and sour and shriveled and bitter? Or have you always been this way? No wonder Papa's life was misery. No wonder he didn't want you when he died. Did you wish him dead too? Do you hate life so very much?"

I couldn't speak. She stood and watched the tears rise in my eyes. She seemed merely curious. Then she walked from the room. I wanted so much to call after her, to tell her that the cruel and hard words I had said were meant for me and not her, I wanted to tell her that I loved life. But I couldn't tell her that because I don't. I hate my life and I hate myself.

Tuesday, January 24, 1865

Lt. Seth Kierney has gone. He came on Sunday to say goodbye. I couldn't look at him. And I cannot look at Annie. I keep remembering. Today, through a strange turn of fate, I learned one of the places where they had been meeting secretly.

This morning we heard a great din out in the street, fire bells clanging, and we all rushed out to the porch. There were great clouds of smoke in the sky and people running wildly in the street. Mr. Weichman called out, asking where the fire was. A man shouted over his shoulder that he thought it was the Smithsonian Institution. I saw Annie clutch at Honora's arm at these words. Honora whispered that the man must be mistaken, that it couldn't be the Smithsonian. I wondered at their concern for this public edifice until I overheard them talking in the afternoon when we learned that the Smithsonian had indeed been burned. I walked past the open parlor door and heard their conversation.

"Annie, it doesn't mean anything."

"It does. I know that it does. Why the Smithsonian of all places? Our lovely castle where we always met, where he asked me to marry him. Why would it burn only two days after he left me to go back to the Army? Why?"

And dear pragmatic Honora had assured her, "It burned because someone was careless, because the Washington Fire Department is notoriously slack and inefficient. That's why it burned, Annie."

"No, it's a sign, an omen. Seth and I are doomed. He's going to die."

"You're being very foolish. You mustn't say such things or think them."

"But it's true, I know it. I can feel it."

My poor Annie. She is my daughter far more than she realizes.

Saturday, January 28, 1865

It has been ten days and there has been no word. I have been unable to do anything. My thoughts are all with him. My life waits for him. I ask why he has gone. I ask where he is. But there is no answer. There is only emptiness and pain. Today I could bear it no longer—the hours spent at the window during the daylight when I might catch a glimpse of him, the hours spent lying in my bed staring up at the blank ceiling during the black nighttime trying to catch his phantom in a dream—even dreams have deserted me, and sleep. Each sleepless night leaves a little of its darkness beneath my eyes and in my heart. Today I stopped waiting. I decided to go to him.

I told them at the house that I was going to Mass. I went to the National Hotel, his hotel. There was such elegance and sophistication, such beauty too, but along with it such dissoluteness, dissipation, and degeneration. The women, all in silk and pearls and flowers, waiting in their carriages for their young men, their lovers. A dark and gleaming young captain in blue would step into a rig, and another would pull up for a languid blond man in shepherd's plaid and fawn-colored trousers. All were eagerly and impatiently awaited by ladies who were slightly old and beautifully groomed.

I approached the desk clerk after circling the red damask and mirrored lobby several times. I had hoped that I might encounter Wilkes before I was forced to ask for him, but that was not to be. The desk clerk was smooth and even of feature, his hair oiled and slick. I presented myself to him and asked for Mr. John Wilkes Booth. It was over in a moment, after ten days of agonized waiting. The man replied that Mr. Booth had gone up North, probably New York City. He had left ten days ago. He gave no word of when he might return. The desk clerk did not even give me the nasty and knowing smile I had expected. It occurred to me that he could not believe that the shabby old woman with the faded gloves which she continually twisted with swollen hands could have any sort of connection with the famous, young, and handsome actor. Obviously any sort of amorous affiliation was unthinkable. Possibly he took me for some obscure country relation of Wilkes', or maybe the mother of some young girl he had wronged. I suppose I should have been glad that I was spared the desk clerk's ugly little suspicions, but I felt cheated. I was one of the women in the carriages. I was like them. Yet I had no carriage, no silks, no flowers, no pearls, no young man to publicly flaunt to prove that I was still attractive, still a woman. All that I had was the memory of his few words of love and an uncontrollable desire for him fulfilled not even in my dreams.

He went to New York without a word of farewell. He makes trips like that often. He is as free as the wind. He indulges his every whim, and does not think twice. I have never seen New York. I never will. I am the antithesis of the wind. I am fettered by heavy emotions, and duty, and obligations. I do not indulge my whims. I do not even have whims. My whims become earthshaking and imperative. I murder whims. I change them into deep, desperate and urgent desires. I hate him for all the things that he is and that I am not, and never can be. He can create images, protective coloring, for himself with great facility, while I have worked years on one image, my mask. I thought it was wonderful protection, but he stripped it from me and left me with nothing. With myself. Oh, how I love and want him. When will he come back to me? Please, God, give him back to me. He is life to me. He is light and shade, happiness and sadness, open windows and closed doors, sunlight and night, goodness and evil–he is everything to me. Please, God, don't take him from me too.

Sunday, January 29, 1865

The Captain and Jebediah have come again. It was so good to see them. The Captain regaled us this time with the story of his surrender last month. It seems that for once the Captain picked the wrong officer. He said he was ashamed of himself for showing such poor judgment. He attributed his error to his age and the weather.

Last month, he began, it was very cold, and not like the cold at home, he said, but city cold, the very worst kind. He and Jeb were most anxious to do their business and get away. He spotted a young officer with a slick black mustache. That should have warned him off, the Captain told us, but his hands were red and throbbing with the cold and he overlooked the mustache in his haste. The officer agreed to take Jebediah to the Commissary Department, and they planned to meet later for the Captain to collect his money. The Captain went to the meeting place, but the officer never showed up. He waited until it grew dark and still he did not come. The Captain walked over to the Commissary Department. He looked through the fence to the pens where the mules were kept, but Jeb wasn't there. He decided to go to the place where they always met after the mule's escape. He went there and there stood Jebediah. The Captain told us how he wished so hard at that moment that Jeb was one of the talking breed of mules so that he could tell him what had happened, but the Captain figured that probably the officer got an offer of more money than the Commissary pays for mules, so he sold Jeb to someone else and pocketed the money. There had been a strange piece of rope around Jeb's neck which he had bitten through. That was the only clue.

The Captain looked around the room at all of us and laughed as he said, "Can you imagine it, Jeb and me was taken in by a slicker? It just shows how poor honest folks from the country can get taken advantage of in the big city."

The Captain had sworn off officers with mustaches forever.

Monday, January 30, 1865

The first month of the new year is nearly gone. People are slipping back into their old patterns and habits. Resolves are fading fast. The new year is no longer new.

I have some new boarders coming, the Holohan family. So far I have met only Mr. Holohan. He came in answer to my prayers and advertisements in the "Star." We made arrangements. There is Mr. Holohan, his wife, and their small daughter. We will be crowded but the extra money will help tremendously.

It feels very strange to be packing once more. I am taking the back parlor on the second floor, leaving this room for the Holohans. Gathering my things and moving them reminds me of coming to Washington last fall. It has been four months. Much has happened and yet nothing really has changed. I am still alone, perhaps more so now that I have lost Annie, but then we were never really close. I just grow older every day.

There will be much added work with the Holohans here. I do not know if I am equal to it. The headaches grow worse all the time. Sometimes I think I cannot bear the pain another moment, but I always do.

I am so used to my things in their proper place. Three times as I sit here writing I have looked up to the mirror hanging over my desk. Each time I have been jolted by its not being there. It's been moved down to my new room already, but I keep forgetting. I never realized before now how I prepare my face before looking into the glass. I can feel it relaxing into its natural lines when confronted with the blank wall. I can feel that it was crimped up in the most unnatural way for the benefit of the glass. If I do this for myself and my mirror, I wonder what I do upon meeting people.

I will be glad to get settled in my new quarters, and have things arranged as I am accustomed to them. I don't like being unsettled. I do not like making uncomfortable discoveries about myself. I like hiding in habit and routine.

Wednesday, February 1, 1865

The Holohans came this morning. I hope that they will be permanent boarders. They do not, of course, completely solve my money worries, but they will ease them considerably. Mr. Holohan is a man who has done many things, and seen much of the world, the rougher side, I think. He is a big Irisher with huge hands. At one time he was a tombstone cutter. He is more vague about his present occupation, saying only that he is involved with the government. He has the look of a bounty hunter to me. His wife, Eliza, is a pretty thing with raven hair and alabaster skin. She gives the impression of intense dissatisfaction with her husband and her daughter who looks, I fear, like Mr. Holohan. She prefers to be called Miss Eliza, and her preferences are thinly veiled demands.

It is very difficult trying to accommodate one's personality to a family of strangers, who, because of financial necessity, live in one's house. Anyway, Mr. Holohan appears to have a great sum of money. He has paid me three months in advance. Miss Eliza made it very clear that she would rather have stayed in one of the bigger hotels, the Willard or National, but evidently Mr. Holohan decided that a home-like atmosphere would be best for the child. So they bring their money and their unhappiness to this house, which may not know much of the former but most certainly is acquainted with the latter. I shall have to smile in the face of Miss Eliza's aristocratic posturing and her feigned delicate sensibilities. She has her reasons, as do we all. I feel the most for the poor unloved little girl, red-haired and sad-faced. Her father has eyes only for her mother, and so too does her mother. Miss Eliza has announced that she lies abed late and likes her breakfast brought up to her at about eleven. And because of her husband's gold I will comply.

Tonight the Holohans are unhappily ensconced in their room, but their blessed bickering presence is gone and now I am once again alone. And it is the same litany-like recital. Why has he gone? Why no word? Will I ever see him again? I have taken the cloak from my closet night after night, and over it I repeat his name again and again. I must see him. He must not dwell for the rest of my life only within my mind. I am helpless to bring him back. Yet he said that he loved me because I willed it to be. Why then can't I will him to return to me? He will return when he wants, when he chooses. Oh, to be a man and have that blessed gift, that wonderful endowment, of choice. But I am a woman, and women are fated, destined, to wait. I blame only myself. I was not beautiful enough, young enough, to hold him. Would he have stayed for an empty-headed egotist like Eliza Holohan who lies in her bed with a gilt-handled mirror and is capable of loving only herself, and not really even herself but merely her mirrored image? Would he have stayed for her, for her selfish white skin and blue eyes and black hair? Oh, he must come back to me. Days of dull ugliness never changing and nights of barren yearning. I cannot stand it. Why did I ever look upon him, know him, love him? If he had never existed for me, my life would have continued as now, but I would not have hated and loathed it as I now do.

And John's words on that last terrible night that I saw him, what did he mean?

Annie stopped reading. She thought of John and of herself and of their mother, and how none of them had known each other. She closed the book and sat with it in her lap. There was a knock at the door.

"Come in."

"I gots yer things fer you, Miss Annie."

"Good. Thank you, Mardella."

"You was restin'?"

"I've been reading."

"Well, I's been listenin'."

"What?"

"Listenin'. Why you not tells me, Miss Annie."

"Tell you? About what?"

"'Bout Miss Victorine. I ain't heard so many words spoke in sech a lit'l time in I don't knows how long. She is de talkingest woman I done ever did seen. Why, she talk fer twenty minutes 'bout her chocolate cake, an' truth to tell, Miss Annie, it look a mite dry to me. I knows all her sisters' names, an de names of all her cousins an' folks in Georgia, Tennessee, an' Missouri. She done wore me out wid listenin'."

"Is your room ruffled?"

"Fer Gawd, Miss Annie, it ain't no joke. It's de worstest place I ever did see. Dat woman, wid her talkin' and her rufflin'. I don't put much store in neither of dem things. Dey jus' ain't needed, not so much of 'em anyways."

"We'll be leaving soon, I promise."

She had started to dress.

"Let me hooks you up dere in de back, Miss Annie."

"I can manage."

"You cain't." She came over to her. "You knows you cain't never do yer own . . ." She trailed off as she saw the red marks on her back through the thin cotton of the chemise. "How long is you 'spectin' to be stayin' in Washington, Miss Annie?" She was quickly and expertly hooking her up.

"I'm not exactly sure, Della."

"When is we goin' home agin?"

"I don't know."

"You is done, all hooked."

She turned. They faced one another.

"Is we ever goin' home agin, Miss Annie?"

"Della, I just don't know."

"It be gittin' 'bout supper time, I 'spect. I knows what you is havin'. Miss Victorine, she done tole me an' tole me an' tole me. You best be goin' down."

"Yes." She walked slowly, leaving the door open. "Mardella, I'll tell you all about it some day."

"Ain't no need, Miss Annie. I knows 'bout it. I's a woman, ain't I? An' I's black. I knows all 'bout dem things."

"Did you ever think that you might, that you possibly could love a man who beat you?"

"I s'pose I could say dat rightfully you should hate de man, but it jus' ain't so. It don't happen dat way. Mos' women dey born to be beat. Some folks says dat's why Gawd he make men de bigger. Every time I done ever had a man he beat me, dat's why I steer clear of men dese days."

"Because you hated it so?"

"No, Miss Annie, jus' de other way round. Dey usta say 'bout me dat I big enough to go bear huntin' wid a switch. I don't 'spect no man ever beat me if I didn't want him to, but I's gittin' too ole to have some man take de hide off of me fer love. Dat's what it always come down to, men talkin' love wid dere hands 'cause dey cain't do it wid words. Dey's right too, makin' love or fightin' 'spresses feelings better dan talkin' do.

"But words express how we feel better than anything else."

"Mebbee so. Mebbee not. I ain't never had much luck wid 'em."

"But they do, they must. We are just like animals otherwise."

"Like I say, Miss Annie, talkin' an' ruffles dey's mighty no account things to me."

"I just can't believe that words are competely useless."

"Our talkin' ain't doin' much good right now. I ain't changin' you an' you ain't changin' me. An' you is missin' yer supper."

"I'm going, Mardella."

"Miss Annie?"

"Yes?"

"I jus' wanna say dese . . . Beatin' jus' don't mean hatin'. 'Cause somebody beats you don't mean dey hate you an' it also don't mean dat you gotta hate dem. Mos' times it mean somethin' altogether different from hatin'."

"Yes, Della."

"You go down an' eat somethin'. You is jus' skin an bones, Miss Annie."

"I'll eat a piece of chocolate cake for you."

XV

It was late. They were sitting by the fire in her parlor. Annie had come down after everyone had gone to sleep and knocked at Mardella's door. They had gone into the parlor at Annie's insistence.

"You sure it be all right, Miss Annie. Mos' white folks don't take to havin' us folks sit in de parlor. Dustin' is one thin', sittin' is another. Miss Victorine, she done strikes me as de kind who don't like de sittin' part."

"It's all right, Mardella."

"It feel mighty strange to me. Miss Victorine, she come down an' see me perched on her pritty lit'l horsehair sofa, she liable to swoon."

"Well, at least if she was in a faint she wouldn't be able to talk."

"Don't be countin' on dat."

"Della, do you remember the first time we ever saw each other."

"I does."

"It was a strange and wonderful piece of luck for me. That was a terrible time. It was the day Mother died."

"Miss Annie, it weren't luck dat brought us together."

"What do you mean?"

"I done planned on meeting wid you dat day. 'Course, I didn't plan how it would be."

"You planned?"

"It time it be tole. I's been lyin' too many years."

"Lying? To me?"

"It weren't 'sactly lyin', Miss Annie, jus' not tellin' all."

"You're frightening me. Tell me what you mean by all of this."

"Dat day when dey killed yer ma, dat weren't de first time I ever seed you. I'd been followin' you fer months."

"Following me? Spying? Were you working for the government?"

"Hole on, Miss Annie. I ain't tellin' dese thin' as it ought to be tole. You 'member a short time back you asked me 'bout my ma an' I tole you dat she die young, dat I never did know her. Dat weren't de truth. I knowed my ma. She be 'bout de bestest person I ever did know. When you asked me, I hated havin' to deny her, but I didn't think it be de right time to be telling you."

"Telling me what?"

" 'Bout me, 'bout my ma. You was so busy wid yer own ma, I didn't think it be de right time fer my story. Now I thinks dat it is. I tole you dat my pa he was white. Dat true. Ma had eight young 'uns, four by a black man an' four by a white man. I didn't know none of 'em. I come de last. Dey'd all been sold off de place or died by de time I was borned. My ma she was de bravest, de strongest, de bestest I ever did know, black or white, man or woman. I was lucky. I got to spend all my young time wid her. I be 'bout nineteen when de war start up. I done had a lit'l girl of my own by dat time. She was de prittiest sweetest lit'l thin', but I was wild. I didn't have no time fer her, fer nobody but myself. De place was in Maryland an' it were real easy to run off from dere. My baby's pa, he had done it, an' I thought to do it too. Dat's jus what I did do. I was wild to be free.

"I left my lit'l girl wid Ma. Runned up to dis place, to Baltimore. Dere was lots of men, white men, soldiers mostly, lots an' lots of em. Dat's how I lived. In three years I never did once go back down home to see my ma an' my baby. An' I could of. I surely could of, but I didn't. I was havin' too much fun. I went by de name of Coffee. A little blond soldier boy gave me dat name. He told me dat be de color I were, de color of coffee wid plenty of milk in it. I done had three names in my life. De name my ma give to me when I was borned, de name de soldier boy give me, and dis one, de one I took fer myself, Mardella. But I weren't Mardella in dem days. Coffee, dat me, an' Coffee she were havin' high ole times in Baltimore, wearin' satin an' silk, takin' men an' boys, takin' and takin'. Coffee she was givin' 'em pleasure an' dey was givin' Coffee money an' presents an' pritty things, but she just weren't happy.

"Den I finds out I's gonna have a chile. I goes to an ole woman who knowed 'bout sech things an' she give me somethin' to take. I swallowed it down an' after a while I started thinkin' I were gonna die, but I didn't. I lived. De little baby it died. I went back to bein' Coffee, but I were scared, real scared all de time dat it happen agin, an' dis time I would die. I got to thinkin' 'bout Ma an' my baby. So I went to see 'em, but dey were gone. Dere was only one ole boy left on de burned-out place an' he tole me dat dey had gone to Washington. I don't know why I didn't go lookin' fer 'em den, but I didn't. I went back to Baltimore. De war was endin'. Things was changin'. All dem boys who fer years had been thinkin' dey was gonna die, dey started thinkin' dey might jus' live after all. Dey started in thinkin' 'bout the lit'l girls dey'd left back home an' forgittin' havin' fun wid coffee-colored gals in Baltimore.

"I finally went to Washington. I looked an' I looked an' I found my ma an' my baby. Dey was jus' a pile of bones lyin' in a black dirty room wid lots of other folks who was dyin'. My ma was holdin' my baby who had died de day before, as she was dyin' too. It were de typhoid. Jus' before Ma died she tole me 'bout a lady, a white woman, who lived on H Street. She'd been feedin' 'em fer months. Ma tole me if it hadn't been fer her, dey would have died long 'fore dis."

"H Street?"

"Yes. She died after sayin' dat. I saw to it dat my ma an' my baby was buried, an' den I went lookin' fer dat woman. I wanted to thank her. If it hadn't been fer her I never would have seed my ma alive. I never would have had de chance to tell my ma dat I was sorry fer what I'd done. I never would of heard my ma say to me dat I was forgived an' dat she loved me. So I went lookin' fer dat woman, but H Street dat a long street. By de time I talked to yer houseboy Dan it were already June, de war were over, Mr. Lincoln dead, an' yer ma on trial fer killin' him. I jus' couldn't believe dat a woman'd feed an ole black woman an' chile could do de things dey was sayin' she'd done. I waited an' watched. I started in followin' you, seein' you got to dat jail an' it broke my heart seein' yer face. Den come de day you went to de White House, an' I waited an' waited fer you to come out. An' den you did. I will never be forgittin' yer face dat day. I jus' had to go to you. So you see, Miss Annie, it weren't 'sactly luck."

"Oh Della, Della. I remember your mother and your little girl so well. Why did you wait so long to tell me?"

"In de beginnin' dere weren't no need of it. You never did want to speak of yer ma. I jus' didn't think you could of beared to hear it much 'fore dis, Miss Annie."

"You were right, as usual. You know me better than I know myself, Della. You know what I'm thinking and feeling right now, I know that you do. I don't have to tell you, do I?"

"You don't. Words is cheap things. All I needs do is look at yer eyes, Miss Annie. Dey tells me."

"Don't ever leave me, Della."

"I cain't. I couldn't of dat first day nor any of de others after it. I always be right beside you. You'd best be goin' upstairs an' gittin' some sleep now. Us is goin' to Washington tomorrow, 'member?"

"Yes, tomorrow. To Washington, to face all the ghosts. I must apologize to someone there. I must tell him that I was wrong and that I am sorry to have hated and wasted so many years."

"He understand, I 'spect."

"I hope so. Mardella, did you pack any of my medicine?"

"Yes, Miss Annie. It in de trunk in my room."

"Will you go and get it for me, please, and bring it up to me?"

"Yes, Miss Annie."

She left the parlor. Annie walked up the stairs slowly in the darkness. She entered her room and turned up the gas jet. She took out the bottle of medicine that she had. There was very little left in it. She drained what there was and put it back in her satchel. She heard Mardella coming and opened the door for her.

"Dere it is, Miss Annie."

"Thank you, Della."

"Dat story of mine, it make you sad?"

"It was a very sad story. Yes. Why do you ask?"

" 'Cause you wants yer medicine so fast."

"I don't take it because I'm sad. That's not the purpose of it."

"Why you takes it den, Miss Annie?"

"I take it because I need it, because I feel ill and it makes me feel better. It helps me to sleep . . ."

"An' it make dat sad feelin' go away."

"Well, what if it does? What's wrong with that?"

"I s'pose nothin', Miss Annie. I don't s'pose nothin' be wrong jus' so long as you knows why you takes it. Dem other reasons you be sayin', dey ain't de real ones. You cain sleep widout medicine an' you ain't sickly, but you is sad an' dat's why you takes it. Dem other reasons, dey's the spoon of honey dat makes the swallowin' easier."

"Sadness is a sickness. I take my medicine because there are times I get so sad, as you say, so sad, that I think I'd rather die than go on feeling that way. The medicine makes it better. Now does that reason satisfy you, Mardella?"

"Do it satisfy you, Miss Annie? Dat be de question. I ain't got nothin' to do wid it."

"Obviously you don't approve of the medicine. Why?"

"How much is you takin' in one day dese days?"

"I don't know. However much I might need."

"How much is dat?"

"I tell you, I don't know exactly."

"Does you takes it in de mornin'?"

"Yes, sometimes."

"An' does you takes it in de afternoon when you lays down fer yer nap?"

"I suppose I do."

"An' at night?"

"Yes, at night."

"You takes dat stuff likes it were food, like meals. You should be eatin'. You makes yer breakfast, lunch an' dinner outa dat stuff. You is gittin' so skinny, you ain't nothin' but skin an' bones. All I ever sees you doin' is swallowin' tea an' dat stuff. Look at de circles under yer eyes. It cain't be helpin' much to make you sleep."

"That's my business, Mardella."

"I 'spect you is right, Miss Annie. Ain't nobody's business but yer own."

"Then why are you doing this? Asking me all these questions? Criticizing me?"

"We be tellin' de truth tonight. Lest ways I be doin' dat. You always sayin' dese days dat you is readin' de truth 'bout yer ma in her book an' how you ain't 'fraid no more to face it, dat's what you tells me. I tells you de truth 'bout me. It ain't pritty, but it de truth."

"Yes, I know that."

"Well, to me, Miss Annie, yer medicine it be a lie. Long as you takes it you is lyin', as I sees it."

"I don't know what you mean."

"I means, first off you tells yerself lit'l lies 'bout why you takes de stuff. You takes it to sleep. You takes it 'cause yer head aches or yer belly or yer back. You takes it 'cause you is feelin' dizzy. Dem's lies, all of dem."

"I told you once, Mardella. I told you why I take the medicine, the real reason. It keeps me from wanting to die, from dying."

"Why you wants to die?"

"I don't know."

"You ain't never gonna find out neither, not so long as you takes dat stuff. You makes sech fine speeches 'bout facin' up to de truth, but it ain't never gonna happen. Ever time you reads yer ma's book you is full of dat stuff. You thinks you really knows what you is readin'?"

"Yes, I think that I do."

"Dat's yer medicine talkin', an' it's lyin', Miss Annie. You ain't never gonna know what yer ma was sayin' in dat book, you ain't never gonna know how you really feels 'bout it till you stops takin' dat stuff."

"I need it."

"You don't, not no more. I done watched you fer years swallowin' down dat stuff an' I tells myself, she need it an' I hush my mouth, but no more. I gonna stop hushin' an' you is gonna stop swallowin'."

"I can't."

"You cain."

"I'll die without it."

"You ain't gonna die. You gonna live. You gonna face up to yer ma an' to yerself, really face up, widout dat stuff. You ain't never gonna see de truth lookin' through a blue glass lie."

"I can't do it alone. I have to have my medicine with me."

"You ain't alone. You gots me, but you ain't gonna have me if you don't stop takin' dat stuff. I'll leaves you, I swears it. Miss Annie, you makes my story a lie when you has to take dat sutff to bear it. You wants dat stuff so you cain change it to suit you. You wants a nice glow from de bottle an' den you listen to what I is sayin', you thinks 'bout my ma an' my little girl, an' you say to yerself, it ain't so very bad, I cain face up to it now. But it is bad an' you ain't facin' up. You is lyin'."

"How can you talk to me like this?"

"Dere ain't nobody else cain do it. I knows I is black an' you is white, an' I knows dat make a powerful difference to de world, but what we feels is de same, Miss Annie. You done watch yer ma die an' dere weren't a thin' you could do 'bout it, same fer me. We hurts inside 'cause dere be a time when you an' me, de both of us, could of done somethin' 'bout our mas, but we didn't do it. We was too busy wid our own selves an' now we is payin'. We is de same, Miss Annie. Dat's why I says dese things to you. 'Cause when you lies an' takes dat stuff you makes me hate you fer a coward, an' dat jus' cain't be. 'Fore yer ma's book, I figure you lives in dat house wid dat man an' you takes yer medicine an' dat be all dat you cain do. I figured dat dey done killed de insides of you long time ago. I 'cepted dat fer you an' fer me, but den dat ole cripple man he show up an' I thinks mebbee, jus mebbee, we gots ourselves a chance. If you'd burned up dat book den I would of knowed dat you done dried an' shriveled up inside, but you didn't. You took it an' you commenced to readin' an' I begun rejoicin', but den I seed dat you was takin' more an' more stuff. You gots to stop, Miss Annie, otherwise dis fine thin' dat you is tryin' to do it ain't gonna mean nothin'. You is still hidin' out an' I is right beside you. I knows dey didn't kill off yer insides 'cause I is watchin' you do dat job yerself. Will you gives dat bottle to me, Miss Annie?"

"I can't do that."

"Miss Annie, don't you hear nothin' dat I be sayin'?"

"I hear you. Would you really leave me, Mardella?"

"I 'spect if you don't stop I has to."

"You're like all the rest. Not more than an hour ago you promised never to leave me. I can't trust you or anyone."

"Miss Annie, de only reason I leave you is outa love, dat de only one dere could be."

"Where would you go?"

"Don't know. It wouldn't be de first time I sets my feet on de road not knowin' where I is bound."

"Della, don't go."

"Den gives me de bottle."

"You won't throw it away? You'll keep it in case I should really need it?"

"I keeps it but you ain't gonna need it."

"But you'll have it if ever I should?"

"Yes, Miss Annie. I promise."

"Here then, take it away."

She took it and turned to go.

"Della, would you really have left me?"

"I don't thinks I could of."

"Will you come back up and stay with me until it's light?"

"I come back."

She watched Della leave the room with the bright blue bottle in her hands. Annie wanted to call her back. She wanted the warmth of it badly. Her stomach was beginning to cramp. There had hardly been a drop in the old bottle. She went over to her satchel, took the old bottle out and tipped it to her lips. There was nothing. She took it over to the basin and wrapped it in a towel. Slowly she brought it down upon the edge of the table. She hoped it had broken in large pieces. With shaking hands she opened the towel and saw one large wet portion of glass. It was jagged. She lifted it to her mouth and began to lick it carefully. She thought she heard footsteps. She reached for another, more hurriedly. She cut her finger. Ignoring that, she put the piece to her lips and sucked it. The taste was wonderful, but somehow strange. She did not realize that it was tinged with her own blood. This would be the last time, the very last, but she must have this. She was sure she heard footsteps this time. She bundled the broken pieces of blue glass in the towel and shoved it into her satchel.

XVI

Mardella returned.

"Della, I can't sleep. I can't possibly. Perhaps I could read aloud from Mother's diary. I would like to share it with you. Would you like that?"

"Did you cut yer lip, Miss Annie?"

"It's nothing."

"It bleedin'."

"It's nothing, I tell you. Do you want to hear some of the diary or not."

"I likes to hear some. Don't you have somethin' else to be readin'?"

"What?"

"De letter."

"Oh, William's letter. I'll read it tomorrow. On the train, that's when I'll read it. When I'm headed somewhere, on my way, then I'll read it."

"Jus' as you say. I wished you'd let me takes a look at dat cut now. Did you fall down?"

"No. I didn't. I assure you it won't impair my reading. That is, if you really want to listen."

"I would. My ma, she could read, dat not a common thin' fer a black woman her age, but she could. She had dis big ole book wid pictures in it. She usta tell de folks dat she liked to look at de pictures. She rarely owned up to knowin' how to read. She real proud of what she could do, but she say it ain't healthy fer black folks to talk 'bout knowin' certain things. She tried to learn me, but I were a real flighty chile. I never could learn. All dem letters jus' look to me like so many chicken prints. I knowed I were a real disappointment to my ma. She had her heart set on me learnin' how to read an' write. I do wished dat I learned now."

"I'll teach you."

"I's too ole."

"That's the first cowardly thing I think I've ever heard you say."

"You thinks dat I's 'fraid?"

"Yes, I do."

"You jus' commence to readin'. I's gonna watch over yer shoulder. Mebbee dem things looks less like chicken prints to me now. I doubts it, but mebbee."

Saturday, February 4, 1865

Life goes on in its endless tedious round. There are so many meals to be prepared–meals and meals, and if they should be late, enraged faces, hungry and tired. There are so many dishes to be washed–and washed and washed, and hands red and sore and chafed from constant immersion in hot soapy water. I never feel any sense of accomplishment. Nothing is ever done, finished, completed. If once, just once, I could scrub a floor and it would remain clean, but no, there is the inevitable boot mark awaiting it, or in summer dust descends, and in winter mud seeps. And all of this has so very little to do with me, my daydreams, my night fears, and the headaches which come so frequently now.

They begin with cold hands gripping my head, and then those

hands place my head into a hot metal vise which squeezes my skull until I grip the sides of my bed and barely hold back screams which would raise the house, indeed, the dead. I roll from side to side, moaning, begging, pleading, praying, for relief, but it does not come. I have no thoughts then—no belief—nothing. I stifle my screams only because I want to be alone with this. When first it comes, I am quiet because I do not wish to disturb the others, but when the vise begins to tighten, and it feels as if shards of hot glass are being stabbed into my brain—then I wish only to scream. I take great bites of my pillow only so the others will not run frightened to my room, and seeing me, from me run away, not in simple fear, but in terror and horror. For the pain makes me wild and bestial. I tear my hair and rend my bedclothes. I know that I do these things, though I have no memory of them. In the morning, in the light, I find great handsful of my black hair in the bed, and my gowns, the sheets and pillows are all torn. Morning after morning, I try to mend and clean away the evidences of my struggle, and I am silent. It looks as if I have done battle with a murderous intruder, and I have—myself.

And every day I descend into the cold of the morning. I light the fires while they sleep. I am the first one up, the first to face the ravages of the night and the cold. I dispel them with warmth and the smell of coffee brewing and food cooking. It is I who does this while they lie in their beds where they have slept all the night, while I have been fighting demons. One by one they come down, asking the same question, "Are you well today?" And I want to say, no, I have been fighting the Devil all night, I have not slept in weeks, I am ill in mind and body. But I know that they do not want to hear all of this. I know what they want to hear, and so I say to them, I am fine, thank you, and how are you? And they say fine. They say, will it be fair today, do you think? And I answer, oh, yes, passably fair, I think. Then they come to the really pressing and important matters. Will we have beef or lamb for supper this evening? And what for breakfast tomorrow? And tomorrow and hateful tomorrow? Those questions I answer because there are still answers to those.

Our world is a world where the insignificant is of the utmost importance—the inconsequential, weighty—and the power of the petty is supreme. Because that is easiest.

Monday, February 6, 1865

This afternoon I tried to fool the cold hands and the hot vise and get a little nap sitting up in the parlor, but as soon as I closed my eyes I began to feel the icy fingers at my temples. I quickly rose and began to dust. I had not been at it very long when I had a visitor. It was Davy Herold, the young boy of the stutter, who used to visit with that German fellow and John and Wilkes. He seemed lonely and frightened, and very disappointed when I told him that John was not here. He turned to go, sadly, I thought, so I invited him in. He appeared to be very surprised at this. He could not know that his face brought the memory of other faces to me. He could not know that I welcomed him as a kind of link to them, as proof that they were real. He had once exchanged words, even shared confidences, with my son, and with Wilkes. Perhaps he knew something, could tell me something which would explain why both my dear ones had left me, deserted me, resigning me to my uncertainties and doubts of their love for me. Perhaps some word of this stammering boy could give me a clue. He had, after all, known them. While I, I had only loved them, love them still, will always.

Of course, I let the poor lad know none of this. He thought the glad reception was for himself alone.

It turned out that Davy Herold could tell me nothing of John or Wilkes. It seems that he only loved them too, and did not know them, as I had thought. He too feels deserted and alone. The only time he grew happier was when he talked about hunting in Maryland. There is a certainty for him in the marshes, a solitary surety that eludes him among people. I imagine that little Davy Herold whom no one ever remembers, who stutters and shies away on streets and in parlors, has the bearing of a prince and the voice of a general in the swamp. He told me that he was headed there, and I was glad for him. But what of me? Where am I sure, and certain, and happy?

Thursday, February 23, 1865

I have neglected my writing here, but there has been very little to record. My headaches grow worse. I mentioned them one day to Anna Ward. She said that she had suffered from headaches as severe as mine. She went to several doctors, and finally one gave her a tonic which she claims worked wonders for her. She takes it nightly. She then asked sadly after John. I told her that I knew nothing, had heard nothing from him. I asked her the name of the tonic and she wrote it down for me.

This conversation took place yesterday. Tonight I sit with the bottle of tonic unopened before me. I have always considered myself a strong woman, country bred, healthy, and sound, my mother's daughter. I never thought that I would have to take a tonic. Perhaps it is my age. I do not understand why all the aches and pains wait until the body is old and feeble to strike it, when it is least able to endure. I have withstood the pains in my hands and my stomach, but this I cannot bear. If I do not sleep soon, I think that I will either go mad or die. I wonder if headaches are solely an old woman's affliction. Anna Ward is not old. Indeed, throughout my life I have known women who suffered from them, all ages and colors. I remember years ago there was a Negress on a neighboring farm who had her child sold away from her. She began to have headaches shortly after that. She would run out into the night howling with pain. One night, the story went, she ran out and dashed her head upon a rock, and her skull cracked open, and snakes poured out, and then she died. I did not see it happen, but I did see her many times doing battle with the pain. There was no helping her then.

To think that love, rather its loss, could cause such misery and even death. I have tormented myself with fears of a huge tumor in my head that causes the pain, but I wonder if headaches are entirely a physical problem. Anna Ward said that her headaches grew worse when the first doctors she saw told her that she should marry and the possibility of marriage for her grew more and more remote. The tonic eases her mind, she told me. She is happy when she takes it. Surely if the tonic does away with the fears and along with them the pain, then it was the fears that caused the pain in the first place. And the Negress. Her headaches came after her child was taken. It must have been the thought of her child being mistreated, starved, or beaten that made her head burst with pain.

I will try some of Anna Ward's tonic. It occurs to me that she led me to Maria Carbini also. I hope that this will be a better remedy. If it will give me sleep for one hour I will bless it, kneel to it, prostrate myself before it. I must be free of this torment. I cannot watch another gray day dawning.

Saturday, March 4, 1865

Washington is intensely occupied today with the Inaugural. A terrific storm broke over the city at daybreak. It has been gray and drizzly all day. I would wonder what the ill weather portends for Mr. Lincoln's next four years in office, but it is always ill weather in Washington. It portends nothing but more of the same.

The people turned out in droves to hear Mr. Lincoln. Mr. Weichman was one of them. He came home with a carefully composed narrative. He said that the President's speech was almost eloquent, high praise from Mr. Weichman, who is not fond of Mr. Lincoln. He said that the President spoke as if the war was as good as over. While this makes me rejoice, it seemed to make Mr. Weichman rather sad. He bemoaned the lost cause of the Confederacy, but then he is perfectly safe in these sentiments. He clerks in the War Department in the utmost comfort and security, while my sons and many others are in constant danger and suffer the severest privations. Mr. Weichman is one of those stay-at-home patriots, verbally vociferous, vehemently vocal, but with little action to back their words. Mr. Weichman told us all about the fine ladies' costumes which were ruined by the weather at the Inaugural speech.

Eliza Holohan seemed particularly pleased by these tales of mud-spattered velvets, squashed crinolines, and dripping laces. She dimpled prettily as Mr. Weichman related the sad fate of all those dry goods, but suddenly her smile faded. She spoke aloud, though I'm sure she did not intend it, but we all received a glimpse into the ugly workings of Eliza Holohan's mind. "Yes, their pretty dresses are all spoiled, but they will simply return home and deck themselves out in even finer plumes for the ball tonight. They have closets full of dresses, while I must be content with my poor paltry wardrobe and never go anywhere, stay in this wretched house and read about the Inaugural Ball in tomorrow's papers or listen to some boring fool tell about it."

Then she trailed off, realizing that she was speaking these words instead of thinking them. Annie and Honora had watched her closely and listened to every word. Their young faces looked sad. Dissatisfaction seems our common lot in this house. However, Eliza Holohan is one of those poisonous women who breed envy, jealousy, and bitter discontent wherever they go. As one knows more and more of her, she ceases to be beautiful. In fact, she grows quite uglier every day. Mr. Weichman, after coaxing, for he was obviously the "boring fool" in Miss Eliza's diatribe, rather petulantly resumed his story of the Inaugural speech, but I no longer listened.

All through the day the sound of artillery had vied with the storm for domination of the city's ear. but as it grew dark, nature and the soldiers signed a truce, and all was quiet. All the so-called important personages had gathered at the Hall of Patents, where the Inaugural Ball was being held. I could see them, dancing and cavorting, greedily gorging themselves on turkey and terrapin, oysters, and mounds of pastel pastries, sugary and thick with cream. But somehow the man in whose honor this was all taking place seems out of place among these false and strutting peacocks. He seems a simple man. I would wager that Mary Todd Lincoln has the Devil's own time getting him into white evening gloves. The entire display seems vulgar and inappropriate, out of keeping with the solemn, even melancholy, man that Mr. Lincoln is. I know that many think him a buffoon, a joker, but I see an intensely sad man in him.

Everyone is acting as if the war is already over while boys still die fighting it. It is blasphemy. I plan on taking an extra dose of tonic this evening. This room is cold and so too are my thoughts. I will look forward to heavy dreamless sleep.

Annie stopped reading.

"Yer ma, she make you feel dem words."

"Yes. I can see all their faces, hear their voices once again. She conjures them for me too clearly. All the betrayers and deserters."

"Dat Weichman boy, he talk 'gainst yer ma?"

"Yes, he was the chief witness against her. I never liked or trusted him, but Mother did. I try to understand why he did what he did, but I don't know that I ever will. He was afraid. They had ways of making you afraid in the Old Capitol. They threatened him, told him that he too would go on trial unless he testified the way they wanted him to. Better men than Louis Weichman would have succumbed to Lafayette Baker."

"An' de boy dat stuttered?"

"Davy Herold. He was like a child. Mother was right about him. He was not memorable. I can't really recall his face. He was captured in Virginia with Booth, but he survived the capture. They took him to an ironclad on the river, manacled hand and foot. They had Booth there too, his body anyway, wrapped in an Army blanket. A most inelegant shroud for Mr. John Wilkes Booth. They hooded Davy Herold. They did that to all the men. Mother escaped that at least. Finally, a doctor said that the hoods would drive the men mad, that they must be removed. Mercifully, that was done. Davy Herold was beside my mother on the scaffold. I remember the day of the execution. I went very early to see my mother for the last time. I did not believe it to be that, but it was. All of Davy Herold's sisters were with him in his cell. You could hear their cries and moans all through the prison. There were many tears shed for him that day, and that was a good thing, I suppose."

"An dem other folks, de Hooligans?"

"The Holohans. Eliza left as quickly as possible when the trouble came. That wasn't a blow. No one expected anything but the most shallow of behavior from her, even her disloyalty hadn't much depth, but she must have cared something for Mother, she took the stand on her behalf. Perhaps that appealed to her sense of the dramatic, testifying at a murder trial. Tom Holohan went to Canada to track down my brother. I don't think his heart was in it really. He was merely trying to protect himself and his family. You've no idea what fear the government struck in the hearts of people in those days. Secretary Stanton and his henchmen wielded supreme power. They could do anything to anyone, and did. But no, the flight of the Holohans did not hurt. They were boarders, not friends."

"An' yer friend, Honora?"

"That hurt. She stood up to it well in the beginning. She was an honorable girl. She was arrested with my mother and me. Honora, arrested! She was terrified. We all were, but she was fine, really fine. She testified at the trial admirably and with great courage, but shortly after that she left me. She packed her bags one day, while I was at the prison visiting Mother, and walked away without a word. I always believed that her father was behind it. I expected, waited, for a letter from her for months, but none ever came. I suppose she felt that she couldn't possibly explain to me, and that it was no use making a try. We were such friends. I'll never understand why she deserted me. Even if her father pulled her screaming from my house, there was a time when she could have written. It was after Honora that I came to expect betrayal and defection from everyone. I was so alone, so completely alone. Then you came, Mardella. And you stayed, for here you are still."

"It nearly light, Miss Annie."

"Dawn, another day."

She closed the book and crossed to the window. She stood silently looking out onto the street, a handful of curtain pulled back and bunched in her hand.

"It's the gray light Mother wrote of. I know the brain-burning red flame too. I know so much now, so much I never even guessed at then. Why must I know it now when it's too late?" She turned to Mardella.

"Mebbee, it ain't. You jus' says it, Miss Annie, it be dawn, another day, a new beginnin'. Mebbee, as long as you is breathin', dere ain't no sech thin' as too late."

"I'm glad you took my medicine from me. I'm glad now. I can't promise you that I will always be."

"You hears me askin' fer a promise?"

"No."

"We be leavin' fer Washington today?"

"Yes, this afternoon, I think."

"You lay yerself down an' git a little rest."

"I will."

"I jus' takes dese things an' pack 'em up."

"Leave the gray silk, please. I'll wear that today."

"Yes, Miss Annie."

"Thank you, Della."

She left her standing by the window, staring out with gray eyes into the gray dawn, her gray silk dress spread out on a chair.

XVII

Annie came down into the kitchen about eleven o'clock.

"Good morning, Victorine."

"Annie, honey, don't you look nice."

"I'm leaving today, Victorine."

"Leaving so soon? You just can't be thinking of leaving so soon. I'd planned on you staying at least a couple of weeks."

"You're very kind, but I know that this visit was very sudden and must have been an imposition."

"Now, honey, you mustn't say things like that. We loved having you here."

Annie smiled at Victorine's fast slippage into the past tense, it revealed much of her true feelings on the subject. "I loved being here, Victorine, but I must attend to some things in Washington. Perhaps on the way back, I'll stop again."

"But you'll be heading south after Washington, won't you, honey?"

"I'm not sure."

"Oh, well, it'd be just wonderful to see you again, I'm sure. My, you're such a lady of affairs. In Baltimore one day and Washington the next. It'd be fun, but I'm afraid my husband wouldn't approve."

"I'm quite sure that mine doesn't either."

She walked out of the kitchen and went to her brother's study. The door was closed. She tapped lightly.

"Victorine, not now. I'm busy."

"John, it's Annie."

The door opened.

"Come in, Annie."

"I didn't want to disturb you, but I'm leaving today."

"Leaving?"

"Yes."

"I had no idea you intended such a short stay as this. We could have spent more time together."

"We could have, but I doubt that we would have under any circumstances. It's been too many years, John. It seems that all we have left to us are emotional scenes like the other day or silence. We can only reminisce, and ours are not pleasant memories. I'm very glad that we talked. I discovered who you were many years ago and why you did what you did. That was very important for me to know. I found my brother, I came to understand his pain, and to love him again, but that was my brother of thirteen years ago, that was a young man who stood in a rainy train depot and learned of his mother's death, and I felt for him. But I don't know who you are now and I don't need to. It's enough for me to know the young man you once were, the one I loved so much, and came to hate so much, wrongly, until two days ago. He's the one I came looking for and I found him."

"I would like for you to know me now too, Annie."

"Can we bridge thirteen years?"

"We could try."

"I know a person it would be far easier with, a person who wants to know you desperately. It's someone who is as much a part of you, more, than I am. She wants and needs you very much."

"I hope that you are not going to say Victorine."

"No, I meant your daughter."

"Miranda?"

"Yes, Miranda. I see so much of myself in her. She is your second chance at knowing and loving me. And she'll give you things I never could. You two can be to one another what we never could have been. You want someone to know and love you as completely as it is possible to know and love. It's Miranda. Don't waste this little girl, John. She may very well be your last chance."

"I want that with my son."

"Your son is like your wife. John, Miranda is starved for what you can give her and Victorine cannot. Willie is a happy and facile youth. He doesn't need you. Victorine may rail and complain that you don't talk to her, but I don't believe she would really have it any other way. She likes things as they are, much as she may complain. Too much depth makes her uncomfortable. Miranda is not yet nine years old, but if you talked to her, she would understand you far better than Victorine would."

"You have us all figured out, don't you, Annie? That's very remarkable in only two days' time."

"No, it's not. I'm a stranger in this house. That makes it very easy."

"You said you were leaving. Are you going home?"

"No, I'm going to Washington."

"Why Washington?"

"There is someone I must see there. Colonel Wood."

"When are you going home?"

"I don't know."

"You have all the answers for everyone else and none for yourself."

"You are absolutely right, brother. That's what I seek, my answers."

"You act as if you were on some sort of mission, a crusade or something."

"It's more a quest really. I'm looking for our mother. Since I've been reading her diary, I've discovered that I never knew her. I want to know her."

"She's dead, Annie, dead and gone."

"But many of the people who knew her are not. They live still. I can reconstruct her from their memories and her own words."

"Why do it?"

"Because in her I find myself."

"Are you lost?"

"I am. Victorine said something to me. I thought that it was very profound and quite true. She called us a cold and silent tribe. And we are, John. Do you know why?"

"No."

"But you agree that we are?"

"I suppose."

"I want to know why. I think Mother can tell me."

"Forget this, Annie. Go home where you belong."

"That's just it. I don't belong there. I am as unhappy in my marriage as you are in yours. We picked very poorly, John. We should have waited and not done what seemed easiest at the time."

"What does your husband say to all of this?"

"I don't know. I've never really talked to him about it, or anything. I have a letter from him, but I've yet to read it."

"You should read it."

"My duty as a wife?"

"You are the one who believes so strongly in words and talking things out. Is it fair to him to leave his letter unopened and unread?"

"No, it's not. I'll read it today. It's just that I feel sure I know what he will say."

"Tell me, what does he say in his letter to you?"

"First he will accuse me of assignations with a lover. He will threaten me, then apologize and entreat."

"A lover?"

"There is no lover, John. Why is it that no man can believe that a woman would leave him unless there was another man?"

"I'm sure I don't know."

"Have I shocked you?"

"Yes, you have. I think this entire thing is disgraceful and shocking."

"I'm sorry that you feel that way, but it is not going to deter me in the least."

"I'm well aware of that."

"John, what do you remember of Mother?"

"Why do you ask?"

"Because I want to know. I want to know if you remember her differently than I."

"She was very pious and devout. She was a wonderful cook. She played the piano well. I always think of her in black dresses . . ."

"That's all?"

"She was not the sort of woman who would have ever thought of doing what you are doing, defying her husband, running away, traveling alone, inviting all sorts of trouble and danger."

"I think you are wrong. I think she would have liked to have done exactly what I am doing. That is one of the reasons I'm doing it."

"I will remember my mother as I please. I don't need you to interpret her for me."

"She wasn't a saint or a martyr. I believed that she was for a very long time. She was a woman of intelligence, capable of great wisdom and folly. She was a woman of passion."

"Stop it, Annie."

"She was in love with Booth."

"No."

"You know it. You knew it that night."

"What night?"

"In January, when you left so suddenly."

"Is that in her diary?"

"Yes."

"You have no right to pry into these things."

"You knew that night that she was in love with Booth."

"Yes, I knew it."

"Why didn't you help her?"

"I warned her about him. But I couldn't stay."

"Why, John?"

"I was afraid. I was sure they knew about us, that they were after us. That was the night we tried to kidnap Lincoln from the theater. He didn't attend. I can still see his rocking chair standing empty in the box. We thought they were wise to us. Booth followed me to the house. He walked into the room while I was packing and told me that the next time we would kill Lincoln. I told him I would have no part of it. I told him he must be mad. He flew into a rage. I had to get away. He tried to persuade me."

"How?"

"What difference does it make?"

"It makes a difference."

"What do you know about Booth and me?"

"Nothing."

"What have you guessed at then?"

"The way Mother described you in her diary when Booth left the house that night. She sensed that you knew exactly how she felt. Mother was in love with Booth. She was desolate at seeing him go like that. She wondered how you seemed to know just what she was feeling. Were you feeling the same things, John? Is that how you knew so well what she felt, because you felt it too?"

"No!"

"She loved him. Did you, John?"

"No. No. I told him from the beginning to leave her alone, but he insisted she could be useful to us, and that she would never know. I told him I didn't care, that I just didn't want her involved. As soon as the words were out of mouth, I regretted them. He hated to be denied anything. After that conversation, the very next day, I was supposed to meet him at the National. When I went there I saw them together. He wanted me to see. They were in the dining room. He held her hand, and she looked, Annie, she looked like a woman.

I had never seen her look like that. He planned it. He was manipulating her like some sort of doll."

"You knew then, you had to know, what kind of man he was. John, why didn't you rid yourself of him then?"

"I couldn't. He needed me."

"In the plot?"

"Yes, of course, in the plot."

"No, I don't think so. He needed you, yes. He loved you."

"It's not true."

"John, you know that it is."

"I can't bear it, I can't . . ."

"Booth couldn't stand to think that you wanted to protect Mother, that you might have loved her more . . ."

"Than I loved him . . ." John put his face in his hands. His words were muffled as he spoke them. "Yes. Yes, I loved him. He was someone. When I was with him, I felt that I was someone too. All my life I had wanted more. God, how I hated it at home when Pa was alive. He was always joking and drinking too much, that big red grinning face of his, and everyone laughing, laughing at him. Then the boardinghouse in Washington. It was so ugly there. You should have seen Booth's rooms at the National."

"Did you go there often?"

"Yes. I was there many times . . . I don't want to speak of it."

"You must, John. You must. I am the only one you will ever be able to tell of this. How much longer can you live with it and not tell someone?"

"You will despise me."

"No. I will understand, finally."

"That night after I had seen Booth and Mother together, I went to his rooms. He opened the door and he was wearing a deep purple, almost black, silk robe. He led me through the parlor to his bedroom. There was a girl there. She had long red hair and the whitest skin. She lay in his bed, naked. I just stood, not knowing what to do. He took my hand and drew me to the bed. He told me that I could have her, if I wanted her. Her breasts were full and her red hair streamed down upon them. She touched them and smiled. I couldn't move. Booth gave her some money and she dressed and went away. We were alone. He sat down on the bed and looked at me. That could have been your mother he said to me. I wanted to kill him, but I went to him instead. I loved him as I could never love a woman. He promised me. He promised that he would never touch her. You see why I had to go, Annie? You see now?"

"Yes."

"I remember when they finally caught up with me in Egypt, brought me back for trial, and how after the trial was over I laid in prison for a year not knowing what was to become of me, that's when I came to hate him, but I never stopped loving him. He told me that he would destroy me if I ever left him. I thought I could escape, but I couldn't. He has destroyed me."

Annie walked over to him and bent down beside him. "I'm so sorry, John."

He looked down at her. "Don't you know that this is what happens when you go digging in graveyards bone-picking?"

"I'm not trying to disinter Mother in doing this. Just as I know that that is not your intention with your lectures."

"My lectures, a futile gesture. How could I ever really tell the true story? No one would believe it. I wouldn't want them to."

"John, I began this by wanting only to remember Mother without the horror and the pain of her death always intruding. I am sorry if I am unearthing other pain and horror, but I must know her. I cannot just remember her as a pleasant soft-spoken woman in black, busy cooking or mending or praying. I will no longer commit the sin of omission where Mother is concerned. I must find myself in her."

He reached out and stroked her hair. "You're still so beautiful, Annie, and so stubbornly self-righteous. You always were those things. If you are bound and determined to do this, there is someone you should see. You haven't even thought of her."

"Who?"

"Grandmother Jenkins."

"Mother's mother."

"Yes, she lives with Uncle Zadoc now. She's very old."

"Have you seen her, John?"

"No, but I did see Uncle not too long ago."

"I've seen her maybe twice in my life."

"Yet she lived very close to us."

"Mother never spoke of her to me."

"Nor to me."

"She mentions her in the diary, but almost as if she were dead. Why?"

"I don't know, Annie."

"Why didn't I think of Grandmother Jenkins? I suppose that I believed that she was dead. I never thought much about the estrangement. It was just accepted. You say she lives with Uncle Zadoc?"

"Yes."

"I'll go there."

"I thought perhaps you might."

"You are very kind to tell me this, John, especially since you disagree completely with what I am doing."

"I'm my mother's son, Annie. She was kind-hearted to a fault. I think we can agree on that?"

"Yes, John. I am so sorry for today. I had no intention of . . ."

"I know that you didn't. Remember hate doesn't change to love in one day, Annie. Don't fool yourself, there is still within you some residual resentment for me. You wanted me to be punished, and I deserved to be, but it's a strange thing this disclosure today did not hurt me so much as I thought it would. I feel almost as if a weight has been lifted off my shoulders. It is good to know that there is another human being who knows my secret and understands. You do understand, don't you, Annie?"

"I do, John."

She kissed his cheek and walked from the room, closing the door behind her. As she turned toward the stairs, she saw Miranda sitting on the bottom step.

"Miranda."

"Hello, Auntie Ann. I was waiting for you."

"Were you? May I sit down beside you here?"

"Yes, please."

"You look sad, Miranda."

"I am. Mama says that you're going away today."

"Yes, I am."

"But why must you go so soon?"

"I must. I'm sorry to leave you, Miranda. I've enjoyed our talks so much."

"Mama probably drove you out with her everlasting talking."

"Miranda, I thought you were going to be kinder to your mother."

"I'm trying. She's my mama and I love her. I do, but Auntie Ann, I just don't like her very much. I don't like the way she talks all the time and I don't like the things she says. Even though I love her, I still don't want to grow up and be like her. Am I a bad girl to feel that way, Auntie Ann?"

"No, Miranda. You're not a bad girl. As long as you love your mother and try to understand her, that's the important thing. You don't have to try and be like her."

"Oh, why do you have to leave here ever?"

"This isn't my home, Miranda. I can't stay here."

"Couldn't you take me home with you for a visit then?"

"I'm not going right home. There are some other places I must go first."

"Oh. Auntie Ann, don't you want to go home? I heard Mama say that you didn't like your husband, that you had run away from him."

"No, I'm not running away, Miranda. And I promise you that just as soon as I'm home, you can come on the train and see me. How does that sound?"

"It sounds like a long time away."

"I have an idea. There's something you could do for me right now."

"What?"

"Go and knock on your Papa's door and say good morning to him."

"I mustn't."

"Why not?"

"I'm not allowed. Mama says he's too busy for me."

"Have you seen him this morning?"

"No."

"I think he would like very much to see you. Go on."

She got up slowly and went to the door. She stood for a moment and then knocked softly.

"Papa, it's Miranda."

"Come in, Miranda."

She turned and smiled at Annie, then she hurried inside. Annie sat on the stairs for a moment smiling at the closed door. She had not slept. Her eyes hurt her and teared uncontrollably. Her stomach cramped, and her hands were shaking, but at that moment, she felt truly happy for the first time in years.

XVIII

She and Mardella were not allowed on the same car. Mardella was sent to the "niggers' car" near the engine. Annie hadn't traveled in so long that at first she did not understand the arrangement, but Mardella had explained.

"Now dat us is free, ain't no more ridin' wid de white folks. I go on back. Don't you worry none, Miss Annie."

She hated what had been done to Mardella, but selfishly she was also concerned with being left alone with William's letter. Reluctantly she broke the seal on the envelope. His words were what she had expected. There was anger and hurt, but also a frightening coda she had not anticipated. He wrote that he thought she was mad to be doing what she was doing. He added that there were things to be done about wayward wives and demented women. He asked that she come home soon before he was forced to do something that he did not really wish to do. She folded the letter and put it away. She wanted to fling it out the window, but she realized that it would do no good, for having read his words she would carry them with her.

She would wonder at and worry about them, but not enough to turn back to him before she had done what she had set out to do. Before she had simply been running away. Now she felt that she was running toward something.

Washington was much changed. She and Mardella walked to the Willard. As they approached the hotel, she was reminded of a cold November night thirteen years before, the night she met Seth, the night she fell in love.

They had arrived at the Willard in a hired rig, bundled in cloaks against the bitter cold. She noticed that Honora's hands shook. She knew that it was from nervousness and not the weather. Her mother was calm and beautiful in black. She paid the driver and they went inside. She had never seen anything so beautiful as the large room, the lights, the orchestra, the crowd of people dancing and talking and laughing together. Everyone and everything seemed elegant and grand to her. She was completely dazzled, happy and excited beyond anything she had ever felt before.

Her mother settled on a couch not far from the dancing. Honora stood on one side of her. She was on the other, waiting. She watched the dancers, mesmerized by the swirling skirts, blue and green, red and white, lavender and yellow, mixing and turning, faster and faster and faster. She watched all the bare white shoulders and arms and breasts, the flushed faces, the big bronzed hands with hair upon the backs coming from blue sleeves with gold braid at the shoulder, the mustaches, blond and brown and black, the smiles both bold and timid, but the hands most of all, the big hands holding the small waists firmly, and the little hands, soft and white, resting on uniformed shoulders.

She watched first with hope and then with increasing despair. Then he came. He bowed before her and asked her to dance. He was tall and slender, his hair auburn, his eyes bright blue with long black lashes, he wore no mustache. His mouth was wide, and when he smiled he showed big strong white teeth. He held out his hand to her. They were large and brown with squared-off fingers. She took his hand. He put his other at her waist. They waited for a moment to catch the right note to begin upon. And then they began. He swept her out onto the floor, and they danced. She focused on one white candle standing in a silver holder upon a table in a corner. She did not take her eyes from it. Spinning round and round, her feet barely touching the floor, twirling in a maze of dizzy movement, the only stationary objects were his shoulder and his hand and the lone white candle across the room. It seemed that it would go on forever, but then the music stopped. They stood for a moment longer than the dance allowed in an embrace before walking off the floor and out onto the balcony.

"Will it be too cold out here for you?"

"No, I don't feel it at all."

"It's very cold."

"Is it? I don't feel it."

"What is your name?"

"Annie Surratt."

"Mine is Seth Kierney."

"Lieutenant?" She touched his epaulet.

"Yes. You are a wonderful dancer, Miss Surratt."

"You're most kind to say so, but I know it isn't true. I haven't danced very much, you see. I'm newly arrived here in Washington from the country."

"Where in the country?"

"Maryland. Where are you from, Lieutenant?"

"Illinois."

"How long have you been in the Army?"

"Only a year. I was in school in the East till then."

"What school?

"Harvard."

"Oh. Surely you could have obtained a substitute, Lieutenant Kierney."

"I suppose I could have, Miss Surratt, but I find the idea immoral and cowardly, paying another man to face danger for you. I wanted to serve my country."

"That's very brave and patriotic of you."

"Not really. Actually, I was tired to death of school and the Army sounded like a lark."

"A lark? I cannot imagine war being fun."

"Nor can I now, but at the time I thought it would be."

"I suppose that all gentlemen think that the Army and war are going to be like the games they played as children."

"Yes, just like ladies believe that marriage and a family are going to be like the games they played."

"Are you suggesting, Lieutenant, that marriage is as dangerous and disappointing as war?"

"Yes."

"What a very strange way of thinking."

"I suppose it is. May I ask you something?"

"Yes."

"May I call you Annie and will you call me Seth?"

"That's two things."

"May I call you Annie?"

"Don't you think it's rather soon . . ."

"Don't you think that's rather a stupid convention?"

"There are good reasons for conventions."

"Give me one good reason why we shouldn't call one another by our first names."

"We don't know one another."

"How will we ever get to know one another if we follow all the stupid conventions? That isn't a good reason, Annie."

"Goodness are you one of those radical-thinking young men who want to crush all of society's pretense?"

"Yes, I suppose I am. I think it's the war, seeing men die. Suddenly, all the little silly rules that were once so important have no place anymore. I want to call you Annie."

"You are already doing that."

"I want you to want me to."

"You ask a great deal, Seth."

"You're a wonderful girl."

"I really must go back in now."

"Are you feeling the cold?"

"No, but they'll be wondering about me. Where I am."

"They?"

"My mother and Honora."

"Is Honora your sister?"

"No, she's our boarder. My mother runs a boardinghouse."

"Will they be very concerned about you?"

"Yes, I'm sure they will be."

"Then, Annie, we must go inside, but I don't want to. Before we go in I would like to shatter one more fraudulent canon."

"I don't think I understand."

"I mean that I want to kiss you."

"Well, you cannot. What sort of girl do you think I am? Do you think that the poor little boardinghouse keeper's daughter is going to be swept off her feet by the Harvard lieutenant, forget herself completely?"

"That is one of the most ridiculous things I think I've ever heard."

"I should never have let you call me Annie. You think you can take all sorts of liberties. You see what the flaunting of convention leads to?"

"Anarchy, and kissing on the balcony."

"Very amusing. I'm going in now, Lieutenant."

He took hold of her arm. "Wait. Please don't be angry with me. I do think you're such a wonderful girl, Annie. Your mother's boardinghouse has nothing to do with my wanting to kiss you. You are just too beautiful to let go unkissed."

He took her face in his hands and touched his lips to hers. They stood looking at one another, their breath coming fast in gray misty clouds that melted quickly into the cold night air . . .

She and Mardella walked up the stairs to the door of the Willard. It did not seem to have changed a great deal. The lobby was much the same as she remembered it.

"Wait here," she said to Mardella. "I want to go into that room over there for a moment."

She walked over and opened the door. The hall was empty and

bare. It was, as her mother had described it, a very ugly room. She tried to conjure the beauty, the enchantment, that she had so long remembered, but she failed. It was only a big bleak and drafty hall. A hotel employee came up behind her.

"Is there something you are looking for, ma'm?"

"Yes. Yes, I was looking for something."

"Perhaps I could be of assistance?"

"I don't think so. This is the room where the hops were held during the war?"

"I believe so, ma'm. I wasn't here then."

She looked at his young face. "Of course you weren't. This is the room, but it's not as I remembered it."

"Things change, ma'm."

"Yes. I'll be checking in for a short stay. My maid is waiting in the lobby. You could go and help her with the luggage, if you would, please."

"Yes, ma'm." He turned and started out. She was still standing looking for the table in the corner with the white candle upon it. "Are you coming, ma'm?"

"In a moment."

She walked over to the door which led out onto the balcony. She turned the knob. It was locked.

"We keep that door locked, ma'm. It leads out onto a balcony."

"Yes, I know that. Why is the door locked?"

"It's been locked since the unfortunate incident."

"What unfortunate incident?"

"A lady jumped from the balcony about two months ago."

"From this balcony?"

"Yes, ma'm."

"Did she, I mean, was she killed?"

"No, ma'm. It's not much of a fall. They took her away to the madhouse."

"Not to a hospital?"

"She wasn't hurt, just crazy, ma'm."

"But why did she do it?"

"I'm sure I don't know, ma'm."

"Is she still in the asylum?"

"I don't know, ma'm."

"Were you sent in here to watch me because I looked like I might try to jump too?"

"No, ma'm. I just happened by."

"I see. Will you go now and attend to my luggage, please?"

"Yes, ma'm."

He stood holding the door open for her to precede him.

"Do I really so much resemble a madwoman that the management will not allow me to be alone in this room?"

"No, ma'm. I just thought . . ."

"It's perfectly obvious what you thought."

She walked from the room. She was angry. She would have liked to have stayed a few moments longer, remembering Seth. Perhaps the management was right about her. It could be that had she stayed any longer she would have forced the lock and jumped from the balcony just as that other poor wretched woman had done. Anything was possible. The boy's words about a madhouse had make her skin prickle. She thought of her husband's letter and the threat it held. She knew that that was what he was menacing her with, a madhouse. She recalled his words, "wayward wives and demented women." He intended to put her in an asylum unless she behaved herself. The idea of it terrified her. Yet she wondered if she couldn't perhaps find there women just like herself, perfectly sane, deviant only so far as obedience to men and husbands was concerned. Perhaps she could even find the woman who had jumped from the balcony. She could ask her why she did it, ask her name. No one else seemed to have asked those things of her. No one even cared.

XIX

She and Mardella were installed in a second-floor suite. It was large and comfortable. She loosened her stays and lay down upon the bed to rest. She wanted some medicine very badly. Her nerves felt raw and exposed. Finally she got up and went into the small parlor where Mardella was sitting and mending.

"Mardella, did you keep my medicine as you said you would?"

"Yes, Miss Annie."

"I am ill. I need some."

"Is you really sick?"

"My head aches fit to burst."

"I gits a cool wet rag fer your head."

"I don't want that."

"It makes you feel better."

"No, it won't. A wet rag won't give me any sleep."

"So it ain't your head achin'. You wants some sleep?"

"My head aches and I need rest."

"Why don't you lay down fer a while longer. Sleep, it'll come, Miss Annie."

"It won't. I've tried. All I do is toss and turn. I need my medicine. Please, bring me the bottle."

"No, Miss Annie."

"What do you mean, no? It's mine. I want it. Give it to me."

"You don't needs it."

"How do you know what I do and do not need? Who are you to tell me?"

"Now, Miss Annie, don't be upsettin' yerself."

"Give me my medicine."

"No."

"Damn your soul. Give it to me."

"No."

"You get out of here. You get yourself on the nigger car and go home. I don't want you here with me."

"I's stayin'."

"If you're going to stay, then you're going to give me my medicine."

"No."

"I'll find it myself then."

The trunk sat open on the floor. She fell down beside it and began to throw things out, digging toward the bottom. Mardella watched as she emptied the trunk. Clothes were scattered everywhere. She ran her hands along the floor of the trunk.

"Where is it?"

"Where you cain't git at it."

"Damn you."

"You be damnin' me all dat you like, but 'long as I breathe you ain't gonna curse yerself wid no more of dat stuff. I seed a gal die of dat stuff."

"Die?"

"Die of it. It were in dat fancy house in Baltimore. Dey found her in her bed one mornin'. She done swallowed three bottles of it an' she done never wake up agin."

"I don't believe it. It can't kill a person. It can't possibly. It's medicine, a tonic. It doesn't kill. It heals."

"It don't an' you knows it don't. It jus' fuzzes up de edges. I tells you it kills. I done seed it wid my very own eyes. It killed dat gal as sure as a gun."

"Mardella, what am I going to do?"

"You gonna go lay down an' I's gonna go gits you a nice cold rag fer yer head. You gonna close yer eyes an' you gonna sleep."

"I can't."

"Why don't you reads fer a while, Miss Annie. Reads 'bout yer ma an' fergits yerself."

"I'll try, but usually reading only makes my head ache worse. Couldn't I just have a drop or two. That wouldn't hurt me, just a drop or two."

"It don't stop at de drop or two an' you knows it. How much was you takin' in one day las' week?"

"I don't know."

"But you does know you was takin' more an' more all de time."

"Not anything near three bottles, never in one day."

"You is on yer way to it, jus' one drop at a time."

"I don't know that I can bear it, Della. Please give me just one drop. I'll ease away from it. I can't just stop like this. It's not just my head now. My stomach is beginning to cramp. Please, Della."

"No, Miss Annie."

"For God's sake, please."

"You go on a callin' de devil an' damnin' me. You call God too. But I ain't gonna do it. I cain gives you de whole bottle right dese minute, but if I do dat I is walkin' out dat door an' I ain't never comin' back. I takes de nigger car, but I won't be takin' it home. You won't never see no more of me. I gives it to you right now. You cain swallow it all down an' then you cain die alone in dese room. You cain lay fer days till strangers comes in an' finds you. What you say to dat?"

"I think I'm dying anyway."

"No you ain't 'cause I ain't gonna let you."

"I'll try to read for a while."

She went into the bedroom and took the book from her pocket.

She sat down in the chair by the window and looked down to the balcony below, the balcony where she and Seth had begun to love one another and a nameless woman had tried to end her life. She opened the book and blessed the thirteen years that had yellowed the pages and faded the ink. Deep black on glaring white would have started the blinding pain behind her eyes which she had so often experienced. Now she had no blue blottle to ease it. She began to read.

Friday, March 10, 1865

I found Annie sitting alone in the parlor today. Little Beauregarde, the kitten, was curled in her lap. She was not reading or sewing, but merely staring out the window into the street. I sat down in a chair opposite her, hoping to speak about Seth Kierney. We have been avoiding all mention of him these days. We are careful to be polite to one another and nothing more.

"That kitten will soon be a cat," I said. "Look how big he has gotten."

She looked at me and stroked the cat's ears. "Yes, he's grown a great deal."

"It is very difficult to accept growth sometimes, Annie. What I mean to say is that it is difficult to let go."

"Is it, Mother?"

"Yes."

Then she picked up Beauregarde and tossed him to the ground, poor thing. He landed on his feet, meowed in protest, swished his tail, and departed. "It's done easily enough if you want to."

"It's the wanting that comes hard."

"Beauregarde can't spend his life in my lap, much as I might want him to. I like to rub his ears, feel his soft fur, but don't you think it would be rather selfish of me to wish that he would always be a kitten?"

"I suppose that it would."

"Even if I tried to keep him here with me, to hold him, he'd run away one day."

"Annie, I feel such coldness from you lately."

"I really don't wish to discuss it. We'll only disagree."

"But it's not right that there should be such distance between us."

"I think, Mother, that we are very different people. We don't seem to see things the same way. I don't understand you at all."

"And you're willing to leave it like that?"

"Yes. I see no other way."

"Like some sort of armed truce? That's a very bitter thing for a mother and daughter. You want to sit across the table or the parlor from me, politely silent, with your battery of opinions and words poised ready to strike, and mine the same way?"

"At least it's a kind of peace. I won't be here much longer anyway, Mother."

"You and that Seth Kierney . . ."

"Yes."

"You can't wait for him to come and take you away?"

"I can't wait."

"Take you away from me. Why is it that everyone I love wants desperately to be free of me?"

The cat returned then and jumped back into Annie's lap. She began again to rub his ears. "Good little kitty. You've come back. You see, Mother, I turned him loose. I didn't try to hold him. I didn't chase after him, grasping and grabbing at him. And he came back to me, freely, willingly. He wanted to come back."

"But suppose he hadn't?"

"He did."

She turned from me then and resumed her contemplation of the street. I suppose that she is waiting already for Seth. I have lost her. I have lost again.

Do I hold too fast? Grasp and grab? Chase away what I want most and love best? Annie is right. I do. But why? If I knew, then I could finally understand why sadness pursues me, why I seek sadness out.

Saturday, March 18, 1865

I summoned all my courage. I even drank a small amount of tonic to steady and warm my cold quaking stomach. And I went to Ford's Theater this evening. I received the most peculiar looks, a lady alone at night is an unusual sight, but I would have braved far more than quizzical looks tonight.

The play was "The Apostate." It starred John Wilkes Booth in the role of Pescara. It was all so unreal and strange. To see Wilkes upon the stage, dark and handsome, but leaping about and making speeches so unlike him. To watch him as merely one in a great crowd of people, to see him look out into the darkness and see not me but merely an audience, it was strange and yet fascinating. He inspires such adoration. It is almost frightening.

During the intermission I stayed in my seat and listened to what was being said about him. I heard a young man seated in front of me tell another young man that Booth was nearly fatally stabbed by a hysterical female in Chicago. There was bright envy in the young man's eye and voice. His friend said that Booth was nothing but an acrobat, that he had ruined his voice, and would never be the actor his father had been or his brother Edwin was becoming. He'll only be famous as long as he is young and handsome, when his looks are gone he will be finished, the young man said. Then they quieted for the remainder of the performance. I thought perhaps that they might be right about Wilkes, perhaps when all was over for him then I could have him. I would take him then, old and embittered, any way at all. I would serve and love him, give him the adoration and applause of a thousand audiences.

It hurts me to think that he has been back in the city and has not contacted me, but he must have his reasons. It was wonderful to see his face again, but from so far away, so very far. It is painful too, to realize that life goes on for him, happily, fruitfully, while my life without him has been barren and dark. There has not even been hope. He not only dominates my dreams, but my every waking thought is of him too. He brought an excitement, a beauty to my life. And what of the poor creature in Chicago, so obsessed by him that she tried to put a blade into him rather than lose him, what of her? How many others are there like her? And like me?

He performed with such grace. He gave light and beauty to the people ranged out beneath him in the darkness. We ceased to think of the price of coal, the length of the winter and the war, the death of loved ones, illness, hunger, or an aching tooth. We lived through him, through his words and his actions, for a few short hours. And all was beautiful and clear and right because he told us that it was. I felt that the audience would take and take from him–feed off his beauty until it was all used up, all the beauty and the life and the shine of him–and then he would be mine, mine alone.

When the spell was broken and he left the stage, the audience was no longer unified by him into a single feeling body. They disintegrated into a lot of cold and miserable individuals. Out in the street again, I was the coldest and most miserable of them all. I want him so very much.

Monday, March 20, 1865

After all the waiting and dreaming, he has appeared again. He came knocking at the door this morning as if no time at all had passed since our day in Maryland when he said so much, or that terrible last night when he uttered not a word to me. Even Cookie had stopped expecting him, she did not go to the door. I opened it and found him standing there, smiling in the sunlight. He was so smooth and charming, and oh, so endearing. I wanted to cry out to him, why have you done this to me? Why did you leave me? Make me suffer so? Why did I have to go to a theater to see you? Why was I forced to be a mere part of the throng, while my heart ached for you? But, of course, I asked none of these things of him. He had no idea, not the slightest intimation, of what had happened to me.

And so he has returned. I ask nothing of him. There can be no accusations. It is impossible. He has come back to me, and that is enough. That is everything.

He seemed very excited this morning. He paced the parlor. He stopped by the fireplace for a moment, flung his arm across the marble mantel, then ran a long white hand through his black hair. How is it possible to love someone completely and know them not at all? I have no idea what he thinks or feels. He neither asks questions nor answers them. He is able to walk back into this parlor and my life without a word. He paced again making a cryptic remark about fulfilling his destiny today. I asked him if he meant a new role in a new play. That seemed a safe enough question, one that he would surely answer. He came over and sat beside me on the sofa, tracing the lace pattern of the doily on its arm.

It seemed that he would never speak, but just to have him beside me, to see him, that was really quite enough. He looked up finally after what seemed an eternity and told me that the stage was not his destiny. Words, even his, are cheap and vulgar. I wanted him to speak to me with his eyes, but again he spoke words. He asked about John. I told him that I had heard nothing from him, that I had not seen him since that night in January. My voice faltered. I said for the first time in words what I have thought and feared for so long. I said that I was afraid that John had joined the Confederate Army.

Then I remembered John's last words about Wilkes and I was frightened for a moment that I had confided in him. He seemed to read my face or my thoughts. He raised his hand, and I know that I flinched as if in anticipation of a blow. He brushed my cheek lightly and said goodbye. And it was true, I had been struck. He was gone again. If he had knocked me to the ground, he could not have wounded me more than by his going.

"How is you feelin', Miss Annie?"

She looked up from the book. "I'm all right, Mardella."

"Is you gittin' hungry?"

"No."

"You gotta eat, Miss Annie."

"I just don't think I could face any food."

"Jus' as you say."

She started from the room.

"Wait, Mardella. What time is it?"

"It nearly six. Why don't you let me go an' see if dey won't bring up a nice tray fer you?"

"I don't want a nice tray. I'm not an invalid." She looked out at the balcony. "I'm not dead, you know. If I felt hungry I would go down to the dining room."

"Why don't you?"

"I think I will. I'm sick to death of this room. It is really very ugly. I thought that the Willard was a first-class hotel. If this is the best that Washington can offer, then I am sorely disappointed. Mardella, bring me my lavender silk. I think that that is suitable for a lady dining alone."

"Mebbee you starts out alone, but mebbee you don't end up dat way."

"Della, what are you suggesting?" She smiled.

Mardella went out to get the dress and Annie's smile faded. She pressed her fingers to her temples and thought of her mother going to the theater, alone and sad. Well, she would be alone tonight but no one would think her sad. She would glide into that dining room, her lavender silk trailing. She would smile. She would eat oysters. They would speak of her grace, her beauty, her elegance. They would never know that her stomach was tied in knots, that the blood was pounding at her temples, that her hands were like ice, that she could barely hold a knife or fork for their trembling. She would sustain through the goose liver pâté to the coffee in the thin blue china demitasse. She would do it for her mother. They would all say the lovely things about her that they never said about her mother when she went in search of him at the National Hotel and Ford's Theater. She would not be pitiful, timid, awkward, or afraid tonight. She would be exquisite, charming and cultivated.

Mardella came in with her dress. Annie looked at it as if it were a suit of armor. Tonight she must be victorious. Victory would be control, of them and herself.

"I thinks you is feelin' better."

"I'm just trying harder, Della. I'm getting ready for tomorrow."

"What tomorrow?"

"I'm going to see the Colonel. First I have to locate him. I have no address. I only know that he lives somewhere here in the city."

"You gonna find him, I knows it."

"Yes, I'll find him, but will he see me? I said some very terrible things to him."

"He see you."

"You think so?"

"I knows it."

"Mardella, will you lend me some of your confidence and assurance? I am in desperate need."

"If I could gives dem things to you, you knows I would, Miss Annie."

"I know that."

"I gives you anythin' I got."

"You are my good and true friend. I'm very sorry I said the things I did this afternoon. I apologize. I didn't mean them."

"I don't hear dem things, 'cause I knows it ain't you talkin'."

"Oh, but Della, who was it talking?"

"Dat I cain't tell you."

Her charade in the dining room was a triumph. She was all the things she had vowed to herself she would be. Then she went up to her room, vomited her dinner, and did not sleep all night long.

XX

The next morning it was far easier than she had expected. The desk clerk on duty was an older man. She decided to ask him if he knew Colonel Wood. He not only remembered him from the old days but he knew where he was now living. He directed her to a boardinghouse not far from the National.

She checked the address twice before going up the stairs of the big old house. She started to knock on the door but stopped and turned as she heard someone greet her from the corner of the porch.

"Hello, Miss Annie."

"Colonel. Good morning."

"You've come to see me?"

She approached him. He drew his blanket closer as if to protect himself from her.

"Yes. May I sit down?"

"Please do. Forgive me for not standing. I've been having some trouble lately." He motioned to his leg outstretched on a low hassock.

"I'm sorry to hear that."

"I can't believe that you've come to see me."

"Colonel, I came to apologize."

"To me?"

"Yes, to you. I said dreadful things, untrue and unfair things to you. I know that now and can only plead ignorance and sorrow. Those were the reasons for my behavior. I am very very sorry."

"You've read the diary then?"

"I'm reading it still. I dread the end. I find I can only bear small bits of it at a time, that's why my progress has been so slow."

"I'm glad that you're reading it. I'm glad that you have come to see me. Though an apology wasn't necessary."

"Yes, it was. It was imperative. I'm not here only to apologize. I want to thank you for saving the book, and I have something further to ask of you."

"What is that?"

"I would like you to tell me exactly how you remember my mother, her words, her actions, everything."

"You've come then for my memories of her too?"

"Yes. I'm working a kind of puzzle, fitting together the pieces of my mother. But I don't want to take your memories from you, I would like only for you to share them with me. Will you, Colonel?"

"She was very ill and very frightened when I knew her. She was dying. She knew it before any of us did. She was only a shadow then of what she must have been. I remember the night I came to her at the Old Capitol. I wanted to tell her of her pending transfer to the Arsenal. There was nothing I could do. She was to be taken at midnight. Her eyes grew large and she began to tremble when I told her. She said to me that she knew she would never leave the Arsenal alive."

"And she didn't."

"She did not. No one thought that it could happen. None of us believed that she would ever be executed. There were horsemen posted at every corner from the White House to the Arsenal on the day of the execution, men ready to ride with word of a Presidential reprieve."

"But there was none."

"The hangman . . ." He began to cough, a deep racking cough.

"Is there anything I can do, Colonel? Are you all right?"

He took the handkerchief carefully from his mouth trying to hide the blood.

"It's nothing."

"What of the hangman?"

"It's not a fit story for your ears."

"I want to hear it. I want to know all of it, everything."

"You've changed much in a very short time. A month ago you wanted to know nothing, now you want to know everything. It has been my experience that people don't change that fast. Are you very sure?"

"It's not that I've changed, Colonel. I know that I must appear to have altered a great deal, but it isn't that. I've come back to myself. I was in hiding for thirteen years. In the last month I've emerged, not changed. Now tell me of the hangman, Colonel."

"The hangman never thought that he would use your mother's noose. He tied but one knot in it. As the time grew near and there was no word from the White House, the hangman was ordered to proceed. I can hear him still. The woman too, he asked? Yes, the woman too. But, he complained, I've only tied one knot in her noose. She's a very small woman, it'll hold her, they answered him."

He began to cough again.

"Colonel, I know that this may sound rather blunt and hard, but you told me that you were dying . . ."

"Yes, but I decided not to."

"I don't understand."

"I've decided not to die, not for a while yet anyway. I decided that once before in my life. I was very young then and very near to death, but said no to it. I'm older now and weaker, but I can still say no. I'm not yet ready to die."

"My mother said yes to death. Why did she? Do you know?"

"It was hardly her choice."

"I didn't mean that it was. I know that Secretary Stanton and the others would have settled for nothing less than her death. It seems now inevitable and unavoidable, but it also seems to me sometimes that she wanted it too, sought it even."

"She wanted relief."

"Yes, the cessation of pain. I know that feeling."

"The last day she was nearly insensible with the hurt and the fear. If the reprieve had come, she would have died very soon anyway, I think. There had been too much, too much to be borne."

He put the handkerchief to his white lips and brought it away stained red.

"I don't want to tire you, Colonel."

"I must be more careful these days. Perhaps you could come again tomorrow. We could talk some more then."

"I would like that very much, if you're sure you want me."

"Yes, it does me good to see you back among the living, even though you are still pale as a ghost."

"Am I pale, pale as all that?"

"In the sunlight it shows."

"I've not been out much."

"Lately?"

"I've not been out in the last thirteen years."

"Waste, terrible waste."

"I may come again then?"

"I will look forward to it."

"Tomorrow?"

"Tomorrow."

"Good day, Colonel."

"Good day, Miss Annie."

She left the porch reluctantly, the warmth and the sun and the old sick man who had decided not to die. She wanted to be very careful where she chose to walk. She wished to avoid H Street for today anyway. But the city had changed and she found herself suddenly close to the old narrow brick building where she had lived. And then she was standing before it. It did not seem as if she had walked there. Some force outside of her had guided her steps toward the boardinghouse. It had not changed, except that the present tenant was not the housekeeper her mother had been. The windows did not shine and the stair needed sweeping. She thought of Mardella and remembered the old thin black woman and the silent big-eyed child who came with her. She could almost see them, just as they had been so long ago, Mardella's mother and child, dead now. Her mother was dead too. She thought of her child, the child she was becoming sure that she carried within her, the child conceived that dreadful angry last night at home. It had been only days, it was much too soon to know, but she had the strangest feeling that a child was growing inside of her. She was not sure if she wanted that life or if she should try in some way to extinguish it. She had thought that she would never have children. She knew how much she would have loved a child, and she was not sure that she wanted to love anything that much. Love to her meant pain and loss, but standing before her mother's house with this new and strong feeling within her, she felt perhaps she could brave love. Her eyes were tearing so in the bright sunlight that she could barely see to walk.

Back at the hotel the room was empty. She did not know where Mardella had gone. She thought perhaps that she too might have been directed against her will to her own place of ghosts. Perhaps the village of shacks near the White House. But surely freedom for Negroes was a common thing by now, and those shanty cities peopled by lost transients somewhere between freedom and slavery were a thing of the past. Then she thought of the "nigger car" on the train and wondered how many other horrible distortions had been made of freedom.

She opened the curtains and walked over to a tall mirror in the corner of the room. The Colonel was right. She was pale. Her skin looked transparent when the sun shined upon it. She was glad the show she had performed last night in the dining room had been in candlelight. She was not sure she could play her part again this evening. She wanted the medicine more, not less, as time passed. She wondered if Mardella had hidden the bottle somewhere in the room. She began leisurely picking up sofa cushions and pulling out drawers. Her search quickly became more frenzied. She stood in the center of the room, breathing fast. Mardella must have taken it with her. Where was she anyway? Why had she been gone so long? She began to pace, looking in the same drawers again and again, then leaving them standing open. She took the pillows into her hands and threw them against the walls. She sank to the floor and put her face in her hands. Where had Mardella gone? Where was her medicine? She had started crawling about the room looking under furniture when the door opened.

"What is you doin' down dere, Miss Annie?"

She looked up. "Where have you been?"

"I was out."

"I needed you. I need some medicine. Where have you hidden it?"

"Git up off de floor, Miss Annie."

"Answer me. Where is it?"

"It ain't down on de floor."

She stood. "Where then?"

"Did you find de Colonel?"

"Yes."

"You didn't stay long."

"He's not well. I'm going back tomorrow. I'm not well either. I got so dizzy walking, I very nearly fainted in the street."

"You ain't usta walkin' an' de sun is real strong today."

"It has nothing to do with that. Dizziness is part of my illness. I need some medicine."

"What de name of yer malady?"

"It has no name."

"Didn't de doctor never gives you no name fer it?"

"I've never been to a doctor about it."

"Den it ain't much of a malady, I should say."

"Are you a doctor?"

"I 'spects I is one of sorts. I knows when somebody is sick."

"I am sick."

"You is makin' yerself dat way."

"Della, please."

"You knows it ain't no good fer you."

"I know."

"You knows you don't face up to things proper when you takes it."

"Yes, I know all of that. Mardella, I could walk into any number of stores in this city and buy as many bottles as I want."

"Some folks dey don't mind sellin' poison to other folks. Well, you goes ahead. You does jus dat. Go buy some of dat stuff, but least ways I ain't givin' it to you. You does dat, you starts in lyin' to yerself all over again. You does dat, you starts killin' yerself again. Go on! Go right now!"

"I don't want to go, Mardella. I don't want the medicine. I just need it so. Please help me."

"It'll pass, Miss Annie. De needin' it dat's bound to stop. It have to."

"Does it? I wonder." She wiped beads of perspiration from her brow. "I feel so sick, Mardella, but I have to go to the dining room again tonight. I must. I don't know if I can do it without some medicine."

"Why you gotta go down dere agin?"

"I promised I would."

"Who you promise sech a thin'?"

"Myself, and my mother."

"You done made another promise, you says you ain't gonna take no more of dat stuff. Dat more important."

"You've thrown it away, haven't you?"

"No. I gots it still."

"Then for God's sake, and mine, and my mother's, give it to me."

"You went down to dat dere dinin' room las' night an' you didn't have none of it."

"It's worse tonight." She wiped her brow again. "It's getting worse, Mardella, not better."

"It git better, I promise."

"How do you know that? How could you possibly know?"

"Dat gal I tells you 'bout, I watched over her once when she tried to stop takin' it."

"But she didn't stop."

"She did dat time. Den she start up agin."

"And then she died."

"Dat's right."

"Give me just a drop, Mardella."

"No. You goes an' buys yerself some 'cause Mardella she ain't gonna gives you none."

"You told me if it got very bad you'd give me some."

"It ain't bad yet."

"What do you mean?"

"When you starts in to shakin' so hard you cain't stands up, when you curls up a ball an' you thinks sure you bound to die, den after dat, den you gits better."

"How long? How long does it take?"

"Ain't no way of knowin'."

She wiped her brow again. "It's so hot in this room."

"Yes, Miss Annie."

"I can't go down there tonight."

"You wants me to git a tray fer you?"

"No. I can't eat. I can't do anything."

"Come lay yerself down."

"That bed has lumps in it."

"No, it don't."

"It does, I tell you, it does."

"I makes it up fresh fer you. I makes it all smooth."

"Please, Della, just give me a little and I'll go to sleep. I'm afraid. I don't want to shake and roll up in a ball and feel like I'm going to die. I'm afraid."

"I cain't gives you none, Miss Annie. I jus' cain't. Come lay down. I fix de bed all up fer you."

"Yes, all right. Hold me up, Della. My legs feel so weak."

They walked into the bedroom. Mardella began to remove the spread and the sheets. Annie turned her back, rubbing her hands on her arms, and looked out the window. Tears were streaming down her face.

"My arms ache. They ache. And my legs too. My legs ache too."

"Sit down in de chair dere."

She sat down. "Is it cold in here?"

"No, Miss Annie."

"Yes, it is. What's wrong with this place? How can it be so hot in one room and so cold in another?" She wiped her brow with a shaking hand. "My arms ache."

"Yes, Miss Annie. I knows dat dey does."

"Please, Della. I need some. I'm so sick."

"It de medicine dat makin' you sick."

"No, it'll make me better."

"Come on, Miss Annie. De bed all made fer you, all smooth. Come an' lay yerself down."

She went over and sat down on the bed.

"Put yer feets up, Miss Annie."

"They're twitching. I can't stop them. Why are they doing that? Make them stop. I don't like it. Make them stop."

"I cain't. Dey'll stop by demselves. Now lay yerself down. I's gonna git you a cool rag fer yer head."

"It's so cold. Im freezing."

"Cover up den. Climb under de blankets."

She did this. She rolled from side to side. "I hurt. I hurt. I hurt. My legs are twitching all over. I hurt." She threw off the covers. "It's hot. I'm smothering. It's so hot."

Mardella brought a cool cloth. She bathed her forehead with it. Annie took it from her and held it to her throat.

"How does you feel?"

"Hot. These sheets are hot like fire. I'm burning. I'm burning. Don't touch me. I'm burning."

"It gonna be all right, Miss Annie. It gonna be all right."

She clutched her stomach. "My baby. My poor baby. Are you burning too?"

"What is you talkin' 'bout, Miss Annie?"

"My baby. My baby."

"You ain't got no baby, honey."

"I do. I do. I know I do. Is she going to die, my little baby? Am I going to die?"

"Miss Annie, you tells me true, is you gonna have a baby?"

"Yes. Yes."

"You knows fer sure?"

"Cold. Cold. I'm so cold." The flesh on her arms was covered in gooseflesh. She began to beat her fists upon her stomach. Mardella took them and held them, rubbing them gently.

"Miss Annie?"

She turned from side to side. Her eyes were wide open and staring vacantly. "My baby. My baby. We're so cold, my little baby and me. We're so cold. Like ice, like ice."

"Miss Annie?"

She turned and faced her. Her eyes focused. "Yes, Mardella. What is it?"

"How you feelin'?"

"I can't explain. It's awful. I've never felt anything like this before."

"Miss Annie?"

"Yes?"

"You was sayin' somethin' a minute ago. Does you 'member it?"

"No, what did I say?"

"You was sayin' dat you was carryin' a chile. Is you?"

"I don't know. I can't think. I thought that maybe . . . I felt like . . . I don't know. Della, I'm going to be sick."

Mardella brought her a beautiful white china bowl. She hurriedly threw the flowers to the floor. Annie filled it with viscous green fluid. A few stray petals floated within it. She retched over and over until she thought that she would vomit up her stomach. Finally, she stopped.

"Take it. Take it away."

Mardella returned with a glass of water. She pushed it away.

"No."

"Try jus' a lit'l."

"I can't. It will start again."

She could not swallow. The taste in her mouth was putrid and foul. She wanted the water but she could not take it.

"How is it, Miss Annie?"

"It's worse, much worse. My stomach. Oh, my stomach. It's grinding itself up."

"Close yer eyes, Miss Annie. Close yer eyes."

Mardella rubbed Annie's forehead and temples softly. Then she took the covers and pulled them up and tucked them in. Annie began to toss and turn. She had fallen into a fitful restless sleep. Mardella sat beside her for three hours watching her lips move, her body twitch and contort itself. Then Annie woke.

"Della, are you here?"

"I is."

"Did I sleep?"

"Fer 'bout three hours."

"I don't feel as if I've slept. It's very warm."

She threw off the covers.

"You should takes dem things off, Miss Annie. You be more comfortable in yer nightclothes."

"Yes, help me, will you, Della?"

She stood and steadied herself on the tall bedpost. Mardella unbuttoned her and removed her dress.

"I go an' gits yer nightdress."

"I think I can do the rest." With shaking hands she took off her chemise and pantalets. When Mardella turned back to her from the bureau, she was standing naked before the long glass. Her thin pale body was covered in goose flesh. She smiled weakly. "Della , I look like a plucked chicken."

"Dat you does, Miss Annie."

She put the nightgown over her head. "I think I'd better lie down again. My legs are beginning to twitch. I'm cold. I've never been so cold. And then it's hot, winter and summer in a moment's time."

"Miss Annie, is dere a chance you might be gonna have a chile?"

"I don't know. It's probably just a sick fancy. I had the strangest feeling standing outside the old boardinghouse today. I thought of you and your little girl."

"You better go back to de bed."

"I'm going to be sick. Please don't bring me that same bowl. Bring me another. Oh, my stomach, my stomach."

She laid back exhausted on the bed. Suddenly she sat up and holding herself, she began to rock back and forth. Her eyes were blank. She began to chant.

"They killed my mother and now they're killing me. They killed my mother and now they're killing me. And my baby too. We'll all be dead soon. Dead and cold. They killed my mother and now they're killing me. And my baby too. Killed us dead. Dead and cold. Cold. Cold. Cold." She rocked and swayed, her fingernails digging into the flesh of her arms.

"Lay yerself down, Miss Annie. Lay down. It gonna be all right. Jus' you lay down now."

But she didn't hear Mardella. She heard nothing but her own litany of pain.

XXI

It had gone on for four days. On the fifth day she turned to Mardella and spoke in a steady voice.

"I think I would like a cup of tea. And then I would like a bath. Something in this room smells very foul and I am very much afraid that it is I."

"Tea first, Miss Annie?"

"Yes, please. Della, what day is it?"

"It Friday."

"Friday. The last day that I remember clearly was, was Monday. Yes, Monday morning. I went to see Colonel Wood. I told him that I would be back the next day. He must have waited for me. I must go and see him, tell him, explain somehow. To think that I have lost nearly a week of my life."

"Tea, right now, Miss Annie, an' den a bath. De Colonel, he come later."

She tried to stand, but swayed, and had to sit back down on the bed. "I'm so weak."

"I beg to differ wid you, Miss Annie. Mebbee you feels weak at dese moment, but you is strong. You beat dat stuff an' you gots to be strong to beat it 'cause it strong. You mebbee cain't stand 'cause yer legs is bucklin' from under you an' you is white like chalk an' jus' skin an' bones, but you is strong. Don't never let nobody try to tells you any different. I go an' gits yer tea."

She walked out of the room. Annie sat on the bed for a moment. Then she slowly got up, and step by step made her way across the room. She stood before the mirror, her nightgown wrinkled and stained, hollows deep in her cheeks, black circles beneath her eyes, her hair matter and tangled. She looked at herself, and she smiled.

"I is strong."

She drank her tea in the parlor.

"Mardella, I want to leave here as soon as possible. And I don't think that I ever want to step inside that room again." She indicated the bedroom. "I feel almost as if I had been born in that room. Can you imagine what pain and anguish it must be for a baby being born, suddenly wrenched from a dark warm safe place where every need is provided, thrust into this, this cold bright frightening world. I feel as if I had gone through it all in that room behind that door. Mercifully, we forget what it is like being born, but I shall never forget what went on in there, my rebirth." She leaned back in the chair. "Look, Della, look how steadily I can hold this cup."

"You is doin' real fine, Miss Annie."

"Miss Annie. Is it possible you can still call me that?"

"Dat who you is to me. I wouldn't feel right callin' you nothin' else. You wants more tea?"

"No, thank you. I have to get ready."

"Fer what?"

"I'm going to see the Colonel."

"You sure you is able, Miss Annie? Why don't you wait till tomorrow?"

"I have to see him today. I want to leave Washington right away."

"Where is we goin'?"

"To a farm, a little farm not far from here. It's my uncle's. My grandmother lives there with him."

"Yer gran'ma? I don't recall you ever speakin' of her."

"She's a stranger to me really. I've only seen her twice in my life."

"She yer ma's ma?"

"Yes."

"How come you don't know yer gran'ma an' she so close?"

"That's what I want to find out. There was a quarrel or something between my mother and her. There must have been. I never gave it much thought as a child, but now I must know. She is a very old woman. She must tell me before she is gone."

"She mebbee dead already."

"No, she's still alive. John told me."

"He done seed her?"

"No, but my Uncle Zadoc came to see him. She lives with Uncle Zadoc."

"You seed her but two times in all yer life?"

"Yes."

"When dat be?"

"At Papa's funeral. I was twelve then. And once before when I was very little, but I don't remember that time at all."

"At de funeral, what you 'member of her?"

"I remember thinking that she was very old. She was small but she stood so straight. When she arrived I embraced her because I thought that to be the proper thing to do. She didn't bend at all. She was stiff and hard, unyielding. I thought at the time that she didn't like me, that she didn't want me near her. And something else, she and my mother never touched, not once. I remember them standing together before my father's coffin and I heard her say something to my mother that I thought was enormously cruel."

"What dat?"

"She said to her, 'You're fated, Mary, destined to lose everything that you love.' And I suppose I have always thought of her from that day forward as a hard and cruel woman."

"She don't sound soft, nor gentle neither."

"No. And my mother was both of those things."

"So it seem."

"Della, it's nearly two o'clock. I must go and see the Colonel. I would not like to spend another night in this hotel."

He was not on the porch this time. She knocked on the door and asked for Colonel Wood. The large old woman who answered took her name and left her waiting outside while she grudgingly climbed the stairs. After several minutes he appeared.

"Shall we sit out on the porch again?"

"Yes, of course, Colonel."

"I'm afraid that Mrs. Bailey is not the soul of hospitality. I expect she is very angry with us."

"Why?"

"First of all she had to climb up the stairs to get me and second she was surprised by you. Being old she doesn't like stairs or surprises."

"I see."

"I had given you up."

"I'm sorry. I was taken ill suddenly."

"You looked ill the day you were here, and you don't look much better today."

"Thank you, Colonel."

"I'm just a blunt old man."

"Well, you look better than the last time I saw you."

"I told you, I've decided not to die."

"So you did."

They were silent for a moment.

"Colonel, there is something I would like to ask you."

"Yes?"

"Was my mother used as bait to catch my brother? If he had surrendered would she have been executed?"

"I think that your brother would have most likely replaced your mother on the scaffold, but there was a chance that they both would have died."

"Both?"

"Yes, Miss Annie. I don't think you realize how narrowly you escaped."

"I suppose that I don't."

"Secretary Stanton was a hard man."

"He was an obdurate bully."

"He wanted to hold your mother up as an example."

"I don't understand. An example of what?"

"During the war, many women acted as spies, for both the North and South. I had occasion to jail many of them at the Old Capitol, but they were almost always released. They used their femininity as a shield. The Secretary had a bitter hatred of Southern women. He wanted to show the world that being female did not afford protection. That's why I say your mother was an example. And that's why it is entirely possible that she would have been executed no matter what your brother may or may not have done. You were very lucky to escape. The Secretary wanted every vestige of your family destroyed."

"What kind of man must he have been?"

"I knew him for many years, but I don't think I ever really knew him, if you know what I mean. I met him when he was a young lawyer. I had been a big burly brawling youth. There had been an accident, a fight it was, and I had been hurt bad. I was trying to get used to it." He waved a hand at his leg on the stool. "It slowed me down, and it set me to thinking. I was fighting hard to believe that I was still a man, the man I had been or thought I was anyway. It was a blessing, but I didn't know it then. A stiff leg can seem an awful tragedy to a young man, but if it weren't for it and Edwin Stanton, I'd be dead by now. I'd have died most likely choking on my own blood on a barroom floor somewheres. I know what you're thinking, I'm choking on my own blood now as it is. Well, that's the truth but it's not because some plug-ugly beat me senseless. I'm just old, and that's part of getting old. What I'm taking so long to say is that I wouldn't be here today if it weren't for that man you hate so much or this leg I used to hate so much. Anyway, I did the lawyer Stanton's dirty work for him."

"Why would a lawyer need dirty work done?"

"Well, there was a time once during a trial a long long time ago when some needed doing. It had to do with the McCormick reaper. You remember it had a special curved blade, different from all the others. McCormick wanted a patent on it or some such thing. Stanton took the opposite side. He found an old farmer who had an old reaper. Then he told me to replace the straight blade with a rusty old-looking new curved blade. That won the case for Stanton's client. McCormick lost."

"But that, that was . . ."

"Illegal? Yes. It's called manufacturing evidence."

"Did you do that often?"

"Let's say that I was of as much assistance as I could be to the lawyer Stanton."

"I don't believe it."

"Happened all the time. Strange though the men that McCormick trial brought together. I'd never thought of it until now."

"Who? What men?"

"The lawyers. They were all a part of your life."

"My life?"

"There was a young awkward lawyer supposed to be assisting Stanton. He got snubbed early on and was mostly just a spectator. His name was Abraham Lincoln. And then there was McCormick's lawyer from Baltimore. His name was Reverdy Johnson."

"My mother's lawyer."

"That's right. They were all there. Strange."

"Are you suggesting, Colonel, that my mother died not despite the fact that she was a woman, as so many think, but because of it?"

"That's what I'm saying."

"It's grotesque. My mother was innocent of any crime. She died because she was a woman."

"It's not that simple. There were many reasons, not just that one.

The people demanded death, revenge, an eye for an eye. They loved Lincoln."

"They only loved him after he was dead. Until then he was reviled and ridiculed by most."

"Not by those who knew him."

"Very few knew him, but Lincoln is not the issue here."

"He is. His death caused your mother's. Links in a chain."

"When was the last time you saw my mother?"

"I went to her early in the morning the day of her execution. That was the last time I spoke with her. Then I was there later, in the afternoon."

"Can you tell me what she said?"

"Yes, I remember it well. When I walked in she was lying down. She tried to rise up but couldn't. She excused herself, saying she was too weak to sit up. She said that her priests were coming soon. I said that that would be a comfort to her. She told me that she no longer thought of comfort or discomfort, that she beyond grief, beyond despair. The end was inevitable and terrible. I hoped that the priests could help her, but I felt that she was beyond help too. She asked me why this was being done to her. She asked if I thought she was an evil woman, if I thought that she had sinned. She kept asking me why, why it was happening. I told her that I didn't know why.

"She turned her face from me and I thought that she was hiding tears, but she turned back to me in a moment and she was dry-eyed. I never did see her cry. She told me that I must take her book, that I was the only one who could remove it from the prison. She said that she knew they would destroy it if they ever got hold of it. She said to me, 'They want to destroy me and all traces of me. I am surprised that I am not being burned at the stake, like a witch, but I know that they would burn my book. Take it, please, and give it to Annie, my daughter. I have tried to write a letter to her, but I cannot. I hope she will read my diary some day and understand me and my fate. I cannot explain it to her in a single letter, and I am so weak. I wasted my life with her. I hope that she will find in my book all the words I wanted to say and could not.' She went on like that for several minutes. The cell was growing very hot. She kept running her hands through her hair and saying words that I could make no sense of. When the first priest arrived, I must confess I was relieved.

"As he was preparing his things, she came to herself again and begged me not to forget her book. She said that it was in her pocket. I took it and put it in my jacket, saying that it would be safe with me. 'I know that,' she said. 'Thank you, Colonel. Go now, quickly.' She said nothing more to me. At the door I turned. The priest was standing over her. She lay there so still, like an effigy on a tomb. And I thought, she is gone already. The guard opened the door for me and I left her.

"I felt that when I saw her that day, as if she had had her own private death and her soul had departed, as if that poor shattered shell only remained long enough to receive the punishment the law demanded.

"We hanged a dead woman."

There were tears in his eyes.

"They, Colonel. They did, not you. You are absolved. It's late. I must go."

"You won't be back again?"

"No."

"You're done with me then?"

"No, Colonel. I shall never be done with you. I shall think of you always, wish you well, and thank you for giving me my life. I had no life until you came and brought her book to me. God bless you, Colonel."

"You have no more questions?"

"None that you can answer."

"I hate to see you go."

"I'll stand here on the step. You go inside and close the door. Don't go to the window. Don't watch me leave. That way, I'll never really go from you. Know that, Colonel, I will never leave and be done with you. My gratitude and love will be with you always. Go inside."

He limped across the porch. She did not look at him. Hearing his tread made her remember, no longer with dread and hatred, but with a new-found feeling of contentment and completion. She heard the door close, and she walked away.

XXII

The sun was setting as she approached the Smithsonian. She had decided to leave behind her memories and her love of Seth, here in this city where they had been born. She felt that it was time to let go of things that could have been but would never be. She could wish all of her life that she had carried a child of Seth's, but it could not be. Seth was dead. She must finally let him die, and perhaps this new and strange feeling within her could miraculously become a life.

She stood before the big red building and thought of all the cold winter days they had spent walking and talking and falling in love. She remembered how Seth had described the flowers which grew in summer. Today it was summer, and there was a blanket of little white wild daisies spread out at her feet. She bent and picked one. It was brown at the edges from a full day under the hot sun. She held it in her hands and remembered.

"Annie, will you marry me as soon as the war is over?"

"Seth, I want to now, right now."

"The war can't go on much longer. I want it to be over when we begin. Do you understand?"

"Yes, I understand but I'm so afraid."

"Afraid of what?"

"That it's all too good, too wonderful, that I'm too happy."

"That's the way it should be, Annie. You deserve nothing but goodness and happiness. Do you doubt it?"

"Yes, and I don't know why. I don't want to go back to the house. I can't explain, but I feel as if something dreadful is going to happen and you're not going to be there to help me, Seth."

"Is it that Weichman character? I'd like to smash that fat coward's face in."

"No, it's my brother and his friends. They make me very nervous."

"What do they do? Do they bother you?"

"No, it's not that. Seth, are you jealous?"

"Yes, I don't want anyone else even looking at you."

He had taken her hands then and kissed them.

"Oh, Seth, I love you so."

"Your hands are like ice. We'd better go."

"Poor Honora, I'd forgotten all about her. She must be frozen through, waiting on that corner for me."

"I wish your mother liked me. We wouldn't have to do this all the time."

"I don't understand her at all."

"Well, like me or not, I'm going to be her son-in-law soon."

"Oh, yes, soon, very soon."

"Annie?"

"Yes, Seth."

He had taken her arm and they had started walking.

"Annie, my leave is up. I have to go back to the lines."

"When?"

"In a few days."

"But you'll get other leaves. You've had three since November."

"Not this time."

"Why not?"

"I'm just a lowly lieutenant, Annie. General Grant doesn't consult with me, but something is happening."

"What is it?"

"A battle, a big one, perhaps the last of the war, is about to take place."

"You mean you're not coming back again until the war is over?"

"It won't be long, I promise. I don't know how the Rebs have hung on this long. I'll be home and we'll be married before summer."

That had been in January of 1865. She had seen him once more, the day he left, at the house. They were alone in the parlor and she was crying.

"Please, Annie, don't."

"It's different this time, different from any of the other times when you've gone."

"Come here." He had taken her in his arms. He was kissing her wet cheeks. "They taste wonderful, your tears do."

"Seth, someone might come in."

"I don't care if they do. You're going to be my wife. I feel as if you were my wife already. Don't you feel that too?"

"Yes, Seth."

He was killed in April, one of the last to die in the war. One of his friends had come to the door early one evening that spring. All she could think was that the war was over and that Seth couldn't be dead. But she knew that he was dead. And she hated the friend, hated him for being the bearer of such tidings. She understood why the ancients had killed messengers of evil tidings. She wanted to kill him, this boy who was going home to Illinois, home to his sweetheart, home to be married and happy, and who on his way had stopped to tell her that Seth was dead. She did not cry. She merely watched his retreating blue back and wished for a gun in her hands so that she could shoot him dead, and then herself.

She had gone into the house and told no one. Later that night there was another knock at the door. She had answered it. There were soldiers standing there, six, maybe seven. She had thought that it was something to do with Seth. The uniform of the Union would always mean Seth to her. At first she had not understood what they were saying. In her mind she was expecting them to speak of Seth, he was all that filled her thoughts. Finally their words began to penetrate. They had come to arrest everyone in the house for their involvement in the Lincoln assassination plot. April 17, 1865, she had marked that night as the beginning of thirteen years of numbness and death . . .

It was growing dark very quickly. She turned to go, stopped, and looked once more at the big red building. She saw she still held the wilted flower in her hand and dropped it to the ground, remembering how she had felt when she had heard that the Smithsonian was burned. She had visualized it blackened and razed. It had not been damaged much after all, but now she was exorcising it from her memory, destroying and demolishing it stone by stone.

"Goodbye, Seth."

She walked away. The hot summer night was beginning to cool.

XXIII

Mardella had everything packed when she returned to the hotel.

"Mardella, I'm afraid we'll have to wait until morning to leave. I dread spending another night here, but it's much too late for the train now."

"One more night ain't gonna hurt."

"No, I suppose not."

"You gonna go down an' eat somethin'?"

"Yes, I think I will. I'm going to sit up tonight. I don't think I could sleep in that room."

"You needs sleep."

"I'm not tired really."

"I sits up wid you den."

"All right."

"Mebbee you reads some from yer ma's book?"

"Yes, that's just what I'll do. That's a wonderful idea."

She actually felt hungry. It had been so long since she had experienced hunger pangs that at first she did not recognize them.

For years food and meals had been things she had dreaded. Now she was looking forward to eating. Dinner was not a show this time. It was merely a meal. She ate lightly, but relished it. Then she walked from the dining room oblivious of the impression she was making. She did not care what the other diners were thinking. She had come for sustenance, not their good opinion. She was eager to get back to the room and begin reading. Mardella was waiting. She had had her supper and brought up a pot of tea from the hotel kitchen. They settled in comfortably for the long last night in Washington.

Saturday, March 25, 1865

Wilkes was back again yesterday. I had thought, had had the strongest premonition that he had come to tell me goodbye forever last Monday. When he rode up yesterday I thought I was dreaming. He had a young man with him, a young giant. He is staying with us now, sharing the room with Mr. Weichman. His name is Reverend Lewis Wood. He is a Baptist preacher. It seems strange that he would come to this boardinghouse. We are all Catholics here and there are many fine Baptist boardinghouses in Washington, but I suppose that Wilkes spoke highly of this place to him. He is a rather strange preacher, Baptist or otherwise. He is huge, slow-moving, and reluctant to speak out. I have become used to Wilkes' odd choice of companions. This one is like a devoted hound. He follows Wilkes with his eyes or actually lumbers after him wherever he goes.

Wilkes left him here to my care. I showed him to his room. He has left it but little in the two days he has been with us. He consumes enormous amounts of food and immediately returns to his room, to sleep, I presume. Around the young ladies he is silent and awkward. Eliza Holohan tried to tease him the first evening at supper. She took hold of his hand, preparing to tell some joke, but he pulled his hand from hers as if it had been burned. Mr. Weichman has said that he tried to engage him in conversation, but that all efforts have been met by blank stares and snores. I have found nothing in common with this strange preacher until now. It seems we both find Mr. Weichman a boring conversationalist. The

Reverend Wood is totally withdrawn except when Wilkes is about. Even then he is silent, but there is color in his cheeks and his hands move, clenching and unclenching continually. When we are alone with him, he is ominously still and his skin is an overall saddle brown color, from too much sun I expect. That in itself is most unpreacherlike.

I have a feeling that he is a young deserter whom Wilkes has befriended out of pity. He knew that this house could be trusted. And in his usual and thoughtful way does not tell us the lad's real identity for our protection from the authorities. I appreciate his concern, but he should know that Washington is filled with deserters now, and always has been. He should realize that people have more important things to do than search boardinghouses for frightened country boys who have run a picket line because they are tired of fighting and afraid of dying. I would rather have the truth of the matter. This preacher pretense is foolishness.

Sunday, March 26, 1865

Today something most terrible happened. The Reverend Wood or whoever he may be attacked little Genevieve, Dulcey's granddaughter and nearly strangled her to death . . .

Annie stopped reading and looked up at Mardella.

"Della, should I stop? I'm sorry to have blundered into it this way. I didn't know if Mother would write of it or not. I intended to tell you, but I didn't know how exactly. Your mother came to my mother and asked if Genevieve could come with her days to the house because men were bothering her where they lived. I didn't know anything about it until I read that entry in the diary, but this I did know of, and I swear I was going to tell you about it. Shall I now? Or would you rather that I just read on?"

Her face was closed. "Jus' read on."

"All right."

I was at Mass when it happened. It seems that little Genevieve was dusting the rooms upstairs. Mr. Weichman had gone and she thought that the Reverend was out also. She walked into the room and saw him sleeping. She started to back quietly from the room when he lunged at her from the bed. He grabbed her by the shoulders and accused her of thievery. She began to cry and told him that she had come only to dust as her grandmother had told her to do. He seemed to calm somewhat at this. He laid back down on the bed and told her to go ahead and dust. She tried to hurry because she was afraid of him.

Then he asked her if she would like to see something pretty. She said yes, that she liked pretty things. He brought out from under his bed a human skull filled with cigar ash. She began to scream and tried to run, but he crossed the room in one long leap and took her by the throat. Annie and Honora, who had been in their room, came running at the sound. At the sight of the girls, he dropped little Genevieve, and ran from the room and the house. The girls revived the poor child and took her down to the kitchen to her grandmother. I arrived shortly after all of this. Dulcey had the story from Genevieve and she told me. I assured her that the man would be punished. I shall never forget her sad resigned face when I said that. She did not believe me. Why should she have?

Wilkes came later that evening and told me that "the Reverend" had come to him and told him what had happened. He told me that he had taken him, poor demented fellow, to a place where he could be safe, but confined. I am sure that he meant the insane asylum here in the city, but that he had the delicacy to refrain from mentioning it. He had sworn to Wilkes that he had not intended to hurt the little girl but only to stop her screaming. Wilkes said that he was remorseful, that the fellow didn't know his own strength. It was then that I said that he could not possibly be a preacher. Wilkes looked at me sadly, and said that he was a boy in trouble, alone and afraid, obviously not right in the head, but that his father really was a Baptist preacher back home in Florida. He was, poor lad, a long long way from Florida now. Wilkes apologized profusely for bringing him into my home. I accepted his apology, of course. Wilkes said that he would collect his things from his room and that we all should forget about the fellow as quickly as possible. He is quite right. However, it may be easier said than done. I can still see Dulcey's face as she held the sleeping child in her arms, the fear, the pain, and yes, the hatred.

"Mardella, I . . ."

"Jus' read on, Miss Annie. I don't wants to talk jus' yet."

Monday, March 27, 1865

The Captain and Jebediah appeared today. After recent events their presence was doubly welcome, but even they seemed sad. The Captain told me that he thought this would be their last visit and their last surrender.

"Jeb's and my game is up, Miz Surratt. Everyone's going to be surrendering soon."

"You think the war is almost over then?"

"I do and I'm glad of it."

"I have prayed for it."

"Jeb and me, we made a nice little piece of cash. We never did consider it stealing. I always figured that stealing was taking something from another person. How is it stealing to take from a department? A Commissary Department, that ain't no living thing. Leastways that's the way Jeb and me figure it. So we're through. Jeb and me ain't greedy. We're going to make one last surrender before the war is over and then we're going to go home and enjoy the peaceable life."

I shall miss the Captain and Jebediah.

Monday, April 3, 1865

Richmond has been taken. That lovely gentle city is in flames. It is nearly over now. Washington has gone wild. Everyone is making speeches, running through the streets, delirious. Richmond is reduced to ashes. Surrender is imminent. Flags are being flown everywhere. Cheers, shouts, artillery salvos, church bells, all declare that the end is in sight.

Late this evening John came home. He did not stay long. It made me cry to look at his face. He wore a long black cloak which made him seem very tall and very pale. His eyes were red-rimmed from tears and fatigue. His hands shook. He told me quietly that he had just been through Richmond. It was horrible, desolate, he said. He stopped suddenly. I tried to think of something to say to him, but there was little comfort I could give him. I blurted out that I had been terribly afraid that he had joined the Army when he left here in January and I thanked God that he had not. He looked at me oddly. He said that he wished that he had joined the Army, had worn a uniform, had not chosen the clandestine route he had taken, but instead the open and honorable way. It was the first time he had ever spoken outright of his activities to me. I have long suspected him of being a courier of some sort for the Confederacy. He said to me that if he had chosen to be a soldier, then the end would have been simpler, more straightforward. I can still hear his words.

"I could have seen our flag hauled down and furled forever. They would have stripped my gun from me and I would have known defeat, irrevocable and bitter, but bearable. Instead, I must go on this nebulous mission, an exercise in futility, and when the end comes I will be far from here, in another country. There will be no finality for me, no clean break. I will not have my pride, my honor, my belief in the cause, amputated swiftly and mercifully, like the soldiers in the field. No, I will have all those things torn, little by little, piece by piece, from me. Though I meant to be honorable, I chose the way of dishonor, concealment, darkness, secrets, lies, and hiding. Spies are never loved or revered. They are despised and used with distaste. I will never be free of this. I wish I had died a soldier."

He stayed a little more than an hour. There are things I have thought of now which might have given him comfort, but I do not know. In the face of such bitter unhappiness, it is very difficult. I could have said that I loved him dearly, would always love him, but somehow that would have sounded as if I was saying that I loved him *still,* no matter what shameful deeds he may have done or how vile and low a person he had become. My saying that would only have confirmed his opinion of himself. Probably my silence did this anyway. It seems that I never do the right thing. I try so hard, but it is never right somehow. I did not mention to John that Wilkes had returned. I did not think that he would want to know.

I wonder if Wilkes was involved in some way in John's activities. He is an ardent patriot of the South. He has even made speeches from the stage stating his Southern sympathies, risked arrest. Wilkes is too well known, too flamboyant to be a courier or secret agent, I would think.

War, and the terrible traps it lays for young men. It is not just those who die, or lose their limbs or their eyes, who are the victims of war. It can destroy in a myriad of clever and devious ways. But surely John will survive. He has not ruined his young life. He will return home someday, vindicated and clear of conscience . . . yet, I had the strangest feeling that tonight was the last time I would ever see him. It seems I feel that way everytime I say goodbye to someone these days. It's all maudlin foolishness–my old nighttime fears. I will take some tonic and go to sleep.

Sunday, April 9, 1865

Lee has surrendered. It is over. Four years of death and destruction. I thought I had seen the wildest of demonstrations when Richmond was taken, but those do not compare with what is taking place in the city now. The people are crazed with joy. It is enough for now that it is over, but how long before the smiles fade and the shouting subsides, and the voices begin to ask calmly first and then in anger, why, why did it ever begin? And who will answer? Who will make speeches then?

Wilkes came this afternoon. He looked like a young Mephistopheles, wild and black, desperate. It is odd how after the incident with the mad "Reverend" that Wilkes is linked in my mind with that violent and deranged individual. Today, I realized that he had lost his fine balance. He was no longer the detached and controlled young man I fell in love with. He seemed capable of any violence, any deed, anything. As he paced the parlor, denouncing all those that the multitudes in the streets were cheering, I watched him with conflicting desires. I wanted to run my hands through his black hair and at the same time I wanted to walk from the room and not look upon his face again. There was danger in his presence. He made this staid, sedate, and shabby parlor an altogether different place, and this staid, sedate, and shabby woman a different being.

There was a moment when I would have gone with him anywhere, done anything. At that moment I loved him, saw only him, heard only him. But he made no offer, and the moment, and my last chance at romance and adventure, passed away together. Then I became once again a middle-aged boardinghouse keeper, too plump, graying, suffering from numerous aches and pains, and growing far too fond of the tonic that eases them. I was brought back to myself—weak, old, and foolish. But for one moment I was a heroine. I was brave and beautiful and capable of riding off with John Wilkes Booth. I was, for one moment, what I wanted all my life to be. That is more than the rest of the world can say.

My moment is gone, and I do not mourn it or wish it back. I only thank God that He gave it to me. I think General Grant must have had his when, as rumor of the surrender has it, he refused Robert E. Lee's sword. Strange that the general and I should reach our peak, know our ultimate moment, consummate our lifelong desires, on the very same day. His was victory and mine defeat. His was the possibility realized, and mine was knowing that at least there had been the possibility. I wonder, had I ridden off with Wilkes would I not have been courting my destruction. Something in his eyes tells me yes. There is something in him that is lethal, and it is that which I love.

Tuesday, April 11, 1865

Made a trip down country today. Mr. Weichman had the afternoon off, and volunteered to drive me. All the clerks in the city were released in an excited flood at noon. No one, it seems, is capable of any sort of work or serious thought. Everything is speeches, parades, and fireworks. No one sleeps past dawn–five hundred gun salutes booming overhead–and I imagine there are those who do not sleep at all. There are cold, made beds with unrumpled sheets and pillows all around the city.

I am beside myself over Annie. She is actually rude to Mr. Weichman, who does what he can to help me. I have asked her why she dislikes him so, and she will only say over and over again that he is a simpering coward, that she doubts his own mother could rely upon him for support. I protest this, saying that he regularly sends a small stipend to his poor mother. And she will look at me so peculiarly then, and frown, and say that money is not everything in life, that there are other, more important kinds of support to be offered. And it is an accusation that she is making, and we both know it. This is dangerous ground, but it seems that every time we talk of Mr. Weichman it comes round to that. Then she will smile and say that I must be having a very difficult time with money these days. She will say, "Papa didn't leave much, and your children don't help, do they? We're selfish beasts leaving it all to you." There is sincerity in her voice but the oddest look in her eyes when she says this. We have had this conversation a score of times and it is always the same. I always feel such a sense of loss and failure as she walks away from me afterward. We begin with Mr. Weichman and end with ourselves. I feel that she is saying to me that I have not given her what she needs, that I have mended her clothes, given her food and shelter, but still she is hungry and cold in this house because I have not given her love, and I will not allow her to find it on her own. I want so much to tell her that she is wrong, but I do not. She is particularly nervous and sensitive since the "Reverend."

After a trip to Maryland with Mr. Weichman, I begin to understand Annie's impatience with him. I suppose she has a lower tolerance for his foolishness, while I am old and have learned to be tolerant. His constant conversation sorely tested my patience and the trip was totally useless. I could not find Mr. Nothey. I never trusted the man. I didn't want Mr. Surratt to sell him that land. He paid half the sum at the time. That was ten years ago and the other half is yet to be paid. I need money so badly, but Mr. Nothey seemed to disappear into thin air upon my arrival in the state. Everyone I spoke with said that he had been about yesterday, but today, well, that was a different matter. So I accomplished nothing except indebting myself to Mr. Weichman. I listened to his tales of woe, his failed ambition to be a priest, his missed opportunity to teach. And it is always circumstance that has defeated Mr. Weichman, cruel circumstance and never any lack of his own.

All through Mr. Weichman's monotonous monologue I thought of Wilkes. How very different our journey in January was from this one, and how very different Wilkes has become in just a few short months. I think of our day together then–the heat, the barrenness of the land–and my love for him. Now the specter of spring brings a strange coldness to the air and to my heart. How it frightens me now to see him. And yet, I long to. Oh, how I long to.

Thursday, April 13, 1865

Tonight was the illumination of Washington. Annie put a small white candle in the window. Mr. Weichman took offense to this. He has always been a great defender of the Confederacy, in the safest possible way. Annie declared defiantly to him that she was glad the war was over, the killing would now stop, the boys would come home, and the world would be peaceful and pleasant again. I watched her as she stood in the window lighting her small white candle in celebration of peace. I too rejoice at the end of the slaughter, but my joy is not so simple and pure as Annie's. I know that peace will bring the return of her lieutenant. And beyond my own petty concerns, I know that victory makes men vindictive. The South will be made to suffer beyond defeat for her rebellion. It is not over yet.

This night seems to last forever. It is like New Year's again. I listen to the merriment in the street below me, and I wonder why it is that I never seem to share in the wild happiness of this city. I partake only of the bleak gray mud-choked streets, the leaden skies in winter, and the terrible killing heat of summer. I always thought that love brought happiness, but it has not to me. Wilkes I am afraid of these days. He has metamorphosed into something strange and desperate. And Annie. We never talk but that we disagree. Her eyes accuse me. They say to me what her words do not. She thinks that I am cold to her, that I do not love her. How can I tell her of the night she was conceived, a night much like this one, cold and damp. It was the last time that her father and I would ever be so close. From that sudden fanning of remembrance, that night perched upon the precipice of spring, a beautiful golden child was born. We both loved her dearly, cherished her as our proof–our testimony–the vindication of our sorry life together. She is close to Honora these days. They hold each other's hands and whisper in each other's ears. And I am shut out, as always.

The amount of empty tonic bottles which has accumulated in my closet is rather alarming. It doesn't seem that I use that much. But the bottles keep emptying, as if by themselves, and I need more and more. I must have sleep. I must. Everyone takes such tonics. There is nothing sinful or evil about tonics. Why then do I hide the empty bottles? Why do I always break the promises I make to myself when I swear I will take no more? I don't know why. I don't even know why I continue to ask these questions of myself. I have no answers anymore, to any of them.

Friday, April 14, 1865

Good Friday. It has been a full day. I am trying very hard not to take any tonic tonight. I rely on it far too much for sleep, and even for comfort. That is why as I write this it is acutally morning, Saturday morning.

Honora and I went to early Mass today. The streets were cold and dark as we made our way there. Annie did not accompany us. She has another cold. Inside the church the statuary and Stations of the Cross were hung in purple. I felt much at home in my black widow's veil. Usually, I feel as if I frighten people or sadden them.

My faith seemed to return to me, to flood through me. I felt a peace that I had not known in years. I felt as if I had been forgiven. There is a change coming. I am ready and willing to accept it. Now that the war is over perhaps we can go back to the country, back to the farm, and leave this dirty city.

On the way home I told Honora that I would probably be closing down the boardinghouse very soon. She seemed distressed. She said that she felt faint from the blast of bright sunlight out in the street, but I think that there were other reasons.

It was sunny as we walked back to the house, an omen of things to come. On the farm we will be happy again. I will no longer have these Washington headaches. I will throw away my tonic bottles. And Wilkes . . . Can I forget my fancies, toss them out with the bottles? Yes. I will love him only as a son. Love can be channeled in many ways if one has the strength to do it.

I have received along with the letter from John another letter, a most troublesome one. It was from Mr. Calvert. I owe him money which I cannot pay until Mr. Nothey pays me. Mr. Calvert wrote that Mr. Nothey told him that he has tried to settle accounts with me on several occasions. This is untrue, as Mr. Nothey has done nothing but avoid me. I found it necessary to go again to Maryland in an attempt to unravel this terrible tangle. Mr. Weichman again offered to drive me. I fear he feels he has found a sympathetic ear. It is a curse when one is chosen by such a tenacious talker as Mr. Weichman. But it was a most kind offer, which I was obliged to accept. This time I insisted upon paying for the rig. Just before we left—Mr. Weichman was waiting in the carriage, I was gathering my shawl and some things—Wilkes appeared. He seemed in a highly nervous state, agitated and wild. He takes the surrender hard, I fear. He seemed to know that I was headed down country though I do not know how. He asked if I would do him a favor and drop off a package to Mr. Lloyd, my tenant, for him. I said that I would, of course. I asked if it had something to do with the hunting trip he had mentioned that he was planning. He smiled. I remember well his words.

"That's exactly it. For the hunting trip. They're field glasses. What a fine memory you have, Mary. Yes, I will finally know the exhilaration of the kill."

I said to him that as a woman it was difficult for me to understand what joy there could be in hunting down poor dumb beasts and he answered me most strangely, I thought.

"I was deprived of the ordinary boyhood pleasures of hunting by my father. I intend to make amends for that. Then too, Mary, there are certain kinds of prey which are more rewarding than others. The prey I seek is large and clever, and very dangerous and evil. It is the kind that needs killing. It is good that it should die."

I assumed that he meant a bear, but it was an extraordinary way to describe an animal. They may be driven mad by hunger or disease, but surely only man is evil. I hope that Wilkes will soon learn to accept the defeat of the Confederacy. He is so young. His life is so bright and promising. I hope that he will not allow this to blight it. It ceases to be an effort to feel motherly toward him. I will never forget my dreams of him, but I now accept them as that–dreams–never to be reality. He must accept that too.

It is my time of the month now. The flow is heavy and has been for days, far too many days. It goes on too long. I think that this will be my last. This is perhaps part of the change that I am feeling–this great change going on within me–this cessation of a ritual I have known since girlhood, this first tangible and irrevocable step toward dying, toward dry barrenness. I feel surely that I am losing my womanhood with this final flow, that when it ends, I will be truly old. And I do not mind. Now that it is here, I do not mind. It was the waiting that was most terrible.

I resolved nothing in Maryland today. I missed Mr. Nothey again. It was very disappointing, but now that I will soon be returning, now that these people will once again be my neighbors, I feel sure that everything will be worked out. Mr. Lloyd gave me the strangest look when I delivered the package from Wilkes. First, I gave it to Mrs. Offutt as he had not returned from Court Day. She set it on the couch and when Mr. Lloyd did come in, falling down drunk, I must say, I gave it to him. It seemed for a moment that he did not wish to touch it. Be careful, I told him. They're field glasses. Was there any word from him, he asked me. I told him that there was no message, but I suggested that he make things ready as it looked as if Wilkes would be ready soon. I said that my late husband had some weapons stored in the attic, and that if Wilkes would like he was certainly welcome. Mr. Lloyd looked so oddly that I explained that Mr. Surratt, Sr., had been an avid hunter, but he seemed not to understand me. I assume it was his condition that prevented him. I decided further talk to him would be a waste and I left. He has not been the best of tenants. I will not be sorry to see him go.

It will be wonderful to be home in Maryland again, to watch the crops grow in the fields. I begin to think that Annie will not be dissuaded from marrying her lieutenant. Perhaps I will have grandchildren soon. There will be life all around me, and I will be able to stand back and admire and love the fertile life all around me. I think that I will finally and truly be at peace . . .

Saturday, April 15, 1865

I left off abruptly last night because of a commotion I heard downstairs. I read now what I had written moments before it began and it seems that it could have been a thousand years ago instead of last night.

President Abraham Lincoln has been murdered. The noise I heard at my door was made by a group of policemen. I went down to see what the matter was. They demanded entrance. They shouted and waved a piece of bloody rag in my face. They claimed it was the President's shirt. They said that John Wilkes Booth and John Surratt had shot him. They said that I was hiding the culprits. They searched the house. Mr. Weichman quaked on the stairs, his nightshirt partially tucked into his trousers.

They asked me questions for which I had no answers. I was able to tell them that I had seen Wilkes that afternoon and that I had not seen my son in two weeks, but that I had had a letter from him on Friday. That was all I could tell them. They left, but not without shouting several dire warnings and threats. It was not until they had gone, not until I was back in my room, that I thought of Wilkes standing in the parlor, in his favorite attitude, arm outflung across the mantel, looking wild and reckless with despair. I remembered his words about the evil prey that he sought. I have never felt so cold. My hands shook. I went to my closet and poured the last drops of all my empty tonic bottles, straight down into my throat.

The city has been plunged into despair. The President lasted through the night and died this morning in a house across from Ford's Theater. All the bunting is being replaced by black crepe. Now the church bells ring but the tone is different. The tolling, the knelling, is heavy and sad. There is no joy. And the sun finally shines. Through all the celebrations and illuminations, it was damp and gray. And now when the city is gripped by death and fear and hatred and unbearable sadness, now spring and sunshine have finally come.

This house is a terrible place. None of us know what will happen next. All that we know is that suspicion has fallen upon us. We have become entangled, disastrously linked, to this villainous crime. Mr. Weichman and Mr. Holohan left this morning to volunteer their services, to help track down Wilkes and John. Mr. Weichman and Mr. Holohan, a coward and an Irish bounty hunter, dubious patriots. Eliza Holohan and her daughter cleared out in a hurry. They will be staying at the Herndon House, which is what Miss Eliza has always desired anyway. So it is just Annie, Honora, myself, and the servants. We walk the floors like restless ghosts, meet coming round corners, and jump at the sight of the pinched white face staring back, so like one's own one might be looking in a glass.

I think that it is best that we leave the city. If our associations should become public knowledge, I would fear for our safety. I have been most of the day by the window, watching the faces in the street, and I am fearful I see in them a mob needing something or semeone to focus their fright and their hatred upon. Annie and I will leave for Maryland as soon as possible. Honora may accompany us if she so wishes, but I will advise strongly against it. She should go to another boardinghouse and wait for her father. That is the wisest course. But Annie and I must get away from here. We must.

Sunday, April 16, 1865

It grows worse daily. We immure ourselves here in this house and torture ourselves with newspaper accounts of the crime. It did not begin or end with the murder of the President. The killing of Vice President Johnson, General Grant, and others too was planned. Secretary of State Seward was attacked in his bed the same night that the President was shot. It is believed that he will survive. The newspapers are all saying that the President's death and the attempt on all the others was a Confederate plot.

Everyone is afraid. The city is like one under siege, not by that tattered and weary gray army across the river any longer, but by fear of plots and murder and mayhem. The average citizen does not feel safe, and even the most petty government official and bureaucrat sleeps with a gun under his pillow these days. They are ready to fend off the attack of wild-eyed Southerns who have come North in hopes of reclaiming the glory of Dixie by killing a clerk from the Treasury Department. The populace is enflamed, terrified, and seething with anger and hatred. And my son. My son, whom I remember used to sleep with his hand gently cushioning his cheek, golden curls on his damp forehead, and breath coming from between parted rosy lips, he is their target. And Wilkes, that elegant and beautiful young man of whom I have thought and dreamt all these long months, he is now the most infamous and notorious of villains. He has dwelt so long in my imaginings that I used to think sometimes that he was purely a creature of my conjuring, but he is real after all. His pictures are in the papers. He has done murder, they say. Men spit after uttering his name and wish they could be the lucky one to kill him and collect the price they've put on his head.

I wonder, did he see this in his poor tormented mind as another role in a play. He told me once that his destiny did not lie upon the stage. In an ironic and cruel way it did. How he must have hated himself, his life, and the theater, to try such an evil and desperate means of escape. The Confederate plot notwithstanding, I cannot believe that his motive was anything but personal. I wonder, does he know that he has failed, that now and forever he will dwell in the darkness of Ford's Theater on the night of April 14, 1865. There will be no escape for him. He will have no other life. To the world he will ever be the assassin in the theater, nothing more.

And where is John? Still in Canada? Could he possibly have been any part of all of this? I think of his last words to me. I try to think of what could have possibly prompted such bitter self-disgust and hatred, and I am afraid. They will hunt him down, and then what?

Monday, April 17, 1865

It is early morning, Monday, three days since the horror at Ford's. My writing here in this little book has been a nightly occupation, the only time I find some solace, some clarity.

My plan to leave Washington has met with some opposition. Annie does not want to go. She will not tell me why, but I can guess. She wants to stay and wait for her lieutenant. She fears he will not find her if she is gone from here. I must try to persuade her. I feel the most urgent need to leave this place.

I told Dulcey that we would be closing the house soon. I also told Cookie and Dan, the houseman. They seemed to accept the situation, but Dulcey was troubled. She has not been the same since the incident with the "Reverend." I asked her if there was something wrong. She said no. I asked again. Finally, she asked if she and little Genevieve could go with us back to the farm. She said that she hated the city, that it was the Devil's home. I told her that I agreed, and that they could certainly come with us. I have very little money, but there will at least be plenty to eat. She seemed relieved and very grateful. I feel in Dulcey a kind of kinship, a shared love of the country and things of the country. It will be good to have her and Genevieve with us.

These events are incomprehensible to me. As a woman, I am most sorry for Mrs. Lincoln. I know what it is to be left alone, a widow, in middle life. I know that pain well, but I cannot conceive of what it must be to have one's husband become the victim of a violent crime–to witness it–to have one's ball gown stained with his blood, to watch, helpless, as he dies. It must be like living one's most terrible nightmare, only to discover that it is not sleep but real.

Perhaps tomorrow I can convince Annie and we can begin our journey home. I will shut up this house without a twinge of regret. Then in Maryland, away from all this horror, I can come to know my daughter as well as I love her.

Annie closed the book and looked up at Mardella.

"We were arrested that night."

"You looks mighty tired, Miss Annie."

"I'm so sorry, Della."

"What you sorry fer?"

"We could have gotten out of the city, Mother, your mother and child, and me. We could have gone to Maryland. But I was too busy, waiting for a dead man."

"You cain't blame yerself. Dey would of got hole of yer ma anyways. Maryland weren't far enough to run."

"But would the typhoid have gotten your mother and little girl if they'd gone to the farm with us?"

"Somethin' else would of got dem. Some folks jus' ain't meant to live."

"You don't hate me then?"

"No, Miss Annie."

"Is there any more of that tea?"

"It cold."

"Della, do you know why my mother died? The Colonel told me today, I mean yesterday. Do you know why they killed her?"

"No, Miss Annie."

"Because she was a woman. That's right. Secretary Stanton hated Southern women. He wanted to punish them all and he used my mother to do it. She was an example, the Colonel said."

"Any man I ever knowed who hated women, it usually 'cause he 'fraid of 'em."

"But there's more to it than just one man's hatred, or the people wanting revenge. My mother thought of running home, to Maryland, but why didn't she think of running to some strange place, farther away? Why? Because it's hard for a woman to run, almost impossible."

"What you sayin', Miss Annie?"

"I'm saying that women are trapped. My brother ran away and hid. When they finally found him after two years, the times had changed, the blood lust had died away. People had calmed and forgotten. He was saved. If my mother had been able to run, she might have been saved too, but she didn't."

"She knowed she hadn't done nothin' wrong."

"Yes, she knew that she was innocent, but even if she had been guilty she never would have thought that she would be hanged. She was a woman. She was waiting, passive, for others to act. That was her role. She couldn't take her life into her hands and save herself because she was blind to the danger. She believed that someone else would take care of her. I killed even her feeble desire to run to the farm, because I am a woman, and I was doing a very womanly thing, waiting for a man, the man I loved."

"Mebbee it so. I 'member my ma tellin' stories 'bout long long ago back in Africa where my folks comes from. It seemed like always in dem stories, de men out huntin' an' runnin' round wid spears an' sech things, an' de women dey sittin' by de fires makin' baskets wid dere bellies full of babies. I 'spect it always been dat way an' it always gonna be. Women is women an' men is men. It don't matter de time dey's livin' in or de color dey is. Nothin' seem to change it."

"I suppose it will always be that way."

"I 'spect so."

"But there must be a better way. Look at the misery that women live. Della, that's why I took the medicine for so long. I hated the life I was living or not living, but there seemed nothing to be done. So I took the medicine to forget and not think."

"I knows dat, Miss Annie."

"I wonder, do more women take the medicine than men."

"I 'spect dey do."

"It's not easy is it, Della?"

"It ain't."

"Della, I do think I'm going to have a baby."

"Dere is a certain feelin' you gits."

"I'm not sure I want this child."

"Miss Annie, I ain't de one to be advisin' you on dat."

"Why not? Who better than you?"

" 'Cause I borned one chile an' killed another, dat what you mean?"

"No, because you're my friend, and you know me better than anyone."

"I cain't be tellin' you de right or de wrong of it. I jus' say dese. Both my babies end up dyin'. I ain't gots no babies left. When I seed my little girl dead 'side my ma, I done wished mere den anythin' in de world dat I hadn't killed dat new little baby."

"Oh, Della."

"But it were done. Dere ain't no changin' once it done, Miss Annie. I gonna live all de rest of my life regrettin'. You gots to think on it real hard, an' decides de right an' de wrong of it yerself. I cain't be tellin' you, but Miss Annie, decides de best you cain an' don't never look back. 'Cause when it done an' decided, it done an' decided ferever. An' cain't nobody change it."

"I just don't know what to do."

"Could be what I done was fer de best. I weren't much of a ma to Genevieve. I done borned her an' gives her dat pritty name an' den I went off an' left her. Mebbee I would of done de same thin' to de other lit'l one, but I would gives mos' anythin' to have de chance to prove different. So you be as sure as you cain be. Dat's all I be sayin' 'bout it."

"The tea is cold, you say?"

"Yes, Miss Annie."

"I think I'll lie down on the sofa here and try to get a little rest."

"Dat be good."

Mardella went into the bedroom and came out with a blanket.

"You puts yer feets up an' I cover you wid dese. Put dat pillow under yer head."

"I think you would have made a wonderful mother."

"De time is past fer it now. I left my little girl to de mercy of big strange white men in bedrooms an' I done killed my other chile. An' now it too late. My time done past. Dat the hurtin' part. Close yer eyes now. Go to sleep, Miss Annie."

XXIV

They arrived at the farm of Uncle Zadoc while it was still early morning. They had hired a rig in the small town where the train stopped. Mardella drove. Annie sat beside her, silent, anticipating the meeting with Grandmother Jenkins with great anxiety.

"I don't even know what she looks like, Della."

"I don't 'spect she know you neither, so you is startin' off even."

They stopped in the yard of a dilapidated farmhouse which seemed a part of the cool foggy morning. There were tall trees all about, and only a strange misty light filtered through them. They walked to the door. Annie knocked, and it was opened by Uncle Zadoc. He looked very old to her. She remembered the last time she had seen him had been during John's trial, more than ten years ago. He squinted his eyes in disbelief.

"Anna, is that you?"

"Yes, Uncle Zadoc."

Now he was looking at Mardella, with suspicion and even fear.

"Uncle, this is Mardella."

He ignored the introduction. "Come in, Anna."

She was jarred by the use of the name Anna. No one called her that. Her mother had only on occasion. It was the mysterious name from the diary. When she had first read it there, she had thought that her mother was referring to her. Later, she thought it might be Anna Ward, but it was neither of them. She had decided that it must be someone she did not know, someone from her mother's past. The strangest thing about her mother's Anna was that she always called her little Anna. She was hoping that Grandmother Jenkins could tell her who little Anna was. It took her aback to be reminded so quickly of one of the purposes of her visit, and by Uncle Zadoc of all people. He could not possibly know her reasons for coming.

"Thank you, Uncle." She stepped inside followed by Mardella.

"It's been so many years, Anna. I saw your brother not long ago."

"I know, he told me."

They were standing awkwardly in the narrow hallway that led to the body of the house. It was darker within than without. There was a musty smell as if no window had been opened in a very long time. Uncle Zadoc had turned his squinting stare to the trunks.

"Uncle, this is not to be a long visit. I have been to see John in Baltimore and then I stopped in Washington for a time. I was so near that I thought I would come and see you, but only for a day or so."

"We don't have much company. There's an empty room upstairs. The house is full of them. All the children are gone now. The wife died last year."

"I am sorry, Uncle. And there's just you and Grandmother now?"

"Just Ma and me. I'm getting as old as she is. It's peculiar how time catches up with us."

His manner was not intentionally rude, but only abrupt, as if he were unaccustomed to speaking with people.

"Miss Annie, I takes de bags upstairs."

"Don't go into the first two rooms on the left. Those are mine and Ma's. Any of the others will be all right. If Ma saw that big strange nigger come into her room, she'd think sure it was the angel of death come to get her."

Mardella did not turn as she walked up the stairs, but Annie could tell from the set of her head on her neck and the arch of her back that she had heard.

"How is Grandmother, Uncle?"

"She's old."

"Yes, well, I mean beyond being old. Is she in good health?"

"She has her good and her bad days. Her mind's been going lately. She'll all of a sudden up and ask for somebody who's been dead twenty years or more. I think she's living back in those days most of the time."

"You see that's really why I've come, Uncle. I want to speak with Grandmother about my mother."

"I don't think she'd cotton to that idea. She and your ma never did get on too well together, but after everything happened Ma really gave up on Mary. I can remember coming back here from her trial and Ma never asking a question. And when Mary asked to see her, she turned her down flat."

"My mother asked to see her?"

"She sure did, just after the trial was over. She asked me if the next time I came to see her if I'd bring Ma with me. I told her that I sure would try. 'Course none of us knew how little time she had left. Anyway, Ma wouldn't hear of it."

"Did she ever tell you why?"

"No, Ma never was one for explaining herself. She just said no, and that was that."

"Uncle, do you remember why they quarreled?"

"They fought over most everything, near as I can tell. I was younger than Mary by almost ten years. I don't remember too much about it. I must have been about five when she came home from school in Virginia. She got married right after that. Mary and Ma didn't agree on much of anything."

"Do you think she'll remember me?"

"I think she will. On her good days she's sharp as a tack. On her bad days she doesn't even know me. It's a terrible thing, getting old, especially for a woman. Women are more vain than men. Sometimes I think your ma was lucky in a way. At least she went quick."

Annie could not believe that she was hearing what he was saying correctly. She supposed he had said it out of fear. It must be truly horrible to watch someone you love disintegrate before your eyes.

"I think I'll go upstairs to my room. Does Grandmother come down?"

"No, she stays in bed all the time now. She used to come down in the afternoons, but it's been months since she's done that."

"What would be a good time to go in to her?'

"Afternoon's still the best, but I warn you she won't talk about Mary. I haven't heard her say her name in thirteen years. And if it's a bad day she may not even know who you are."

"I'll take my chances, Uncle."

"I don't want her getting upset."

"I understand your concern."

"It'll just make more work for me. It's not easy taking care of an old sick woman and working the farm too."

"You should have someone in to help."

"An old nigger woman comes here days. She goes home at night. I still can't get used to paying niggers money. It just doesn't seem right somehow."

He walked out and Annie went upstairs. It occurred to her that her uncle had not asked once how she was. She also thought of his announcement of his wife's death, so matter-of-fact and cold. She had not even offered her sympathies. It didn't appear that he would want them.

She walked quietly past the first two doors on the left. Down the hallway to the right she saw an open door. Inside, Mardella was hard at work with a dust rag. She looked up at Annie.

"Filthy ole man. I jus' don't know how folks cain live dese way."

"I doubt that anyone has been in this room in years."

"You is tellin' me. I mos' broke my arms off tryin' to pry open dat dere window. Dese is de darkest, dirtiest place I done ever seed. I cain jus' imagine what de kitchen look like."

"We won't be here long."

"I's glad of dat. I knows dat man is yer kin, Miss Annie, but if I had to stay under de same roof wid him fer very long, I'd strangle him. I jus' knows it."

"He's grown worse with the years. I know that during my mother's trial they suggested that he had been involved in some sort of illegal business ventures and they questioned his loyalty to the Union. They tried to use him to blacken Mother's reputation, but that is about all I recall about him. I never was very fond of him. The years have not improved him."

"He sure ain't much of a host. You done seed yer gran'ma?"

"No, from what Uncle says she is very ill. She doesn't leave her room. Without actually saying it, I think Uncle wanted me to leave here and not stir up trouble, to let the old woman die in peace. Maybe he's right."

"I thinks dat you is 'fraid of yer gran'ma."

"I know I am."

"Ain't nothin' fer you to be 'fraid of."

"I know, she's just an old woman who is dying quite naturally of age, of living too long, but I cannot help but think that she is the reason my mother was a stranger to me. I'm frightened."

"Miss Annie, you is here at yer own choosin'."

"Yes, that's true. I came because I felt I had to. I felt compelled to see her, but that doesn't make it easier or make me less afraid."

"What 'sactly you think is gonna happen?"

"I don't know. I just don't know, Della. Uncle Zadoc told me that she refused to come and see my mother in prison. What kind of woman must she be?"

"I wouldn't believe a thin' dat ole man said. 'Sides dere's two sides to every story."

"Yes. Two, three, four, however many people are involved, but I remember her as such a cold woman, and hard. Look at her son, a stingy, narrow, spare man. Look at what the years have done to him."

"You is still lookin' fer villains, ain't you?"

"What do you mean?"

"I means dat you is still lookin' to blame somebody. First it were de Colonel. You done hate him wid a fury till you seed dat he jus' a man, an' a right good one, as men goes. Den you tries to hate an' blame yer brother, but you finds you cain't do dat neither. Now it's yer gran'ma. You gots it all figured out 'fore you even sees her. When is you gonna stop doin' it, Miss Annie? When is you gonna puts de blame where it belongs?"

"And where is that?"

"On all dem men who was so sure dat dey was right. So sure dat dey couldn't seed nothin' but dere right. All dem law-abidin' men in dem blue uniforms who was so full of hate an' so bound to be blamin' somebody dat dey hanged yer ma widout ever once seein' her or what she was. All dem blind men, jus' like you, Miss Annie, hatin' an' blamin' an' not never seein' nothin' but what dey wants to see, what dey thinks is right."

"I never thought I was doing that."

" 'Course you didn't. You cain't always be judgin' folks."

"But there are standards to live by. There is right and there is wrong."

"You gots yer standards, yer rights an' yer wrongs, but don't be tellin' other folks. Dey gots dere own."

"Della, there are things that are right and there are things that are wrong. Those things don't change."

"Mebbee so, an' mebbee not, but folks gots dere reasons fer doin' things. But you cain't always be judgin' an' blamin' an' hatin' or even lovin' folks fer de things dey does or de reasons dey does 'em. It ain't yer place, Miss Annie. It ain't yer right."

"There has to be good and evil in life, right and wrong. Otherwise there is nothing to believe in."

"Was yer ma a good woman or a evil one?"

"She was good. She was kind and gentle."

"Does you thinks dat mos' folks would say she a good woman? Or does you thinks dat mos' folks would say she bad, she real bad, she done helped to kill a good man?"

"But they didn't know her."

"No, Miss Annie, dey didn't. Dey didn't know her, not her reasons fer doin' de things she done, not nothin' 'bout her. Dey jus' hates her an' blames her, say she a evil woman an' she done wrong."

"But still, Della, had they known her they would have judged her good."

"Mebbee so, mebbee not. I say it 'fore an' I say it agin. You is jus' not an acceptin' woman, Miss Annie. You gots to take folks fer what dey is an' not be judgin' dem or tryin' to make somethin' else outa dem."

"I can't do that, Della. I know what's right and what's wrong . . ."

"Fer you, Miss Annie. It jus' may not be fer somebody else."

"No, I can't believe that."

"You 'member tellin' me 'bout yer gran'ma's back at yer pa's funeral, how it so ramrod straight an' it never bend?"

"Yes, I remember."

"Well, you is jus' like dat. I thinks dat you is 'fraid to see yer gran'ma 'cause you knows you is gonna be seein' yerself. You thinks you did to yer ma jus' what yer gran'ma did to her. You thinks you is cold like her an' hard like her, not yieldin' an' forgivin' like yer ma. You an' yer gran'ma hated dat in her, blamed her fer it. Dat's who you really blame fer dis whole thin', yer ma, blame her fer bein' what she was. You say to me dat it good to be kind an' gentle, but you don't believe it. You thinks bein' dose things killed yer ma. So do yer gran'ma. You is 'fraid to go into dat room an' look at dat woman 'cause she is you."

"I never wanted to be like my mother. She always seemed so weak to me. But I loved her, I did, Mardella. And I don't think my grandmother could have. If she loved her, how could she have refused to see her?"

"Mebbee she done thought it be wrong fer her to go."

"Oh, Della."

"Yer gran'ma have her reasons too, I 'spect. Mebbee it be time to find out what dey was an' stop hatin' an' blamin' her an' yerself."

"It's not quite yet noon. That might be too early."

"I don't think so, Miss Annie."

"I'll go and knock at the door. If she answers I'll go in. If there's no answer I'll be back."

She walked slowly from the room.

XXV

As she walked down the hallway, she realized that she did not know which room was her grandmother's and which was her Uncle Zadoc's. She knocked on both closed doors and waited. She was about to turn and go when she heard a voice, a voice which was surprisingly strong and steady.

"Come in, Zadoc. Or is that you, Betsy?"

She opened the door and stepped inside. The old woman was propped up by many pillows in a big bed with a tattered and graying lace canopy. Her long gray hair was loose on the pillows.

"Who is it? I don't know you."

"Yes, you do."

"Come closer then. And don't tell me. Don't tell me. Let me look at you first." Annie approached the foot of the bed. "I'm old and my eyes are old. Come closer. Your face is still in a shadow. This infernal room is like a bat's cave. They won't open a window. It's as if I were dead already." She watched Annie's face closely with sharp clear gray eyes. "It's terrible always to ask people to come to you. I do know you. It's Elizabeth Suzanna."

"Yes, Grandmother."

"What do you want here? You must want something or you wouldn't have come. What is it?"

"I wanted to see you."

"Why? You've gotten along without seeing me, for what? How old are you now, thirty? Yes. For thirty years you've managed without seeing much of me. Why have you come now?"

"I had to come."

"Why? To watch me die? I warn you, I have nothing to leave anyone. You will not be made an heiress by my passing."

"That was the farthest thing from my mind. Do you really believe that you are dying, Grandmother?"

"Stupid child. Of course, I'm dying. I've outlived everyone I know. It's high time I died."

"You seem well."

"As compared to what? I'm well for a woman nearly eighty. I'm well for someone who is dying, you mean? I can't get out of this bed. I can't walk. I can hardly see or hear. My teeth are gone. And sometimes my mind isn't right. That's the worst of all. I think that I am making perfect sense and Zadoc looks at me most peculiarly, but then Zadoc has a peculiar face anyway. Then I know that I'm not thinking or talking properly, so I just shut up like a clam. Am I making sense now? I don't know your face. I can't tell how you're looking at me."

"You're doing just fine."

"I'm glad to hear it. I'm glad to hear most anything these days with these ears of mine. I don't remember, have you told me why you've come here?"

"I've come because I want to speak with you."

"Well, I'm pretty much stuck, aren't I? I can't get out of this bed. You talk away. I will reserve the right not to talk back, Elizabeth Suzanna."

"Elizabeth is your name too, isn't it?"

"Yes, I suppose your mother was trying to make things up to me when she named you that. She was called Elizabeth also until she saw fit to change it."

"Her name was Mary Eugenia."

"Don't I know it. That's just what I'm saying. It was Mary Elizabeth first."

"Why did she change it?"

"She did it when she joined up with the Papists. It was probably one of their infernal rituals. I don't know for sure."

"I came to talk about Mother."

"In that case I'm going to choose to be clam-like."

"Uncle Zadoc told me that you wouldn't want to speak of her."

"That surprises me. I have always thought that Zadoc was rather stupid. I suppose I'll have to change my opinion now, not an easy thing to do at my age."

"Please, Grandmother. This is very important to me."

"It's important to me too. I have nothing to say about your mother."

"I think that you do."

"Well, you're wrong. I'm not sure I like you. You have eyes like mine."

"It's not only your eyes I have, but your chin and your stubborn character too."

"How can you tell about my chin through all this wrinkled skin?"

"I can tell."

"Hmmm."

"Tell me about my mother."

"I would imagine you could tell me more than I you."

"No, I'm afraid not. I knew her so little, it turns out. I never really knew her at all."

"What on earth sort of gibberish are you talking? She was your mother. You lived with the woman for seventeen years. Of course, you knew her."

"I didn't. We never spoke of how we felt or the things we

thought. I've been reading her diary and I know now that she never spoke her mind or her heart to me. She wrote it all down in that little book, but never told me."

"Mary always was better at writing words than saying them."

"Did she ever write to you?"

"Yes, she wrote me letters from the convent school in Alexandria."

"Did you keep them?"

"No, I burned them."

"Why?"

"That's my concern and none of yours. You think you're very clever, don't you? You think you're going to lead me around and that I'll begin to talk about her. Well, I won't."

"Will you talk about Katherine then?"

"Katherine who?"

"In her diary Mother wrote down the story of Katherine, the story you told her when she was twelve years old."

"Katherine. I don't suppose I would mind talking about her. She was a brave woman. She had courage. I admired that when I was young. I admire it still. I don't like women who sit back with folded hands and take it all the time."

"And you think that's what my mother did?"

"Speak up. I can't hear you."

"You can hear me."

"What's that you say?"

"About Katherine, did you ever hear from her again? Mother said not in her diary."

"I never told your mother, but I got a letter from her. It was years later. She wrote to Ma actually, but she was gone by then. Katherine raised a fine family of boys out West."

"She had a happy life then?"

"I doubt that. I expect it was a hard life, but Katherine lived it well. She had a hard core, Katherine did. She was a fighter. I liked her."

"Grandmother, who was Anna?"

"That's what you're called, isn't it?"

"Yes. Anna. Annie."

"Then why ask such a stupid question. You're Anna. Are you touched in the head. I'm old. I have enough trouble making sense of things."

"There was another Anna."

"No."

"Yes there was. Mother wrote of her in the diary."

"What are you doing reading other people's diaries anyway? Don't you have any life of your own?"

"No, I don't."

"That's a fine thing."

"When Mother died I crawled into a shell. I went into hiding."

"I heard that you married."

"I did. My marriage has been my greatest hiding place."

"What made you decide to come out?"

"Her diary. I thought it had been destroyed, but it wasn't. It was brought to me a few weeks ago and I began reading it."

"I can't think of anything your mother could have said to bring anyone out of hiding. She was hiding all of her life. She didn't crawl into any shell. She crawled into the Roman Catholic Church."

"You disapproved?"

"I did."

"Why did she do it?"

"Do what?"

"Join the Church."

"She just did, that's all."

"That's no answer."

"Make the best of it. It's the only one you're going to get."

"Who was Anna?"

"Your mother's twin sister."

"She never . . ."

"Anna was your mother's twin."

"What happened to her? Is she . . ."

"Anna did what we all do sooner or later. Only she did it sooner. She died."

"When?"

"1832."

"That's forty-six years ago."

"That's right."

"How did she die?"

"Most unpleasantly."

"But how?"

"She died of cholera. So did her daddy, within a day of one another."

"Cholera?"

"Yes. Have you ever seen anyone die of cholera?"

"No."

"It's horror. In '32, in Baltimore, they were dying like flies of it. Everyone looking at his friends and neighbors and praying, Please, God, let it take them next and not me. The lucky ones died quickly. The strong ones, the ones who fought and lingered, their limbs shriveled up as if they had been burned, their lips turned whitish-blue, their stomachs were sunken, they vomited constantly, their bowels were like water, and if they managed to speak it was always the same, a prayer for death. In the streets there were great bonfires. People hoped to burn the cholera from the air. Thousands died. Their bodies were heaped in the streets. It was hell on earth, the end of the world. I shall never forget it.

"The only sanity and serenity came from the nuns. They were an island of peace and faith in that sea of pain and terror. Their pale faces surrounded in black, their cool hands, and quiet voices. They made you believe that perhaps all was not lost. They were a force, strong and powerful. They inspired you to live. I've never witnessed such bravery before or since. They nursed us all. Mary and I lived through it. So did Zadoc, which was a miracle because the cholera fed on babies. But my husband and Anna did not. It left as swiftly and mysteriously as it came. One day no one got sick anymore.

Those who were sick either recovered or died. It was gone. The fires in the streets were quenched. The bodies were buried. And the vision of hell receded, it became Baltimore once again."

"And Mother . . ."

"She asked me, 'Mama, why am I alive? Why did Papa and Anna go and leave me behind? I want to go too. Why did Papa take Anna and not me?' I couldn't answer her. I couldn't believe what she was asking. Instead of being thankful for being saved, she was sorry. She began to go to the nuns at the hospital. I grew to hate them. I knew they were exacting her soul as payment for her life. She gave it to them and when she did that she turned from me forever, and I from her."

"But you couldn't answer her. You said so yourself. Perhaps the nuns gave her a reason, an explanation why she lived and her father and twin sister were taken."

"Why did she need to know that? She was alive. Life should have been enough for her."

"It was for you but not for her."

"I loved my husband. I wanted him to live. I wanted to stand beside him, and watch our daughters and our son grow. I wanted other babies. I have never stopped wanting him. I wish even now that he was here. I wish that I could have seen his hair grow gray, and he mine. But he was dead and I was alive. I couldn't hate myself for that or wish myself dead. I was glad to be alive. I didn't want to die."

"But Mother did want to die."

"She didn't love them any more than I did. Being willing to die is not proof of love. Going on and living is. I wish she had died of the cholera."

"In a way, I suppose, she did. That's what it was about Mother, the thing I could never understand. She was never completely alive. There was a part of her that was dead always."

"It would have been better if she had died. As it was she killed everything around her, everyone. Death clung to Mary, and she to it. I told her that."

"At the funeral, my father's funeral. I remember."

"There's some of her in you, but I think there's more of me. You're a fighter. I think you want to live."

"I do, Grandmother, but sometimes it's so hard."

"She makes it hard. Close the door on her. She brings only death. In the Bible, Job it is, there is a line for Mary. 'Where the slain are, there is she . . .' That's your mother."

"You're wrong. She returned me to life, her book, her words. She brought me to you, to a final understanding of her and myself."

"She wanted to be a nun."

"Perhaps you should have let her."

"I was willing, perfectly willing. I would have preferred it if she had cloistered herself in a convent and I would never again have had to look upon her cowardly white face again. She made the decision not to become a nun, not I."

"But why?"

"She met a young man."

"Who?"

"John Surratt, your father."

"She fell in love with him."

"Yes. He was everything that she wasn't. I liked him in those days. He was tall and handsome and not afraid of anything or anyone on earth. When he walked into a room he filled it. He was more alive than anyone, man or woman, I've ever known. He rode a big black horse no one else dared ride. He would come to the house on it, and if anyone touched even the reins that horse would rear and rage. They were like kin to one another. For some reason, John Surratt began to look at Mary."

"But she was beautiful."

"Yes, she was beautiful, I suppose. Not the sort of beauty you would have thought would have appealed to a man who rode a horse like that. She was barely fifteen, so pallid and silent. She had no spirit at all. She looked out from behind those big gray eyes of hers and watched the world. She had a soft quiet tread, so even when she moved there was little sound. There had been another boy in love with her too."

"Henry Warfield."

"She told you about him?"

"No, never. His name was in her diary."

"She turned him down, told him she was going to be a nun. Well, he slunk off like the poor-spirited wretch that he was. He was far better suited to her than John Surratt."

"That's what the woman who told fortunes said to her. In the diary she speaks of this woman, Maria Carbini, a seer. She told Mother that she should have married Henry Warfield. He died in a hunting accident and the woman said it would have been best had Mother married him and been made an early widow, that she would not have had children then."

"The seer was right about that, but if she was any seer worth her salt she would have known that Henry Warfield did not die in a hunting accident."

"How did he die?"

"He killed himself, shortly after your mother married. He went into the woods and put a rifle in his mouth and pulled the trigger. You think that was an accident?"

"No."

"No, indeed. His family covered it up with the hunting story."

"He killed himself because of Mother?"

"I suppose that's the reason he gave, but he would have done it anyway. People who want to take their lives will always find some excuse. If Henry and your mother had married, he would have found some other reason. God knows she would have given him plenty."

"You're very hard on people."

"I'm hard on myself too. I just see things clear, that's all. I don't believe in lying, to myself or anybody else."

"Did you and Mother ever talk about Henry Warfield, his death, I mean?"

"Yes. She decided to believe it was a hunting accident. I told her the truth but she wouldn't accept it."

"But she gave up the idea of a convent. She must have wanted to live. She must have loved my father."

"I'm not saying she didn't try to. Your father was the sort of man who was easy to love."

"She said that too."

"Yes, but she couldn't manage to do it. She infected him with her sadness and her defeat and her death. She killed him bit by bit, over the years. Your mother just wasn't a fighter. She should have died young or become a nun. She should never have tried to live in the world. She was incapable of it. She kept reaching out for death. The nuns had convinced her that she had been chosen, singled out to survive the cholera by God so that she could give her life to Him. She believed them. She was going to do just that when John Surratt came along and tempted her. When she was not true to the nuns, when she married your father instead, she hated herself. Her desire, her wish, for death grew even stronger. He was passion, sensation, and life, but he wasn't strong enough. I had always felt that Mary had been spared from the cholera, as Zadoc and I had, to go on and live fruitful and happy lives as best we could. I thought that when Mary decided to marry your father that she had come to believe that too.

"I remember once before she was married. John had been to the house to visit. She stood at the window, watching him go. I was behind her, close behind her, but I don't think that she was aware of me. He was riding his big black horse away when something frightened it. It reared. His thigh muscles bunched and gripped and he held firm. It reared again, tossing back its black mane and a thin spray of saliva from its open mouth. Again your father's legs tightened and he remained astride. The horse calmed finally and he rode off. Mary put a hand to her throat. She was breathing rapidly, her breast rising and falling heavily. With both her hands she rubbed her neck and slowly down to her breast, feeling her heart pounding. Then she turned and saw me. She told me then that she was going to be married. And I was a happy woman, but it was short-lived. What I had seen was only a moment of love and living. She was unable to sustain it. After a year or so of their marriage, I couldn't watch anymore. That's when the physical break came between your mother and me. We no longer saw one another, but our spiritual parting had come long before that."

"I don't think Mother ever understood the break, as you call it."

"Yes, she did."

"But why, when you knew she was dying, did you refuse to go and visit her in prison?"

"To me she was already dead. She had wanted to die since her father and sister had gone. Her wish was being granted. I had no desire to see it."

"Because you loved her."

"Yes, I loved her. She was my flesh, my blood, my child. I loved her, but she didn't want my love."

"She did love you."

"No. If she had loved me, she wouldn't have wanted to die."

"In her diary before her arrest she spoke of going back to Maryland, to her farm, raising things, growing them, being a grandmother. I think she realized that she had wasted much of her life, but she was ready then to live."

"And it was too late."

"Too late. She was trapped in a web . . ."

"Of her own spinning."

"Perhaps, but she did want out. She was very sick. She wanted you, Grandmother. She loved you. You could have brought life to that cell, but you refused. I call you a coward for that."

"I didn't want to see her dying. I wanted to remember her as I saw her that day at the window as she watched your father on his big black horse. That's how I wanted her in my mind. You should understand that. I don't have to explain it to you. You have worn me out."

"You look very tired."

"I am. I'm old."

"I've stayed too long, asked too much of you."

"That's true. I'll take a nap now."

She leaned back on the pillows and closed her eyes. Annie bent and touched her lips softly to the old cheek. She stood and looked down at the face for a moment. Mardella had been right. It was as if she was looking at herself. The eyes opened.

"You may come back later, Elizabeth Suzanna. And make yourself useful, bring me some tea when you come."

"I will. Rest well, Grandmother."

She left the room and returned to her own. Mardella was still dusting and yet it seemed years since she had left her. She was not yet ready to speak of the conversation, even to Mardella.

"Della, I'm so tired. I think I'll lie down for a while."

"You gots to wait jus' one minute. I wants to shake out dat spread. It probably full of spiders an' sech like. You waits jus' one minute now." She shook out the spread and returned it to the bed. "Dere now, dat better."

"Thank you, Della. Do you never get tired? Are you always ready to talk, or not talk? Are you always just what I need?"

"I don't do much sleepin', Miss Annie. I don't eats much neither. It jus' don't seem as 'portant as it usta in my younger days, sleepin' an' eatin', dat is. As fer talkin' an' listenin', I knows de times you needs it an' de times you don't. I jus' knows you, Miss Annie, dat all."

"Thank God for you, Della."

Annie slept well into the afternoon. It was dusk by the time she brought tea into the dark room. The old woman was lying very still, her eyes staring up at the frayed gray lace. Annie stepped closer.

"You are awake, Grandmother?"

She did not stir. Then slowly she turned her eyes toward Annie.

"Yes, I'm awake. You brought tea, that's good."

"Would you like a cup?"

"Yes."

Annie poured her a cup and watched as her grandmother shakily brought it to her lips.

"Take it away."

"Is there something wrong with it, Grandmother?"

"Nothing is right when you get as old as I am. Nothing tastes good. Nothing looks good. Take it away."

Annie took the tea tray and put it on a far table. She returned to the bed.

"Are you back again?"

"Would you like me to go, Grandmother?"

"No. Stay. I hope you're satisfied, child."

"What do you mean?"

"You disturbed my afternoon nap. I had a dream."

"What did you dream of?"

"Your mother."

"Do you remember it?"

"Clearly. Your mother was standing on a hill. The sun had set, but the sky was still light behind her. She was silhouetted against it. A wind came up. It blew her skirts. She beckoned to me. She wanted me to come to her."

"And did you, Grandmother?"

"I don't know. I only know that I woke up wanting to go to her."

"Then you've forgiven her. You two are reconciled at last."

"I have not forgiven her. I feel as I have always felt. I think that death will be Mary's and my reconciliation. It's very near. That means that she wins, I suppose."

"She never wanted to win, Grandmother."

"You're right, child. Will you please go now?"

"Yes." She stood and started to leave, but remembered all the unspoken words between her mother and herself. She felt the regret. She stopped and turned.

"I love you, Grandmother. I am part of you, and you of me."

"I believe that. Come here, child, Kiss me. Kiss me goodbye."

"But I'll see you tomorrow."

"Kiss me goodbye, Elizabeth Suzanna."

She kissed her.

"Goodbye, Grandmother."

The old woman said nothing. Annie left the room. Grandmother Jenkins stared up into the lace. Her eyes dimmed for a moment with tears. Then she slowly closed them.

XXVI

That evening Grandmother Jenkins died in her sleep. Annie came upon her uncle crying in the hallway. She did not think that the man was capable of tears. She asked him what was wrong and he told her. He said that she had been all his strength and now he had none.

She stayed for the funeral, which was the next day. The old woman was put into the ground with little ceremony. She had outlived all of her contemporaries and friends. The grief, except for Uncle Zadoc's, which was really for himself, was tempered by the inevitability of her death. What struck Annie was the choice of cemetery. Grandmother Jenkins was buried at Saint Ignatius Catholic Cemetery. She asked her uncle about it and he said that it had been his mother's request. Annie could only think that it was a final show of appreciation to the nuns who had saved her life during the cholera epidemic. She had been unable to thank the nuns and their faith during her lifetime because of her bitterness over her daughter. She would do it in death then. Annie hoped that she was attributing the right reasons to her grandmother's choice. As Uncle Zadoc had said of her, she was not a woman to explain herself. Her burial place would remain her last mystery. She probably had wanted it that way.

On the way to the train, the wagon bumping over the rutted, muddy road, Annie told Mardella of her decision.

"I want to visit Mother's grave, Della."

Mardella said nothing to her.

Mount Olivet was not far. They took a room in a boardinghouse close to the graveyard.

"I'll go tomorrow, Della. It's late. I'm not ready to brave it in the darkness. I think I'll read some in the diary."

"First you ought to eats some supper, Miss Annie."

"Later, perhaps."

She sat down by a window and took the diary from her pocket.

Thursday, April 27, 1865

You have been returned to me, dear little book. I cannot believe it yet. Yesterday, you appeared with my meal—I am given but one. A young silent soldier brings it upon a tray without benefit of dishes or cutlery. I took you into my hands and prayed that it was really you. The feel of you was blissfully familiar and there was a small stub of pencil inside. Did someone know how much I have missed you, and returned you to me? Or did someone know how much I have missed you and decided to play a cruel joke upon me? I had to wait until now, for my hour of sunlight, to be absolutely sure. Through the night I tormented myself with thoughts that the little leather book I held might not be my beloved diary at all, but something entirely different. Perhaps my little book, but its pages filled with hateful ugly words and threats. In the sunlight I saw it was you.

I have kept count in my mind. Ten times the sun has risen and come slowly to my window and left swifty. Today then is April 27, 1865.

I do not know who my benefactor is, but I have a guess. I believe it to be the Colonel who is in charge of this place. When Annie, Honora, and I were brought here by the soldiers, we were greeted by him. Then we were separated. I have not seen Annie since. I do not know if she is still here or if she has been released. All my inquiries fall on deaf ears. It is rare now that I see anyone but the soldier who brings my meals. In the beginning, at all hours, there was a regular procession of the curious past my door. They would look in through the tiny barred window, mostly soldiers, and peer at me. Some of them said things, terrible things. Some of them spat upon me. I have done nothing to deserve such hatred. Thank God they stopped after a while. All of this is a horrible mistake.

That first night, the Colonel took my arm and led me away from Annie down a long dark corridor. I noticed for the first time his peculiar way of walking. It was difficult to keep pace with him. He took out keys and opened the door of a large dark cell. I could see the dim outlines of three bodies sleeping upon the floor. He pointed to a pallet of straw and started to leave. Am I to stay here, I asked. Why must I stay here? For how long? He seemed not to hear me. The only answer to all my questions was the sound of his key turning in the lock.

I was feeling my way along the wall with my hands when one of the bodies from the floor rose up and spoke. I nearly jumped from my skin. She quite calmly introduced herself, saying that her name was Miss Lomax. Miss Lomax was very loquacious and surprisingly cheerful considering her circumstances. We talked for a very long while, but I cannot remember what was said. She talked so steadily that it occurred to me that she might be mad, but I decided that she was merely lonely and afraid. As it turned out, I was never to see Miss Lomax's face. Early that morning, before dawn, a soldier appeared and brought me here, to this smaller and darker cell where I am alone always. I am a short woman but I can barely lie upon the floor without touching the walls at my head and toes. They gave me a blanket. There is a bucket in the corner which the soldier takes when he brings my food and returns when he comes for my tray. I had to ask repeatedly for cloth, rags, before they would give me any. I suppose they thought I meant to make a noose and hang myself. It is for my bleeding. It has continued for weeks now. I am weak from its flow. I finally made clear my need and now I am given cloth, but the bloodied ones I must deposit in the bucket daily. It is very humiliating. I have no desire to end my life here, to scrag myself with rags saturated in my own blood.

I have no candle and the sun is deserting me. I have only a few moments left. Why won't they give me candles? They are afraid that I will make a human torch of myself. They fear I may deprive them of killing me. Don't they know? My life and my death, that is their choice now, not mine.

Where is Annie, I wonder. Could she really be beside me, suffering as I suffer? No, I think that I would sense her presence if she were near. And where is John? Have they hunted him down and killed him? And Wilkes? I must not even think of him. And Isaac? The war is over. Has he survived it, only to return to a deserted home, and possibly prison, because of his unfortunate kinship? And Dulcey and little Genevieve? And all our little cats? Are they back on the streets, starving, dying? I cannot do a thing to help any of them. I cannot even help myself. I wonder if any of them have realized, as I have, that our lives are in the hands of others. Of them all, I think that Dulcey always knew.

The sun is gone. I know that it still shines somewhere. It must. It is spring. The sun somewhere is riding high in a blue sky. It is only gone from me. I can no longer see to write. The words I have put here may be running together in a hopeless and incomprehensible tangle. I cannot see. I stop now and perhaps forever.

Friday, April 28, 1865

They have allowed me the sun once more. I have spoken to the Colonel. It was, as I had thought, he who gave me back my diary. He came to my cell last night, and though he brought ill tidings, it was wonderful to share conversation with a human being. He has read my little book. He told me that it was his duty. The soldiers searched the house and brought all of my papers to him. They could have been used as evidence, he said. He seemed uncomfortable, even embarrassed, by his actions. I asked him how many others had read my things. He said that no one but himself had seen the inside pages of my diary.

He told me that he wished more than anything on earth that he could free me at that very moment, but that it was impossible. In fact, I am even being taken from his custody. That, he said, was the reason he had come. He was afraid for me. He knew they would be coming for me soon. He guessed that I would be taken to the Arsenal. He told me that he realized that I must think I had been mistreated at his hands, but that he had done the very best he could do. Others under suspicion had been arrested and confined on ironclads on the river, hooded and tortured. The Colonel told me that he had done his best to protect me and provide for me. He has felt from the beginning my innocence. It was confirmed by my diary. He tried to have it read by a very influential person, but he was turned away with orders to burn it. That he could not do. So he disobeyed and returned the book to me. Who is this influential person, I asked him. For the first time I felt close to the source of the power. But the Colonel answered that he could not say. I asked, would this person talk to me? The Colonel sadly shook his head. He said to me, "There are no reasonable men in Washington these days. Everyone is filled with hatred and fear. No one wants reason. They want only revenge."

Then it is hopeless, I said. I am to be taken against my will to an even worse place than this, and then what? And the Colonel said that he did not know. I told him to go and talk to the influential person again. Tell him, I said, tell him that I am nothing but a poor widow caught in circumstance. Tell him that please, I begged. Take my diary, give it to him, make him read it, make him see. But the Colonel would not take it from me.

"Keep it. You must keep it hidden. It is your only solace. I cannot provide any other, for I must confess I have little hope to give you. You are doomed unless your son returns."

"My son?"

"Yes. It's not you they want. You are being held in hopes of ferreting out your son. He is the one they seek, but he eludes them. They hope that you will bring him to them."

"Who are these men who would do this to an innocent woman? Who are they?"

"You will know soon enough. They will begin questioning you soon."

"And Annie, my daughter?"

"She is safe for the moment."

"She is no longer here then?"

"No, she was released with Miss Fitzpatrick after a few hours."

"She is home then, thank God. But she is alone."

"Surely there must be friends with her."

"Friends? I thought that all had turned against us."

"You have friends, Mrs. Surratt. We will help quietly, but all that we can."

"Colonel, are you saying that you are a friend?"

"Yes. Your secret friend, that I must remain to be of any use to you."

"When will they be coming for me?"

"Tomorrow night, probably."

We spoke last night. They gave me another tomorrow, and that is today. After the sun is gone and I finish here, I will hide you, dear little book. We will wait for them. I will take you wherever they take me. We shall see, you and I, where we wake tomorrow, if we wake.

Sunday, April 30, 1865

They came for me in the darkness, early Saturday morning. I was manacled at the wrists and my legs ironed. They were so heavy that I could barely walk. I was put in the back of a wagon which was covered over with canvas. I could not sit upright but had to crouch. Two soldiers sat at the open flap, their legs dangling, their backs to me, their rifles resting on their shoulders. At least they trusted me enough to turn their backs on me, or perhaps they did not want to look upon my hateful face. I was told coldly that I should have walked through the streets, but they feared that the populace, should they discover who I was, would rend me to pieces. So I was privileged to ride.

The journey was not a long one, but at one point I asked one of my guards if the iron on my one leg could be loosened as it pained me greatly. He did not turn. I did not see his face as he told me that he would do nothing to comfort me, that he hated me, wished fervently for my death, that his only brother had died in Andersonville Prison. And so I learned that I must now take responsibility for a prison camp I never laid eyes upon, and be punished for the deaths which occurred there.

This is a terrible place. I feel that I am lost completely now. I write this very quickly and furtively. They searched me upon my arrival here. God knows how they missed finding you, my dear little book, but they did not. In my cell at the Old Capitol I had the morning sun for a brief time. Here, there is one hour of light in the afternoon. Yesterday I was afraid to try to write anything. Today they watch less closely. There is straw upon the floor, that is my bed. I have no covers, not even the old thin blanket. There is a bucket in one corner as before. The walls are damp. I have seen no one but soldiers. They have obviously been ordered not to speak to me. Again I am a novelty, a sight to be seen, as I was in my first days at the Old Capitol. They come and peer in at me. I have turned my back to the door and crouched over my book so that if any should come they will not be able to see what I am doing.

I have the terrible fear that the Colonel was correct and that this is the Arsenal. It was so very dark and I was moved so quickly that I could not get my bearings. God, let it not be the Arsenal. This place has meant death to me for so long now. I think of all the lovely young girls who were shattered to bits in the explosion, and I feel their presence here. This must be the Arsenal.

I cannot believe that I am in a cell. It is horrible and inconceivable. I have done nothing. Yet I am hated, chained, spat upon, abused, and locked in dank dark chambers. I am humiliated, degraded, and despised. This is happening but it cannot be. I have done nothing wrong. I wonder how long I can be treated this way before I begin to believe that I deserve it.

Monday, May 1, 1865

Still I bleed, profusely and continually. It has gone on for so long now. I grow weaker every day. They bring food to me here twice every day, a kind of mush on a tray. I eat it in the darkness with my hands. Sometimes I feel as if I must push it down my throat with my fingers because the effort to swallow is too great.

I feel so unclean. That terrible bucket and the stench. Two soldiers passed my cell the other day and the one asked what the reeking was. The other answered that it was the Surratt bitch, that she has the disease of the womb. His companion said he had not smelled anything so bad since the field hospital at Shiloh.

Again I am forced to beg cloth, rags, anything, of strange soldiers. This is a woman's disease not understood by men. They show little compassion. Besides I am a she-devil to them, and I think that they enjoy my pain.

I wonder how it is with my family. I am allowed no visitors. I know nothing of the outside world. This is my world now—this shrunken, ugly, fetid place.

Do they intend to keep me here forever? Am I to be put on trial? Charged with some crime? As of now, I do not know. It could be that I must remain in ignorance and darkness, in this atmosphere of hatred, forever. But forever cannot be long. I will die. I must speak with another human being. I must be given some understanding of why this is being done to me.

I am guilty of being a fool, for that I am culpable.

I may be censured for blindness.

Blame me for weakness.

I confess to these misdeeds and offenses. I am a felon of the mind and heart. I have done wrong. Yet I know that these are not the reasons for my imprisonment. I could not believe it, the first time the police arrived at my door, but they did not frighten me as the men who came next did. The ones in their uniforms, so stiff and cold and sure of their duty. They terrified me. And then that ruffian appearing at the door right after their arrival, claiming to have been asked to do some work around the house for me. I had never set eyes on him before. I told the soldiers that, but they took him too. Is everyone to be swept up in their net?

Lincoln is dead. Does that make everyone who lives on somehow guilty?

What is to become of me? And those I love? I worry so about Dulcey and Genevieve. Will they return to starvation, go back to that miserable hovel and die? They are not stray cats. They will continue on, somehow. And Annie. I did very little for her these last months, except make her unhappy. I wish that I could see her now. Now I would try to tell her what I feel. Perhaps I would still fail, but at least now I would try. Now she will never know that I was not being intentionally cruel or cold to her. She will never know how I love her. I am sorriest of all for that.

This is my best hour of the day. There is light and I am able to write. I am wearing down the point of my pencil. I don't know how I am to sharpen it. I can just see myself asking one of my guards for a dagger to whet the point of my poor pencil. Oh, I am a desperate character.

Thursday, May 4, 1865

Today I believe I met with a devil. This morning they pulled me from my straw bed, shackled me, and led me down a long corridor and into a small room. The sun filled it. I was allowed to sit in a chair. And it seemed to me that this particular morning anyway it was not intended that I should die.

The door opened and a man entered the small sunny room where I sat. He seated himself behind the desk and put some papers down upon it. He seemed ordinary enough, until he looked up at me and I saw his eyes. They were like mirrors, silver, smooth, and glassy. I could not see past their glazed surface. I truly believe he is a devil.

He goes in this world by the name of Lafayette Baker. He

introduced himself to me, then looked down to consult his papers. His eyes are inhuman, not to feel them upon me was blessed relief. He told me that he was going to ask me some questions. It was an insidious interrogation, but in my terror I can only remember pieces of sentences, unrelated words. He asked me about Wilkes—"Booth, the fiend."

When he said that, I wanted to say that fiend Booth may very well have been, but you, Lafayette Baker, are his brother.

"Your lover."

No, he never loved me. He couldn't have. I loved him, but he never, never . . . But instead I said, "He was not my lover. He was a youth. He could have been my son."

"Your son. Where is he?"

"Where am I? How can I know where anyone is, if I do not know where I am?"

"Booth, the fiend, your lover, assassin and murderer."

"Is he here?"

". . . dead."

Wilkes is dead. From this moment on that will be the only time that the present tense can be used for him. Is dead. Wilkes is dead. Was beautiful. Was loved. Was evil. Was mad. Is dead. Is dead.

"Your son. Where is he?"

"Isaac was in the Army, but the war is over now."

"Not Isaac. John. John Harrison Surratt, where is he?"

"I don't know. He was in Canada."

". . . Booth, the assassin and murderer, the fiend, your lover. Booth?"

"Is dead."

"You planned. You plotted with him . . ."

"No." I only loved him. There was no plot or plan to it.

"You aided. You abetted. You assisted. You assassinated."

"No."

". . . Booth, your lover, the fiend, the assassin and murderer . . ."

And that is all, except for silver eyes glaring at me, that I remember of it. And Wilkes is dead. The sun is gone again.

Saturday, May 6, 1865

I have not slept. Every moment I expect to be taken once again to Lafayette Baker. I remember when I anticipated death. That was preferable. I have not been summoned to him again. I cannot imagine that he got enough from me in our last interview. I doubt that my answers suited him or his purposes. As I remember them, they were hardly answers at all. They were more the meanderings of a mad woman.

They torment me. They bring my food at different times. It may come in the early morning and late afternoon one day, and then early afternoon and late at night the next. I am not allowed to expect anything. All control has been taken from me. At first I welcomed that. My headaches have ceased since I have been in prison. Perhaps the pressure of being responsible for myself created that pain. But now I would gladly take back the pressure if only I could have some say in what was to become of me. I have grown to hate them most for their trespasses against my humanity and my autonomy.

I have been a prisoner nearly a month now.

I keep thinking that someone will come to me and say, "I'm sorry. This has been a terrible mistake. You are free to go." But my hope for those words fades as the days go past and they go unspoken. If it was a mistake they would have discovered it before this. I have been plighted, promised to this cell.

Lately I've been visualizing a keyboard in my mind. I play upon it, and I am splendid. I am as good as I was when I was young—better. That's the wonderful thing about imagination. I can imagine myself as good as I want. And I no longer have to spend my evenings doing the mending. The sewing must be piling up at home these days without me there. But no, I suppose not. There's only Annie there now, and she has always been so careful with her clothes. To think of that house, once so full, nearly empty now. It has been many days since I spoke with the Colonel, perhaps now the house no longer even stands. It could be that they have razed it. Things happen so swiftly, and their loathing and rancor is so strong and destructive. I believe that I must be homeless now.

I am a wanderer locked into a prison. I am a criminal who never thought of doing harm. I am a woman who is bleeding away her purpose in life onto a straw bed which lies on the cold stone floor of a cell.

Sunday, May 7, 1865

Colonel Wood came to see me this morning. It was so dark. I thought that he was my breakfast. He ordered two chairs brought in and a candle. I could see his face then.

"Mrs. Surratt, this is a disgrace."

"I'm usually a much better housekeeper, Colonel."

"I am truly sorry for this."

"It is not your doing. I know that."

"You are ill."

"Woman's illness. It will pass."

"A doctor should be called. I will see to it."

"You're very kind. It was good of you to come. You're my first visitor here. I hope not the last. Colonel, have you any word of my family? My daughter? My son? Do you know anything? They will tell me nothing."

"Your daughter is still free. She insists on living in your house, as usual. It is very dangerous since many know of the house, but she declares she will hide from no one, that she will wait for your return in her own home, your home."

"She is a strong-willed girl."

"Yes, very brave."

"Is there a chance that she might be taken . . . that they might . . ."

"I cannot lie to you. There is a chance of anything these days, Mrs. Surratt."

"But she is safe for now?"

"Yes, for now."

"And my son, John?"

"He has disappeared completely. Mr. Weichman and Mr. Holohan did not find him in Canada. Mr. Weichman is here now."

"Here? In prison?"

"Yes. I am sorry to be the one to tell you this . . ."

"You are the only one who tells me anything, Colonel. I know that you would like to tell me hopeful things. I also know that you cannot. Tell me about Mr. Weichman."

"He has given witness against you."

"Against me?"

"He made a statement to Lafayette Baker. It is very bad, Mrs. Surratt, very bad for you."

"What kind of statement? What could he possibly say about me? He lived in my home. We went to church together. He could not testify against me."

"He could and he has. They've brought in your tenant Lloyd too. They've both buckled under to Baker."

"Lafayette Baker, the man terrifies me."

"He should."

"Colonel, I'm very frightened. What do they mean to do to me?"

"You're going to be put on trial for your part in the Lincoln assassination plot."

"I had no part in it."

"They intend to prove that you did."

"When does it begin, this trial?"

"Soon. I don't know exactly."

"Oh, God. God help me. They want me dead."

"Mrs. Surratt, you know who they want. They want your son. They believe that he was co-leader with Booth in the plot. I believe that too."

"No. That cannot be."

"I believe as much in his guilt as I do in your innocence. You know that you are being used to bait a trap for your son. If they put you on trial, if there is danger for you, he'll come out of hiding. That is their plan. I think it will work."

"And when he does come out of hiding . . ."

"He'll be executed."

"He mustn't then."

"Mrs. Surratt, he must."

"Or else I will die, I know."

"I don't think they would go that far, but you could very well spend the rest of your life in prison."

"That won't be a very long time, the rest of my life. I feel dead right now. Besides, Colonel, I think that they are quite capable of executing me. However, it would be far more appropriate for me to die of a female ailment. How very indecorous of the government, to hang a middle-aged widow lady."

"I'll see that a doctor is sent to you."

"You would do me a very great favor by not doing that. Let nature take its course. Let's cheat the government. Let me die."

"Your son will come, Mrs. Surratt."

"Colonel, is it true what Baker told me? Is John Wilkes Booth dead?"

"Yes. He was killed in Virginia in late April."

"Shot?"

"Yes."

"Was there a fire?"

"Yes, a barn was burned. But how did you know that? Did Baker tell you?"

"No. Maria Carbini told me."

"Who is she?"

"It doesn't matter. It's far too late to heed that warning. Colonel, can you make a guess as to when the trial will begin?"

"A few days from now. A week at the most."

"That soon?"

"Yes. I must go now. I'll see to a doctor. One of these chairs will be left for you. I'll do whatever I can to help you, Mrs. Surratt."

"Thank you. Oh, Colonel?"

"Yes?"

"Might you have a pencil with you? I've worn mine down to a nub."

I have Colonel Wood to thank for my darker, deeper, bolder words here today.

Monday, May 8, 1865

Another visitor. This time during my hour of sunlight. I thought that he would never leave and that I might miss writing today, but he has gone finally and left me about fifteen minutes with you. His name is Dr. Gray. He came to examine me. Colonel Wood must wield some power and influence outside his realm of the Old Capitol. This was very fast action.

I have been so isolated and alone, it is hard for me to believe that I could resent the presence of any human being, but I did indeed resent Dr. Gray. Colonel Wood, in doing the part of a friend, I fear, has convinced them that I am dying. They are very afraid of losing their bait. Hence Dr. Gray.

I want to die. There have been many times in my life when I wanted to live no longer. After Papa and little Anna had gone, I wanted to go too. I could not understand why they had not taken me with them. I grieved. Yet I did not wish them alive again. I wished myself dead, wished it with all my might and strength. I never wanted death more until this moment. I pray to God that John does not come back here to save me. He loves life. He should have it. On me life is wasted and always has been.

Tuesday, May 9, 1865

This morning I was awakened and brought here. It is a larger cell. I have three windows. Of course they have bars upon them, but bars cannot keep out the sun. I have a couch. A chair. And a rug upon the floor. I even have a table with a lamp. And I am to be allowed books to read. Breakfast was a revelation–eggs, and ham, and two slices of bread toasted with butter, and coffee–and a knife and fork and spoon to eat it with. I had forgotten how good coffee tastes.

They are bound and determined that I should live. And though it sounds hollow, it is easier to want to live when one has sunlight and coffee and a soft spot to sit. Yet I am not deceived by all of this, even if I am rather dazzled. I realize that this ease and comfort is just another of their tortures. My resolve is firm. I will die. The only question that remains is, will my death be at their hands or my own, my choice or theirs? It is the only choice they have left me. I intend to exercise it. God give me the strength.

Dr. Gray arrived close on the heels of the soldiers who deposited me here. He brought with him little white pills which I am to take. And tomorrow he promises me a tonic.

After he left, another soldier arrived with a box. I opened it. Inside I found my best black alpaca dress, a black bonnet and veil, and some of my underclothes, even one of my lace handkerchiefs trimmed in black. I asked the soldier why I was being given these things. And he answered me. They are allowed to speak to me now, it seems. He told me that an order had come down that I was to be given other clothes. It wasn't much of an answer to me, but to a soldier, I suppose, an order is an answer of sorts. He left me alone with my black alpaca. I held it next to my face, hoping that Annie had packed it for me, that she had touched these things only a few hours before. It must have been she. Who else would have included my favorite hanky?

The trial must be coming very soon. This dress I'm wearing would invite far too much sympathy and pity. The alpaca makes me look rather prosperous. Though I imagine it will hang on me now. I have lost a great deal of weight. I'm surprised they don't hold off on the trial until they have fattened me up a bit. Perhaps they will.

I wonder who my judge and jury will be. I was right to distrust Salmon P. Chase and his promises. Have I been treated justly? No. Will I be? No.

There is only revenge, no thought of justice, in their hearts and minds. I am innocent. I have done nothing. But death is no punishment to me. I want to die. I am so tired of this unjust world of theirs. They think that it is punishment to send me from it and from them? It is bliss. I want nothing more than that. I choose death. I! They do not condemn me to it. I choose it!

* * *

Annie closed the book and looked up at Mardella. There were tears in her eyes.

"Miss Annie, please you try now to eats some supper?"

"I'll try. Oh, Della. I wish that it was morning. I wish that I was beside her, by her grave, this very moment."

"De morning, it come fast, Miss Annie."

XXVII

It was bright and sunny. She walked to the cemetery slowly. When she reached her mother's grave, she realized she should have brought flowers. Her mother had always loved flowers. She sat down on the ground. It was early and there was no one about.

"I'm sorry that I forgot flowers. I'm sorry for so many things, Mother. Someone tends this place very nicely. I'm glad of it. It was such a struggle to bring you here. They had you in such a dreadful place. It took years before they would release you to me. I hope that you know somehow that you are no longer in their hands, but in this pretty quiet place, in Maryland, Mother. I brought you home.

"I've been reading your diary. I feel that I have to come to know you finally. I wish that we could have talked together more than we did. I wish that I could have understood more, but at least I do now. It's not too late, is it, Mother?

"I have been to see John. He is well. He has a wife and two children. I don't know that he is truly happy. I don't think that any of us could be completely happy ever again. John blames himself for your death. I suppose he always will. I blamed him for a very long time, but I do not any longer. I told him that. I hope that it was some comfort to him, but I don't know. I think that if you could tell him that you did not blame him, that it wasn't his fault, then he might begin to believe it, but it is, of course, impossible for you to speak to him. I think that his little daughter may help him. She is a lovely child, bright, warm, and sweet-natured, your grandchild, Mother. I told her about you. She wanted very much to hear. She can give John the opportunity to love, unselfishly. He can give to her the things he blames and hates himself for not giving to you. I hope with all my heart that he does this, and I believe that he will, Mother.

"And Colonel Wood, good and brave man, I would not be here now if it were not for him. He saved your diary and he gave it to me, as you asked. He gave you to me. I had driven you from my life and memory, Mother. I could not think of or remember you because all I saw was horror and all I felt was pain when I did. It was not just you, Mother, and your memory that I avoided. I had isolated myself completely. But as I began to read your book, I began to feel again.

"I had not even thought of Grandmother Jenkins until John said her name to me. Then I knew that I must go to see her. We talked for a long while, Mother, just hours before she died. It was almost as if she had been waiting for me. She loved you very much. She told me that. It hurt her, Mother, to think that you wanted to die. She couldn't bear it, because she loved life so very much and you so very much. I realize now that you did want to die, but Mother, I believe there was a time when you wanted to live.

"I've been a long time reading your diary. I'm not yet finished. I would never have begun, had it not been for Mardella. You don't know Mardella, but you knew her mother and her daughter. Mardella's mother was Dulcey and her child was Genevieve. They both died, shortly after you went to prison, of the typhoid. Mardella felt that you kept them alive, and that because of you she was able to see them one last time. Mardella has kept me alive, Mother. She has done this in thanks to you. She knows me better than any other living creature. I owe her my life.

"I'm going home, Mother. I'm going to try to make it a home at last. It has never been that. I believe that William is a good man. I have been brutally unfair to him, and unkind. I have never shared a thought with him. I never tried to love him, or feel anything for him at all. I used him as a shelter, as I would a house or a room. I never gave anything to him, nor did I ask anything of him. I want to know him now. I want to try to love him. I believe that I am going to have his child, Mother. This child did not begin with love, but I hope to carry it with reverence for the love and life that it will bring.

"Mother, I don't want to leave you now that I have found you at last. I want to believe that you will always be with me. Life has become precious to me once more. I remember the day I begged for your life, so many years ago. It was summer then, as it is now. I went to the White House to plead with the President, but he would not see me. I was turned away. There was nothing I could do and I began to hate life then. Seth had been taken from me, and you were being taken. I was powerless to stop it. It all seemed so horrible and hard and unjust. I wanted to die then, and I did, in a way. It has been thirteen years, Mother, thirteen long years of feeling nothing, desiring nothing, being nothing.

"I have a picture of you in my mind. You are at the piano in the parlor at the H Street house. Your head is bent over the keys and your face is in profile. Your hair shines. Your fingers move and beautiful sounds come from the old instrument. There is such love and peace and pleasure in this picture. You are happy. It is like this that I shall forever see you."

Annie stood and looked down at the plain stone marker. The night's rain had spattered it with drops that looked like tears. She bent and pressed her lips to it.

"I'm sorry, Mother, that I forgot flowers. I know what I shall do.

In the picture I carry in my mind of you, I will place a crystal vase of red roses upon the piano. That will do, I think. I love you, Mother."

She turned and walked from the graveyard.

XXVIII

She and Mardella arrived home early that evening. They walked in the front door.

"Della, it's the same."

"You 'spect it gonna be different, Miss Annie?"

"Yes, I suppose that I did. I feel so different. How can it be the same?"

"It jus' is."

"Do you suppose he's here, Della?"

"Cain't say, Miss Annie. I 'spect he be turnin' up soon."

"Do you think he will have changed?"

"Mebbee so, mebbee not. You has changed. You gotta let him do dat too if he be so inclined. You cain't grudge him dat."

"I want him to have changed. I do, Della. It's just that I'm a little frightened. I don't know what to expect."

"Don't 'spect nothin'. Jus' look an' try to 'cept what you sees."

"Yes, I'll try to do that."

"I gonna go an' take a peek at de kitchen. I cain't help but 'spect what I is gonna find dere, a man alone in de house all dese days."

"I think I'll go upstairs. Just leave the trunk for the time being, Della."

She stood for a moment looking up the stairs before she took a step toward them. Finally, she began the climb.

The room was closed off and dark. She pulled the curtains and opened the windows. It had grown dark outside. She stood looking out into the purple light of the steet. The air was soft and warm.

"Hello, Annie."

She turned. "Hello, William."

"You're back."

"Yes. Yes, I am."

"Are you planning on staying?"

"I thought that I would."

"Then I will pack and go."

"But why?"

"Because I don't want to be in the same house with you."

"You don't want . . ."

"That is correct. Just as you don't want to be with me, I don't want to be with you."

"But that's not . . ."

"Did you run out of places to visit? You had to come here, didn't you?"

"You wrote to me asking, demanding, that I return."

"Begging would be the better word, I would say. You never even bothered to answer my letter."

"I intended to, but so much has happened. There is so much I want to tell you about."

"It's not that simple, Annie. You cannot just walk back into this house and pick up again where we left off."

"That's not what I want, that's the last thing I want, to go back to where we were. I want you to know what has happened to me. I've changed."

"I don't want to hear. I don't care anymore."

"Anymore? Since when did you ever want to hear me, listen to me?"

"I don't want to argue."

"I had forgotten how much you disliked raised voices. We will try not to argue, but we must talk."

"Suddenly you want to communicate, to tell what has happened to Annie. Do you ask how I am? Do you want to know what I have been through since you have been gone? No. Well, I do not call that talking, conversing, or communicating, my dear."

"You didn't give me a chance. You came in here talking about packing and going before I could say a word. Besides, why should I think that you would answer my questions? You never have. You have never told me once how you felt, or what you felt. You've never once wanted to share with me anything that you have been through."

"Nor have you."

"I was trying to do just that a moment ago."

"It's too late, Annie. I feel too bitter toward you."

"Because I went to visit my brother and my grandmother, because I needed to talk to them about my mother, you hate me for that?"

"You left me, left me for another man."

"I did not. There's never been another man. There's not been anyone in my so-called life for thirteen years, no one, not even you. You, who slept beside me every night, made love to me, even beat me, you never touched me."

"Don't you think I know that? I knew what you were when I married you. I thought that was what I wanted. I had watched my mother and father, watched them year after year. He was a drunken beast, and she was a weak-willed woman, how do they say it in melodramas, ruled by love. Love! He would come into that little room late in the night, reeling and stinking, slap her and strike her. They would scream at one another, but always they would end up on the big old bed in the corner, grunting and moaning like animals, the new baby crying in its cradle while they thoughtlessly, endlessly made more and more new babies. I wanted a wife as different from my mother as I was from my father. And I chose you. I wanted cold unfeeling beauty, and I chose you. You opened your thighs to another man. You became my mother, weak and wanton.

You made me become my father that night. You question my bitterness? I hate you."

"There was no other man. I left you for a woman."

"What?"

"I left you for my mother."

"I could beat you again. You are such a cheat and a liar. I cannot believe that I actually wanted you back. Did you and your lover laugh over my letter together? Did you tell him about all the times I made love to you while you pretended to be asleep, how you never once returned a kiss, but would just lie beneath me like a cold marble statue? Did you tell him those things while you were in bed together?"

"You threatened me in that letter. That is one reason I didn't answer. I was afraid."

"Afraid of what?"

"Afraid of an asylum. That's what you were warning me of, wasn't it? If I didn't behave, you would have put me in a madhouse."

"I could still do that."

"Do you want your child to be born in an insane asylum?"

"Child?"

"Yes, I think I'm going to have a child."

"It's not mine."

"Whose is it then?"

"Your lover's."

"I have no lover. This child is yours. Don't you remember the night before I left . . ."

"I remember."

"You didn't pull away from me . . ."

"Stop it!"

"You didn't wet the sheet beside me . . ."

"Stop!"

"For once you stayed within me until the end."

"You could not possibly know this soon."

"But I do know. I think I knew that night. It's growing inside of me, our child."

"It is his child, not mine."

"It's yours. There is no lover."

"There was a man who came here. I know it."

"Yes. His name is Colonel Wood. He was my mother's jailor. He saved her diary for me. I began reading it. That was the change you saw in me. I did not acquire a lover. It was my mother and her words that made me feel alive again."

"You felt so alive that it was impossible to live with me any longer. You had to leave me."

"I didn't leave you. That was not my intention. My brother was planning on giving public lectures about the Lincoln assassination. I wanted to stop him. That's why I went to Baltimore."

"And did you succeed?"

"I did not succeed in stopping the lectures, but I had a much greater victory. I came to understand my brother, and to love him again. That was a success, I felt anyway."

"You've been all these days in Baltimore?"

"No. I went to Washington. I wanted to apologize to Colonel Wood. And I went to my Uncle Zadoc's farm to see my grandmother."

"I didn't know that you had a grandmother living."

"I don't any longer. She died while I was there. I stayed for her funeral. The last stop I made was at my mother's grave. And now I'm home."

"This is true, what you are telling me?"

"Would I invent such a story?"

"I don't know. I don't know what you're capable of doing."

"Do you want to know?"

"Do you really believe that you are with child?"

"Yes."

"Yes. You look different to me."

"There are so many things I want to tell you. So many things I want you to tell me. Shall we try?"

"I will only ask once more, and then I will never mention it again. You did not take a lover?"

"I tried to tell you that night about Seth. I loved him, loved him as you can only love someone when you are very young. He is dead. He died in the last days of the war. We had planned to be married. I confess to you that even after thirteen years I had never really said goodbye to Seth. There were nights, many nights, when I wished that you were Seth, wished it with all my heart, but I will never do that again. I've let him go, at last. I loved my memories of Seth, but he was a ghost-lover, not flesh."

"You're certain?"

"Yes."

"You want to stay? You want me to stay?"

"Yes. I want you, William."

He walked over to her, put his arms around her, drew her close to him. With his face buried in her hair, she heard his muffled words. "I've missed you, Annie. I thought that you had gone forever. I wanted to die. I love you. I love you."

She lifted his face from her shoulder and looked into his eyes. "If I should be wrong about the baby, I know that I am not, but if, by some chance I should be, let's begin one now."

XXIX

She woke in the darkness. The windows were opened wide and a warm breeze billowed the white curtains. The night outside did not frighten her. He slept still. She looked at him closely and she knew that she could come to love him. She got up from the bed and put on a wrapper.

"This is the last time, the last time I will leave you like this, but I must finish. Tomorrow night I will begin sleeping nights through with you, I promise, William." She kissed him lightly. He did not stir.

She carried the book down to the parlor and lit a candle. Before opening the diary at the ribbon-marked page, she held it in her hands for a moment, rubbed its soft leather cover, and remembered the first time she began reading it and thought of all that had happened since. She began to read, to reach the end, and to begin again.

Wednesday, May 10, 1865

I was taken from my new cell this morning. I guessed that it might be to Lafayette Baker again. Then it occurred to me that I was being returned to my old cell, that they had decided to let me die there after all. These thoughts were running through my mind as they walked me down the corridor. It was very difficult for me to walk. My legs were in irons, but they had not manacled my hands. We arrived at the end of the hallway, my two young guards and myself, and I thought surely that they would lead me down the stairwell to the lower level where my old cell was awaiting me, but they did not. They opened a door instead, and I stepped inside.

The room was very large. There were barred windows all around. There was the smell of whitewash and the walls were bright with it. It was very sunny, but even with the sun the room was not warm. I felt that this was the first time in a long time that human beings had been within this chamber.

As I walked through the door, immediately to my left there was a long dock about four feet high. There were several men sitting there. I was turned to the right, where I was seated. One of my guards sat beside me. It seemed that I was somehow bound, joined, to this group in the dock. I looked at the men closely. I counted seven in civilian clothes. They also wore chains. I recognized the three closest to me. Davy Herold was nearest. Then the "Reverend" whom I had thought Wilkes had confined to an asylum after his attack on little Genevieve. Then there was the funny little German, Atzerodt, whom we had called Port Tobacco. The others I had never seen before. They were a rather rough-looking lot, except for one gentleman seated nearly in the middle. He looked a cut above the rest. I noticed that his hands were not ironed like the others.

Directly in front of me, in the middle of the room, there was a stand, a sort of podium. There was a large empty table beside it, and it faced the far wall, where there was a long high bench with nine men in uniforms sitting upon it. There was much gold braid and buttons. I assumed that they were all generals, or colonels at the very least. To their left there was another table where three men were seated. Only one of them was in uniform.

It appeared that I was the last to arrive, because after I had been seated one of the generals began to speak. He was a fierce-looking white-haired man, clearly in command. He said that he wished to open the proceedings with joyous news. I, for one, welcomed this. He announced that Jefferson Davis, archrebel and conspirator, had been captured by Federal troops this morning. The general's joyous news was received most quietly. I wondered if we had been assembled only to hear this, but then he started to read the charges against the prisoners.

I realized then that my trial had begun. We, the prisoners, were told that we were accused of traitorously conspiring with John Surratt, John Wilkes Booth, Jefferson Davis, and others unknown, to kill and murder Abraham Lincoln, Andrew Johnson, William Seward, and Ulysses S. Grant. We were then asked how we pleaded. Everyone, including myself, said not guilty. Then the white-haired general said that we would move on to the individual charges. There followed a great deal about aiding, abetting, laying in wait, conspiring, comforting, and counseling. My memory fails me here, but I do recall the specific charges made against me. I was accused of receiving , entertaining, harboring, concealing, and aiding Booth, my own son, Herold, Atzerodt, and three men whose names I never before heard. They were Paine, O'Laughlin, and Arnold. When the name Paine was called and the charges read for this man, I was most surprised to see the "Reverend" stand.

We were told that we were sworn to secrecy and that none of the accused in the course of the trial would be allowed to take the witness stand. The general also said that the defense counsel for the prisoners would be present tomorrow, but that they would not be allowed into court unless they took the Oath of Allegiance to the Union.

I was returned to my cell. I have no lawyer. I don't know how to go about obtaining one. It all seems so unavailing and empty.

I was not frightened today. There was a dream-like quality to the proceedings. I was very weak and dizzy, which added a strange and fanciful dimension. This is the first time in a long long while that I have been in a well-lighted room, seated, with many other people about. I am not used to it. I am also unaccustomed to being referred to as "the prisoner" and "the accused." It makes it difficult to realize that they are talking about oneself. I could hardly find my voice to say that I was not guilty. It seemed so unnecessary. I know that I am not guilty. They know that I am. I will say what I believe and they will hear what they believe.

Thursday, May 11, 1865

This morning my attorneys introduced themselves to me, Mr. Aiken and Mr. Clampitt. I, in turn, introduced them to the court. I was told by them that this was procedure. They are very young men, capable, I am sure. I suppose that my brother Zadoc obtained them for me. Perhaps Annie did. Only one other of the accused had lawyers to present to the court. The rest had not yet retained counsel. It seemed very strange to be represented by these young men whom I had never set eyes upon before this morning. All so formal and official.

We were taken back to our cells. We, our, I begin to feel a kinship with my fellow prisoners. The trial will begin in earnest tomorrow. My lawyers were allowed to visit in my cell with me. Except for the Colonel, they are my first visitors.

They told me the names of my judges. I cannot remember them all, but there was a plethora of colonels and generals. There was a Hunter, a Harris, and a Howe. I never knew of my predilection for H's before this.

My young lawyers are most optimistic–a condition endemic to young lawyers I would expect. I told them that there was an attorney whom I did not know personally but of whom I had heard a great deal. They straightened at the mention of his name, Reverdy Johnson. I told them that I wished they could consult with him. Mr. Aiken and Mr. Clampitt seemed agreeable–perhaps with all their optimism–they would like to share the burden of my defense. It is good that they have young strong backs. I just feel that perhaps we also need an old head.

Friday, May 12, 1865

There was one battle in court today that had nothing at all to do with any of the accused. It involved the man whose presence I had desired, Reverdy Johnson. He did indeed appear in court for me today, much to my wonderment. He was presented to the court and one of the generals, Harris, I think, raised an objection to him. It is necessary that all attorneys take the loyalty oath before they can appear in court. Reverdy Johnson had not taken it. When he answered the court on this, I knew that I had picked the right man. He stood before all those men in blue perched high on their bench, and told them that he had been a senator and had taken the Oath of Allegiance on the floor of the United States Senate and in the Supreme Court. He clearly held them in contempt. The objection was withdrawn, and I went through the day with such hope until it was dashed by the very man who had given it to me, but that came later.

I do not pretend to understand legalities or fine constitutional points, but I do know that as a civilian I should not be tried by military tribunal. I believe that I am guaranteed a jury of my peers. There are civil courts open and operating in the city. This was pointed out in court today. It was asked if the accused could be tried in civil court. The court was cleared for deliberation, we were marched back to our cells for a time out, the plea was overruled. Which means that our judges decided that they were to be our only judges. We were also denied separate trials. We are to remain in a bunch, like grapes. They will have it no other way.

Today I saw my first witness. Though it is my trial, I had no idea who the man was. He said that his name was Richard Montgomery. He talked a good deal about Canada and secret ciphers. It was a puzzle to me what he was doing there at all. I surmised that the man was a spy of some sort. He spoke of a raid on St. Albans and the burning of New York City. The things he said were so fantastic, I could not separate what had actually happened and what was only planned. He also mentioned Halifax, which, unless my geography has totally deserted me, is a city on the Nova Scotian peninsula. All of this is completely alien to me. Richard Montgomery's testimony consumed most of the day.

Afterwards I went back to my cell and was lying upon my couch in exhaustion. It is very difficult for me to sit all day long. I was resting with visions of burning cities in my head when Reverdy Johnson was admitted to my cell. He sat down and looked hard at me.

"Why did you ask for me, Mrs. Surratt?"

"I don't know exactly. You are from my home state. I have heard your name spoken for many years. Seeing you in court today I can well understand the accolades you have gathered. You gave me hope today. This is something I have not had in a very long time."

"Please, madame. You make a difficult task impossible."

"I don't understand you, Mr. Johnson."

"I came to tell you that I will not be in court tomorrow."

"But the following day . . ."

"No, not the following day. Never again."

"But why, sir?"

"Don't you see, I angered them today."

"But you won. They withdrew their objection. They backed down."

"Do you think that any of those things make them less angry? Of course not. It only incenses them. I would only hurt your cause, madame. I must withdraw."

"Please don't."

"I must. I will work in the background. I will help your young men in any way that I am able, but I will not again appear in that courtroom."

"Please, I want you there."

"I tell you my presence will damage your case."

"Mr. Johnson, you and I both know that my case cannot be damaged."

"You have so little faith in your innocence?"

"I am certain of my innocence. It is their justice I doubt. I feel that only you can help me. Mr. Johnson, you cannot hurt me."

"I would, I assure you of that."

"Hurt me? What sort of harm could you do me? A soldier crossing a battlefield sees what he thinks to be a corpse. He notices a slight twitching of the hand. He drags the body to a field hospital, where the doctor pronounces it dead. Or perhaps the doctor might just possibly say that there is still life. That passing soldier has another choice when he sees the body with twitching hand. He can think that it is most definitely a corpse and for fun drive a bayonet into it. What sort of hurt is that? It was only a corpse after all. I see that you have made your choice, Mr. Johnson. You see me as a corpse."

"It is not so hopeless as that, madame."

"Isn't it? Isn't that the real reason for your desertion of me? You like victories, Mr. Johnson. In that courtroom you smell death and defeat. And that is why you will not return there."

"You are filled with bitterness."

"Yes, I am bitter. I speak and think nothing but recriminations these days. I do apologize. You were my last hope."

"I'm not leaving your case. I will help."

"You will give counsel to my counsel. Remember, they are young. You would do well to advise them of the uses of the bayonet. Good day, sir."

And he left me alone in my cell.

Saturday, May 13, 1865

Familiar faces today. Mr. Louis Weichman and Mr. Lloyd. I had been warned by Colonel Wood about Mr. Weichman, that he had made a statement to Lafayette Baker. My former boarder seemed most nervous today. I suspect that he was very glad that the witness stand faced the men in blue, and that his back was to me. Mr. Weichman has a conscience. He knows that he lies.

He talked about going to school with John, living in my home, accompanying me to church, doing errands for me, and driving me around the countryside. To save his soul he feels he must testify to my goodness, kindness, and general Christian approach to life. While at the same time to save his life he swears to my disloyalty, my plotting and planning murder, and my assisting and associating with villains and conspirators. One of whom was my own son, his friend and former schoolmate. It must be truly untenable for him. He is not evil. It is the men who prey upon his weakness and cowardice who are evil.

And poor Mr. Lloyd. I cannot hate him either. His trembling hands, his quavering voice. He turned once to Mr. Clampitt to answer a question, and one of the generals shouted that he would face the court at all times. The abject terror of the man at that moment was really awful to see. He is in fear of his life. To save it he has concocted a story of my telling him to have "shooting-irons" ready at the tavern for the conspirators, and my carrying messages and packages to Maryland like a spy or courier. I am depicted as a sort of Belle Boyd character. Obviously this could be nothing but one of Mr. Lloyd's wild alcoholic delusions. It is almost laughable, but I do not laugh.

This is tragedy. I do not think only of myself. This will ruin and destroy lives in a far-reaching way that I am sure none imagine at this moment. I may die of this. It is probable that I will, but Mr. Lloyd and Mr. Weichman will live. They have purchased their lives with their testimony, but I doubt either will be happy or content after all of this is finished. Mr. Lloyd may manage to live a kind of life, relying heavily on the bottle. It can be very supportive, the bottle, but all the while it is killing slowly. And Louis Weichman. I believe his counterpart to the bottle will be self-deception. As time goes on he will convince himself that he spoke the truth today.

This trial is like dropping a pebble in a still pond, the rings of disturbed water keep growing and growing. It does not stop with the prosecutors, the witnesses, the accused, and the judges. It reaches far beyond us.

Wednesday, May 17, 1865

I should try to recall some of the trial and record it here, but it is difficult. The heat grows more intense every day and my ability to make sense of all the words lessens.

Today, Emma Offutt, Mr. Lloyd's sister-in-law, testified. I could not see her clearly, but from a distance she looked most unwell to me. She was questioned about April 14, when I visited the tavern in Surrattsville. In recalling that day I was almost positive that upon finding Mr. Lloyd not at home I gave the package Wilkes had given me to Mrs. Offutt. She said on the stand that I did not.

Upon returning to my cell I checked in my little book and I had noted on that day, April 14, that I had given the package to Mrs. Offutt. She put it on the couch. When Mr. Lloyd came in I gave it to him. I don't know why this is so important to me, but when Mr. Clampitt arrived, as is his habit every day after the trial, I asked him about the matter of the package, if there was any significance to it. He said that there was, a great deal. If I had handed the package to Mrs. Offutt it proved I was not being in the least secretive or furtive in my activities, an important point, he said. Of course, I could not tell him about my little book. It was a promise I made to the Colonel when he first returned it to me. I know that young Clampitt, in his zeal and exuberance, would want to involve it in the trial if he knew of its existence. He could not know that my prosecutors, and probably my judges, perused it and found it not incriminating enough, and ordered it destroyed. So I simply told young Clampitt that I very clearly remembered giving the package to Mrs. Offutt and asked that he check with her again.

Thursday, May 18, 1865

Louis Weichman was recalled to stand today. It is as I thought, he is already well on his way to convincing himself. He answered today with much greater conviction than the other time. I myself could almost believe him today. I know that he did.

This morning when I came into the courtroom I noticed that

something new had been added. There was a table placed next to the prosecution table. There were several men seated at it who were busy writing. They did not wear uniforms. Some had even removed their jackets and sat in their shirt sleeves, an irreverence this courtroom had not seen before. It occurred to me that they were journalists, reporters.

One of them in particular seemed to be staring at me. He was not writing on his pad. He was sketching, and I realized that he was drawing me. I tried to imagine seeing myself in the papers. It was impossible. Then the man got up, crossed the room, and approached me. I was not sure of his intention. Neither was my guard, who is always beside me in the courtroom. He would not let the man near. Next he went over to my attorney, Mr. Aiken. He asked him something and Mr. Aiken came over to me, seeming somewhat embarrassed. I asked him what the man had said. He told me that he had asked if I would lift my veil so that he could draw my face. Otherwise, he would just have to imagine what I looked like and draw that. I told my young lawyer that I would not remove my veil. I said that an imaginary sketch of me would be quite appropriate since this entire trial and most of the testimony had a distinctly fanciful air to it. I am sure the man will give me the face of a villainess. My face wouldn't sell any papers at all. I just don't look like a creature of crime and depravity as they would have me.

Friday, May 19, 1865

Today several things were cleared up for me in regard to the "Reverend" whom they refer to as Paine. His name is not Wood and he is certainly not a Baptist preacher. His name is Lewis Paine and he is the man, they say, who attacked Secretary of State Seward.

What shocked me most today was the discovery that he was the ruffian who came to the house the night of my arrest claiming I had called him to dig a gutter or some such labor. I denied knowing him that night. That is what several witnesses testified to today. They are honest men. They do not perjure themselves. I did deny knowing the man. I no more recognized the gutter-digger as the Reverend

Wood than I would have thought him to be my son. I thought that the "Reverend" had been locked away in a madhouse. Besides, the Baptist preacher who had stayed at my house in March had always been dressed in a tight gray suit, his hair was combed close to his head. The man who appeared at my door that night was dressed in workmen's clothes, with a sleeve pulled over his forehead. The hair that escaped from under this makeshift headgear was long and wild. My eyesight is bad. I simply did not recognize the gutter-digger as the "Reverend Wood." I did swear that I had never seen the man before. The young officers speak truly.

Now that I think of the "Reverend" or Lewis Paine or whoever he may be, I remember his devotion to Wilkes. He must have come that night to my home thinking to make some connection with him there. He must have wanted Wilkes desperately to tell him what to do, where to go. It was pure accident, probably the creature's usual bad luck, that brought him to my door at that particular moment. Looking at him in the courtroom, so sinewy and huge, he is not a figure to elicit pity or compassion. He will receive none, except from me. I know what it is to be caught in the web of John Wilkes Booth, to love him, and be blind.

There was a man who testified today who especially interested me. His name was R. C. Morgan. He is with the War Department. He was the first man to search my house after my arrest. He told of the pictures that he found there, pictures of Jefferson Davis, General Beauregarde, Vice President Stephens, and John Wilkes Booth. Yet he mentioned not a word about my diary. He must have found it and carried it to his superiors. I wondered for a moment if he read it. I decided that most likely he did not. He seemed to me to be a man who did his duty, unswervingly. His testimony was correct and incomplete. He had made the omissions ordered. He had done his duty. He could be proud. He could go home and forget.

Thursday, May 25, 1865

Poor Mr. Aiken. Today he came up against a most skillful deceiver, a Mr. George Cottingham. It seems that Mr. Aiken and

Mr. Cottingham had a conversation at the Metropolitan Hotel last Saturday night. Mr. Cottingham had been in charge of Mr. Lloyd after his arrest, and Mr. Cottingham suggested to my young and gullible lawyer that he had obtained Mr. Lloyd's confession through strategy. Mr. Aiken became very excited over this, hoping to discredit Mr. Lloyd's confession by calling upon Mr. Cottingham to tell the court exactly what he had told him in the Metropolitan Hotel.

Unfortunately when Mr. Cottingham was called to the witness stand today he confidently declared that he had lied that night at the hotel to Mr. Aiken. He continued that while it wasn't perjury to lie in a hotel, it was in a courtroom under oath, and now he intended to tell the truth. Mr. Cottingham's present and most recent version of the truth is that Mr. Lloyd, like a good citizen, willingly and voluntarily told the government all that he knew about Mary Surratt and her nefarious intriguing. Lloyd, he said, confessed like a man. He testified that no strategy, no threats, and no force had been used against him at any time while in custody. O, poor Mr. Aiken was crestfallen, but then he is young. He'll learn. Mr. Cottingham was one of the first witnessess for my defense. An auspicious beginning, I must say. I hardly recognized it from the prosecution. Things did improve somewhat, however.

Mr. George Calvert testified in my behalf. He told of my debt to him, and Mr. Nothey's debt to me. He tried to explain our convoluted financial relationship. This, he testified, was the reason for my trips to Surrattsville in April. He also accurately described Mr. Lloyd's drunkenness on April 14th. He referred to him as "tight." I do thank Mr. Calvert for coming forward, but I fear that his main motivation was his fear that if I am hanged he'll never get the money I owe him. It's as legitimate and as honest a reason as any witness has had so far.

Honora Fitzpatrick returned to the stand today. She has now been both witness for the prosecution and the defense. She said much the same thing on both occasions. Her comments were confined mostly to my good Christian character and my being blind as a bat. My lawyers wish to emphasize my defective eyesight. That helps to explain my not recognizing the Reverend Wood/Lewis Paine.

Eliza Holohan also testified today. She carefully patted her hair into place before putting her hand on the Bible. Though I could not see her face, I could almost feel her smiling prettily to the judges. I don't remember what she said.

And finally, there was a Mr. George B. Woods from Boston. I had never seen him before in my life. He seemed a very nice little man. His testimony consisted of telling how often he had seen pictures of the leaders of the Rebellion for sale in the streets of Boston. I suppose that my lawyers' thinking was that if those pictures were for sale in that bastion of Unionism, then it could not be disloyal of me to have had those same pictures in my home. My judges did not seem impressed by this logic. I cannot say that I was either, but I did appreciate Mr. Woods coming all this way. I hope that his train fare back to Boston was paid for by someone other than himself.

Friday, May 26, 1865

This was the day of the Fathers. I thank those good and dear men. There was Reverend Wiget, Reverend Boyle, Reverend Stonestreet, Reverend Lanihan, and Reverend Young. They testified to the length of time they had known me, my loyalty, my piety. Reverend Wiget called me a "Christian and a lady."

It means much to me that they should come to my defense. I was especially glad of my veil today. It hid the tears. Those good men believe so completely in my innocence, but my faith is gone. I believe that I am doomed, and that this trial is God's instrument of my destruction. The good Fathers cannot save me, even though they are God's emissaries on earth. I broke faith with God long ago and this is my punishment. I am to be tried, found guilty, executed, and then I will burn in hell.

I am more tired today than I have ever been. Fifteen days of this, listening to all those voices—raised in anger, low and frightened, soft and harsh, male and female—but the words, all the same. I must sit in that straight-backed chair, with so many eyes fixed upon me, and the heat nearly strangling me. It all weighs far too heavily, and I am not strong. I am weak. I have always been.

Tuesday, May 30, 1865

The faces of the witnesses grow more and more familiar. My brother Zadoc testified today. Zadoc is a fine-looking big man. He is in his prime. He thrusts out his chest and his voice booms. He defiantly refuses to be intimidated by the court, though I know that he is cowering inside. Zadoc is all bluster. He was meant to be a successful farmer, involved in local politics and intrigues, shouting his opinions, and drinking a little too much, but I fear for him now. He will collapse under the pressure, I fear. He was Mother's favorite child. He has such broad strong shoulders, but he cannot bear the burdens of the mind.

He tried so hard today. He told the court about my feeding Union troops and their horses, and never asking payment for it. He also spoke of my eyesight. I believe he said I could not see my hand in front of my face. My guard is convinced by all this testimony. I have noticed lately that he takes my arm and guides me around as if I were totally blind. It is very sweet of him. I see far more than any of them realize. The court, with their unerring ability to scent out weakness, did not attack Zadoc's testimony, but instead Zadoc himself. His loyalty to the Union was questioned. He withstood that rather well. I think only the judges and I noticed the beginning of a crack in his wonderfully strong and sure facade. They did not pursue it. I was very surprised and can only suppose that they feel they will have another opportunity to reduce my cracking brother to rubble.

When Annie entered the courtroom I wanted to rise up out of my chair, but I could not. I wanted so to go to her. It has been over a month since I have seen her. She is paler and thinner, but she looked beautiful, so straight and tall, her hair the color of the barred sunlight. She answered all the questions in her clear soft voice. She did not falter except at the very end. They asked her about the pictures of Booth and the Rebel leaders found in the house. She told them that the pictures of Beauregarde and Davis had been given to her by her father and that she prized them on his account. She went on to say that she and Honora had bought the pictures of Booth when they had gone to a studio to have their pictures made. They had been excited to be able to buy the picture of a famous person with whom they were acquainted. She told them that she also had pictures of McClellan, Grant, and Hooker. Would they like to ask about those? They declined.

She told a story about my now famous failing eyesight, how I was too vain to wear spectacles, that I thought they would make me look too old, and that I couldn't see a thing. Her voice trembled a little just then.

Then they began on Wilkes. The prosecutor made terrible accusations. He declared that Wilkes had been my lover and Annie's too. Annie fainted. There was an outcry in the courtroom. She was carried out. The judges decided that the prosecution had, for once, gone too far. The prosecutor's words were struck from the record. The reporters were ordered to delete any reference to the subject from their notes. But the words, though ordered erased, could not be forgotten even if they are never printed in any newspaper.

I am worried about Annie. I have asked over and over that she be permitted to visit me, but it is not allowed.

Annie closed the book for a moment and thought of the small room in the prison where she had waited to be called to testify that day. She had been so eager to take the stand. Even after the cruelties and frustrations of her several interrogations she had still felt that somewhere someone would listen to her, and understand, and believe. She had convinced herself that her mother could be saved, and that the judges in the next room were the men who would do it. They would hear her testimony and they would know that the woman they had imprisoned and shackled, her mother, was innocent.

Mr. Clampitt had come for her. She was unprepared for the huge hot white room, and the silence as she entered, the staring faces, and then the rush of voices, but most of all the still, black-veiled figure in the prisoner's dock. They had asked all the wrong questions. She had begun to realize that she was in their power, that they could control the things that she said, that they did not want to hear the truth, that they did not want to believe her mother's innocence no matter how she protested it. Then they had accused her of taking Booth as her lover. The white walls grew suddenly bright and blinding. She had felt the blood rushing and pounding at her temples and then there was blackness.

When she had opened her eyes again she was back in the small room, and there had been a doctor, and he had given her medicine. And she remembered wanting to cry, but not being able to.

Now Annie cried. The tears fell on the closed book in her lap. She brushed them away and opened the diary again.

Friday, June 2, 1865

How can it be nighttime and remain so hot? It is becoming exceedingly difficult for me to see or write in candlelight. Sometimes I can barely discern the words I have just moments before put to the page.

The trial goes on and on. It reminds me of the war. The constant circling of the opponent, looking for a weak spot.

Today in the courtroom Mr. James Lusby appeared. He is from down in the country. I do not know him well. He spoke of Mr. Lloyd's drunkenness on April 14th. He testified that they had ridden home together from Court Day and shared a bottle along the way. It occurs to me that Mr. Lloyd and I would have made a wonderfully efficient pair of conspirators. What with his being drunk and my being blind, it would be a wonder if we ever chanced to see one another, much less plot together

Also a Mr. Smoot and Mr. Roby testified against Zadoc. They declared that he was disloyal to the Union. It was clearly an attempt to discredit him, but the only trouble there is that Zadoc is not on trial. I am, I think. It is hard to be sure sometimes.

Saturday, June 3, 1865

Miss Anna Ward testified today. It is very interesting how certain words can paint a certain picture. From what Anna Ward said today no one could possibly guess that she is a young woman who is desperately unhappy, plagued by headaches, frequents fortune-tellers, and takes considerable amounts of tonic nightly. She did not lie certainly and yet she revealed nothing of her true self.

I am reminded of a conversation Wilkes and I once had. We decided then that none of us are what we seem. We were correct, Wilkes and I.

Wilkes. I do not want to think of or remember you. Oh, Wilkes. You managed to evade this circus, this trial. It would have been far more interesting with you here. Your conspiracy is represented by a very raggle-taggle lackluster band, I fear. You would have lent some dash to the proceedings. The reporters would have been very grateful to you.

Monday, June 5, 1865

More gentlemen attacking Zadoc's character and loyalty today. I only wonder what Zadoc's politics have to do with me. I can only guess that as a woman I am expected to have no political loyalties or opinions. So they will use the ones of my closest male relation as interchangeable with mine. It is quite true that I know nothing of politics, but I object to having to take on Zadoc's. My brother and I have agreed upon very little in our lives. If I should choose to study politics, I'm sure we would disagree there too.

Colonel Wood testified today. It was a very brave thing to do. So far most of the people who have come forward for me, though I am grateful and do not mean to belittle them, have been under suspicion already. When I think of all that the Colonel has done for me, I really cannot believe it. I suppose there are those who would say that his position is so strong and protected that he could afford to be magnanimous, but there is no position that is safe from these men. They could bring him down quite easily. He risks much and there is no need of it, except that he is a man of conscience. A rare thing.

Wednesday, June 7, 1865

Annie was in court again today. This time she remained calm and sat erect throughout the questioning. Wilkes was not mentioned. She told how she came by the card with Virginia's motto upon it. They found that too in the house. They dwell on that because that is what Wilkes shouted after shooting the President. A cousin had given the card to her years before. Also she was asked if she had ever seen Dr. Mudd. He is one of the prisoners, the one I marked the first day as being a cut above the rest. Poor man, he evidently set Wilkes' broken leg. He was told to stand. Annie swore she had never seen him before. I am sure that she never has, but I doubt that even his own family would recognize him at this point. He is so changed from the man I saw the first day of the trial, if I did not know better, I would not think him the same person. He is so thin, and drawn, and white-faced. He fears, I know, that his mercy and his doctor's duty may have killed him. Annie walked from the courtroom today with such dignity that my heart swelled just looking at her.

Then there was a succession of war clerks who testified to what a fine and loyal fellow Mr. Louis Weichman is. The prosecution must have been worried about my former boarder's testimony, and the impression he made, to go to such lengths to bolster him.

Mr. Holohan took the stand and announced that he was unaware of my defective eyesight. Then he told how many times he had seen Atzerodt and . . . I suppose I will call him Paine, at the house. I cannot make out Mr. Holohan. He is an enigma, not just the external and internal lives and conflicts I have found in everyone, but even his surface behavior is contradictory. He lent John money on occasion, and yet he was one of the first to volunteer to go and hunt him down. I have seen him touch his little daughter's face so gently with his huge stonecutter's hands and I have seen purple bruises on Eliza Holohan's arms many mornings. He is a paradox.

My vision of him is unclear and yet he is the only one to have claimed ignorance of my blindness.

Friday, June 9, 1865

My days and nights are nightmarish. They blend together. I cannot tell anymore what I have dreamt and what is real. My dreams are filled with the other prisoners and the words said of them. Never about myself. I dream only of the others, and then I forget the dreams. I know only that I am never included in them. I have never dreamt of myself, except that one terrible recurring dream that I first had at the H Street house here in Washington. I would dream that I was at the funeral of the girls who died in the explosion at the Arsenal. I would approach the long line of their coffins and I would lift each lid and look inside. Every girl was dressed in white and wore my face, staring up open-eyed at me. I have not had that dream since I have been confined here at the Arsenal prison. Its prophecy is fulfilled, or soon to be, I suppose.

Tuesday, June 13, 1865

Mrs. Emma Offutt returned to the stand today. I was correct about her. She was ill the day she testified that I had not given her the package. She told the court that she had taken a great quantity of laudanum for the pain and was not thinking clearly that day. She said that she remembered now that I had given her the package and that she had set it on the couch. She could not recall if I had picked up the package and given it to Lloyd when he came in. I might have done that, but she couldn't remember. She too spoke of my failing eyesight. She told of the time last December after visiting my sick mother down in the country. She testified that I had taken her arm and said, "It is all so dark. I cannot find my way."

Mrs. Offutt has a fine memory. I did say those words and she did help me into the parlor. It was only her interpretation of them that was wrong. I was thinking how incomprehensible it was, this falling out between my mother and me, the dark reasons for it which I could not see. I remember so well that visit I made to her in

December. She was very ill. I walked into her room and sat beside her, but she never opened her eyes. I spoke her name, but it seemed that she did not hear me. I left after a while and sat outside the door. Zadoc went in to her. I heard their voices.

"Zadoc, why did you bring her here?"

"I was worried. You were so ill. I thought she would want to know it."

"Yes, so she could come and pull that funeral face, and talk softly as if I was dead already."

"She just wanted to see you, Ma."

"Doing her duty as a good Catholic, visiting the sick. That's the way those people try to buy their way to Heaven. Make her go away. I don't want to see her."

I remember so well that day that Emma Offutt spoke of on the stand today. It was so very dark and I could not find my way. It is still dark but it is not my eyes that cannot see. My heart and my soul, they are blind.

The Hoxton brothers, William and John, from down in the country, testified in my behalf today. John, always more eloquent than William, called me "truthful . . . a Christian and kind lady." I think that in the Hoxtons I have found two people who are exactly what they seem.

I cannot think of anyone else whom prosecution or defense could call upon to speak about me. There is one glaring omission, my mother. If any of them approached her, she probably scared them senseless. I would match Mother against any number of judges in blue. I know who would emerge victorious. If only she were on my side.

Thursday, June 29, 1865

They did not come for me today. I can only assume from this that it is over. It began in confusion and uncertainty. It is appropriate that it should end in the same way. My trial, it seems, is finished. For over a month I have been escorted down the corridor to that great white room. And each day the air grew hotter and the words more meaningless.

They cannot know that they expect my son with far more eagerness that I. They want him desperately to come. They believe that I want that too. I have come to resent very much being misunderstood. My declarations go unbelieved, unheard, by everyone. It is because I do not declare them. I know that I am going to die. I want to die, to be punished for my sins. I can say this to no one. No one would understand.

I have become a cause to those who love and want to save me. I am equally an issue to those who hate and would have me destroyed. I am not a woman any longer. I do not know what I am. I am something that others speak words over, squabble over. I am innocent to some. I am guilty to others. I am nothing to any of them.

Friday, June 30, 1865

I wait. They believe that I wait for my fate to be decided. They are wrong. I am waiting to die.

The Colonel visited me this morning. I wonder what censure and danger he has invited by befriending me. He is a brave man. Just before he left he reached into his pocket and brought out some pencils. He said that he was sure that I was provided with them now, but he remembered the time when he had been the only one who could give me what I wanted so badly, such a simple thing, a pencil. He said that he would like to think that he was still that important to me. I told him that he would never know how much he meant to me and I took his pencils with tears. I waited until he had gone and I wept over them.

Dr. Gray continues to come to me. His tonics and little white pills do no good. I frustrate him. He will be glad to be rid of such a resisting patient, I am sure. Whenever I take the tonic he gives me, I think of Anna Ward. I see her swallowing from a spoon every night the medicine that drives away her headaches and her loneliness. I cannot help but think that she will spend her life teaching foundlings, for she is an orphan of the spirit. Today the good doctor had blue pills for me instead of the usual white. What could it mean?

I thought today that I might read some of what I had written in the beginning of my little book, my thoughts and words when I first arrived in Washington. I turned to the first page, but I was so shocked by the handwriting I did not see any of the words. It was so close and tight and small—so even. I look at what I have just written and it is large and loose, slooped downward on the page, and undisciplined completely. It looks as if two different people have been writing here.

Can it be that not even a year has passed since I first began this book? Can it be but nine months that separates these two women? Nine months. The time it takes for a child.

Saturday, July 1, 1865

Annie came today. I had not seen her since the day she testified at the trial. She is so very pale and thin. She paced nervously about the cell. I don't think she knew what to say to me. I tried. I truly did. Why is it that Annie and I both fall short of what we want to be and what we want to give to one another?

"Annie, please sit down."

"I'm sorry."

She sat for a moment and then got up again and looked out the window.

"You are staying on at the house?"

"Yes."

She walked over to the other window, and then back again.

"Annie, please sit down."

"I'm sorry."

She sat.

"I wish, Annie, that you would stop apologizing."

"But I am sorry, Mother. I'm sorry that I can't be still. This place feels like a cage."

"It is."

"I'm sorry . . ."

"Stop it, Annie, please!"

"Anna Ward comes to visit me often."

"That's good of her."

"She is very worried about you, Mother."

"Tell her please that I think of her often."

"I will."

She began to tap her fingers on the arm of the chair.

"And Honora, how is she?"

"Fine. I think that she is finally beginning to recover from being arrest . . ."

"Arrested."

"Yes."

"Is that difficult for you to say?"

"Should it be easy?"

"No. Annie?"

"Yes, Mother."

"Seth Kierney. I'm glad for him and for you. I want you to have someone. It is very important that you do. I don't think that I will leave this place, ever. I don't want you to be alone."

"Mother, Seth is dead. I've known it for a long time. The soldier who came early in the evening the night that we were . . . that we were arrested, he came to tell me about Seth. I think I knew it even before that."

"Annie, I'm very sorry."

"Yes."

She got up then and started toward the door.

"Annie, stay a moment longer."

"I can't. I'm sorry."

The entire conversation consisted of our apologies to one another. I'm sorry. No, I'm sorry. All in all we are a very sorry pair, my daughter and me. How did it happen? I love her, but I can't touch her. And I feel that she loves me too. Does she blame me for all of this? Could I blame her if she did?

Sunday, July 2, 1865

This cell is so hot that it smolders. The heat began during the first days of the trial. It has been relentless, this summer, my least favorite of seasons. Everyone is so exposed. They are out on the streets and on their porches, outside trying to catch a breeze. And the clothes. The light white cottons, the unbuttoned collars, the glimpses of strange and ugly skin. Oh, no, I have never liked summer. The odors of it—warm bodies damp with sweat—and even the flowers, heavy sweet magnolia and Cape jasmine. It is felicitous that I should die in summer.

Father Wiget came to me today. I finally told him today about the steady corrosion of my faith. He told me that I must put my faith in God, resign myself to His will. He could not know that I turned from God's will long ago and then planted the seeds for this harvest.

I asked the Father if he believed that it was God's will that I should die at the hands of these men. He said that that would soon be revealed to us.

"It has been revealed to me. I know that I am to die, Father."

"If you die it is God's will that you should, but you are most unready. You must not die without faith, Mary. You are doomed if you do."

"Father, I have examined my conscience, and I am afraid."

I confessed to him then that I had denied and doubted my religion, that I had said my prayers in distraction and disbelief, that I had had thoughts of hatred and contempt and resentment for those men who had put me here and who thought to judge me. And with John Wilkes Booth I was guilty of sin. I had dwelt with pleasure on impure thoughts and imaginings of him. I had consented to these things in my heart. I had desired them.

I confessed all of this to the Father, but these are venial sins. My mortal sin I cannot confess or escape.

The passing from this life I do not mind, but what goes after. The one sin I did not confess to Father Wiget is the greatest. He cannot give me absolution. I have broken a promise made directly to God. I promised to serve Him, to be a nun. My life was saved long ago to serve Him in this way, but I disregarded His will, His divine plan for me, and I took another path. Because of this I know that I will never look upon His face. I know that I will burn in Hell forever.

This cell prepares me for it, I think. This room, this place, in which I am locked, trapped. It is filled with scorching air. Surely no summer on earth could be like this.

Monday, July 3, 1865

Today it was my brother Zadoc's turn to visit. I feel sometimes as if I were an invalid and that this is a deathbed vigil. I am sick, but I do not believe that I will be allowed to die of it. They have other ideas concerning my demise, far more spectacular ones. But the analogy between cell and sickbed is a valid one. The faces are the same, nervous, sorrowful, watching. And no one ever knows what to do with his hands.

I asked Zadoc about Mother.

"She's fine now, Mary. You know Ma. She gave us a scare this winter, but she came back. She's ageless. I'd swear by the look of her that she was still a young woman."

"Does she ever ask about me?"

"She keeps herself real busy around the farm. You know Ma."

"She's too busy to ask about me?"

"Well, you know."

"Yes, I know."

"Say, Mary, have you heard? They're going to change the name of Surrattsville."

"Change it? To what?"

"Clinton, they say."

"But why?"

"Well, you know."

"It's so unfair. It was named for my husband. He was the postmaster there. He was so proud. Oh, that's very cruel. He had no part in any of this. Why should his name be despised and defiled? Why that one achievement taken from him?"

"Folks are funny about those things. It's kind of an honor, you know, having a town named for you, even if it is a little bitty one."

"Yes, Zadoc. I understand."

"Guess I'm lucky to be a Jenkins. I miss some of the trouble that way."

"Yes, you are certainly lucky, Zadoc."

"You know, this isn't such a bad place. I expected worse. A person could be right comfortable here."

"You can say that, Zadoc. You can call the guard and have him open the door and walk out at any time."

"Guess you're right. Maybe if you asked him real nice he might do the same for you." And he began to laugh. "Just a little joke. I never do remember you having much of a sense of humor, Mary."

"There are things I find difficult to laugh at, Zadoc. Freedom is one of them."

"Guess I ought to be going."

"Zadoc, I would like to ask a favor of you."

"If I can, I'll be glad to do it."

"I want you to ask Mother if she will come and visit me."

"Well now, Mary, I don't know about that. I don't think she'd come."

"Zadoc, all that I am asking of you is that you ask her."

"Well, I can sure do that."

"Thank you."

"One thing, though. You don't have priests and nuns running in and out of here all the time, do you?"

"Priests and nuns?"

"Well, I mean, you being Catholic and all. Have you got those kinds of people around you a lot?"

"Father Wiget visited me yesterday."

"You know how Ma feels about that. If she were to come and then find one of them kind here, there'd be trouble."

"Tell Mother that she needn't worry, Zadoc. I only want to see her. I am not going to have priests and nuns lying in wait to forcibly convert her to Catholicism. I would just like to see her once more."

"Of course, now, I wasn't speaking for Ma, you understand. I don't know what her reasons are for not wanting to come."

"I know that no one speaks for our mother, Zadoc. She speaks for herself. She always has."

"You're dead right there. She's a strong-minded woman. You might even call her stubborn."

"You might, Zadoc, but I doubt you'd do it to her face."

"Right again, Mary. Funny a woman like her having children like you and me."

"Weak, you mean?"

"I guess that's what I mean. Do you think Ma knows about us?"

"Yes, she knows, and she hates it. Yet she still loves you, Zadoc."

He left me shortly after that. He promised that he would return and that he would ask Mother to come with him. Poor Zadoc, I wonder if he will.

I want very much to see her. My mother and my daughter, how did I get so far away from them, or they from me? Annie reminds me of Mother in many ways. And because of me, they don't even know one another.

Tuesday, July 4, 1865

Annie was back again today. She seemed happier, excited. She had obtained a special treat for me. We were allowed to walk in the prison yard. It must have taken her most of the day to get this request granted. It was late in the afternoon when she came to me. As we stepped outside, I tried to think how long it had been since I was outdoors. Even in the dusk the light hurt my eyes. A guard followed close behind us, but I tried to pretend that Annie and I were alone in an open field somewhere in Maryland.

"Mother, I know that you'll be coming home soon."

"May I take your arm, Annie? I feel a little weak."

"Of course. Perhaps this wasn't such a good idea after all."

"It was a wonderful idea. I haven't felt so good in ages. I'm just not used to walking, that's all."

"You'll get accustomed to it again. I was thinking, we should sell the house here and the tavern in Maryland. We should buy a new place. Start all over again."

"But in Maryland still."

"Yes, in Maryland."

"Oh, Annie, if only we could."

"We can and we will."

"I almost believe you."

"Believe me, Mother."

"Maybe Isaac could be with us again, and John."

"Mother, it will be a very long time before John can come back, maybe never. Can you be happy without John?"

"No, not completely, but if I had you and Isaac and a little farm, I could come close, closer than I ever have to being happy."

"That is how it will be then."

"That's how it will be."

The sky was growing soft dark blue. There was a purple cast to it. Suddenly a Roman candle climbed in the quiet sky and burst nearly over our heads. I remembered then that it was the 4th of July.

"I'd forgotten, Annie. It's Independence Day.

"Yes, Mother. Independence Day. Freedom. For you, and soon."

The guard approached us and said that it was time, that he must return me to my cell. Annie asked if she couldn't come too. He said no, that she had to leave. I tightened my hand around her arm. She smiled at me and I asked the guard if I might take his arm. I could feel her standing there and watching. Just before we entered the building, I turned back and saw her. She was so beautiful in the twilight. Another Roman candle burst in the sky, but she did not look up. She looked only at me. And then I was taken into the darkness.

I will never forget the beauty and the grace of this day of lies. The plans we made which will never happen, the farm we will never have, the sons I shall never see again. I will cherish our words of life and living while we stood knowingly in the shadow of death. Most of all, I will treasure our loving perjury, this pious myth, this dear distortion, forever.

Wednesday, July 5, 1865

My young lawyers came today. I could see in their faces that something was wrong, terribly wrong. Young faces have so little guile.

"We have had bad news today, Mrs. Surratt," said Mr. Clampitt.

"I surmised that from your face, and Mr. Aiken's there."

"I simply don't know how to begin."

"Just say what needs to be said. I know what you are going to say anyway."

"You couldn't even guess at this. None of us expected this."

"Only I did, Mr. Clampitt. Shall I tell you the bad news? I am to be executed."

"Yes. That is the sentence. We are doing everything in our power to stop it, postpone it, at the very least."

"When? When is the execution to take place?"

"The seventh."

"Of July?"

"Yes."

"That is the day after tomorrow, Mr. Clampitt."

"Yes."

"They are anxious, aren't they?"

"It won't happen. We'll see to it."

"I've been hearing that for a very long time. I have always known that they wanted me dead. I had very little doubt that they would accomplish it. I do not blame you, Mr. Clampitt. Or you, Mr. Aiken. No one could have done any better, tried any harder. It was destined, fated to be this way."

"You mustn't talk like that, Mrs. Surratt. I know that you are shocked and frightened, but you mustn't give up."

"And I tell you that I am not in the least shocked. I expected this verdict. It was decided long ago. Now it is finally decreed."

"It is not finished yet. We are making every effort to stem the tide."

"Just as it is necessary for you to make that effort, it is necessary for me to believe that it will fail. I am very sorry. Do not cling too long to me, for you might go under too. Day after tomorrow. That is very soon."

They did not stay too long. They must not have heard me, for they left full of optimistic drive and ambition, wanting so desperately to be my saviors. They want to save me, but they do not want to look at me or hear me.

How does one prepare for death? I have thought so much about it in the past months. Yet, with the reality of death not more than two days away, I find I am not ready for it. I thought by now that death would seem a friend to me, an old friend, but it is still a stranger. And so close I feel its cold breath upon my neck.

Thursday, July 6, 1865

I could not get up off my couch today. I have no strength left me. Annie came in the afternoon. She had been told the verdict and knew that the execution is to be tomorrow.

"It will not happen, Mother. It will not. There are things being done at this very moment to stop it."

"You sound like my lawyers, Annie."

"I've been talking to them constantly. They are about the only people I talk to anymore."

"My poor girl, what a terrible thing this is for you. I'm so very sorry."

"Mother, I wasn't complaining. You are hardly to blame for any of this."

"And yet you do blame me. I can see that you do, Annie. So please accept my apology."

"It is not necessary."

"What's wrong, Annie? Something has happened."

"Something has happened! I would say that, yes! My mother has been sentenced to die on the gallows, tomorrow. That is what has happened."

"There is something else too."

"No, Mother."

"Yes, there is. Tell me, please."

"It is a small thing, not even worth mentioning in this conversation."

"What is it?"

"Honora has gone."

"Gone where?"

"I don't know."

"She just left? With no word?"

"Yes. Day before yesterday when I came home from here, she was gone. All of her things were gone."

"There was no letter from her?"

"Nothing. One more desertion."

"Annie, do you feel that I have deserted you?"

"Is there any other window that can be opened? It's stifling in here."

"Annie?"

"It is so hot I can't bear it. You must be suffering terribly. Can I get you a cool cloth for your head?"

"Annie?"

"I'll call the guard. You have no water left in this pitcher. You must learn to ask for things, Mother. You're far too self-effacing."

"I do ask for things, but it seems that no one ever hears me."

She looked at me then. Stopped fussing. She stood holding the pitcher in her hands, and looked at me.

"You mustn't wait so long, Mother. This pitcher is dry."

She called the guard. He brought the pitcher back full. She sat down beside me on the couch and put the wet cloth to my forehead. She performed a little ritual with the cloth. She would take it from my brow, wave it in the air, and replace it cool again. She did this over and over. Her motions reminded me of something, something long ago and far away. Finally it struck me. I was twelve years old lying in a big high iron bed in a large white room with many other beds all around. I was hot and feverish. Then someone in the bed close beside me moved, came toward me. It was my mother. Her hands were so thin, not like my mother's hands at all. And her face too, drawn and white, but my mother's face all the same. She took a cloth and put it to my burning forehead. Then she removed it, and waved it in the air, and returned it to me.

My mother and my daughter. Then and now.

I wanted very much to tell Annie of my recollection, to tell her everything, but I did not. I feared it was, as she had said, too late. I had waited too long.

Annie put her face in her hands. It hadn't been too late then, but now it was. Her mother's voice was stilled forever, except for the words she had written in her diary. At least she had those, but she wanted more. She wanted to sit beside her mother and hold her hand and ask her questions which were not answered in this little book, but that could not be.

It was close to dawn and she dreaded what was to come, the ending, the last words on the last day. Annie thought of that day, that hot July morning so long ago. She had gone to the White House and it was big and forbidding. Her mother was to die that day and no one seemed to care. They were happy even.

She had made her way to the second floor, fought her way through the guards with guns and secretaries armed with words. She had heard laughter coming from within the President's chamber. She had knocked on the door and two men had emerged. They were very grand, dressed in white linen suits with silk cravats, and their wide faces were flushed and smiling until they saw her. She had pleaded for a word with the President, but they had refused. They had closed the big doors upon her. She had pounded upon them, begging for admittance. Her hands had begun to swell and ache. In desperation she had continued until at last the door had opened again. One of the men, the younger one, had poked his head out and told her that the guards would forcibly remove her if she did not leave immediately. And then the doors had been slammed. She had turned and walked the corridors without seeing or hearing, never feeling such helplessness and grief. She had known then that she and her mother were in the grip of something terrible and unchangeable, something totally devoid of pity or compassion.

Outside in the sunlight she had felt herself falling. She had not even seen the long flight of stairs before her. She was falling and falling. She had had no power, no will, to stop herself. Then finally, as she laid at the bottom of the steps, she had known that her mother would die and that nothing and no one could stop it.

Annie looked down at the book of the dead woman that she held open in her hands and she thought of those men who had kept her from the President that day. They had not discovered what she had. They had believed that possibly they could have prevented the execution. They had both killed themselves within months of her mother's death.

She wondered how many remembered the woman in black who stood on that scaffold in July with an umbrella held over her to shade her from the sun while she waited for death. She wondered how many thought of her and were troubled or saddened for a moment. She wondered how many had forgotten her completely. And she held that woman in her hands, and that woman was her mother, and she would have this of her always. Annie brought the book into the circle of candlelight and began the end.

Friday, July 7, 1865

It is morning. There have been so many here. They are just the same as always. Dr. Gray came very early, silent as usual, his hands full of blue and white pills. I took all of them. I feel as if I am floating, disembodied. The doctor did not say goodbye, but then he never does. He just walked away from me as always, but we both knew that this time was the last time.

Then Annie came. She looked like a wild ghost, desperate and distraught. She kissed my hands and told me that she was on her way to the White House to plead with President Johnson for my life. Annie and I did not say goodbye.

My attorneys arrived, rustling papers and trying to look official. They pin their hopes on a writ or some such thing. I did not discourage them by reiterating my lack of hope. They have faith in their little document, and in justice. We did not say goodbye.

Next was my brother Zadoc. He brought Mother's refusal to me. She will not come. And so, she and I will not say goodbye.

I am alone now and scribbling here. Outside my door and down the hall somewhere I hear women weeping. It must be for one of the other prisoners. Hearing them, I realize that I will not die alone today. There will be another on the scaffold beside me, perhaps all the others, just as they were in the prisoners' dock at the trial. I am not alone in this. Yet I am separated from the rest somehow, just as I was at the trial. Perhaps it is because I am a woman. I did not even think to ask who would die beside me today. Soon I will know.

I have one more visitor. I can hear him walking toward me. It is the Colonel. I suddenly know that it is to him I will give you, dear little book. If it had not been for him I would not have had your dear companionship through all these dark days. It is fitting that I give it to him. I will ask that he take you to Annie.

The Colonel has come in. He looks so sad as he approaches me. Soon the priests will be here too. They will bring what I need. They will stay with me. They will say goodbye. The Colonel, I know, will not, cannot.

It is time then to write the last words that I shall ever write and close the book. I was born to die, as are we all. The end is there, held within the beginning.

It was dawn. Annie sat with tears all down her face. She felt very cold. She gathered the wrapper closer and tucked her bare feet up under her. She put a hand to her stomach. It felt larger, fuller, to her. She smiled, wondering if the child would be a girl. She wanted a daughter. She would give this book to her when she was old enough to understand. She would name her Mary Elizabeth, name her for her grandmother and great-grandmother. They could finally come together in this child. She heard footsteps, looked up, and saw Mardella.

"Miss Annie, you should be in bed."

"I know. I'll be going up soon. You should be in bed too, Della."

"I is like de owl, Miss Annie. You knows dat. I don't never sleep."

"Della, come sit down for a minute."

She walked over and saw the book open in her lap. "You still readin' on dat?"

"I just finished it."

"You does well to be puttin' it aside now, Miss Annie."

"You were the one who was so anxious to have me read it, Della."

"I knows dat. It were a fine thin' fer you to be doin', but now it time you sets it aside fer a while. It a real sad tale, Miss Annie, an' now it yer time to be happy."

"You're right. I was just thinking, wondering when my little girl would be old enough to read it."

"She ain't even been borned yet. Don't you thinks you is plannin' jus' a little far ahead."

"I suppose I am. Oh, Della, she is going to be beautiful, so beautiful."

"Don't I knows dat?"

"Of course, you do. You know everything."

"I knows you should be in bed. Dat chile gonna come into dese world wid big black circles under her eyes if you don't start gittin' some rest."

"I will now. I just wanted to finish the diary. Della, I am going to put it away, but I am not going to put my mother aside, never again. I want her with me always."

"Yes, Miss Annie."

"Della, if it were not for you I think that I would be dead by now. But what of you? Is this any kind of life for you?"

"Is you tryin' to send me away?"

"It is the last thing in the world I want for me, but I am selfish. We both know that. I'm trying not to be, just this once. I want you, Della. I also want you to be everything that you can be. Is it enough for you? Here with me?"

"It is, 'specially now wid de chile comin'. It too late fer me to have any more babies, but I feels like dese one be part mine. Don't turn me out, Miss Annie. I needs you an' you needs me."

Annie went to her. They embraced. "Oh, Della. I wouldn't turn you out. I love you as my sister. I just wanted to make sure that what you have here is enough. I don't want you to sacrifice your life to me. I don't believe in sacrificing lives anymore."

"My place is wid you. I is too ole an' I hates to leave you too much. I is happy wid you, Miss Annie, you an' dat little chile dat is comin'."

"I'm glad. I want you to be with us forever, Della."

"Ain't no sech thin', Miss Annie. Ferever is jus' today, an' mebbee if you is real lucky a long string of todays. Ferever be a promise dat nobody shouldn't be makin'. Now, will you please go upstairs an' git some rest? How many times does I has to ask you to do dat?"

"I'm going. Della, you took such good care of Mother's book before. Will you keep it for me again?"

"Yes, Miss Annie."

She handed her the diary and they walked from the room together.

The sun was beginning to shine through the glass window panes in the front door.

"Lookit you, Miss Annie, in yer barefeets. Is you crazy? Walkin' 'bout at night wid no slippers."

"I wasn't walking very much. I was sitting mostly."

"You is walkin' now, ain't you?"

"Yes, Della."

"Well, you should have yer slippers. Lookit dat sun an' it ain't even six yet. It gonna be another scorcher."

"That's July for you. Today is the seventh of July."

"Yes, Miss Annie."

"But today's the day . . ."

"Yes, Miss Annie. Is you gonna dawdle all mornin' or is you gonna go an' gits some sleep fer you an' de baby?"

"The baby, yes."

"An' 'bout de way you eats, Miss Annie. Dat gonna change too."

"Yes, Della. I'll eat more, I promise." She started up the stairs, but looked back. "The trunk. You'll bring it up for me, Della."

"I brings it up an' unpacks it. I thinks we be stayin'."

"Yes, Della. We'll stay for as many todays as we can string together."

And she started up the stairs again.